MEGAMAN
NT WARRIOR

D1226229

# MEGAMAN NT WARRIOR

Vol. 5
Action Edition

Story and Art by Ryo Takamisaki

English Adaptation/Gary Leach
Translation/Koji Goto
Touch-Up & Lettering/Gia Cam Luc
Cover Design & Graphic Design/Mark Schumann
Special Thanks/Hiromi Kadowaki & Jessica Villat (ShoPro Entertainment)
Editor/Eric Searleman

Managing Editor/Annette Roman
Director of Production/Noboru Watanabe
Editorial Director/Alvin Lu
Sr. Director of Licensing & Acquisitions/Rika Inouye
Vice President of Sales & Marketing/Liza Coppola
Executive Vice President/Hyoe Narita
Publisher/Seiji Horibuchi

Printed in the U.S.A.

Published by VIZ, LLC
P.O. Box 77064
San Francisco, CA 94107

Action Edition
10 9 8 7 6 5 4 3 2 1
First printing, December 2004

For advertising rates or media kit,
e-mail advertising@viz.com

store.viz.com

www.animerica-mag.com          www.viz.com

Viz Graphic Novel

# MEGAMAN
## NT WARRIOR
### Vol. 5

Story and Art by
**Ryo Takamisaki**

# CONTENTS

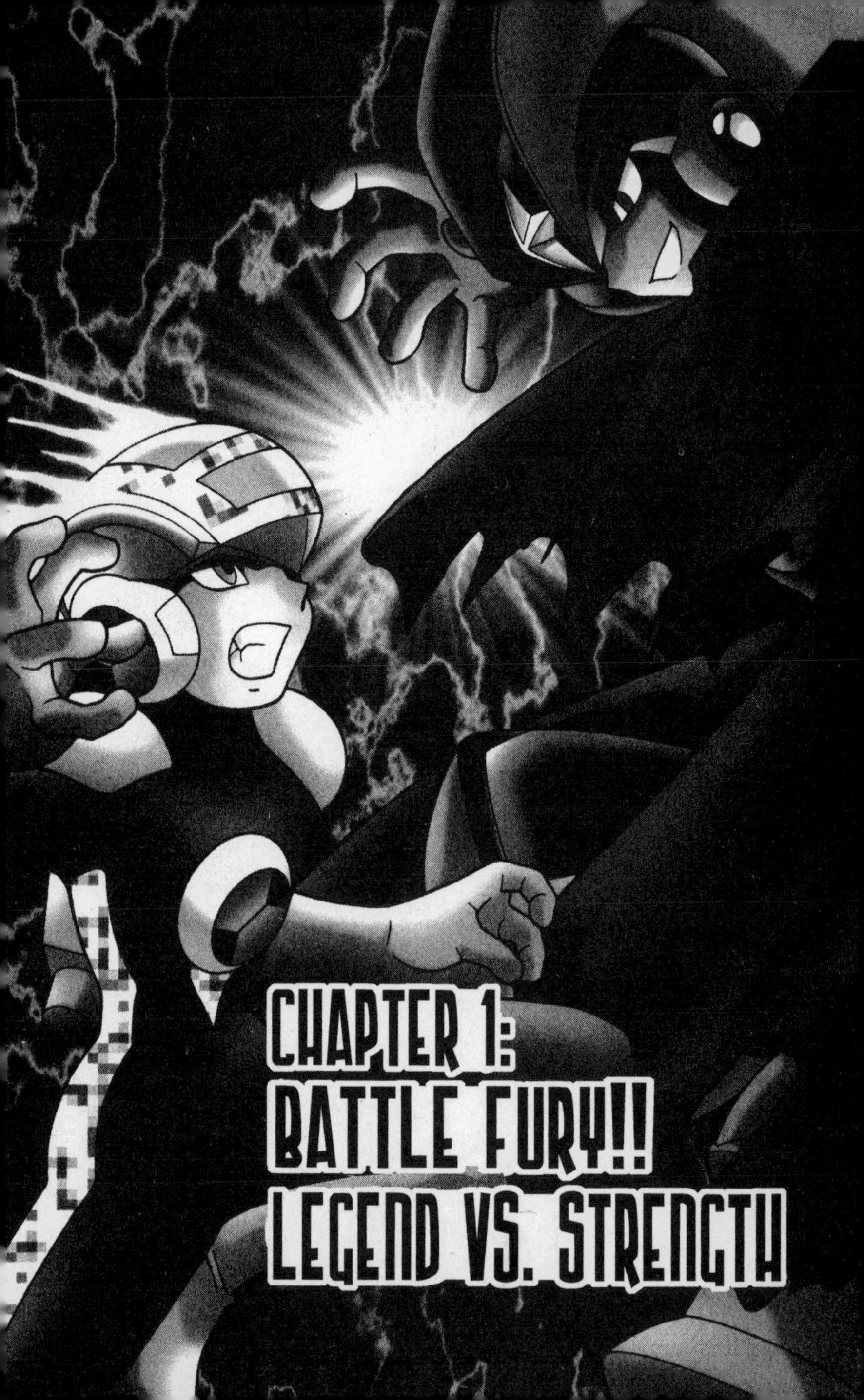
CHAPTER 1:
BATTLE FURY!!
LEGEND VS. STRENGTH

...HAS COME...

SO, THE TIME...

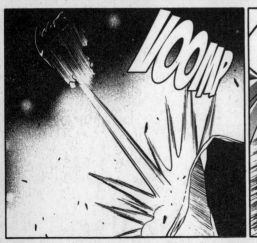

VOOMP

WHUFF

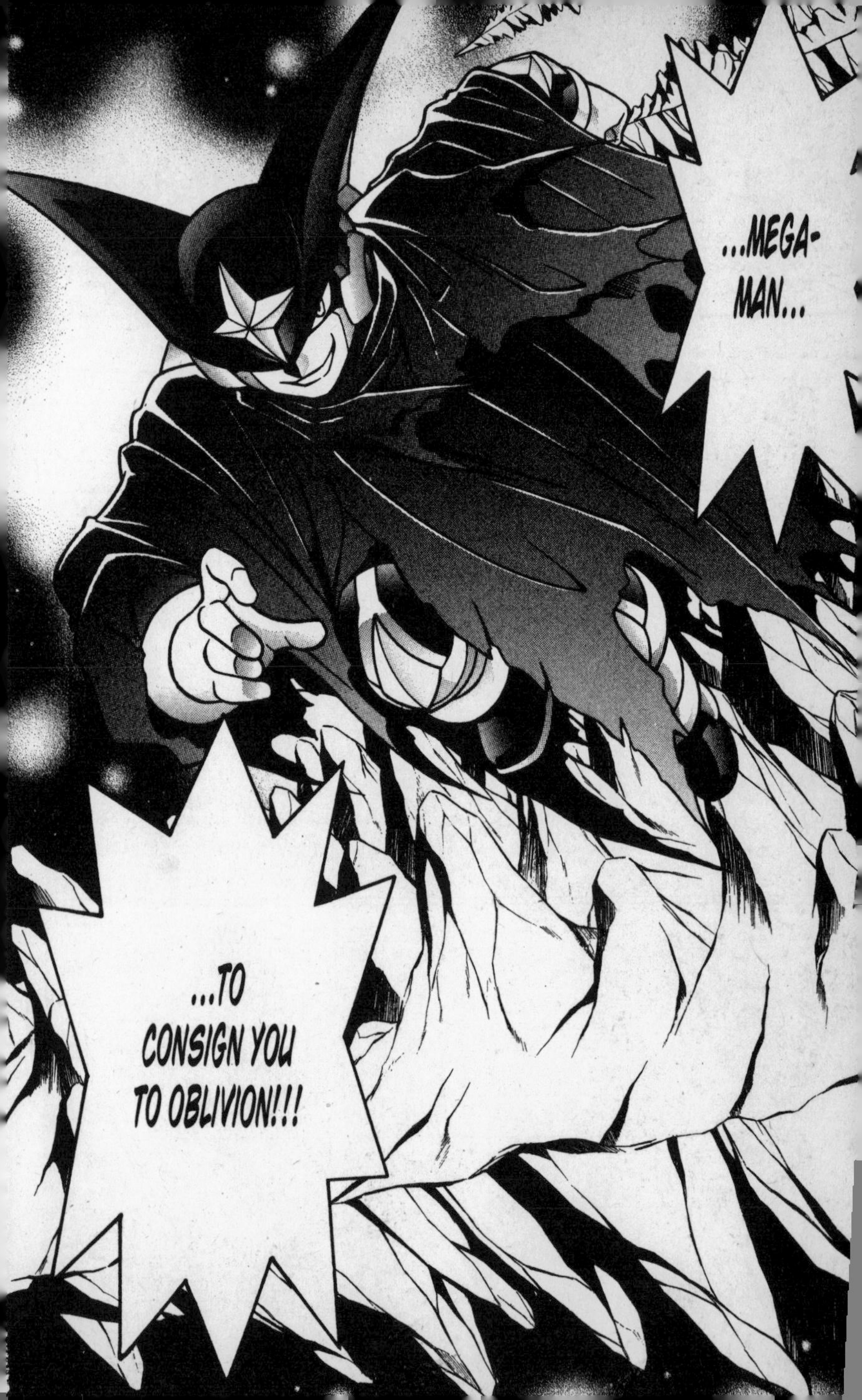
...MEGA-MAN...
...TO CONSIGN YOU TO OBLIVION!!!

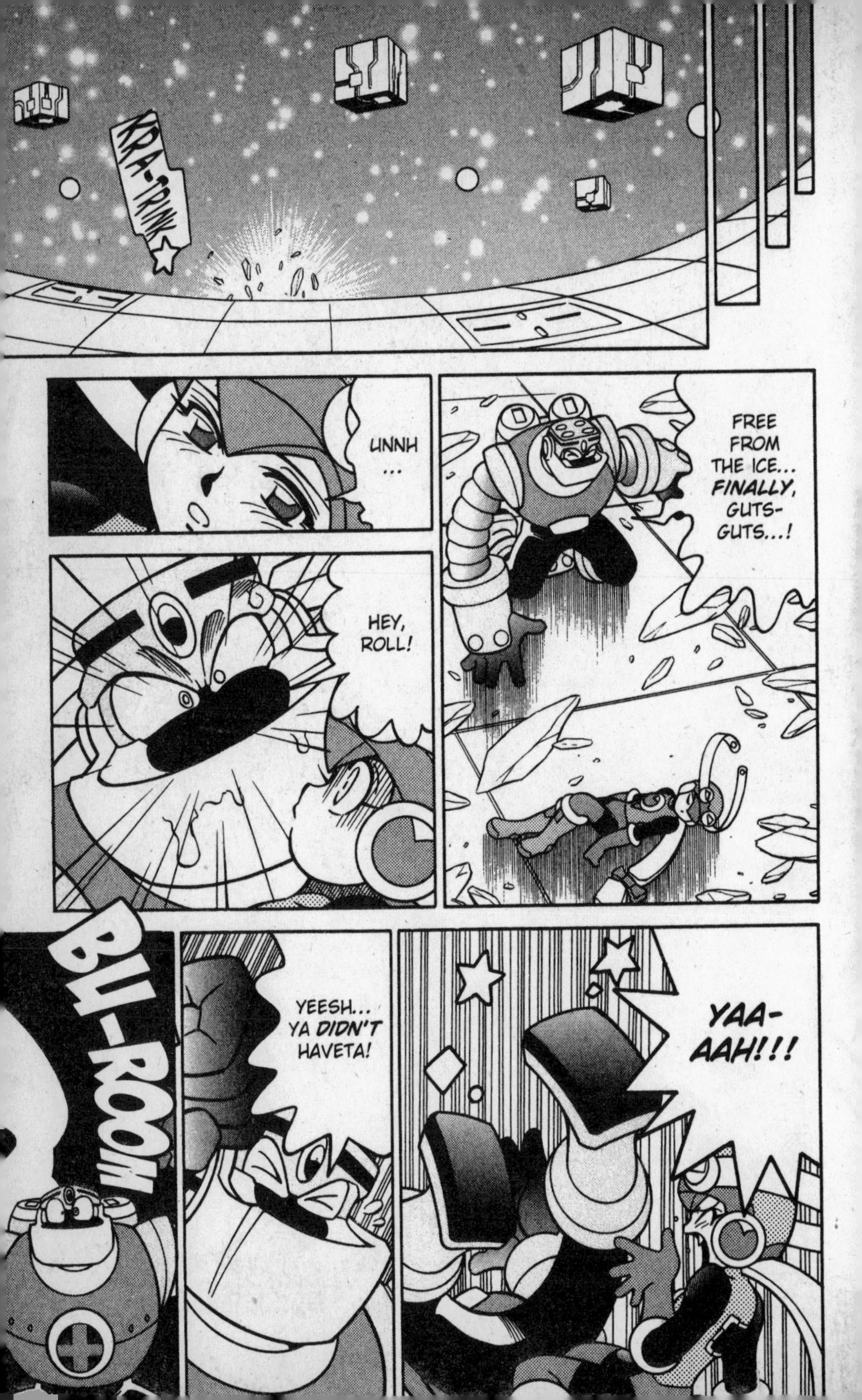
KRA-TRINK☆
FREE FROM THE ICE... FINALLY, GUTS-GUTS...!
UNNH ...
HEY, ROLL!
YAA-AAH!!!
YEESH... YA DIDN'T HAVETA!
BU-ROOM

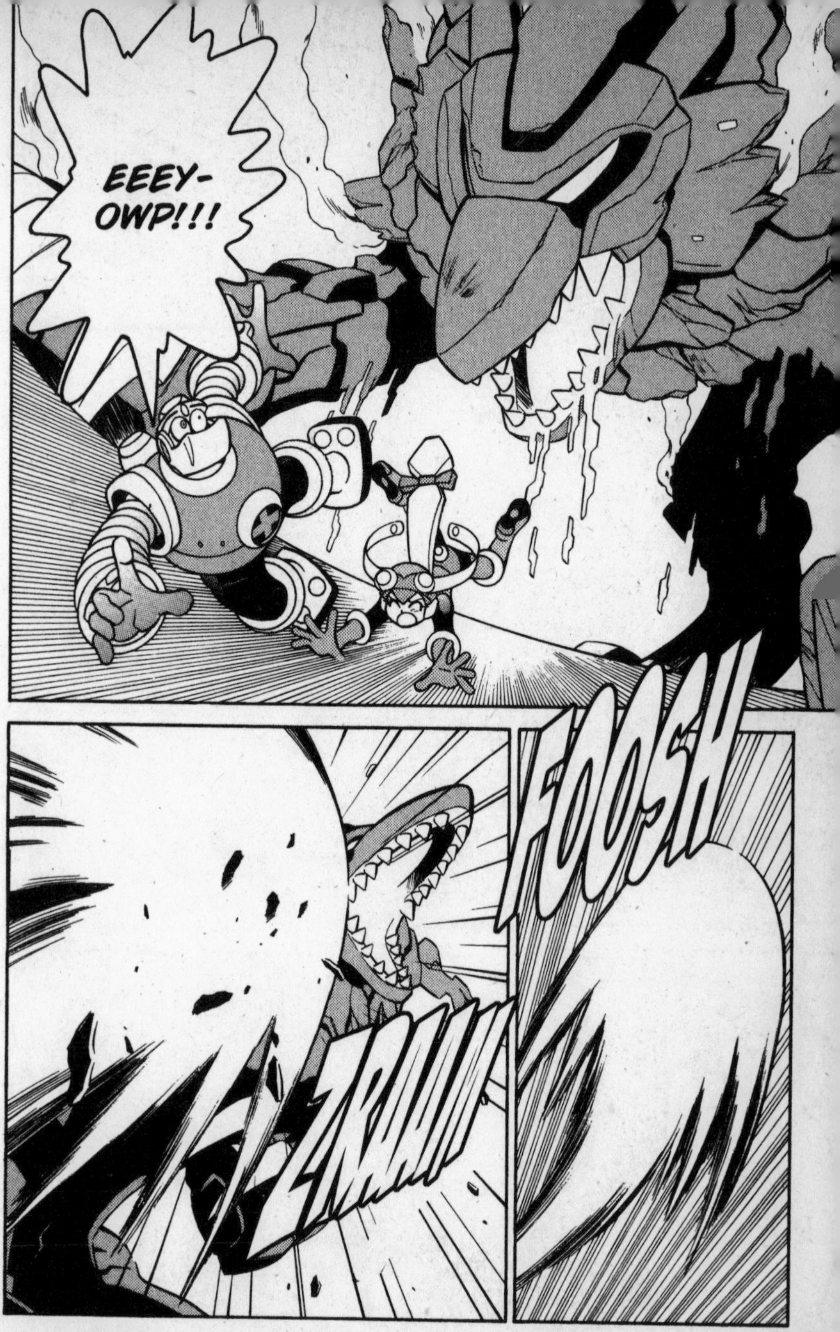
EEEY-OWP!!!
FOOSH

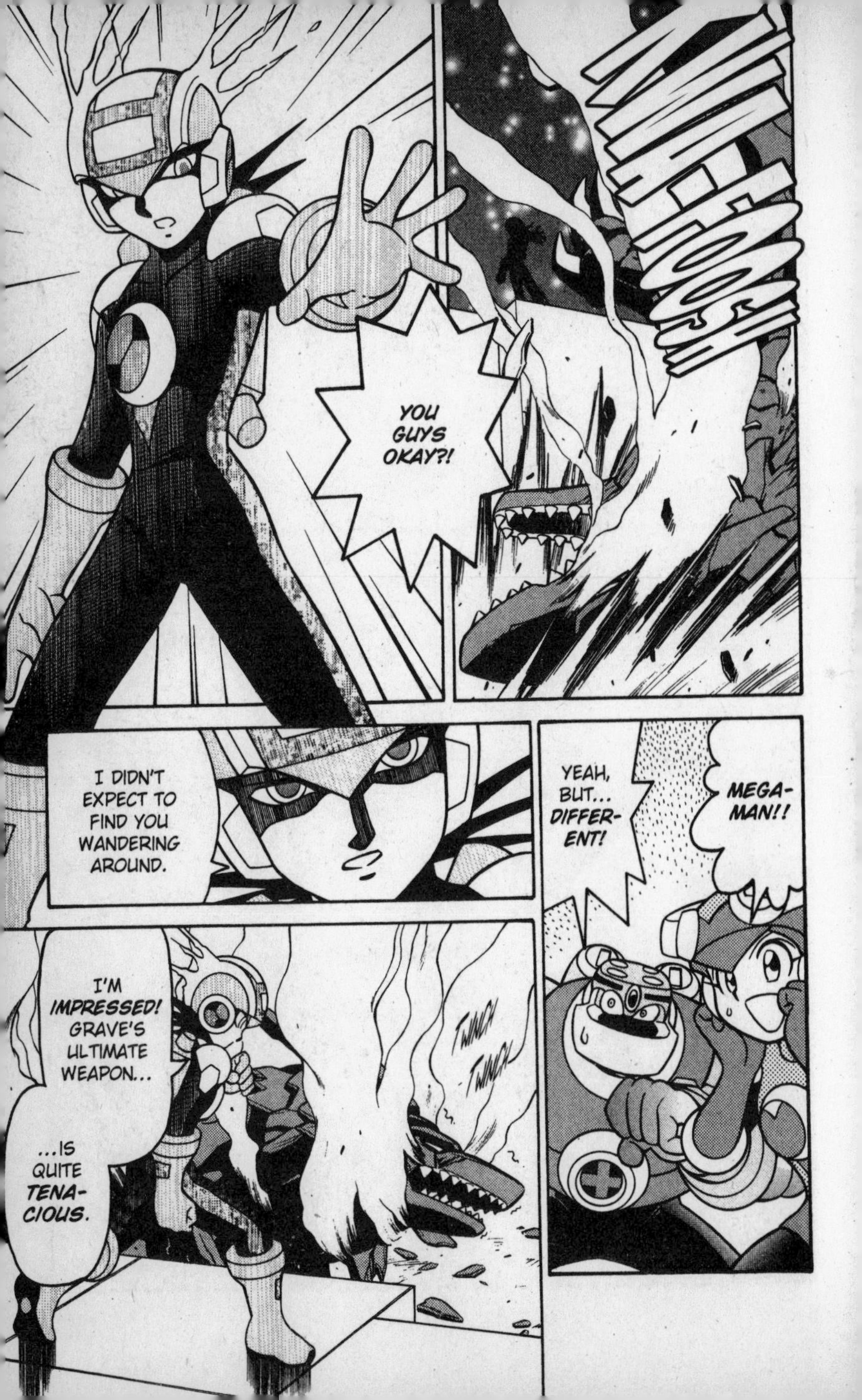
WHOOSH
YOU GUYS OKAY?!
MEGA-MAN!!
YEAH, BUT... DIFFER-ENT!
I DIDN'T EXPECT TO FIND YOU WANDERING AROUND.
I'M IMPRESSED! GRAVE'S ULTIMATE WEAPON...
...IS QUITE TENA-CIOUS.
TWINCH
TWINCH

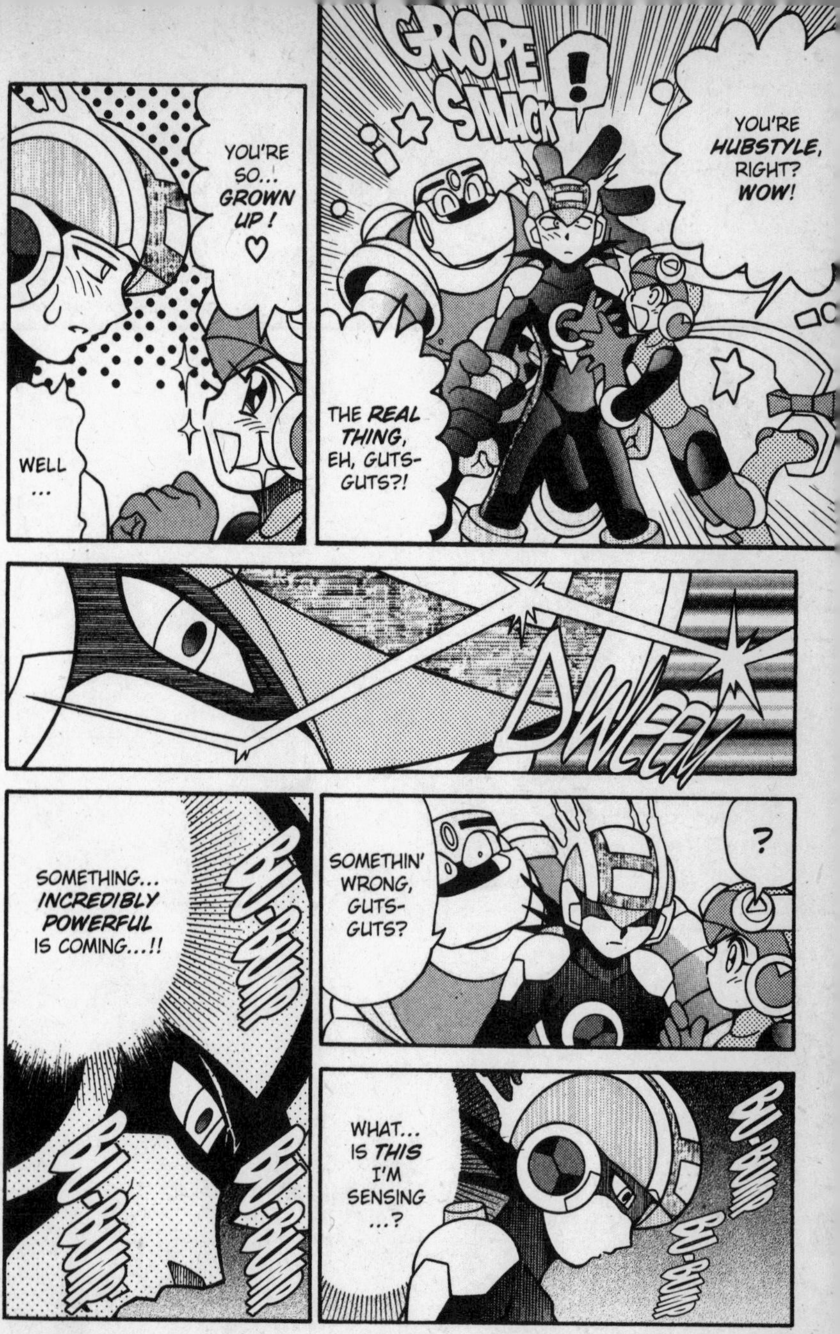
GROPE
SMACK
!
YOU'RE HUBSTYLE, RIGHT? WOW!
THE REAL THING, EH, GUTS-GUTS?!
YOU'RE SO... GROWN UP! ♥
WELL ...
DWEEN
?
SOMETHIN' WRONG, GUTS-GUTS?
BU-BUMP BU-BUMP
WHAT... IS THIS I'M SENSING ...?
SOMETHING... INCREDIBLY POWERFUL IS COMING...!!
BU-BUMP
BU-BUMP
BU-BUMP

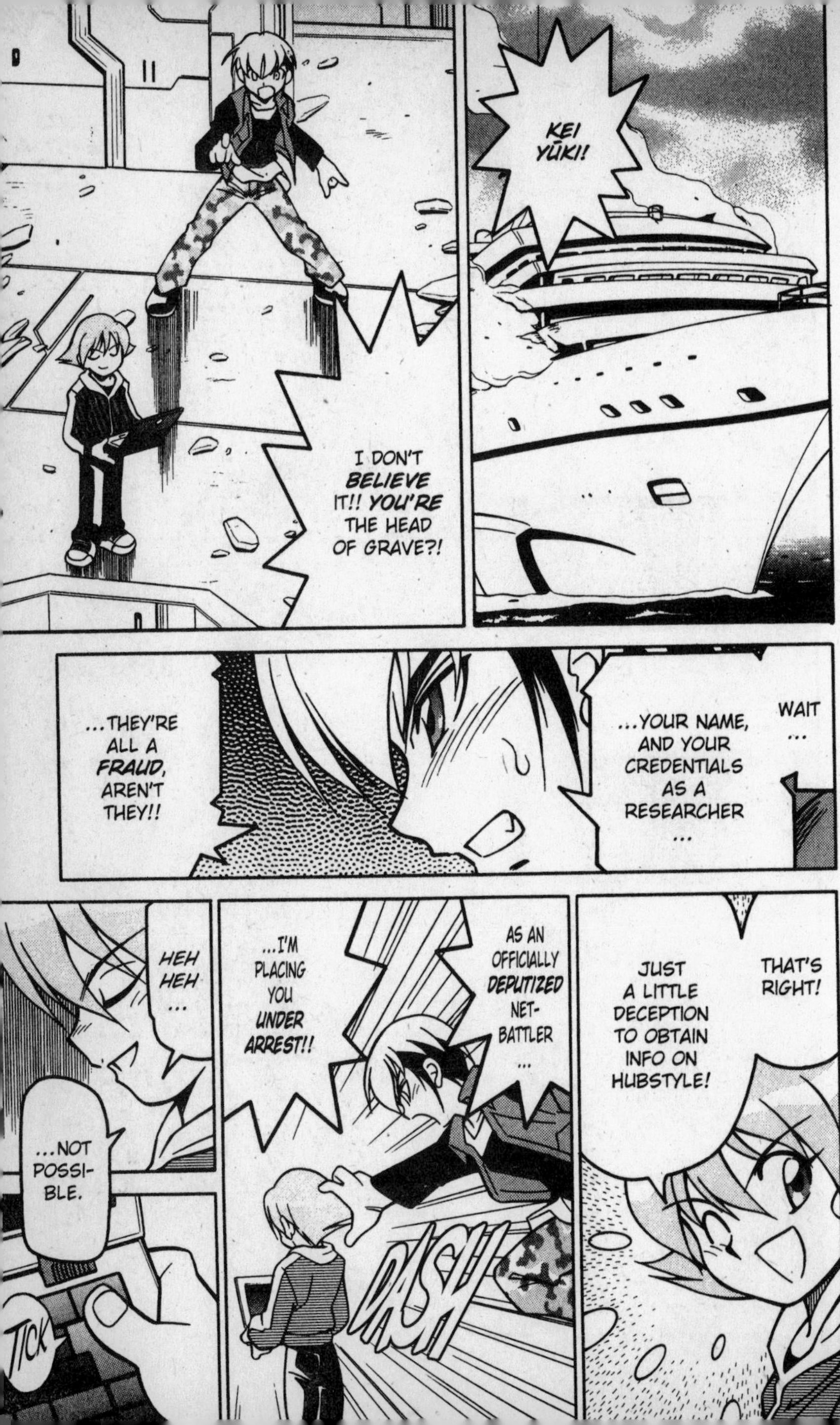
KEI YŪKI!
I DON'T BELIEVE IT!! YOU'RE THE HEAD OF GRAVE?!
WAIT ...
...YOUR NAME, AND YOUR CREDENTIALS AS A RESEARCHER ...
...THEY'RE ALL A FRAUD, AREN'T THEY!!
THAT'S RIGHT!
JUST A LITTLE DECEPTION TO OBTAIN INFO ON HUBSTYLE!
AS AN OFFICIALLY DEPUTIZED NET-BATTLER ...
...I'M PLACING YOU UNDER ARREST!!
DASH
HEH HEH ...
...NOT POSSIBLE.
TICK

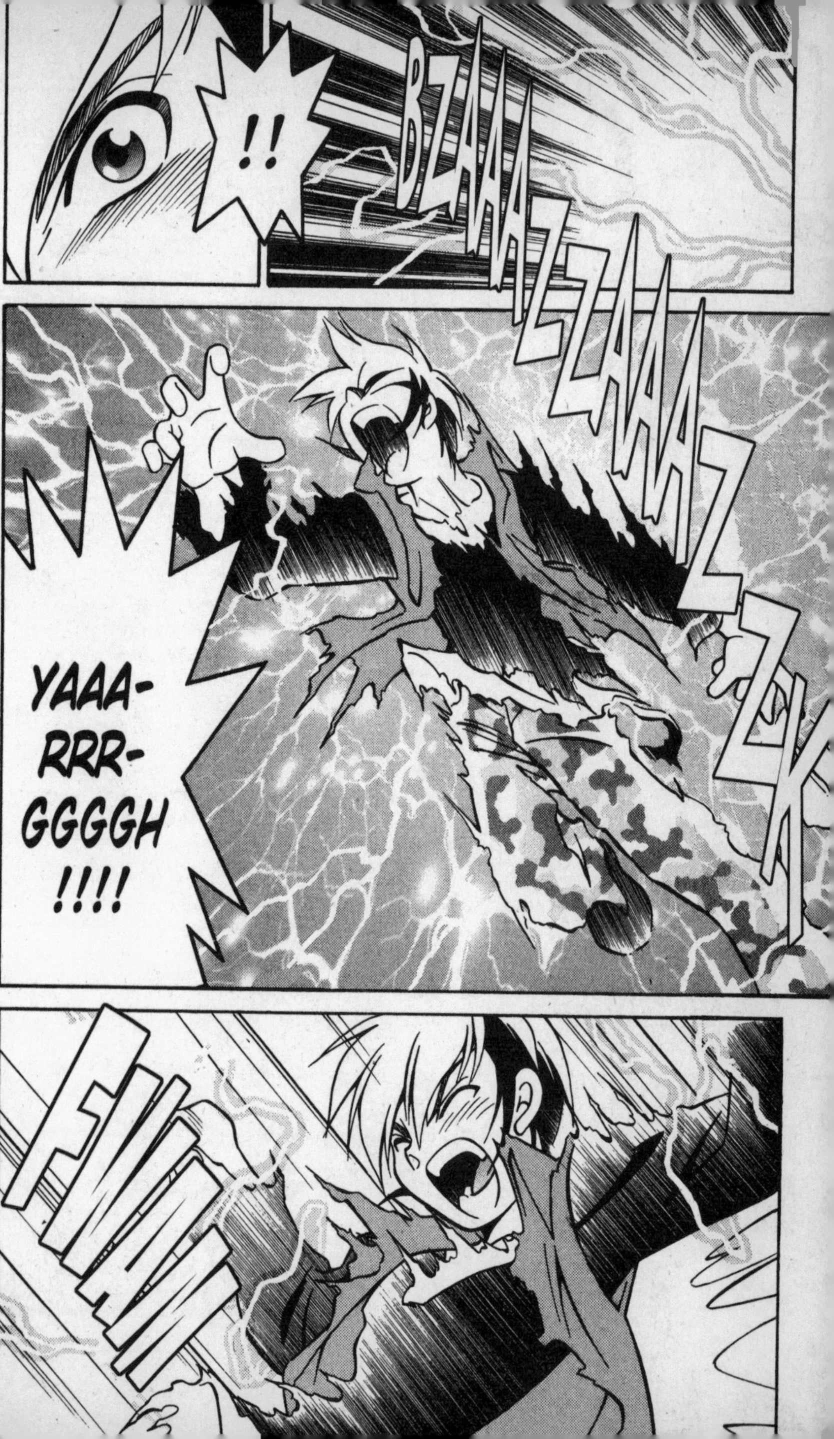
BZAAAZZAAAZZZK
!!
YAAA-RRR-GGGGH!!!!

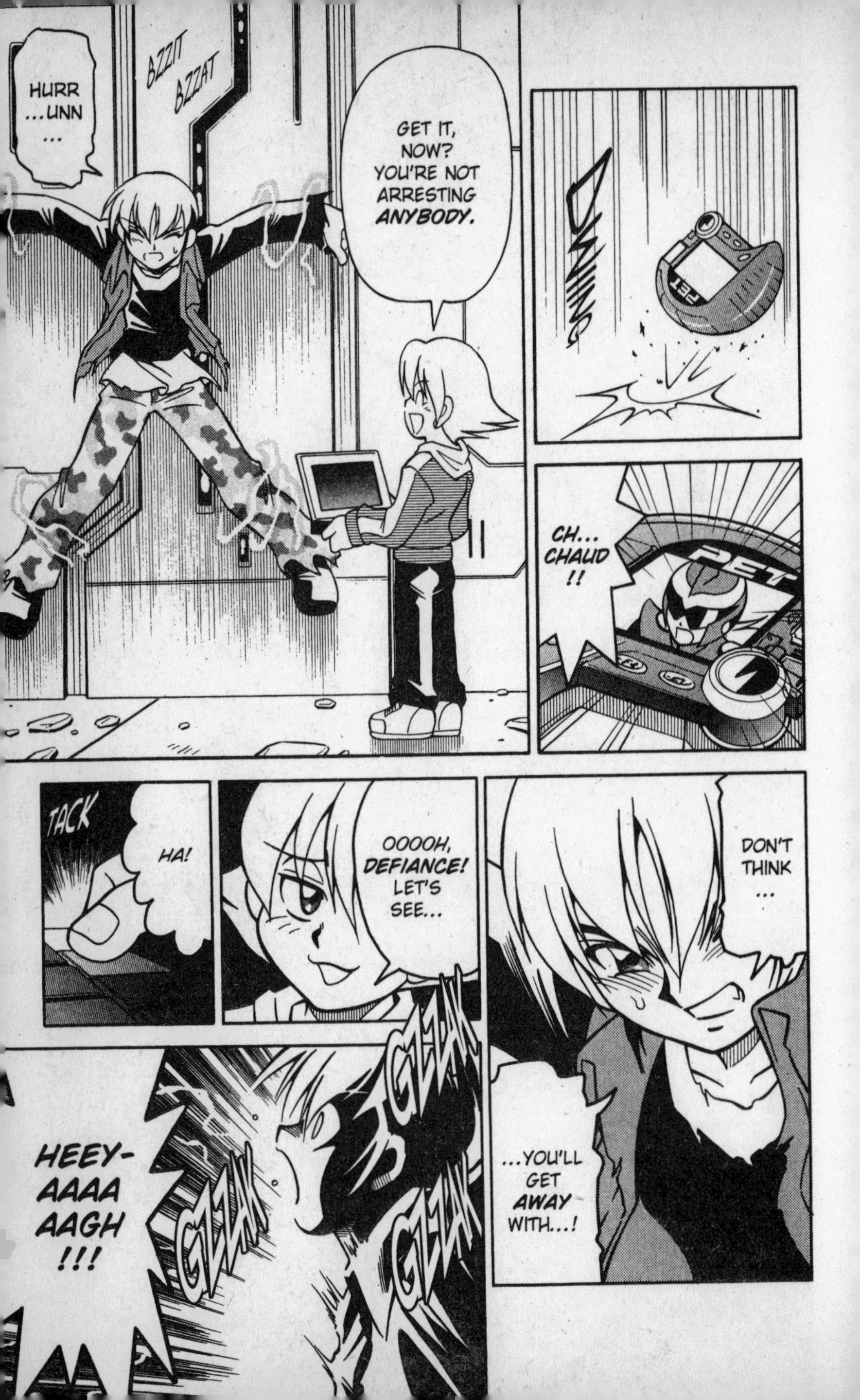
DWIING
PET
CH... CHAUD !!
GET IT, NOW? YOU'RE NOT ARRESTING ANYBODY.
BZZIT BZZAT
HURR ...UNN ...
DON'T THINK ...
...YOU'LL GET AWAY WITH...!
OOOOH, DEFIANCE! LET'S SEE...
TACK
HA!
GZZAK GZZAK GZZAK GZZAK
HEEY-AAAA AAGH !!!

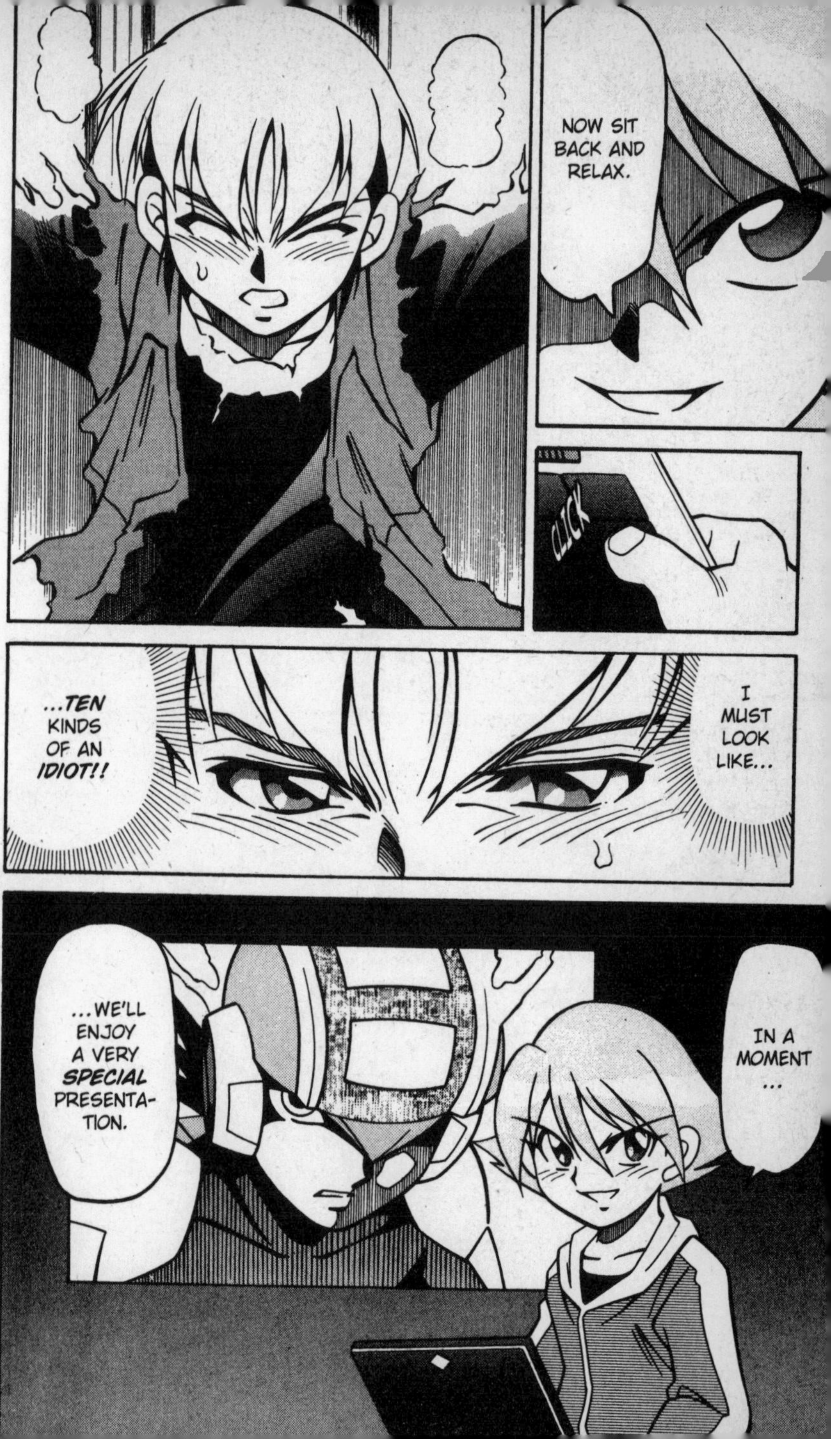
NOW SIT BACK AND RELAX.
CLICK
I MUST LOOK LIKE...
...TEN KINDS OF AN IDIOT!!
IN A MOMENT...
...WE'LL ENJOY A VERY SPECIAL PRESENTATION.

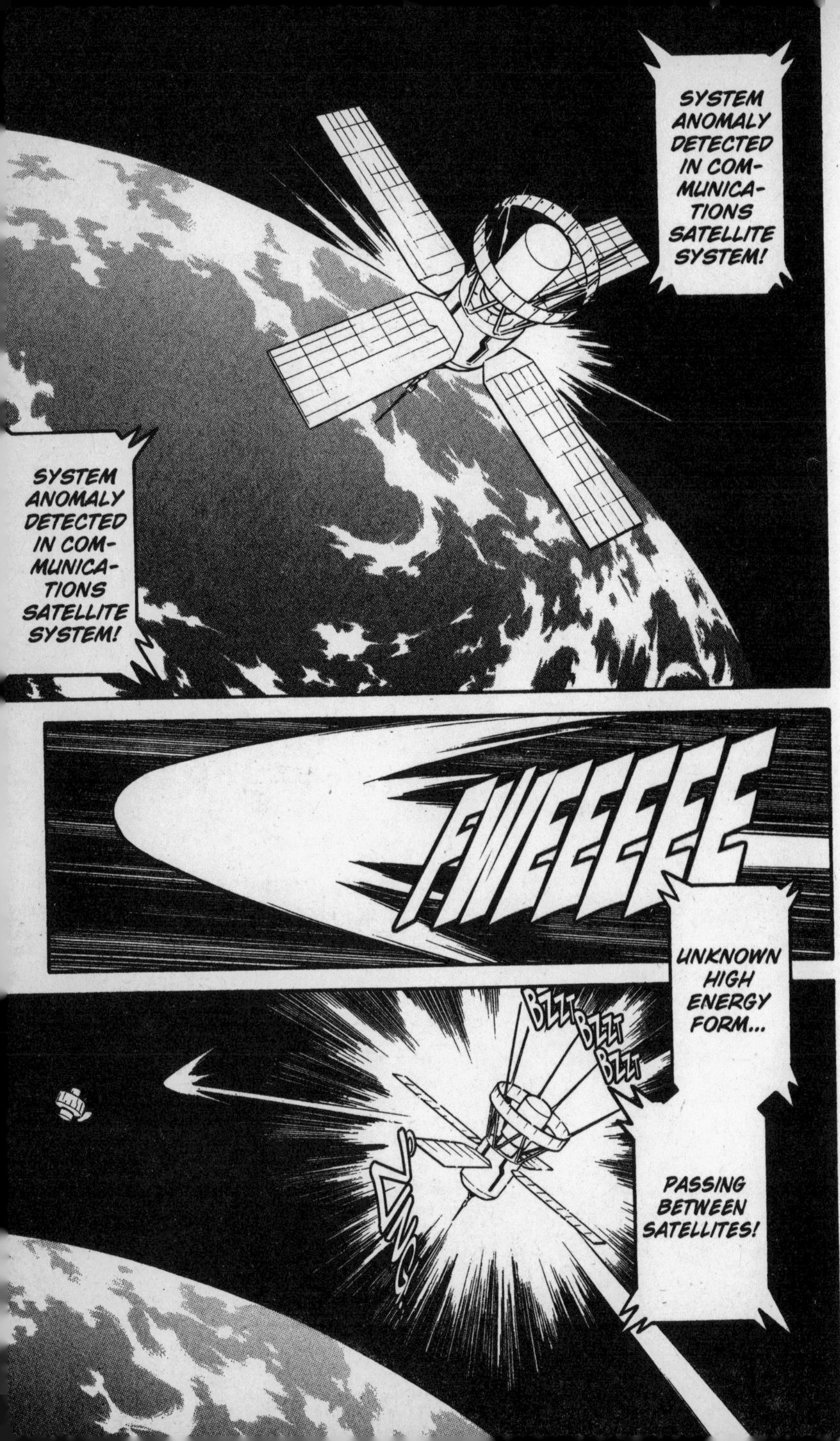
SYSTEM ANOMALY DETECTED IN COMMUNICATIONS SATELLITE SYSTEM!
SYSTEM ANOMALY DETECTED IN COMMUNICATIONS SATELLITE SYSTEM!
FWEEEEE
UNKNOWN HIGH ENERGY FORM...
BZZT BZZT BZZT
PASSING BETWEEN SATELLITES!
ZING

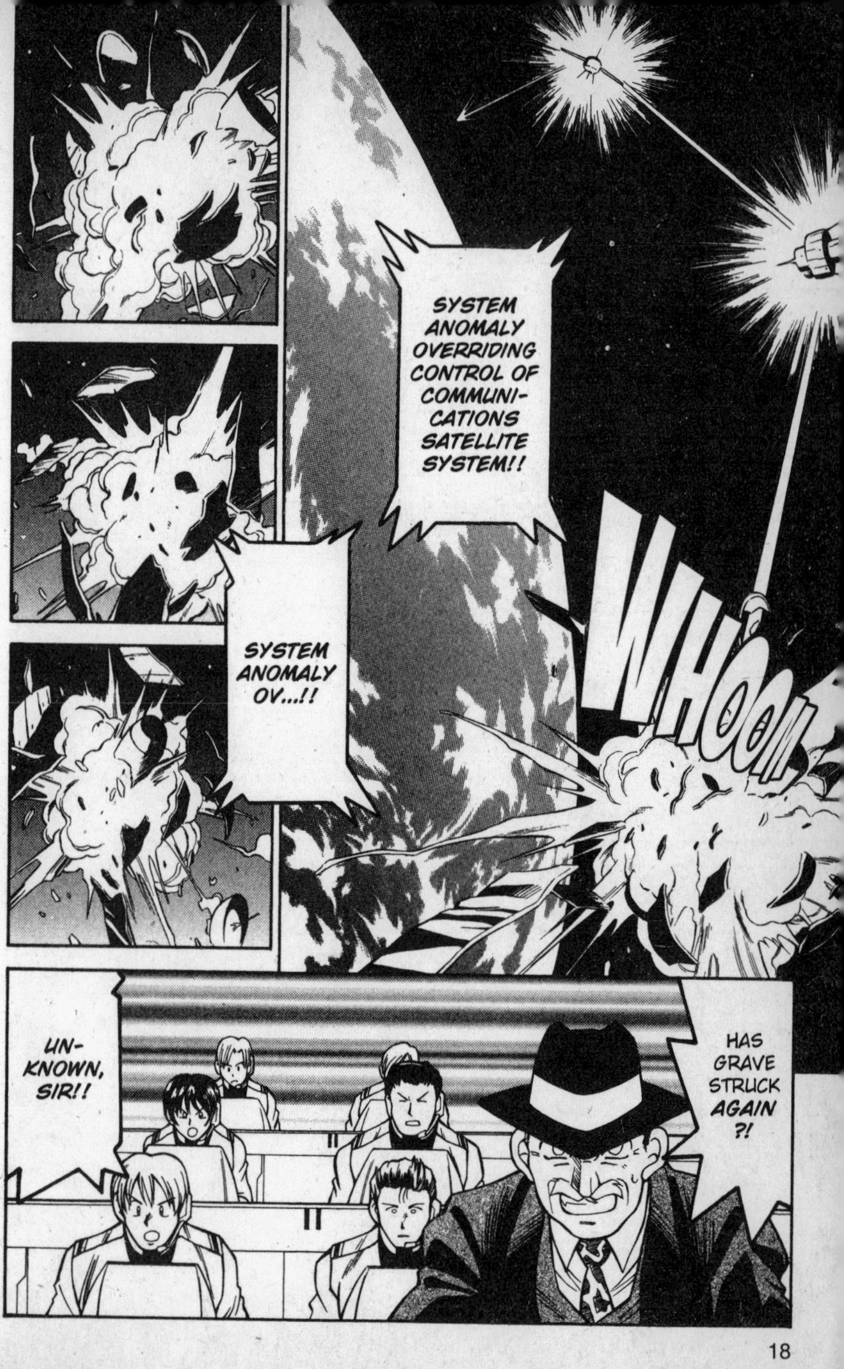
SYSTEM ANOMALY OVERRIDING CONTROL OF COMMUNI-CATIONS SATELLITE SYSTEM!!
SYSTEM ANOMALY OV...!!
WHOOM
HAS GRAVE STRUCK AGAIN?!
UN-KNOWN, SIR!!

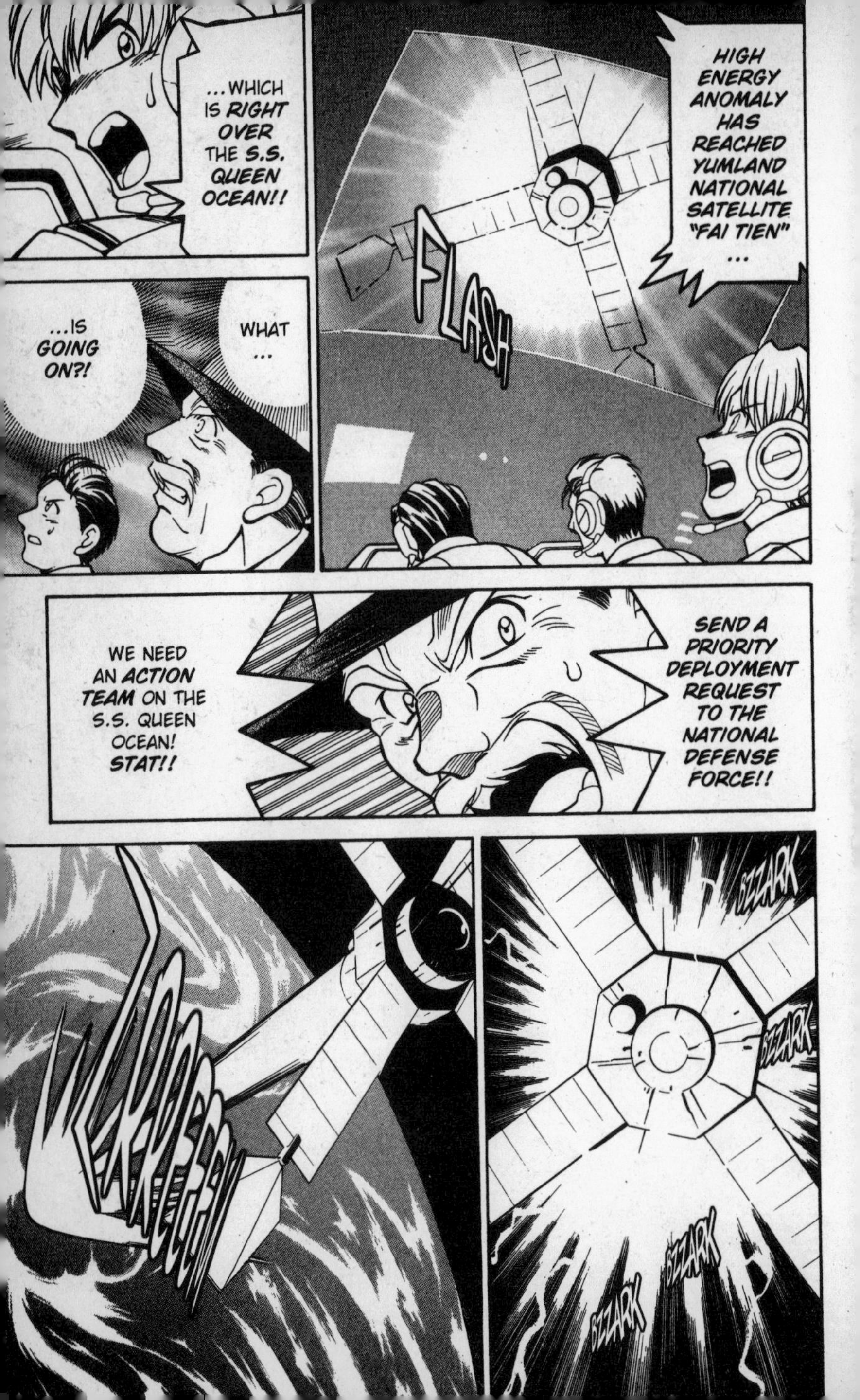
HIGH ENERGY ANOMALY HAS REACHED YUMLAND NATIONAL SATELLITE "FAI TIEN" ...
FLASH
...WHICH IS RIGHT OVER THE S.S. QUEEN OCEAN!!
WHAT ...
...IS GOING ON?!
SEND A PRIORITY DEPLOYMENT REQUEST TO THE NATIONAL DEFENSE FORCE!!
WE NEED AN ACTION TEAM ON THE S.S. QUEEN OCEAN! STAT!!
BZZARK
BZZARK
BZZARK
BZZARK

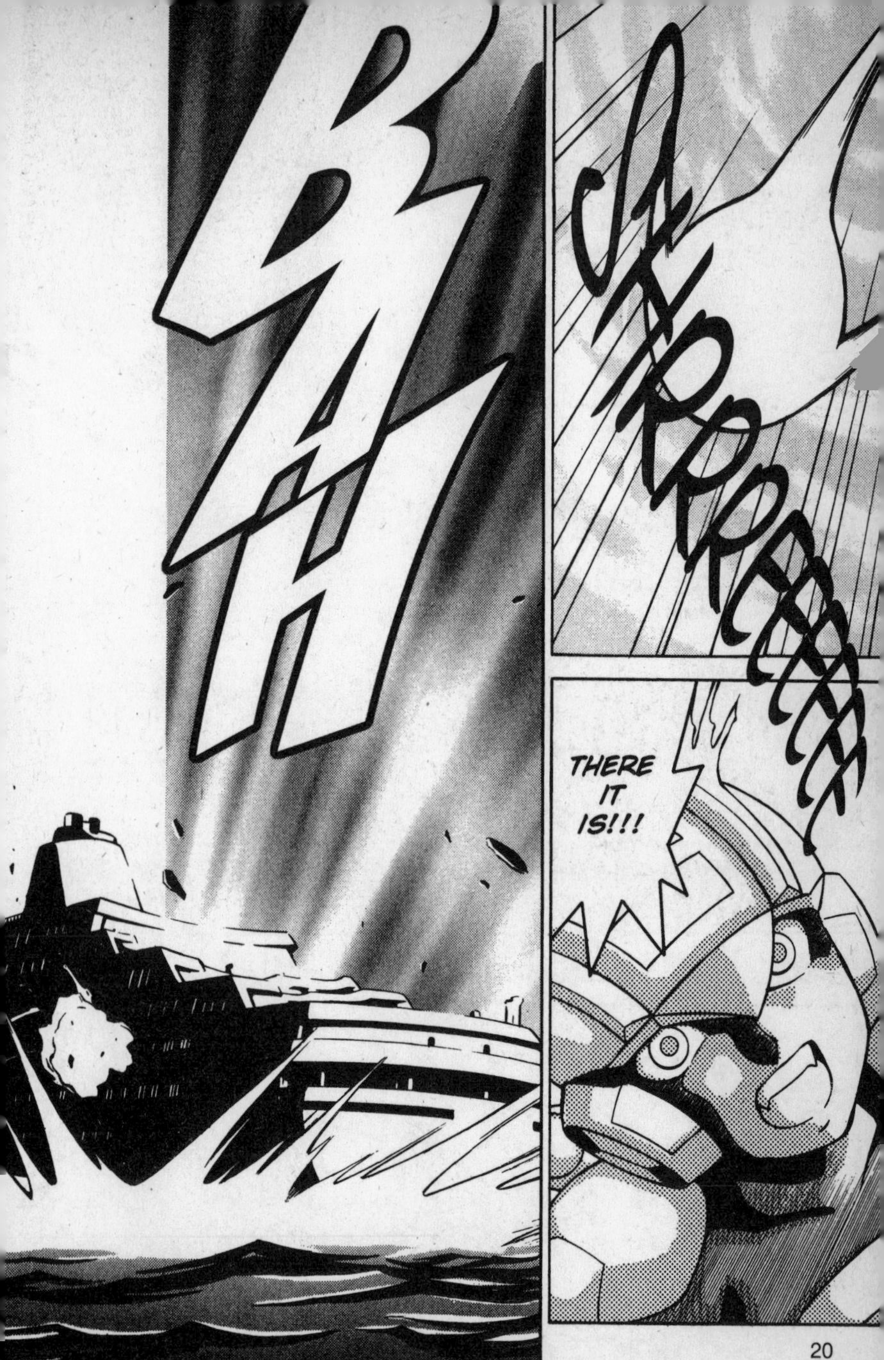
THERE IT IS!!!

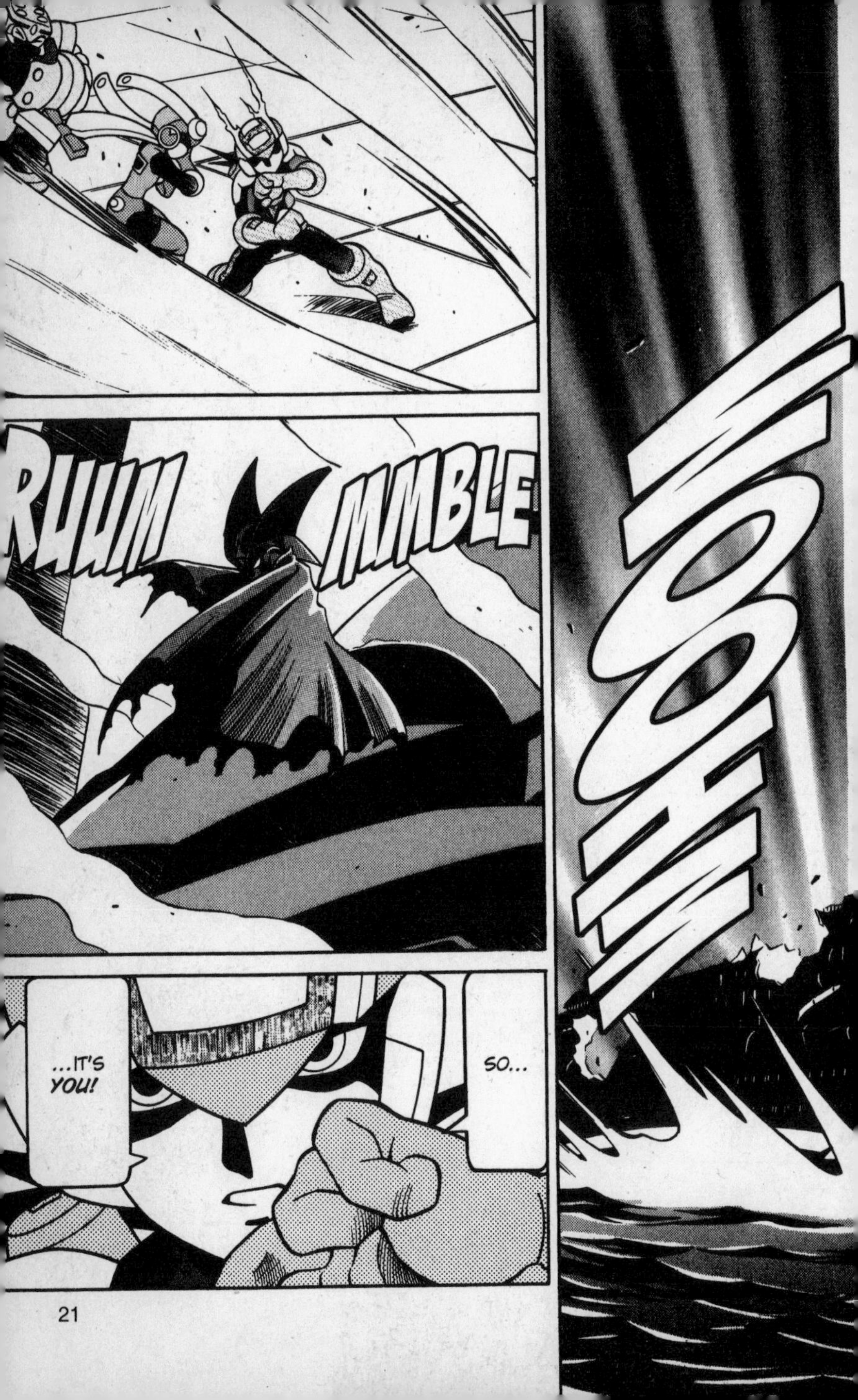
WHOOSH
RUUM MMBLE
SO...
...IT'S YOU!

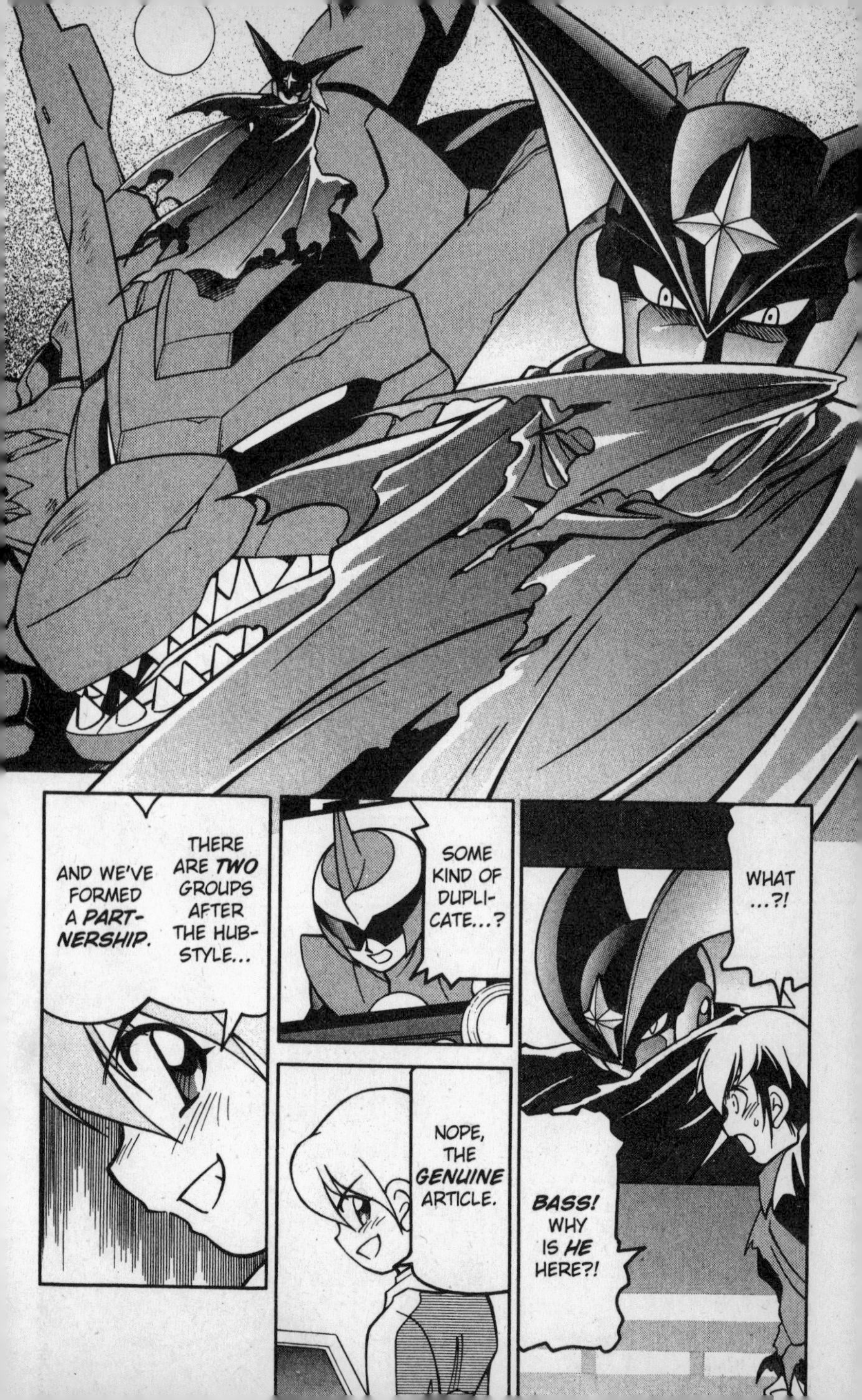
WHAT ...?!
BASS! WHY IS HE HERE?!
SOME KIND OF DUPLI-CATE...?
NOPE, THE GENUINE ARTICLE.
THERE ARE TWO GROUPS AFTER THE HUB-STYLE...
AND WE'VE FORMED A PART-NERSHIP.

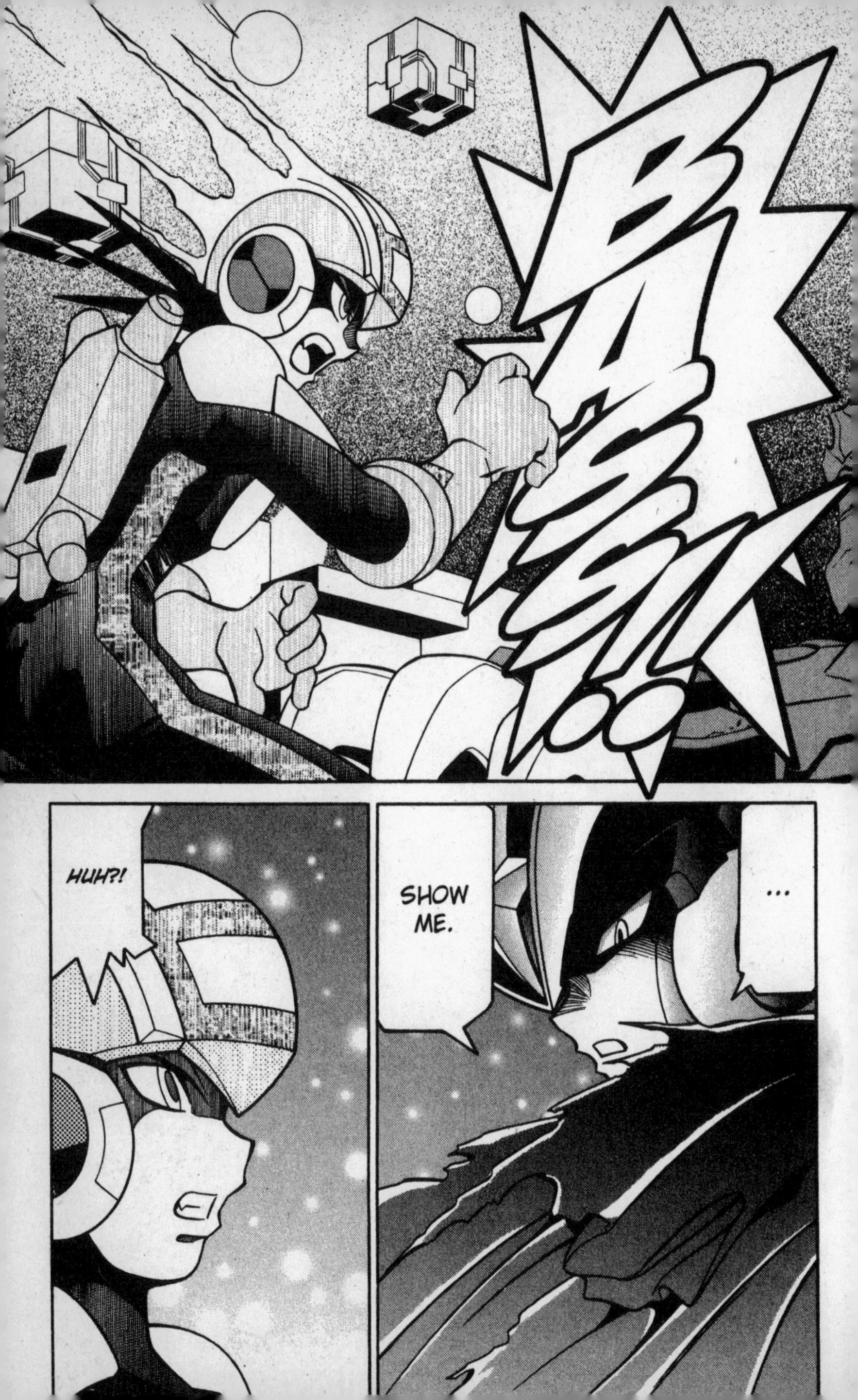
BASS!!
...
SHOW ME.
HUH?!

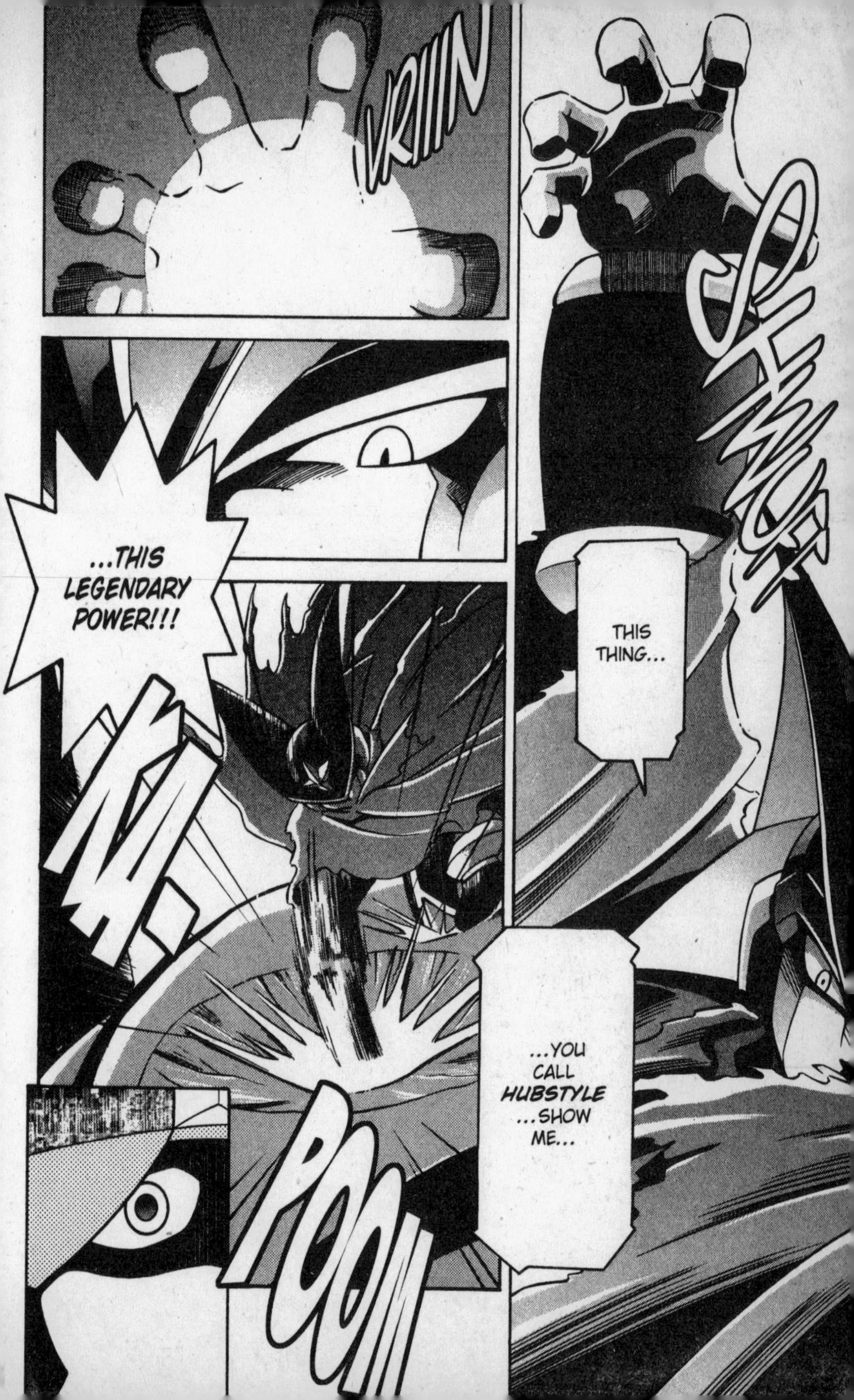
SHWUFF
THIS THING...
...YOU CALL **HUBSTYLE** ...SHOW ME...
VRIIIN
...THIS LEGENDARY POWER!!!
POOM

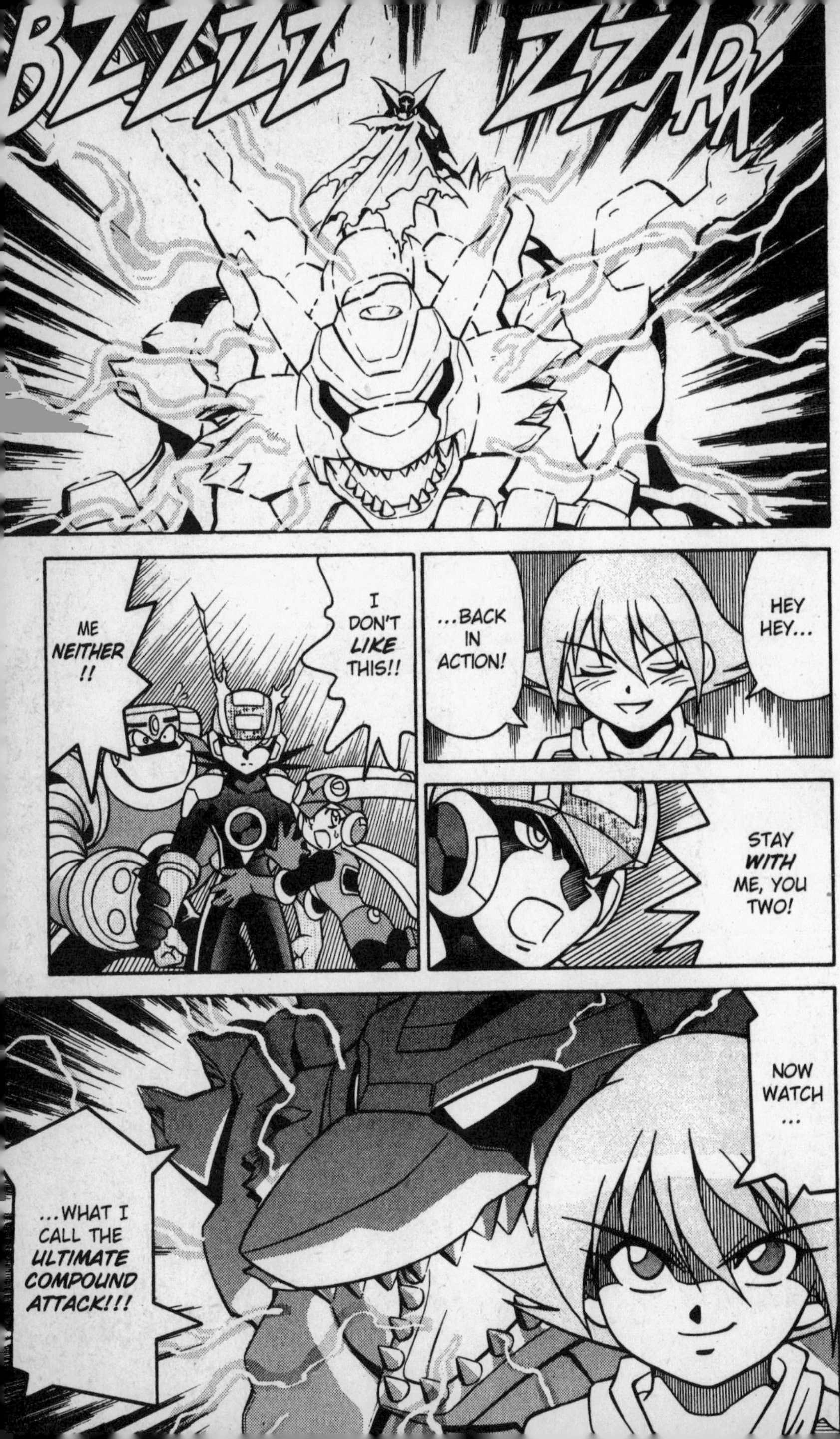

BZZZZ ZZZARK
HEY HEY...
...BACK IN ACTION!
STAY WITH ME, YOU TWO!
I DON'T LIKE THIS!!
ME NEITHER!!
NOW WATCH...
...WHAT I CALL THE ULTIMATE COMPOUND ATTACK!!!

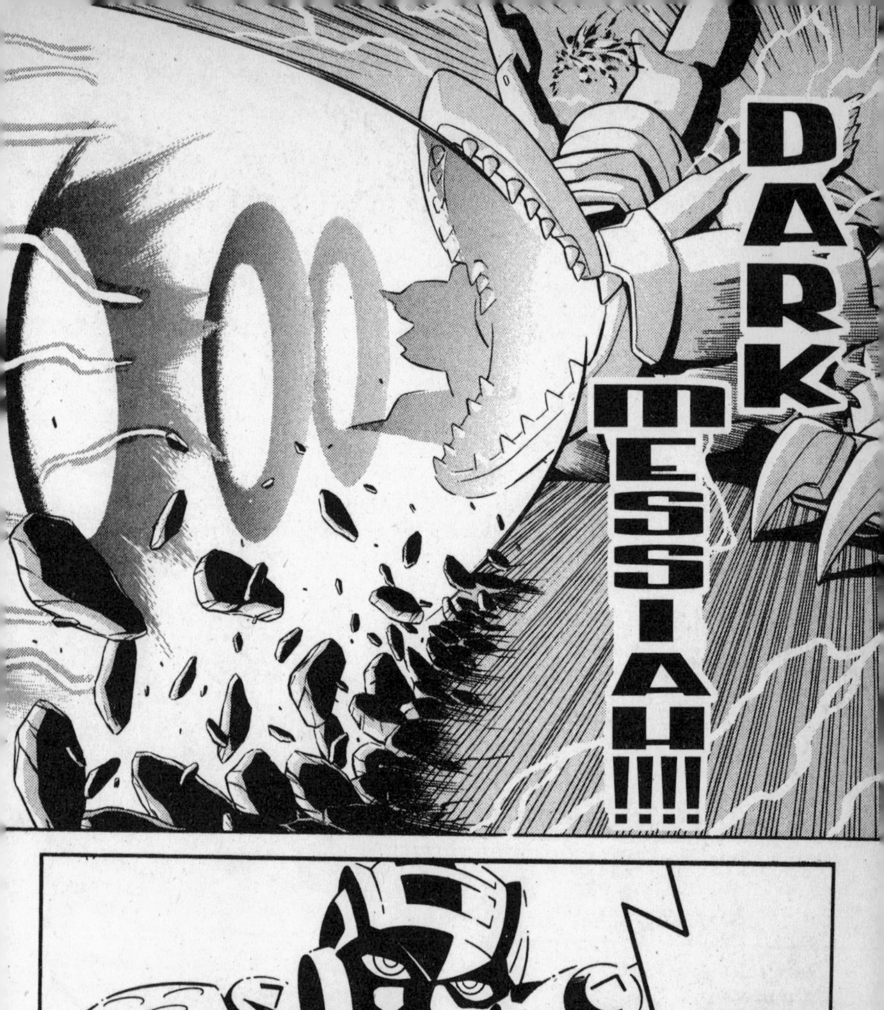
DARK MESSIAH!!!!

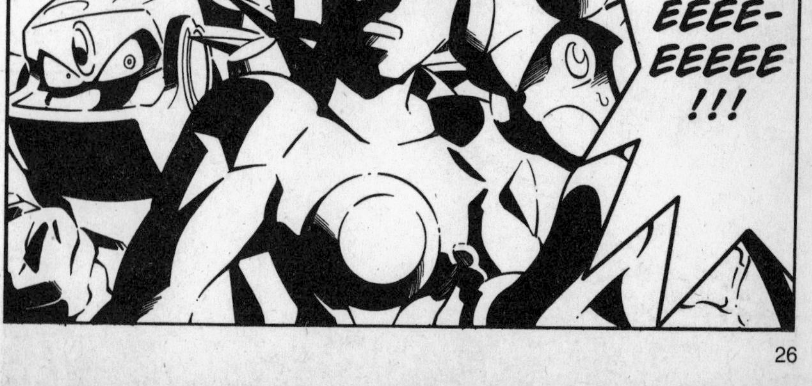
EEEE-
EEEEE
!!!

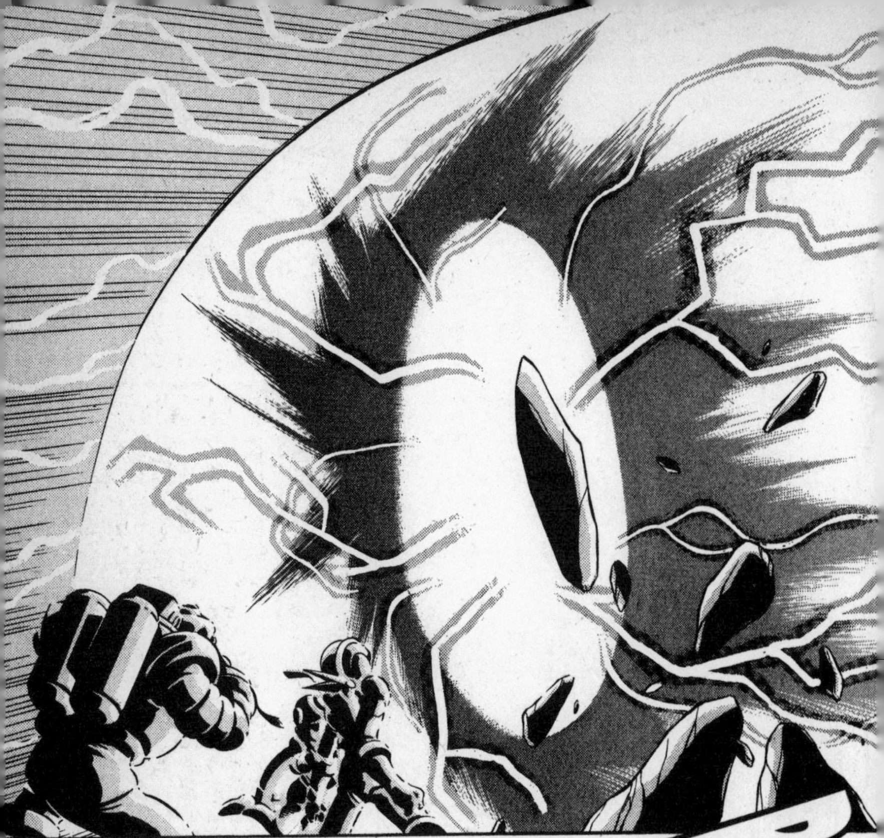

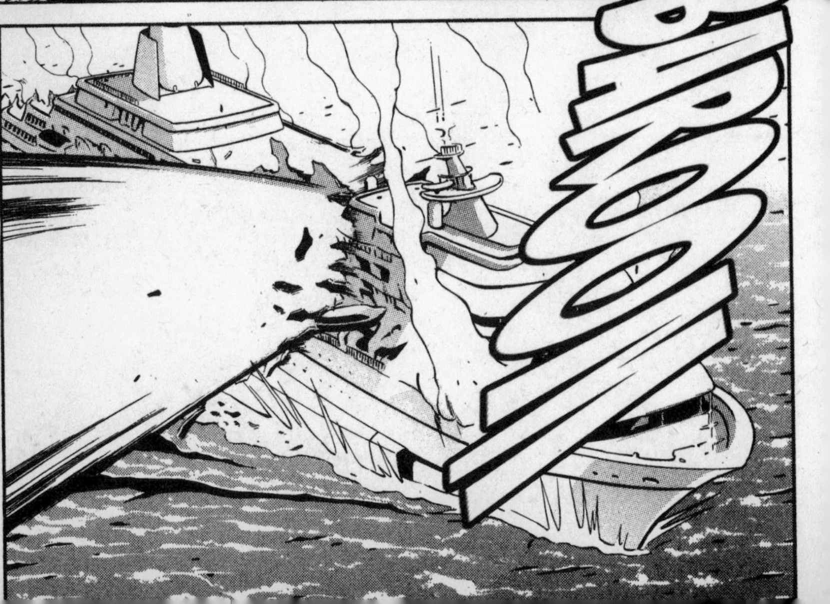
BAROOOM

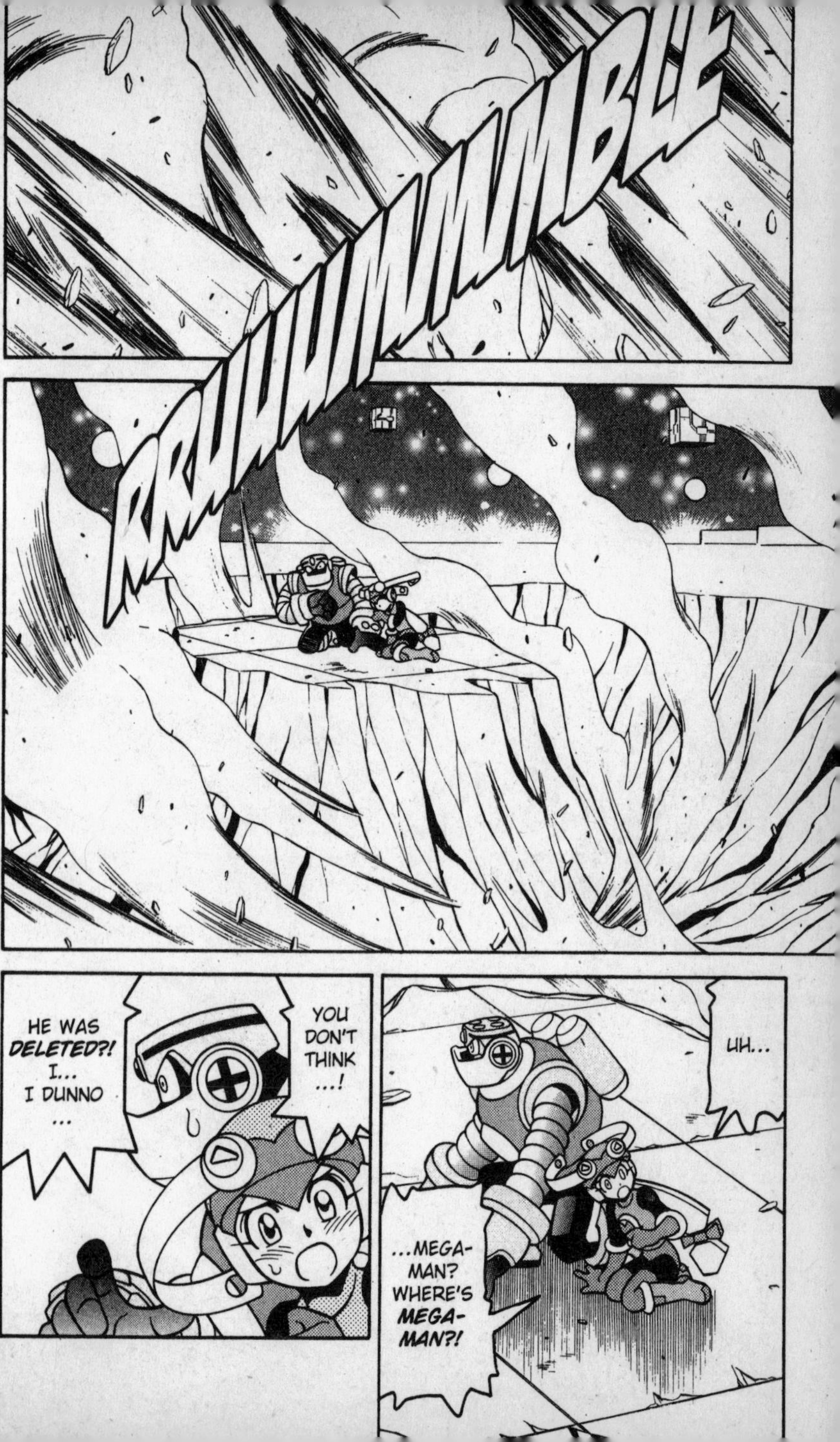

RRUUMMMMBLE
UH...
...MEGA-MAN? WHERE'S MEGA-MAN?!
YOU DON'T THINK ...!
HE WAS DELETED?! I... I DUNNO ...

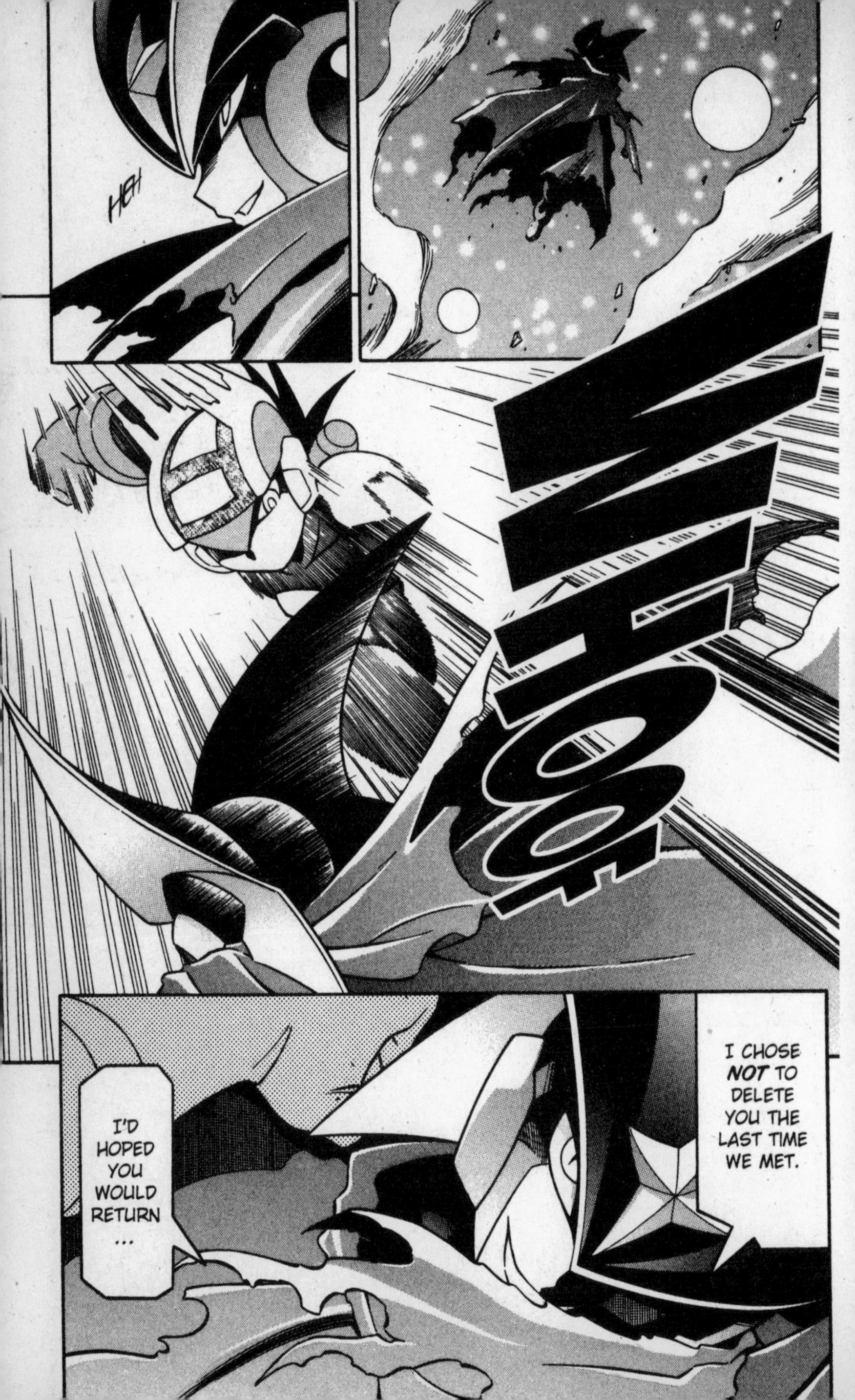
HEH
I CHOSE **NOT** TO DELETE YOU THE LAST TIME WE MET.
I'D HOPED YOU WOULD RETURN ...

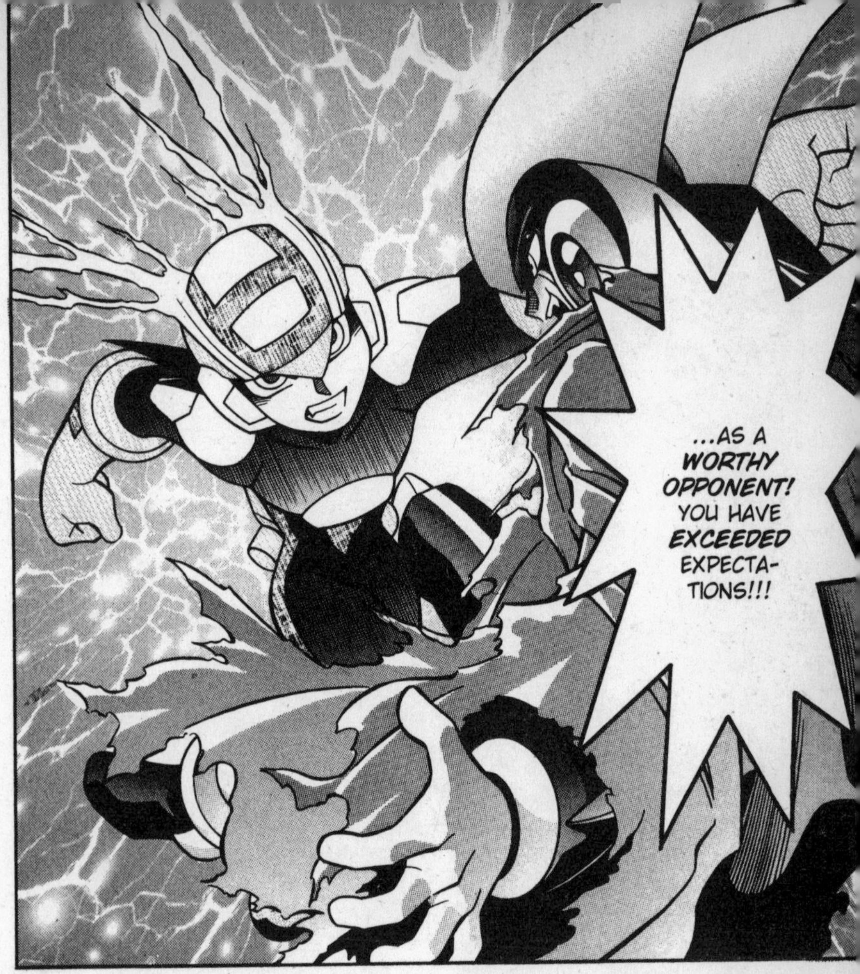
...AS A WORTHY OPPONENT! YOU HAVE EXCEEDED EXPECTA-TIONS!!!

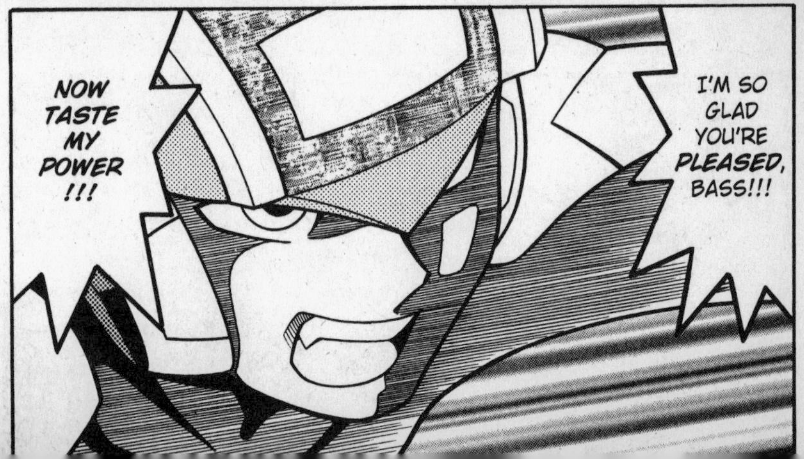
I'M SO GLAD YOU'RE PLEASED, BASS!!!
NOW TASTE MY POWER !!!

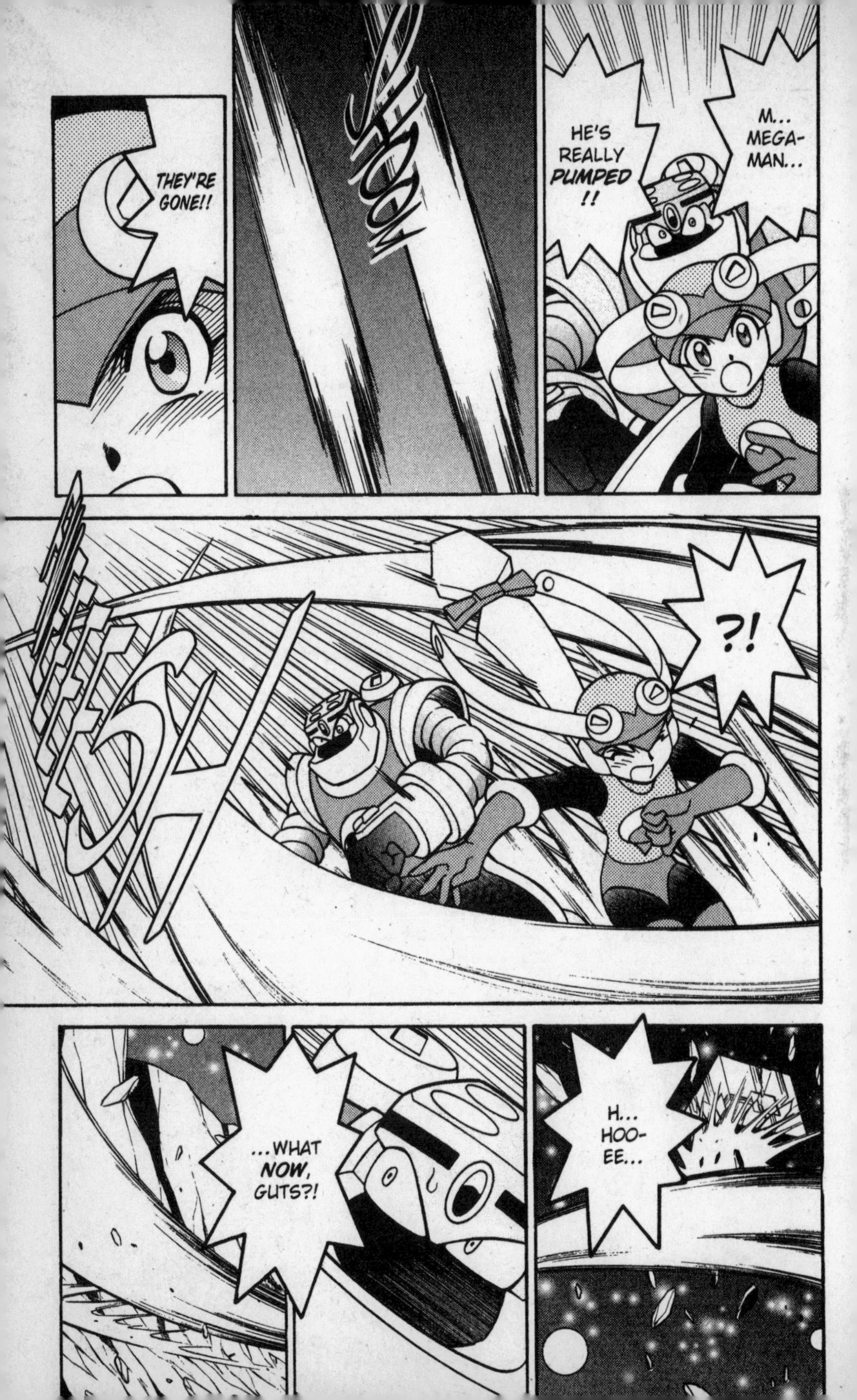
M... MEGA-MAN...
HE'S REALLY PUMPED!!
SHOOM
THEY'RE GONE!!
?!
H... HOO-EE...
...WHAT NOW, GUTS?!

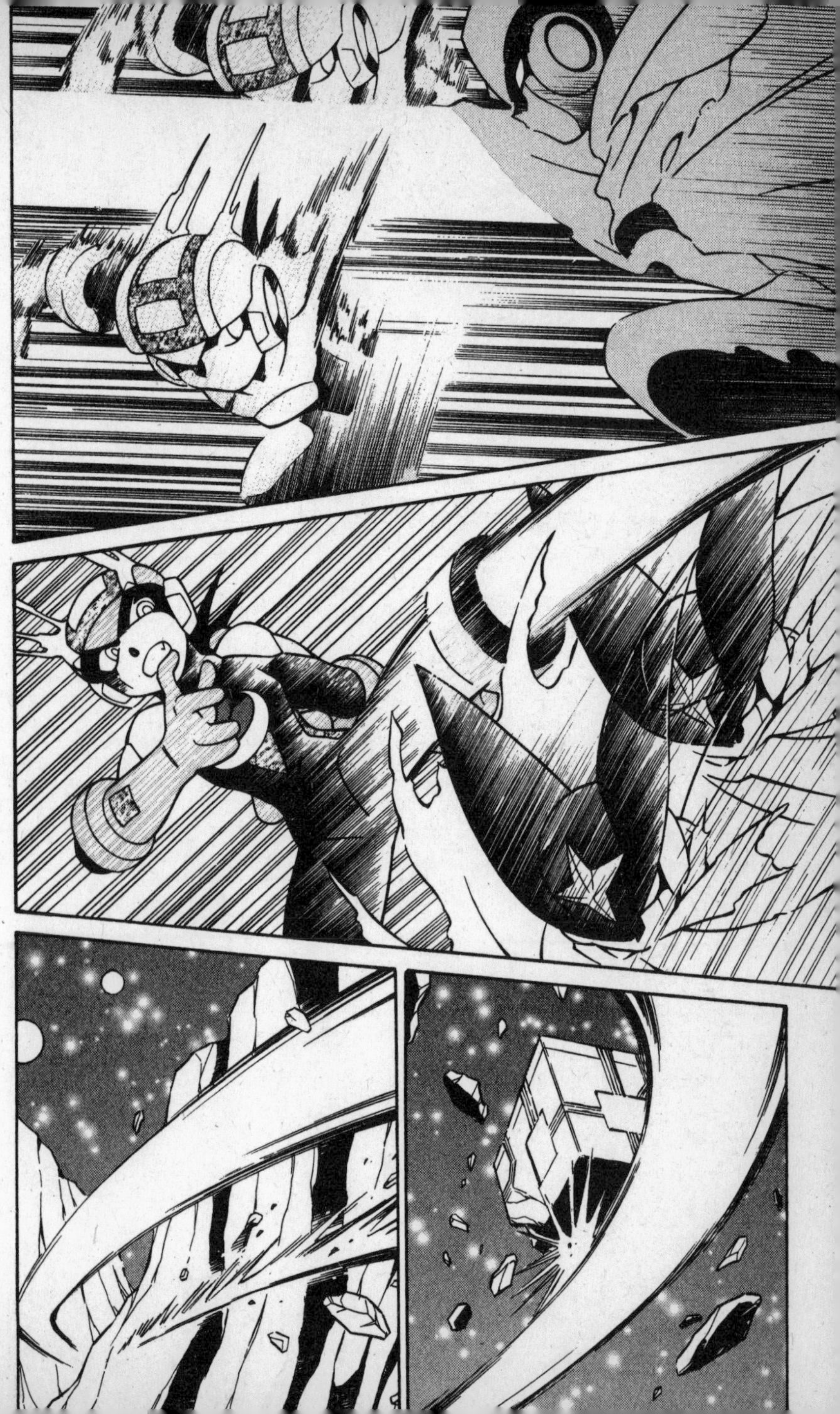

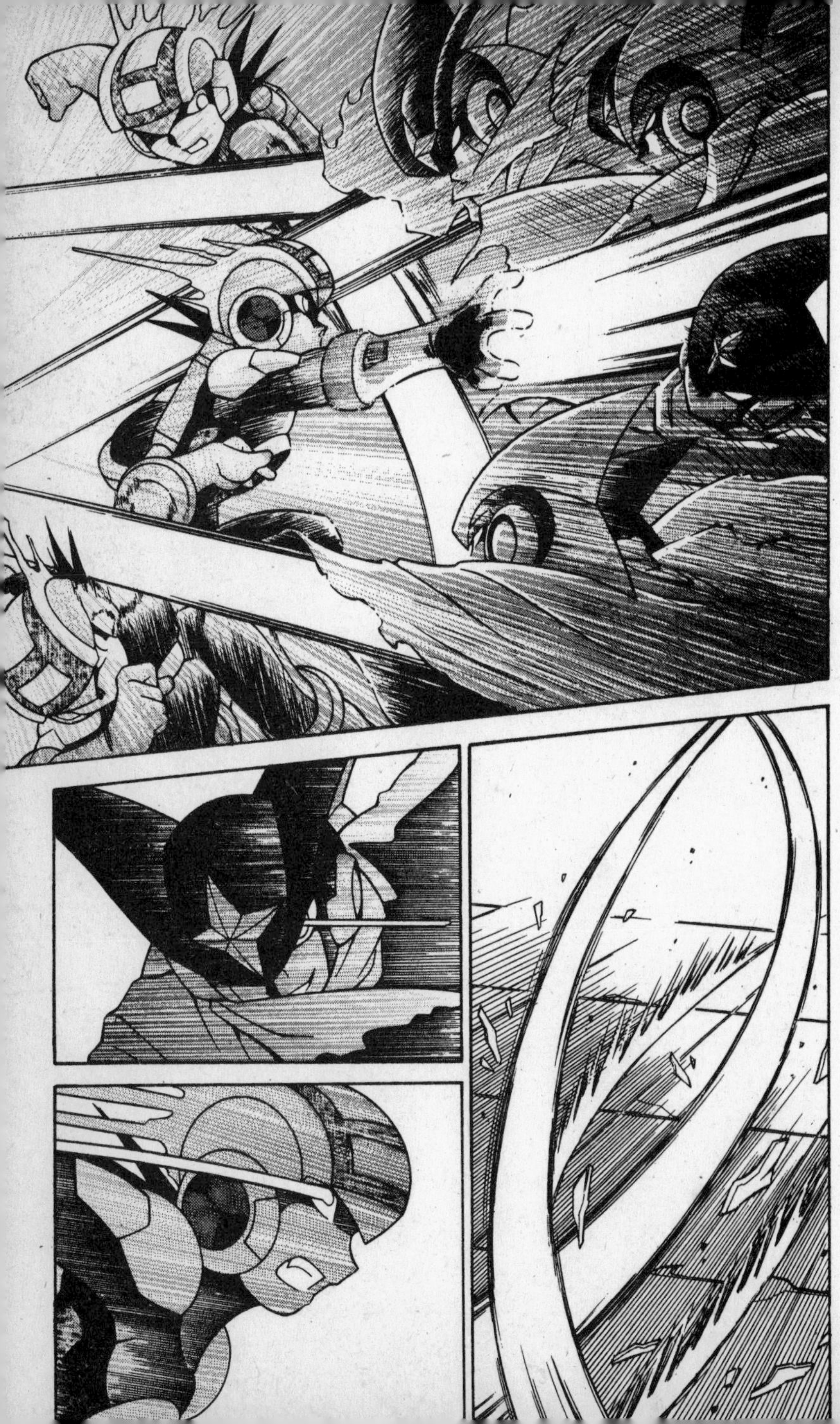

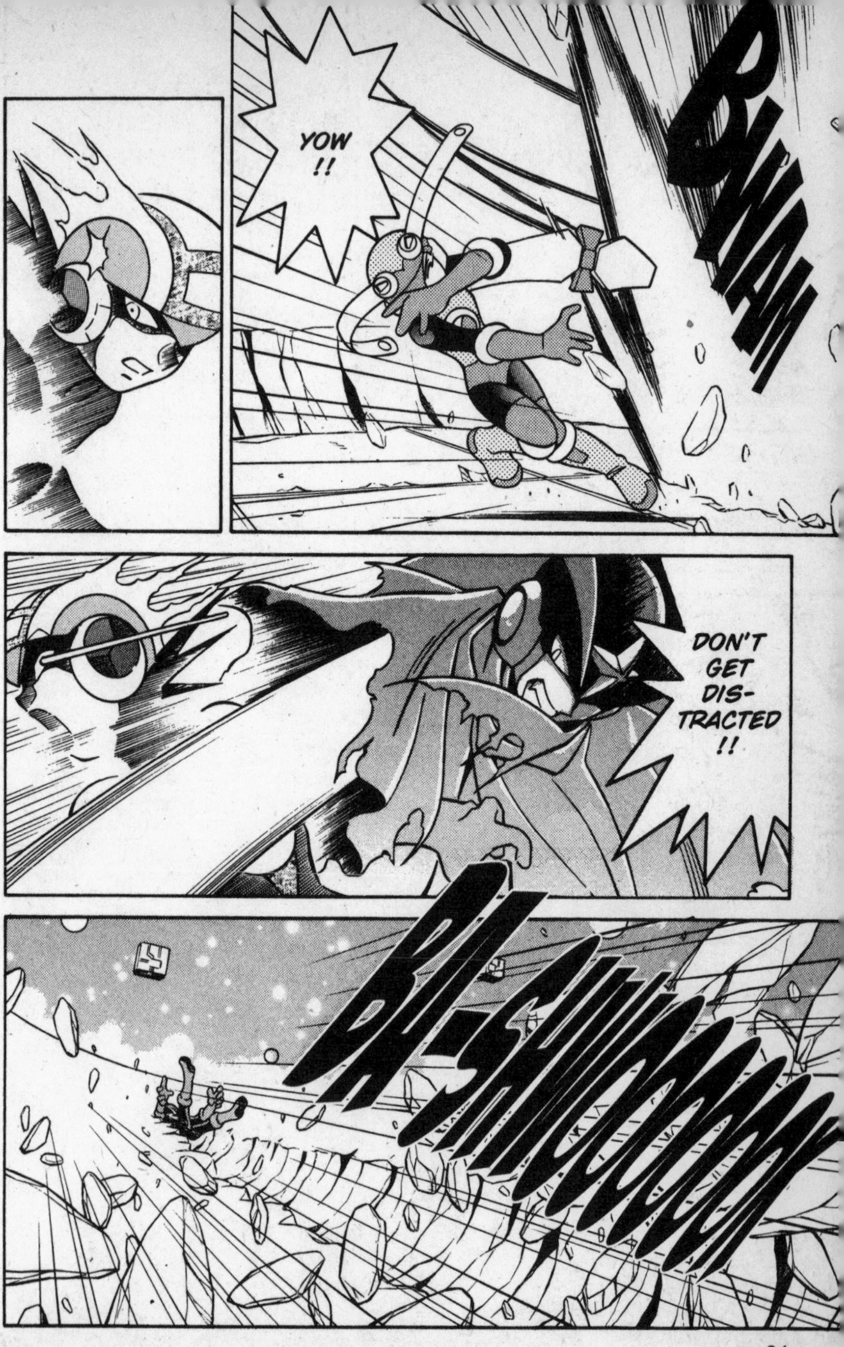
BWAM
YOW !!
DON'T GET DIS-TRACTED !!
BA-SHOOOOOM

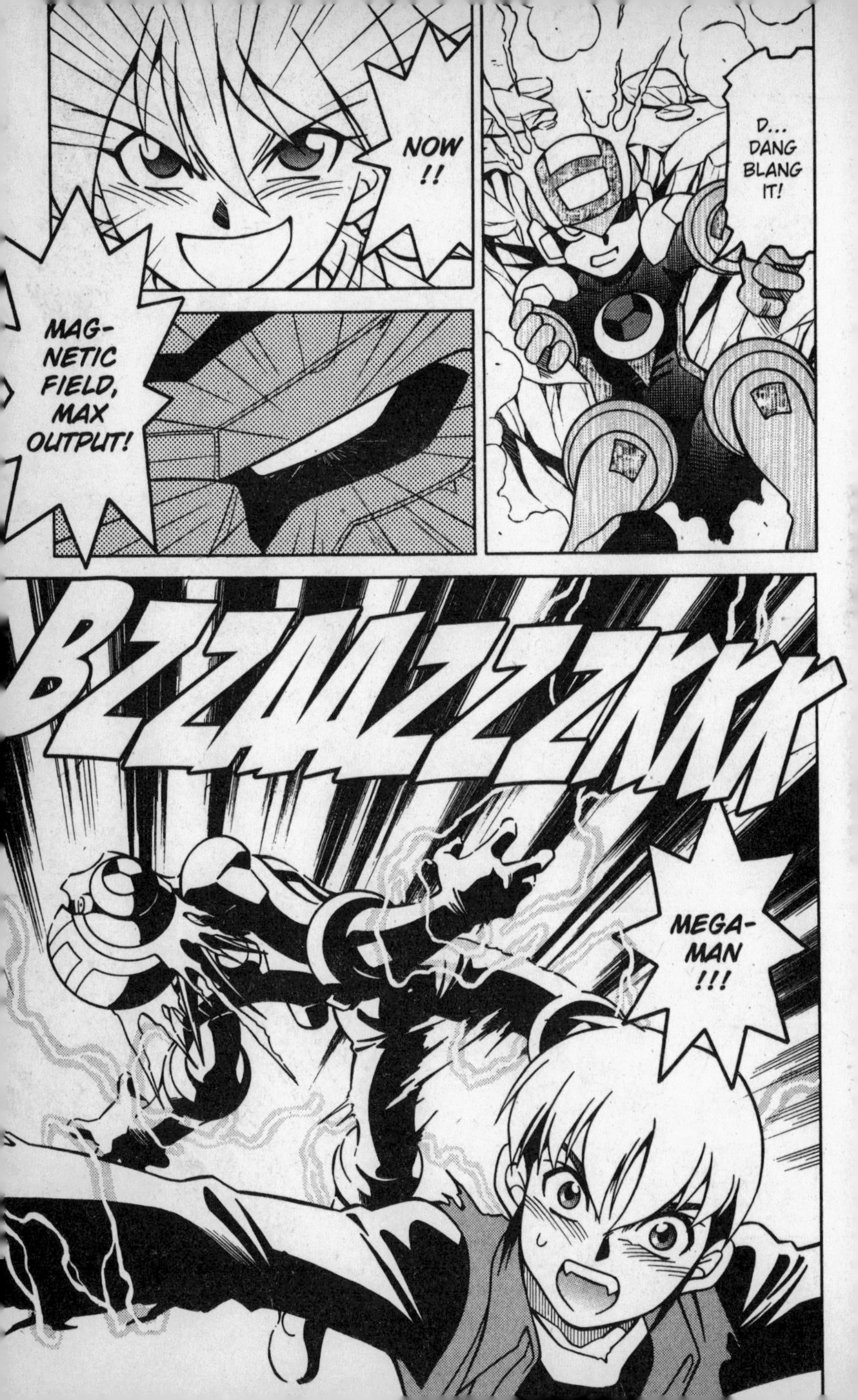
D... DANG BLANG IT!
NOW !!
MAG-NETIC FIELD, MAX OUTPUT!
BZZZZKKK
MEGA-MAN !!!

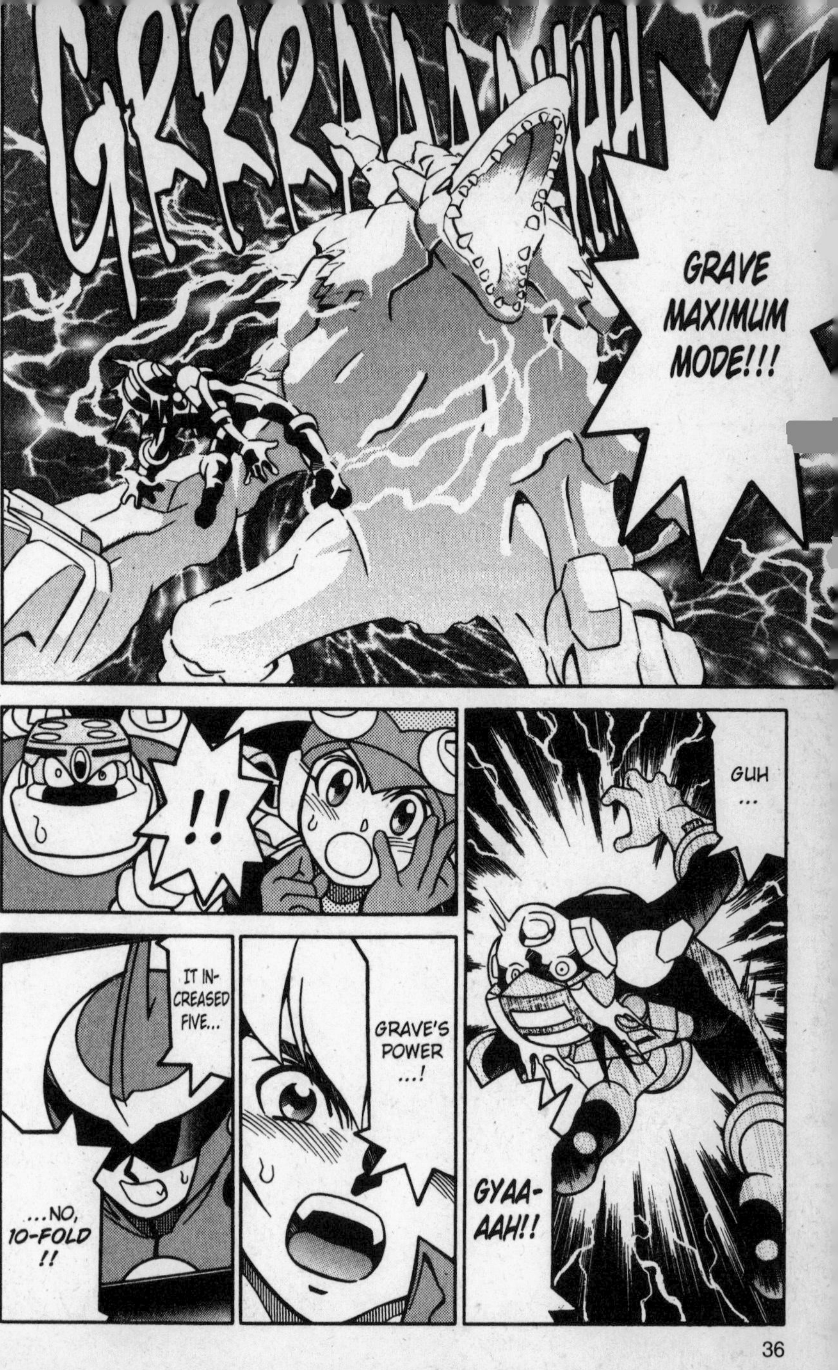
GRAVE MAXIMUM MODE!!!
GUH ...
GYAA-AAH!!
!!
GRAVE'S POWER ...!
IT INCREASED FIVE...
...NO, 10-FOLD !!

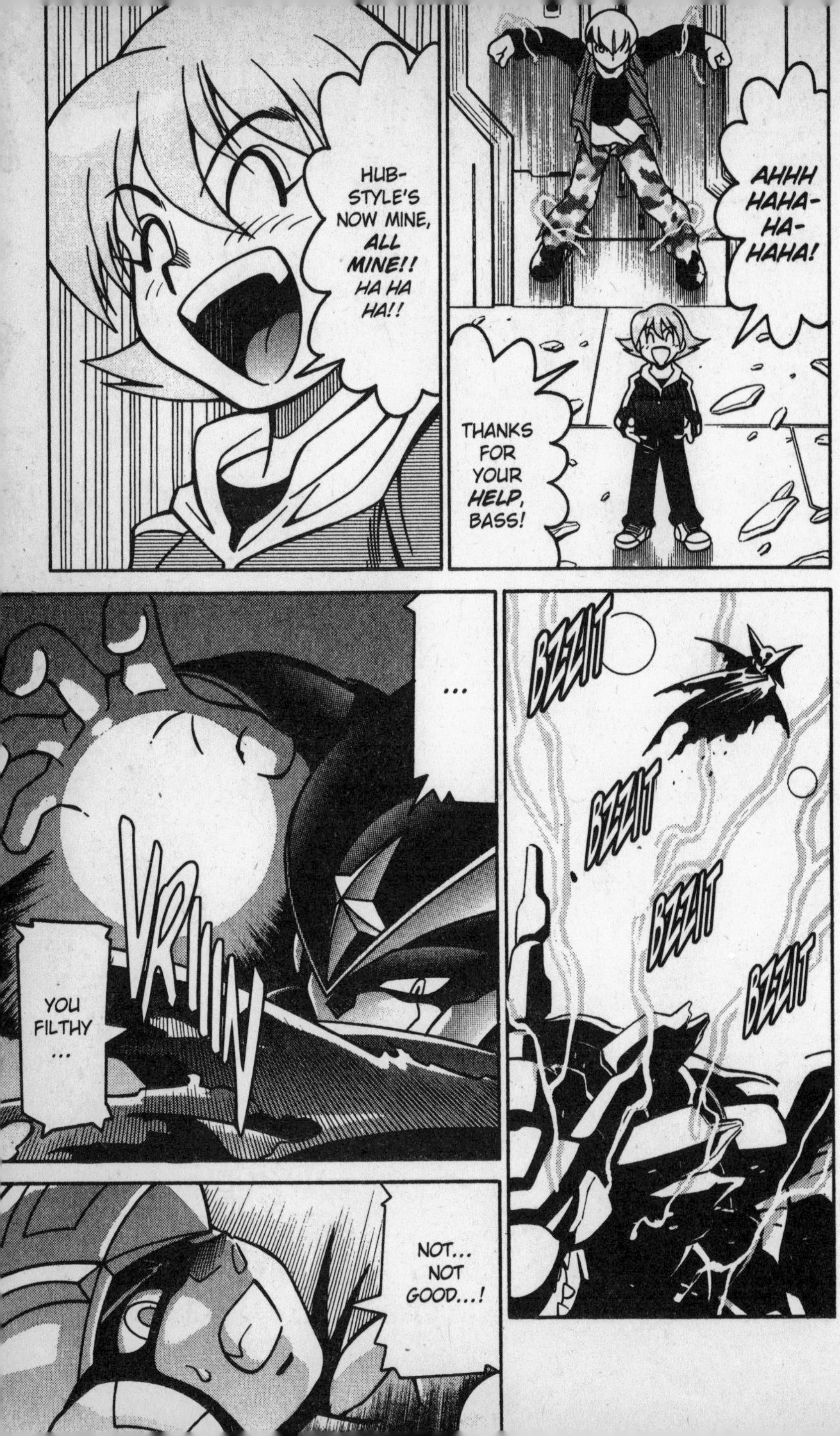
AHHH HAHA-HA-HAHA!
THANKS FOR YOUR HELP, BASS!
HUB-STYLE'S NOW MINE, ALL MINE!! HA HA HA!!
BZZIT
BZZIT
BZZIT
BZZIT
...
VRIIIN
YOU FILTHY ...
NOT... NOT GOOD...!

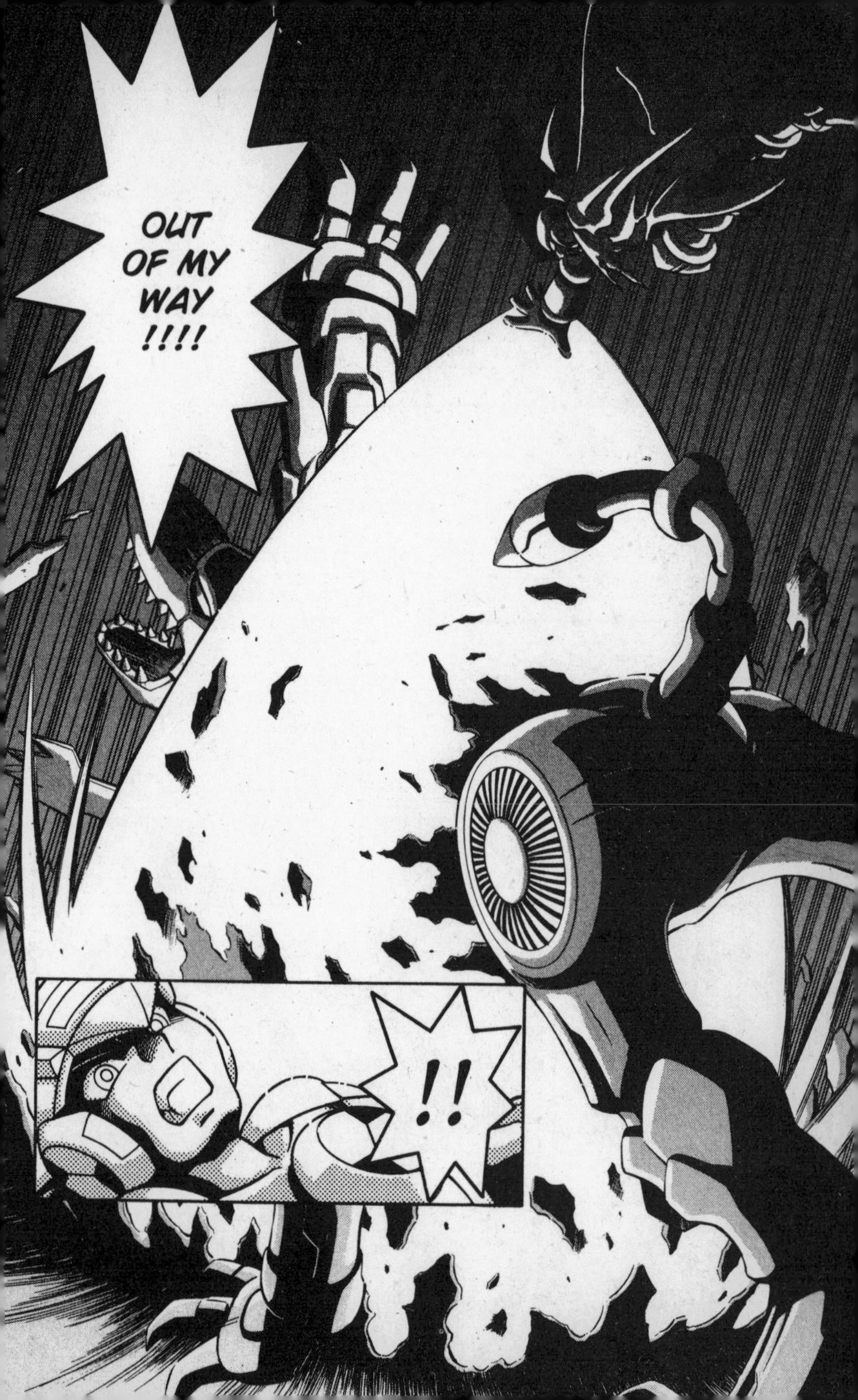
OUT OF MY WAY !!!!
!!

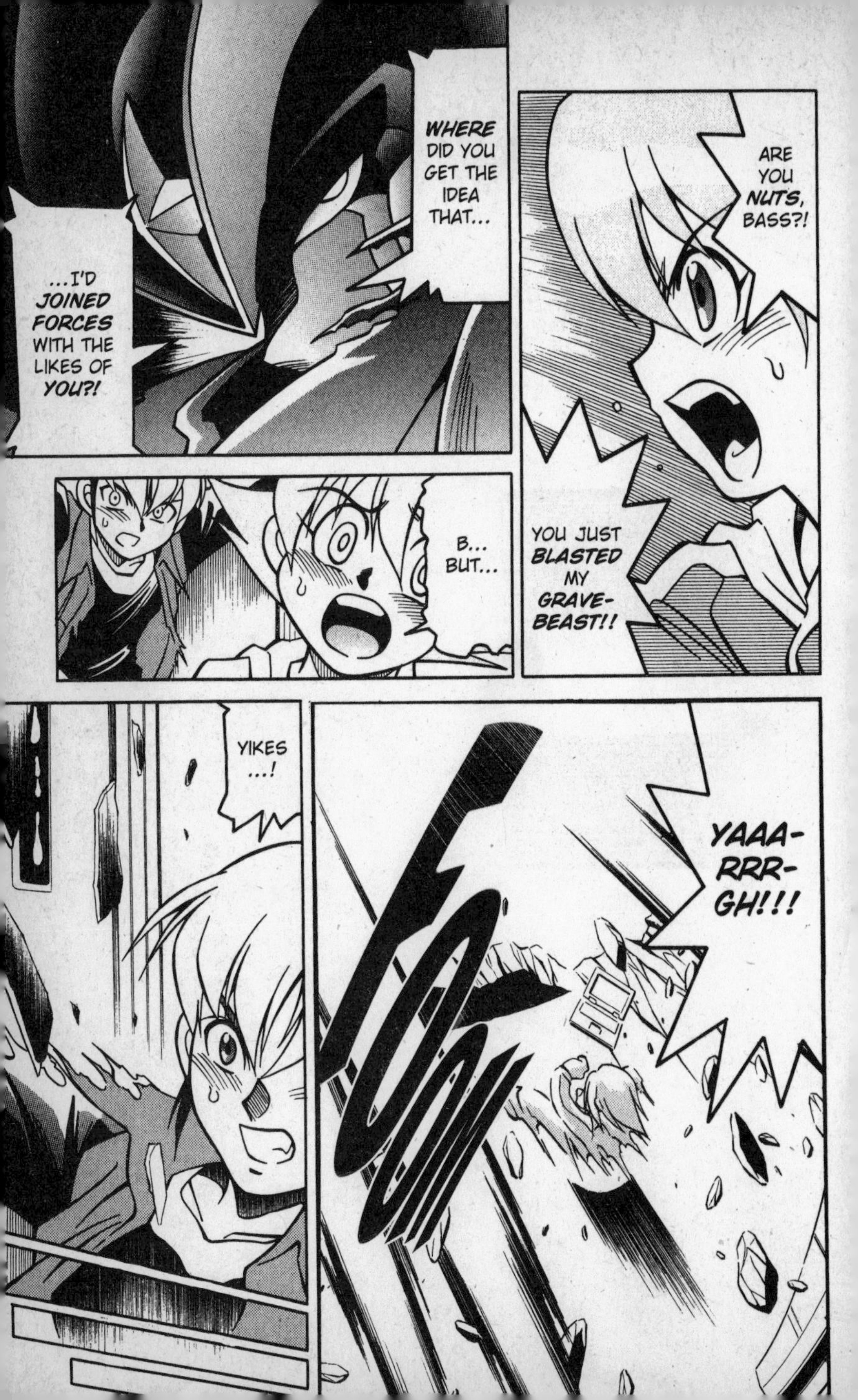
ARE YOU NUTS, BASS?!
YOU JUST BLASTED MY GRAVE-BEAST!!
WHERE DID YOU GET THE IDEA THAT...
...I'D JOINED FORCES WITH THE LIKES OF YOU?!
B... BUT...
YAAA-RRRG-GH!!!
YIKES ...!

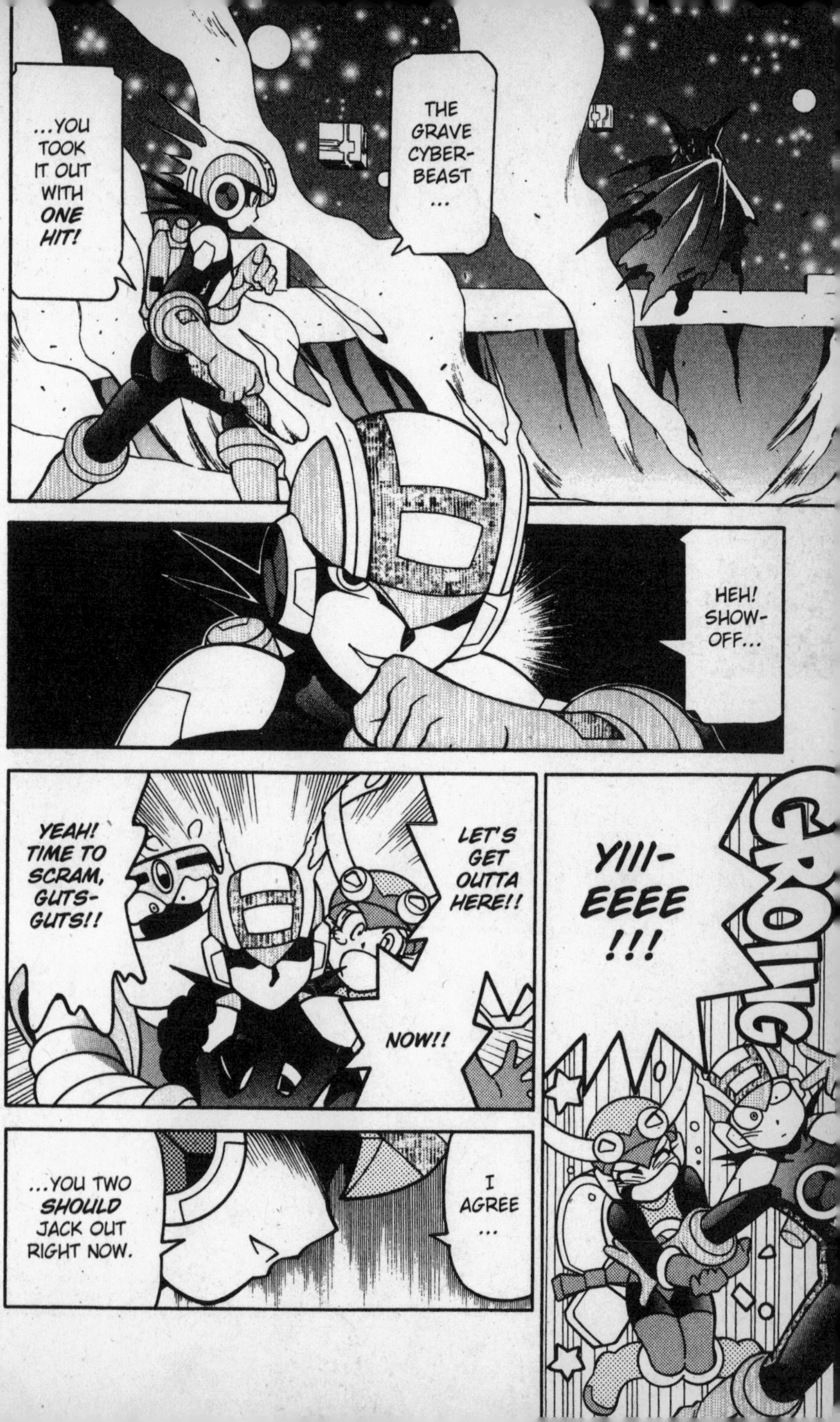
THE GRAVE CYBER-BEAST ...
...YOU TOOK IT OUT WITH ONE HIT!
HEH! SHOW-OFF...
GROING
YIII-EEEE!!!
LET'S GET OUTTA HERE!!
YEAH! TIME TO SCRAM, GUTS-GUTS!!
NOW!!
I AGREE ...
...YOU TWO SHOULD JACK OUT RIGHT NOW.

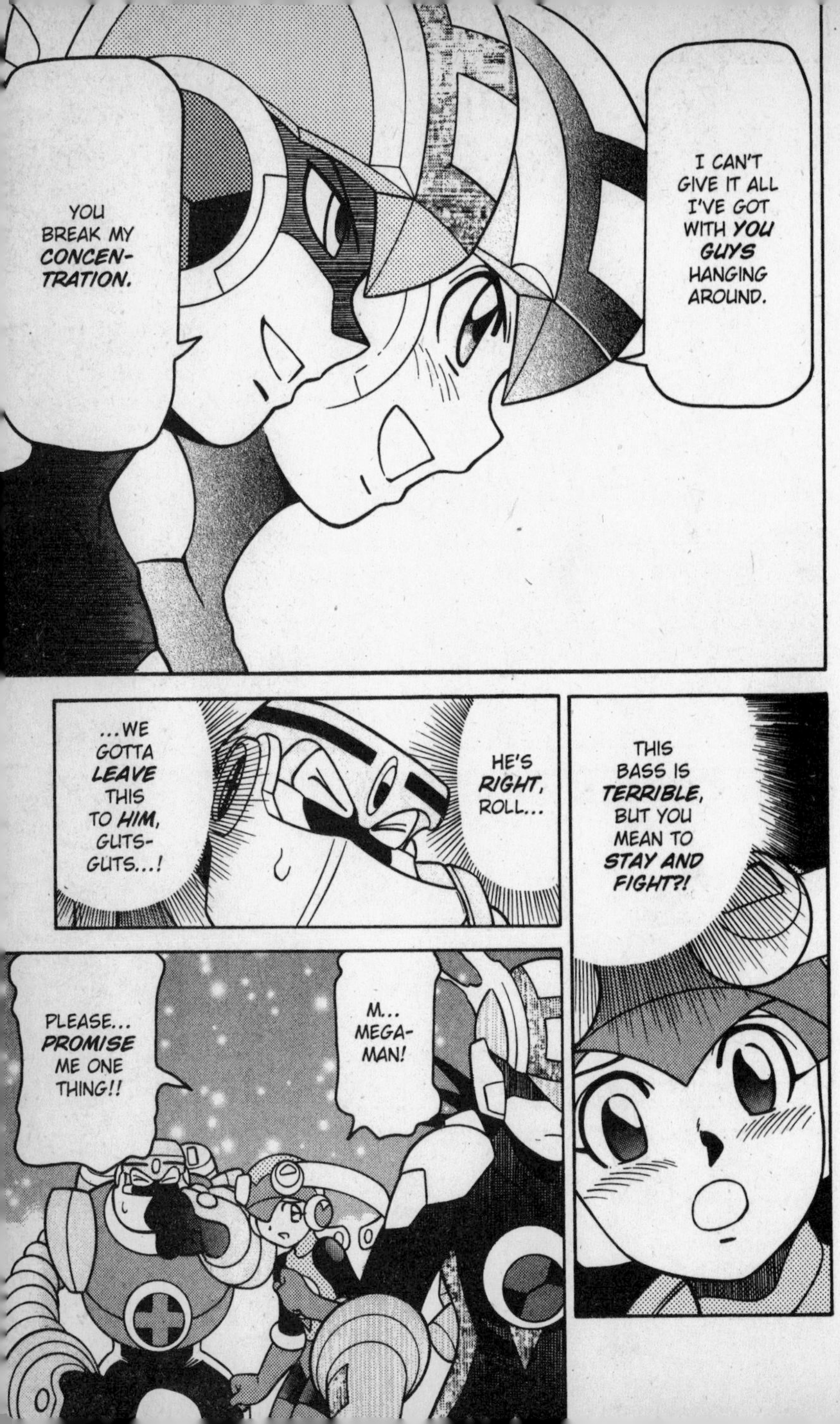
I CAN'T GIVE IT ALL I'VE GOT WITH YOU GUYS HANGING AROUND.
YOU BREAK MY CONCEN-TRATION.
THIS BASS IS TERRIBLE, BUT YOU MEAN TO STAY AND FIGHT?!
HE'S RIGHT, ROLL...
...WE GOTTA LEAVE THIS TO HIM, GUTS-GUTS...!
M... MEGA-MAN!
PLEASE... PROMISE ME ONE THING!!

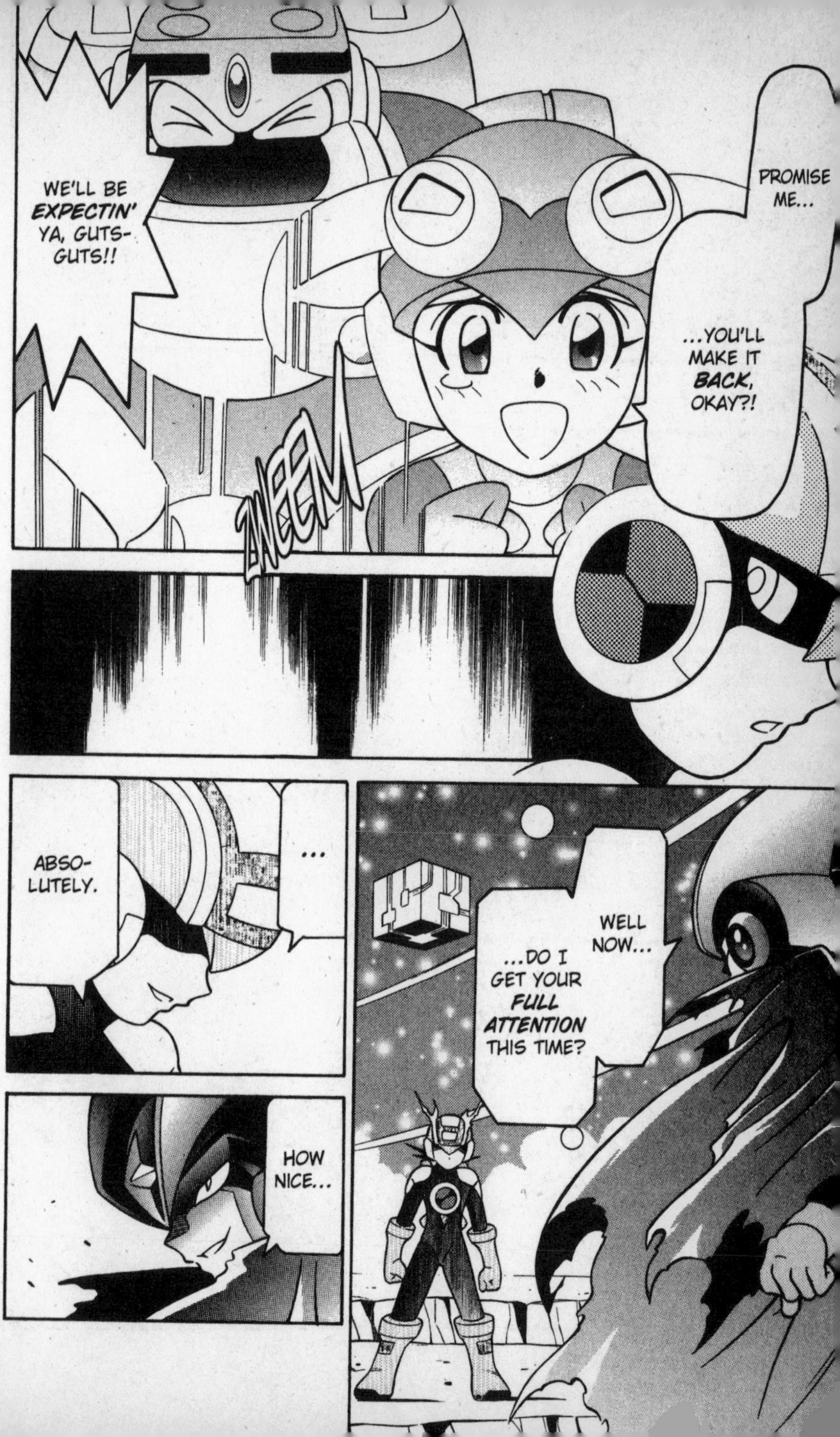
PROMISE ME...
...YOU'LL MAKE IT BACK, OKAY?!
WE'LL BE EXPECTIN' YA, GUTS-GUTS!!
ZWEEM
WELL NOW...
...DO I GET YOUR FULL ATTENTION THIS TIME?
...
ABSO-LUTELY.
HOW NICE...

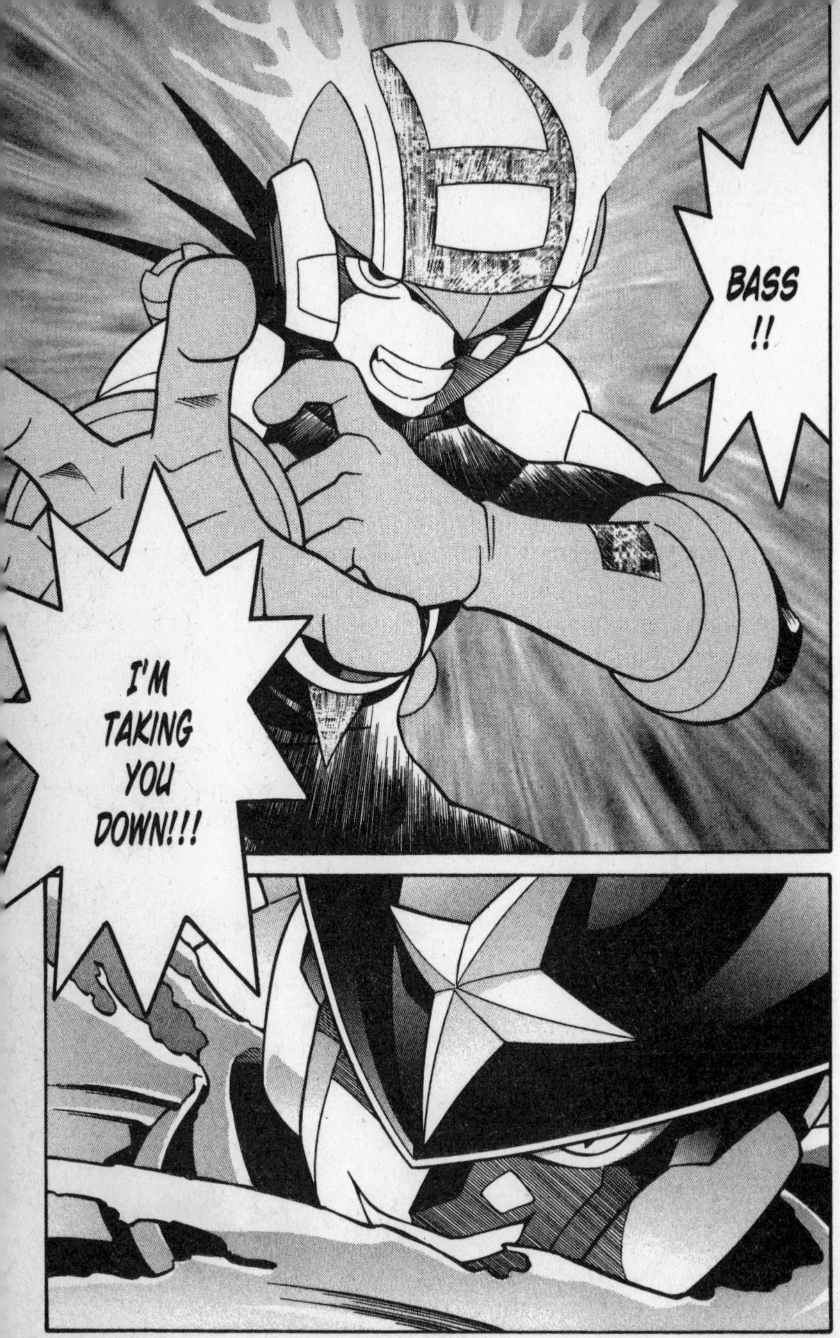
BASS !!
I'M TAKING YOU DOWN!!!

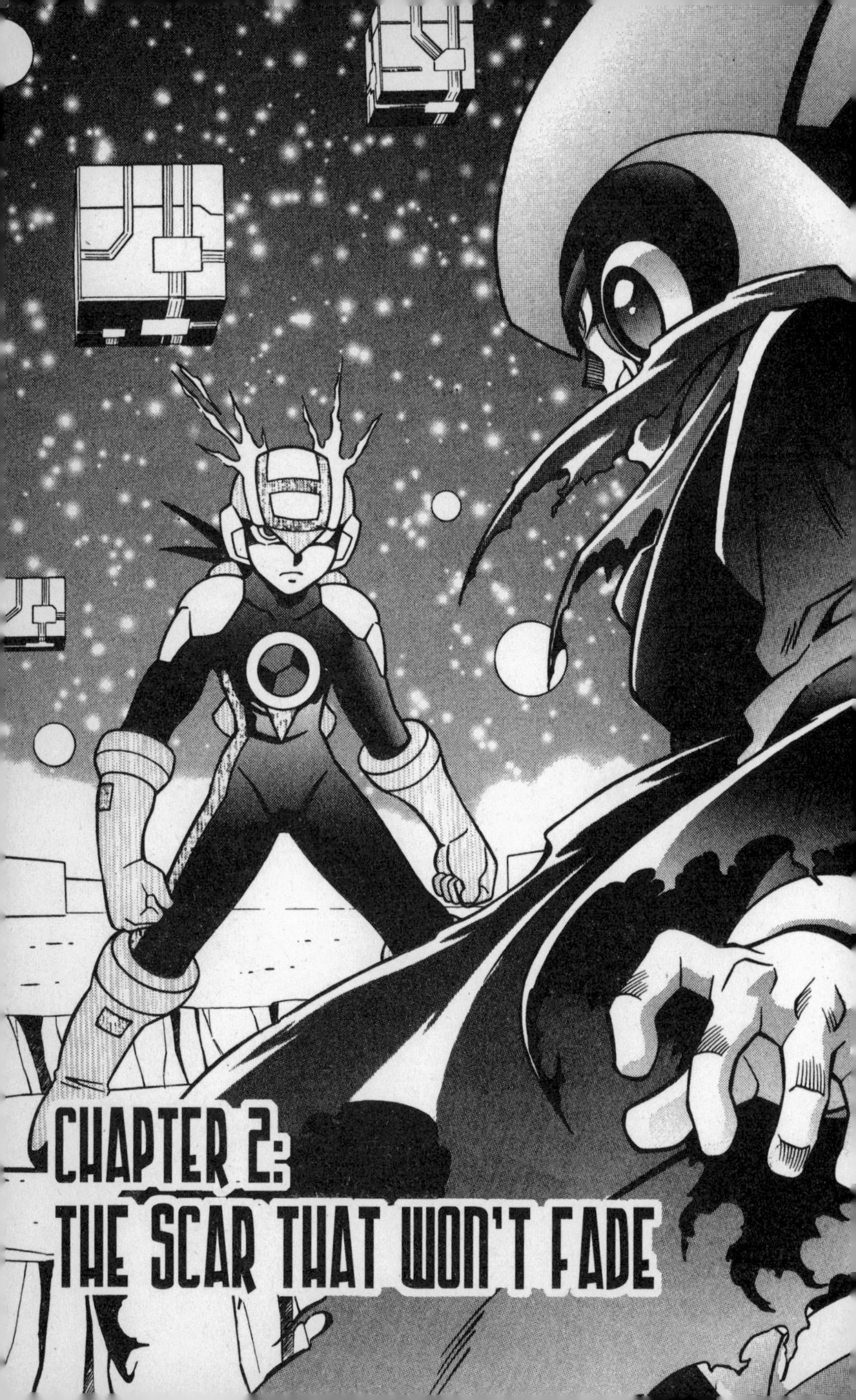
CHAPTER 2:
THE SCAR THAT WON'T FADE

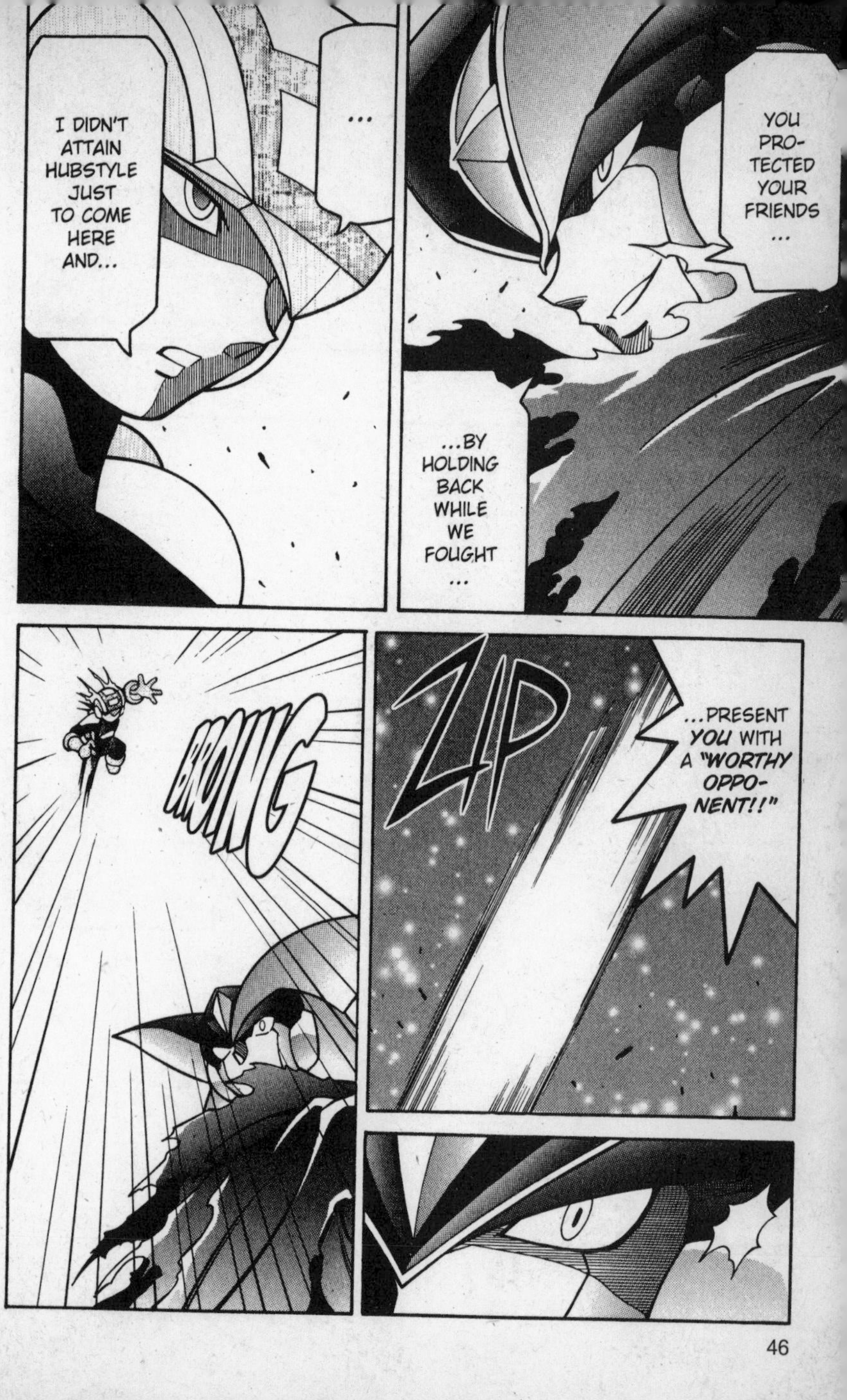
YOU PROTECTED YOUR FRIENDS ...
...BY HOLDING BACK WHILE WE FOUGHT ...
...
I DIDN'T ATTAIN HUBSTYLE JUST TO COME HERE AND...
ZIP
...PRESENT YOU WITH A "WORTHY OPPONENT!!"
BROING

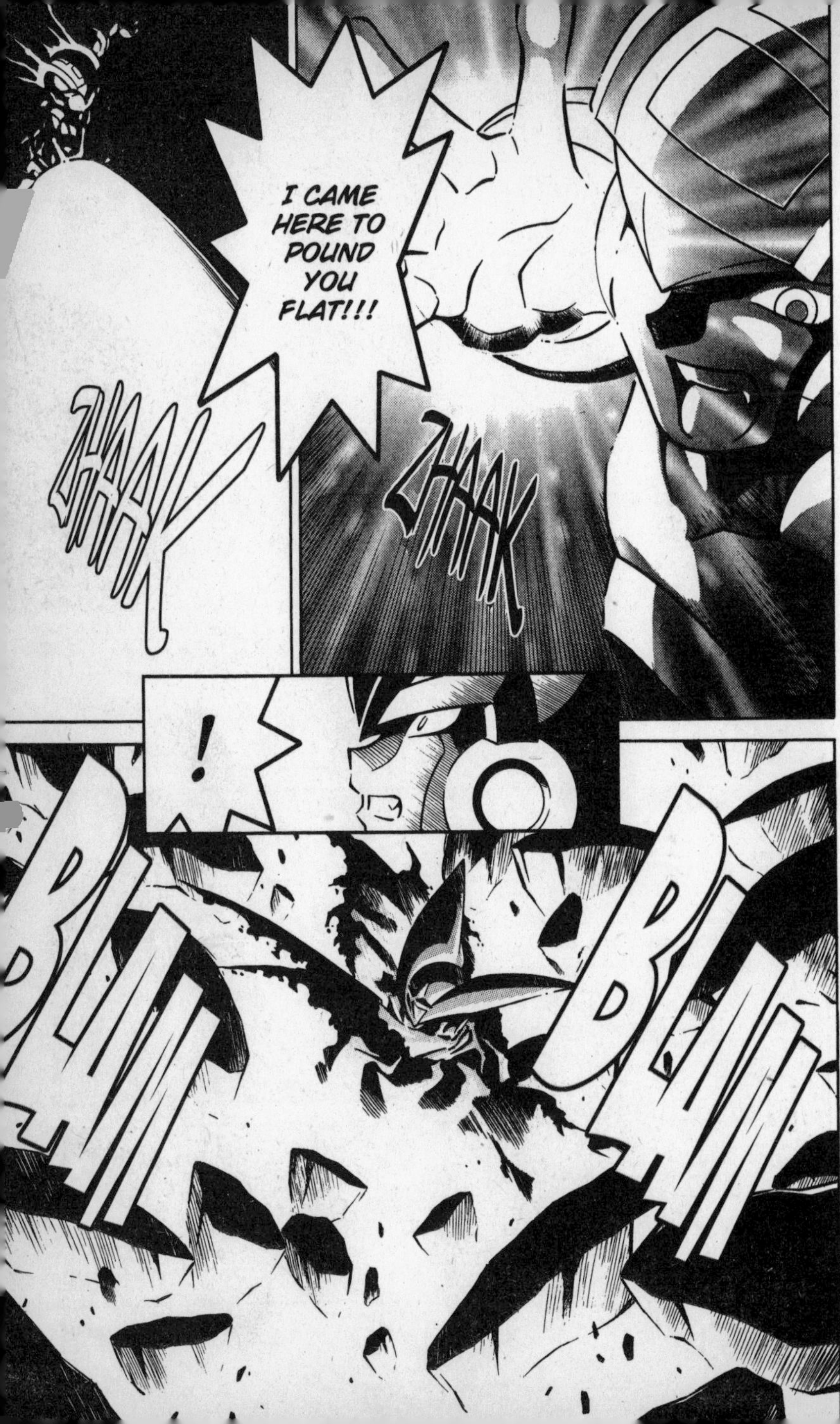
I CAME HERE TO POUND YOU FLAT!!!
ZHAAK
ZHAAK
!
BLAM
BLAM

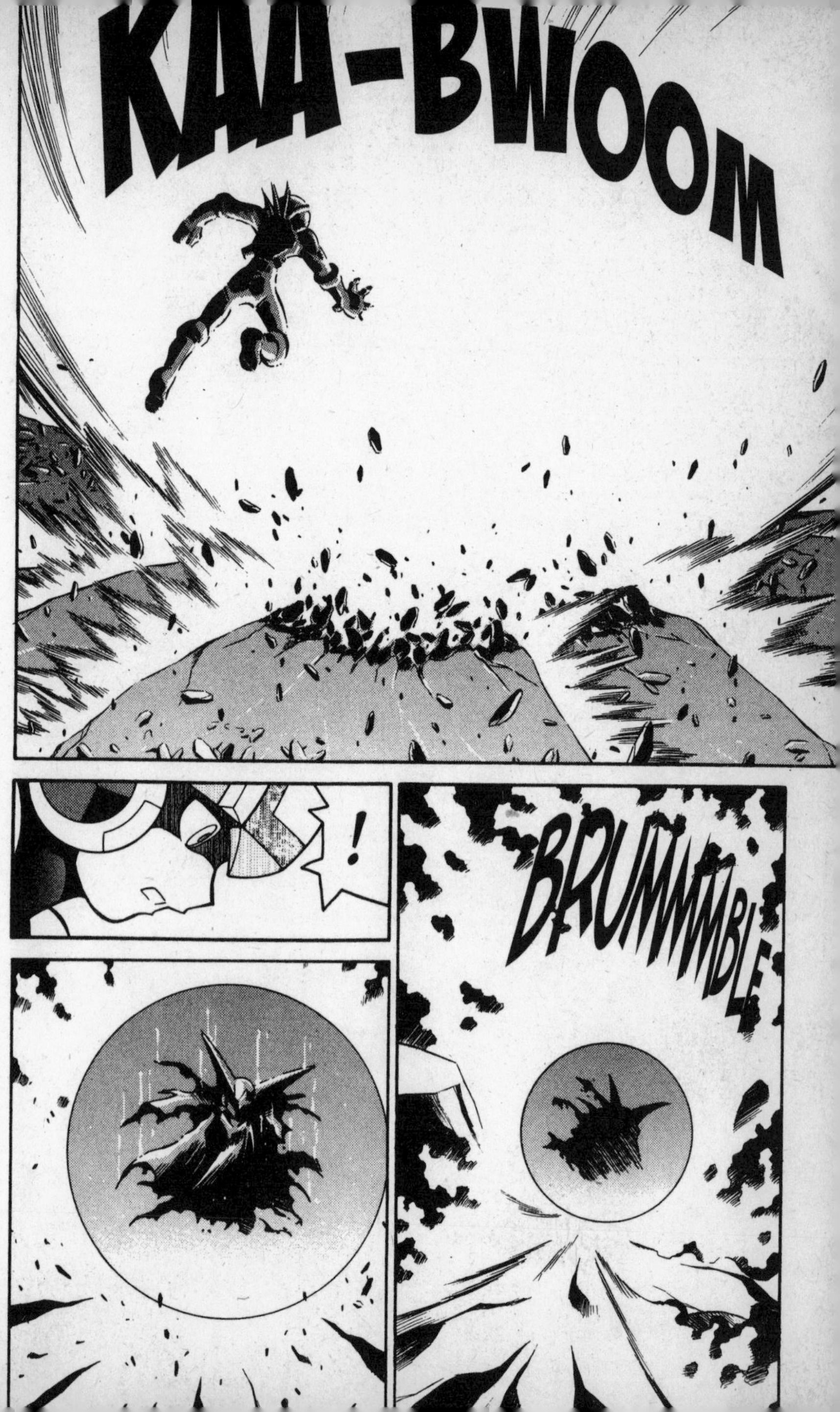
KAA-BWOOM
!
BRUMMMBLE

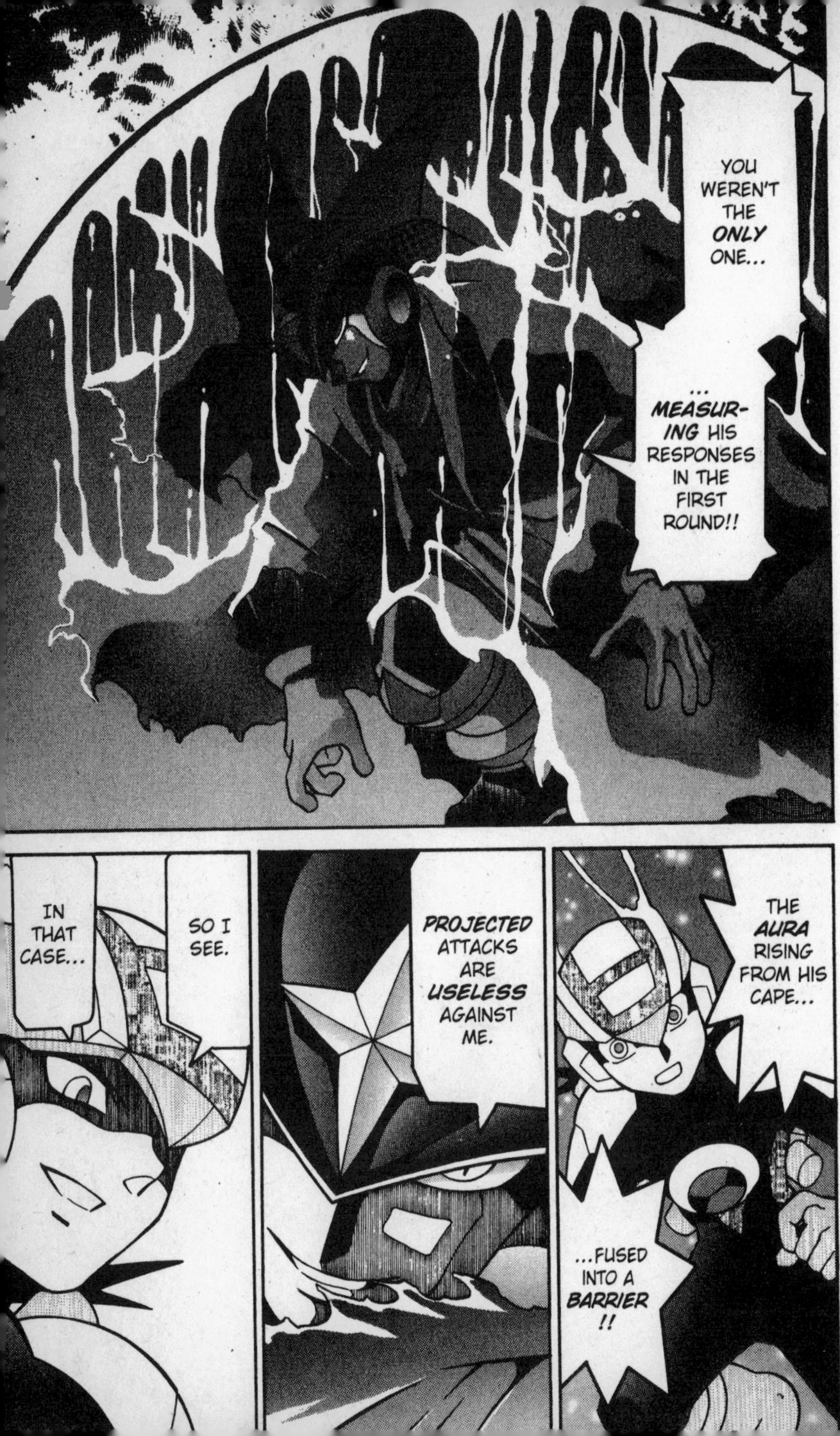
YOU WEREN'T THE *ONLY* ONE...
...*MEASURING* HIS RESPONSES IN THE FIRST ROUND!!
THE *AURA* RISING FROM HIS CAPE...
...FUSED INTO A *BARRIER* !!
*PROJECTED* ATTACKS ARE *USELESS* AGAINST ME.
SO I SEE.
IN THAT CASE...

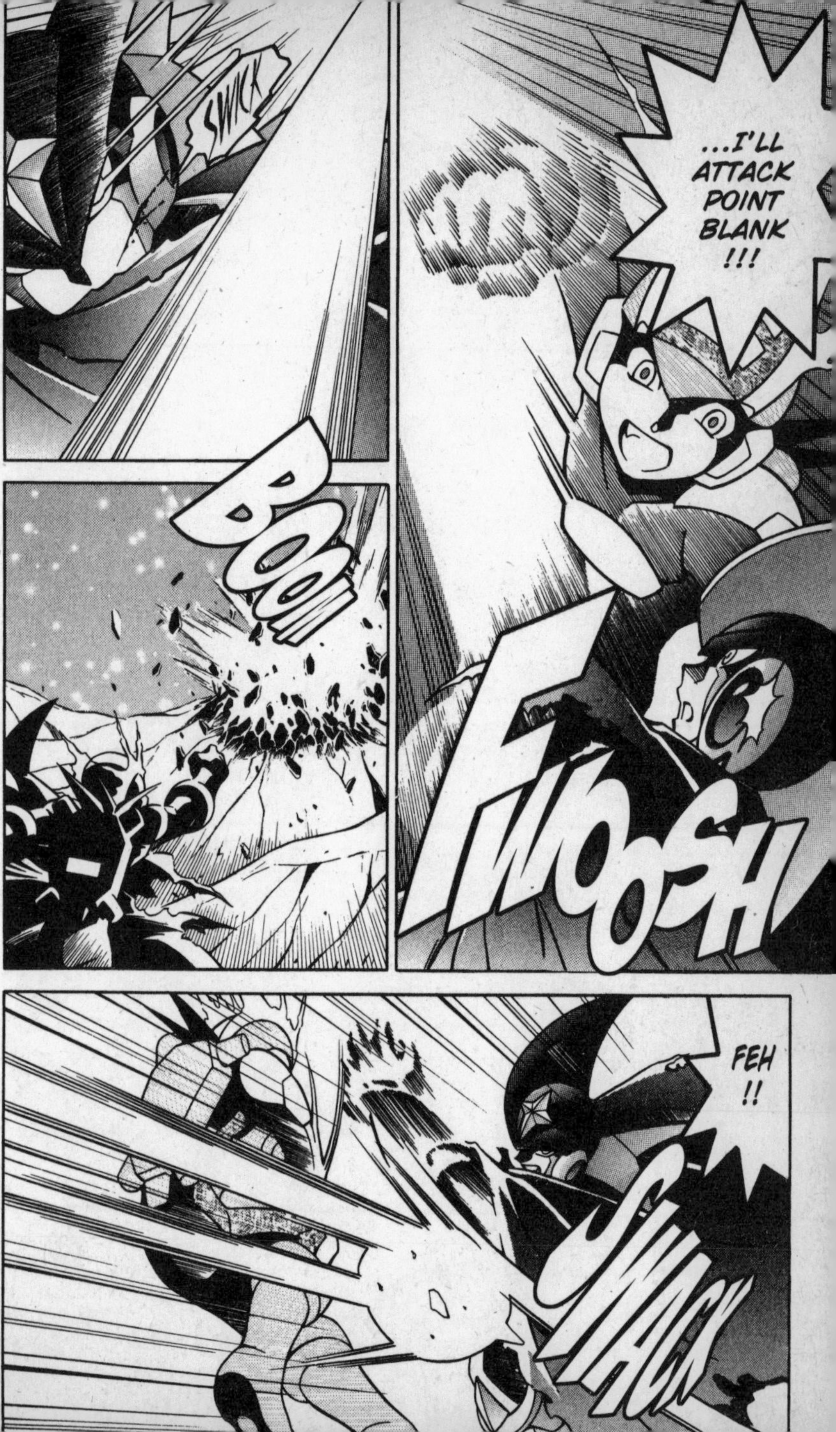
...I'LL ATTACK POINT BLANK !!!
WHOOSH
SWICK
BOOM
FEH !!
SWACK

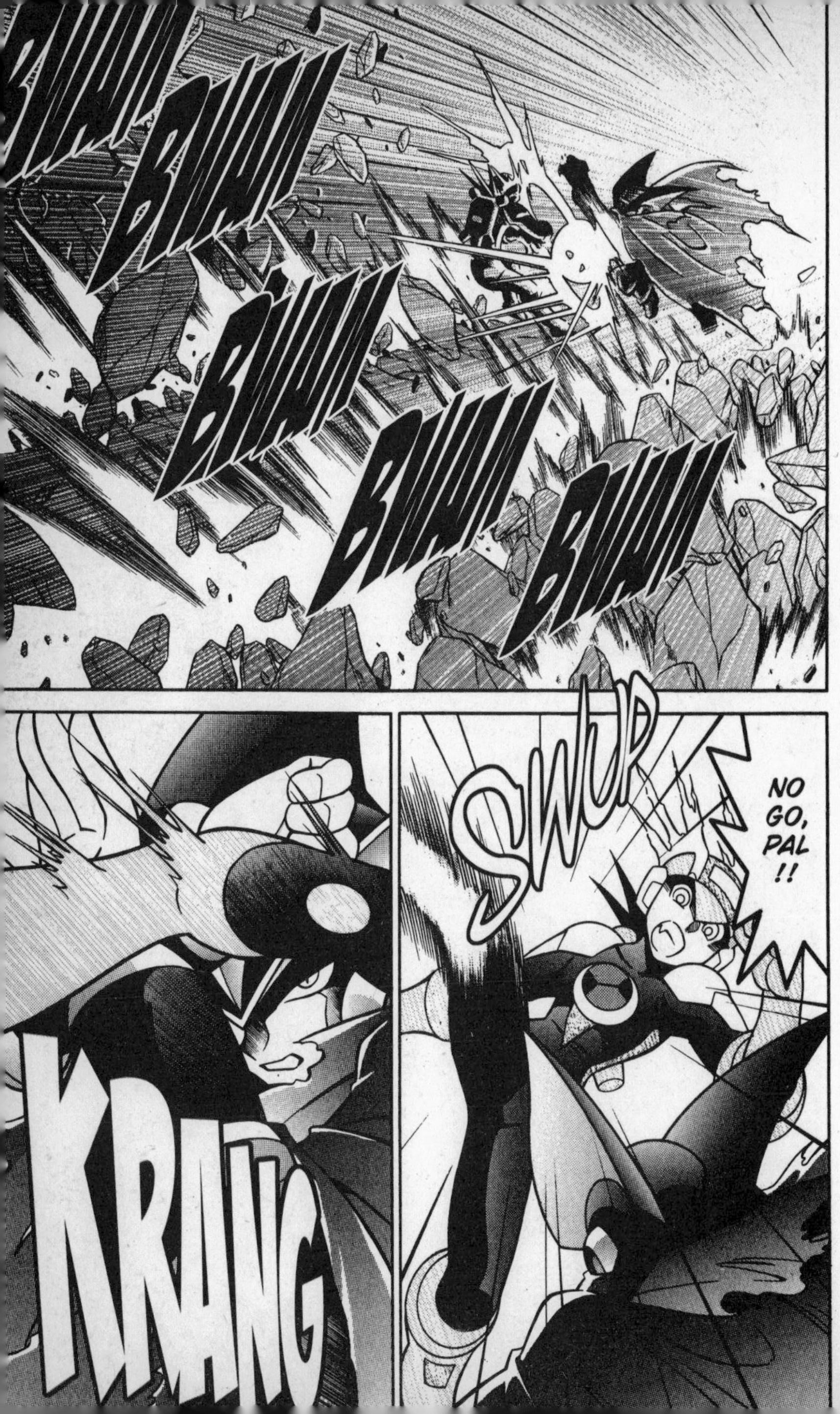
SWUP
NO GO, PAL!!
KRANG

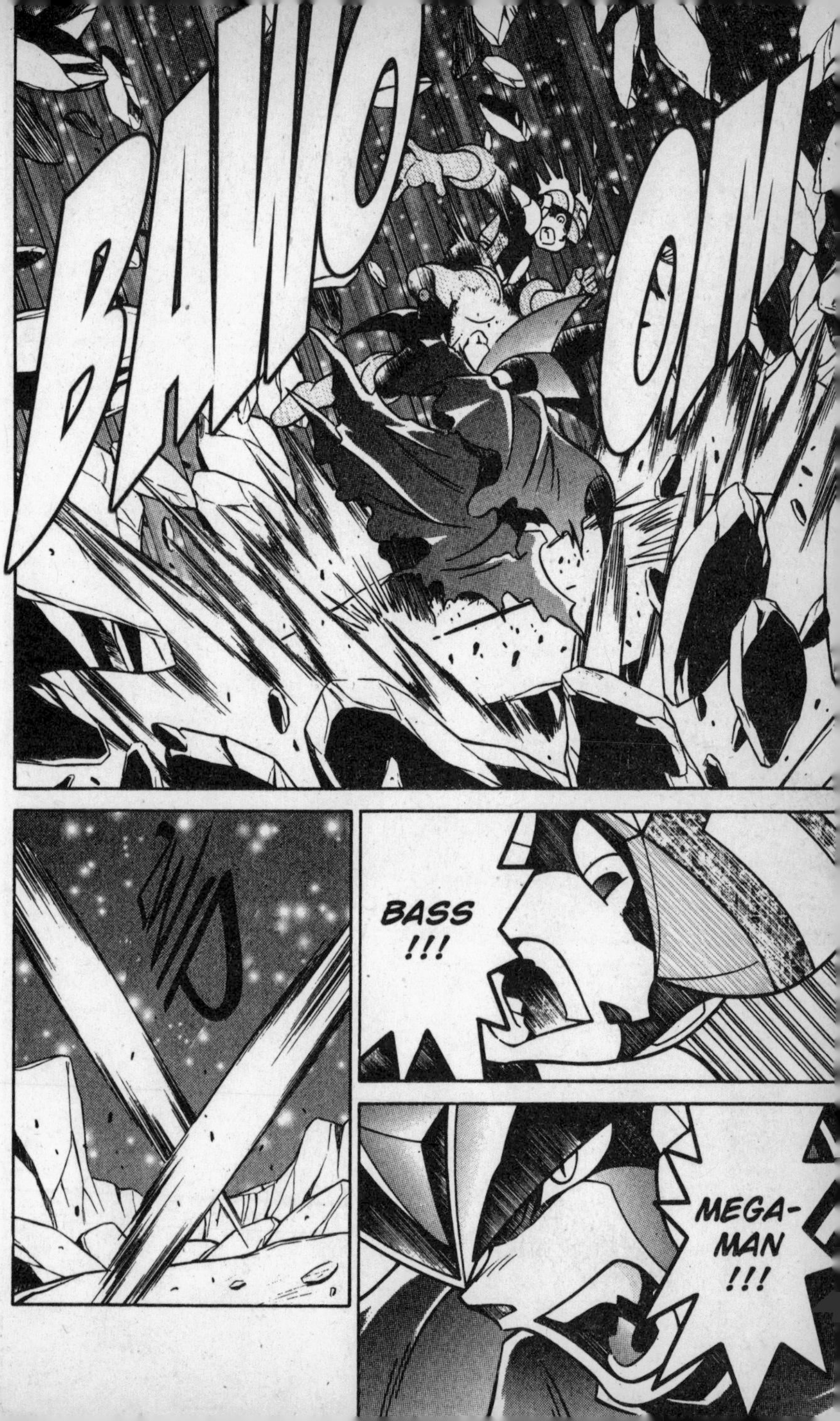
BASS !!!
MEGA-MAN !!!

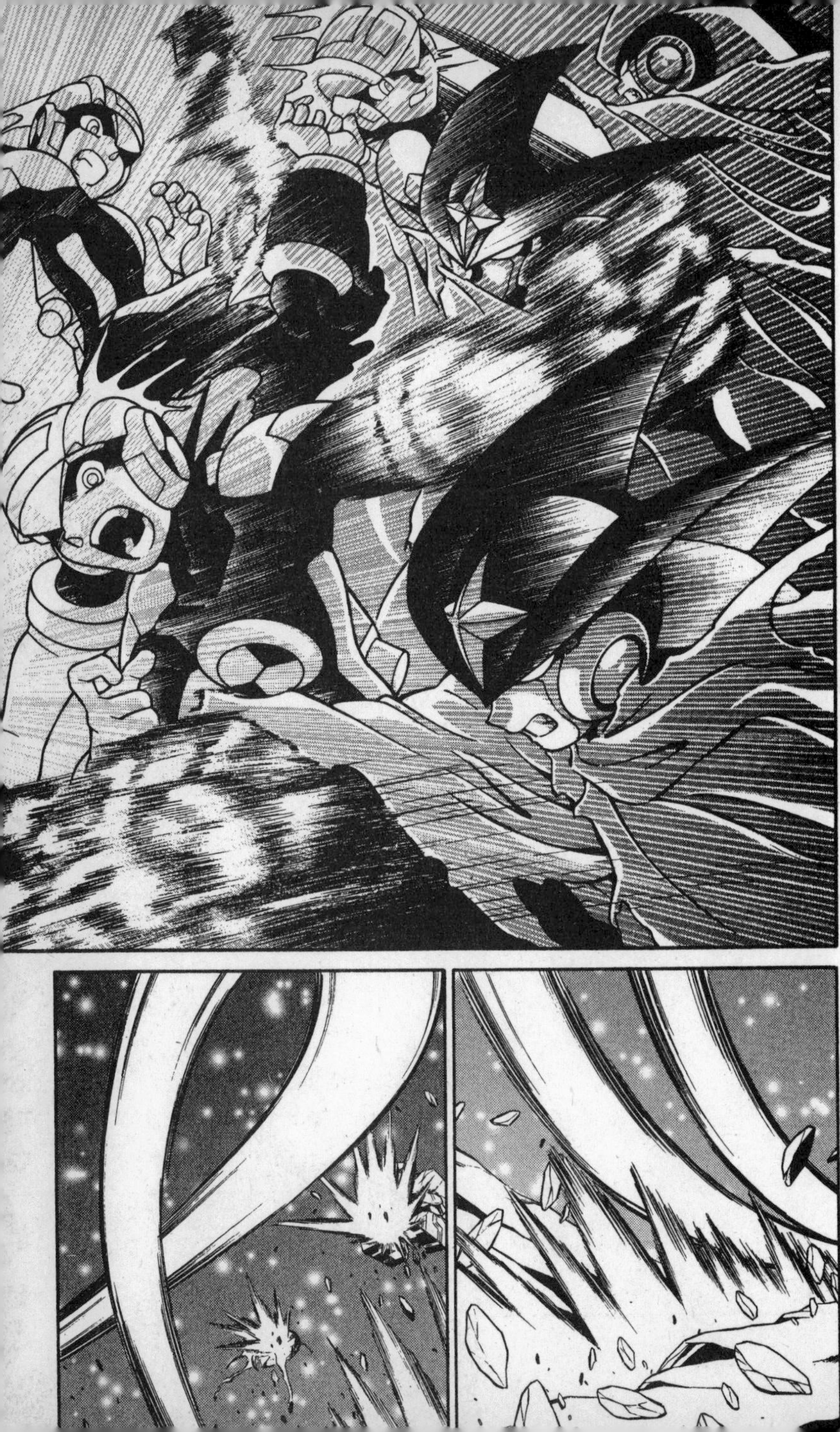

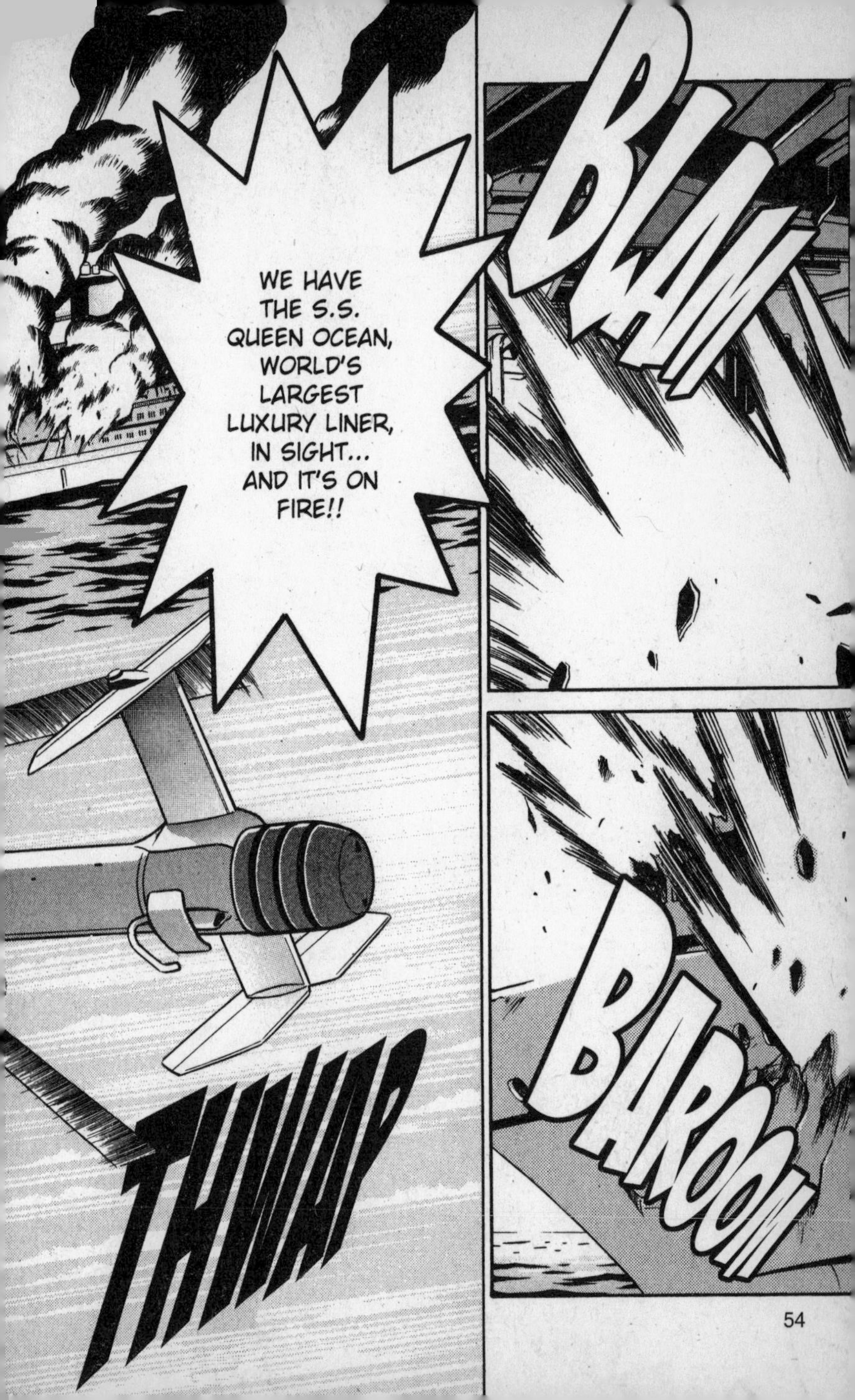
BLAM
BAROOM
WE HAVE THE S.S. QUEEN OCEAN, WORLD'S LARGEST LUXURY LINER, IN SIGHT... AND IT'S ON FIRE!!
THWAP

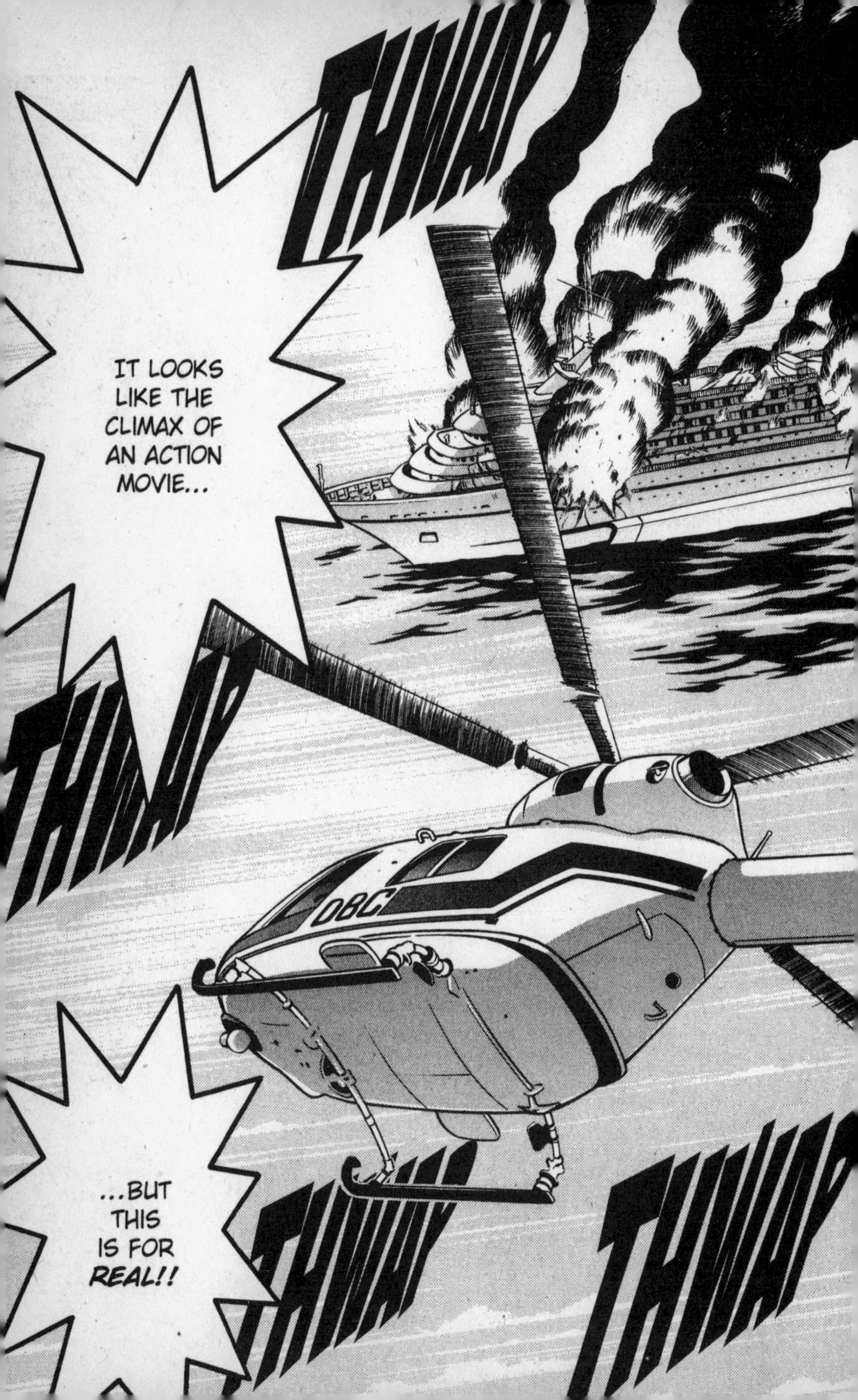
THWAP
IT LOOKS LIKE THE CLIMAX OF AN ACTION MOVIE...
THWAP
THWAP
THWAP
...BUT THIS IS FOR REAL!!

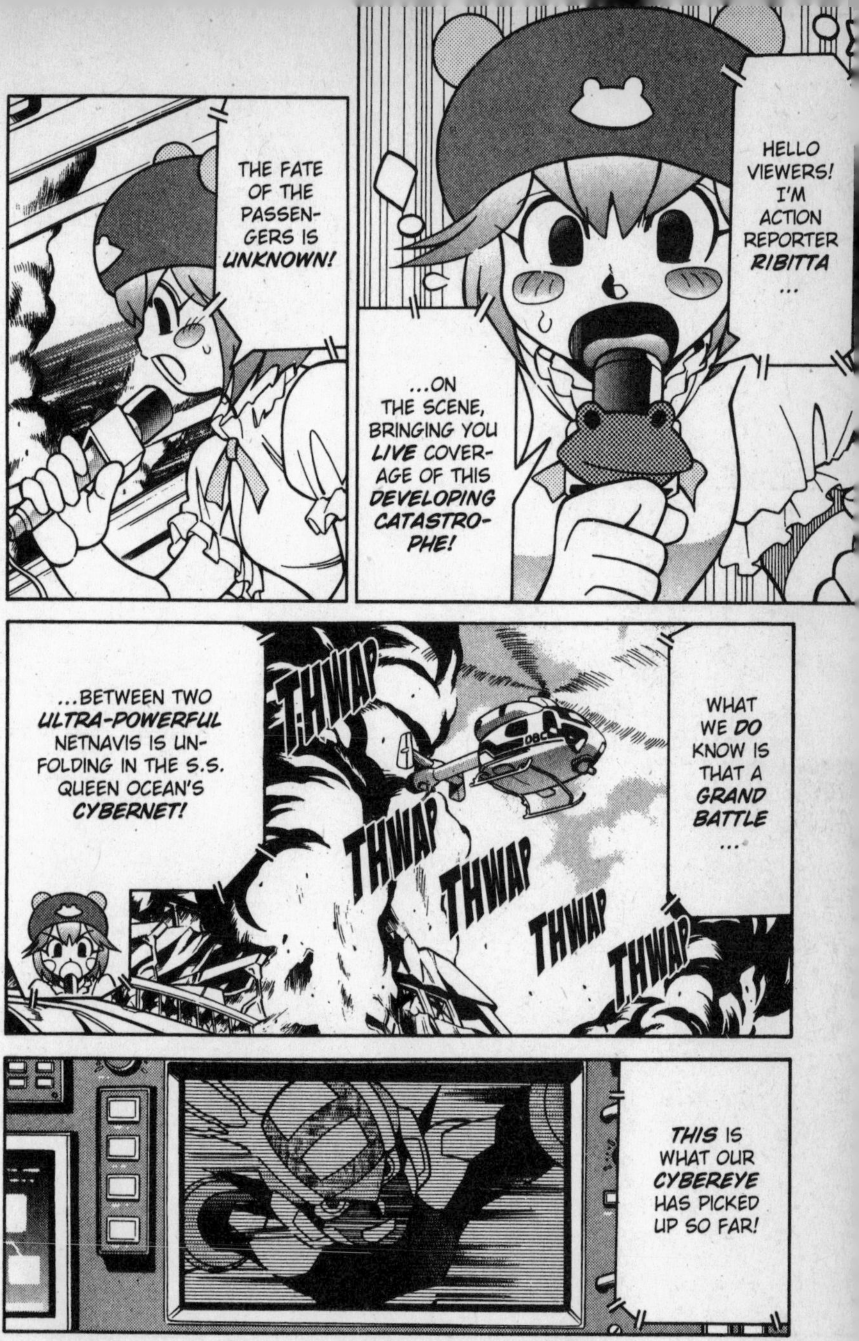
HELLO VIEWERS! I'M ACTION REPORTER RIBITTA ...
...ON THE SCENE, BRINGING YOU LIVE COVERAGE OF THIS DEVELOPING CATASTROPHE!
THE FATE OF THE PASSENGERS IS UNKNOWN!
WHAT WE DO KNOW IS THAT A GRAND BATTLE ...
THWAP
THWAP
THWAP
THWAP
THWAP
...BETWEEN TWO ULTRA-POWERFUL NETNAVIS IS UNFOLDING IN THE S.S. QUEEN OCEAN'S CYBERNET!
THIS IS WHAT OUR CYBEREYE HAS PICKED UP SO FAR!

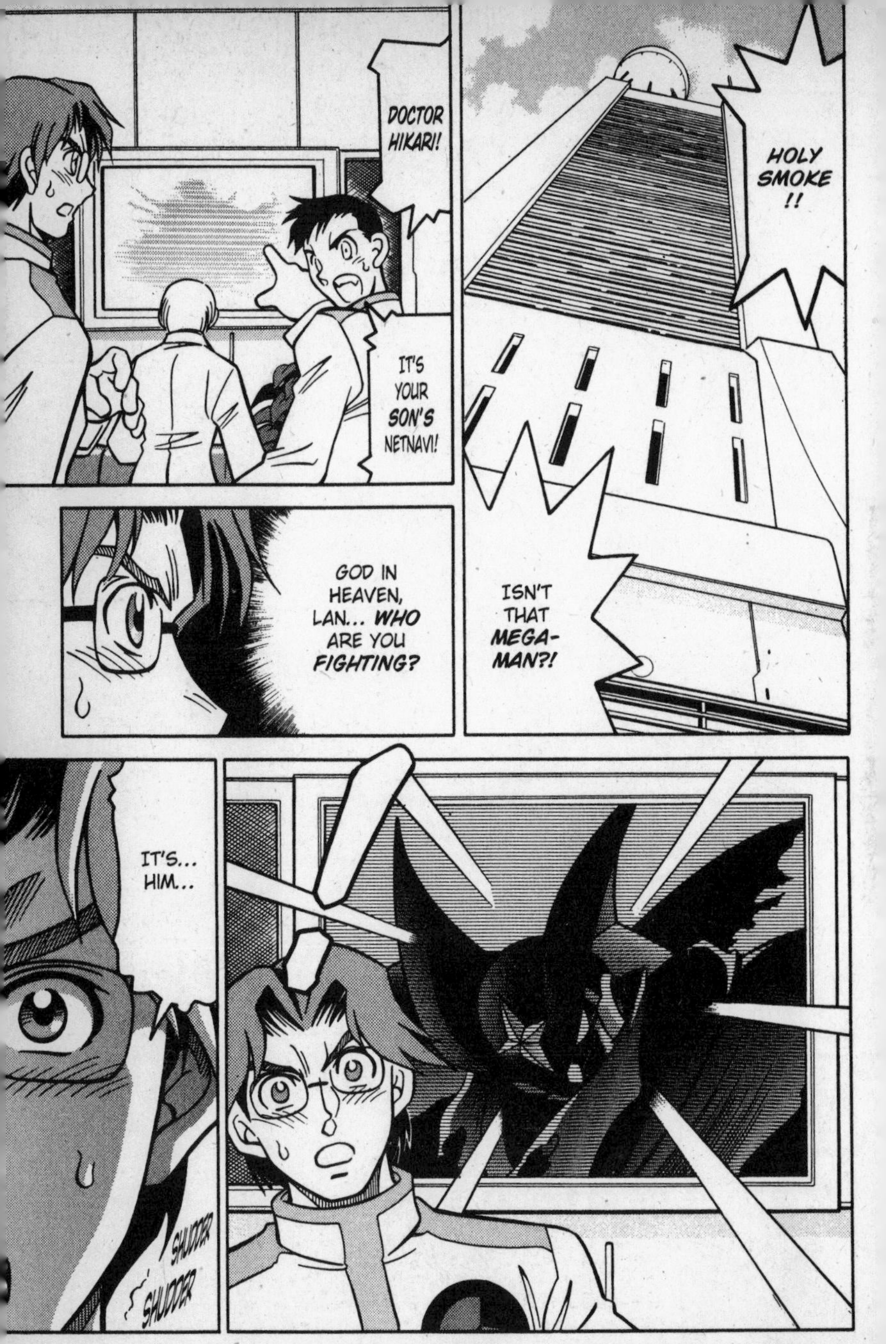
HOLY SMOKE !!
ISN'T THAT MEGA-MAN?!
DOCTOR HIKARI!
IT'S YOUR SON'S NETNAVI!
GOD IN HEAVEN, LAN... WHO ARE YOU FIGHTING?
IT'S... HIM...
SHUDDER
SHUDDER

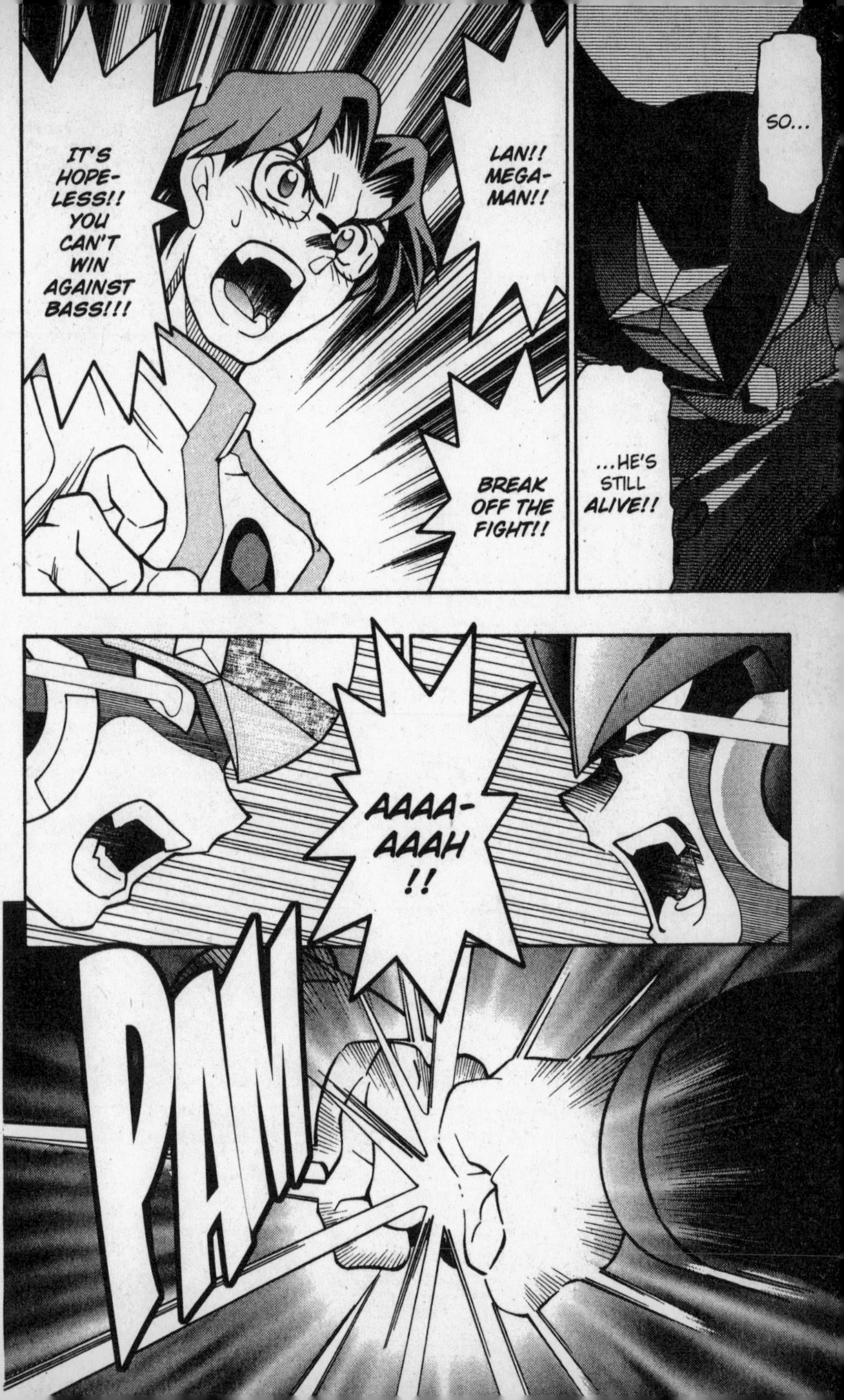
SO...
...HE'S STILL ALIVE!!
LAN!! MEGA-MAN!!
IT'S HOPE-LESS!! YOU CAN'T WIN AGAINST BASS!!!
BREAK OFF THE FIGHT!!
AAAA-AAAH!!
PAM

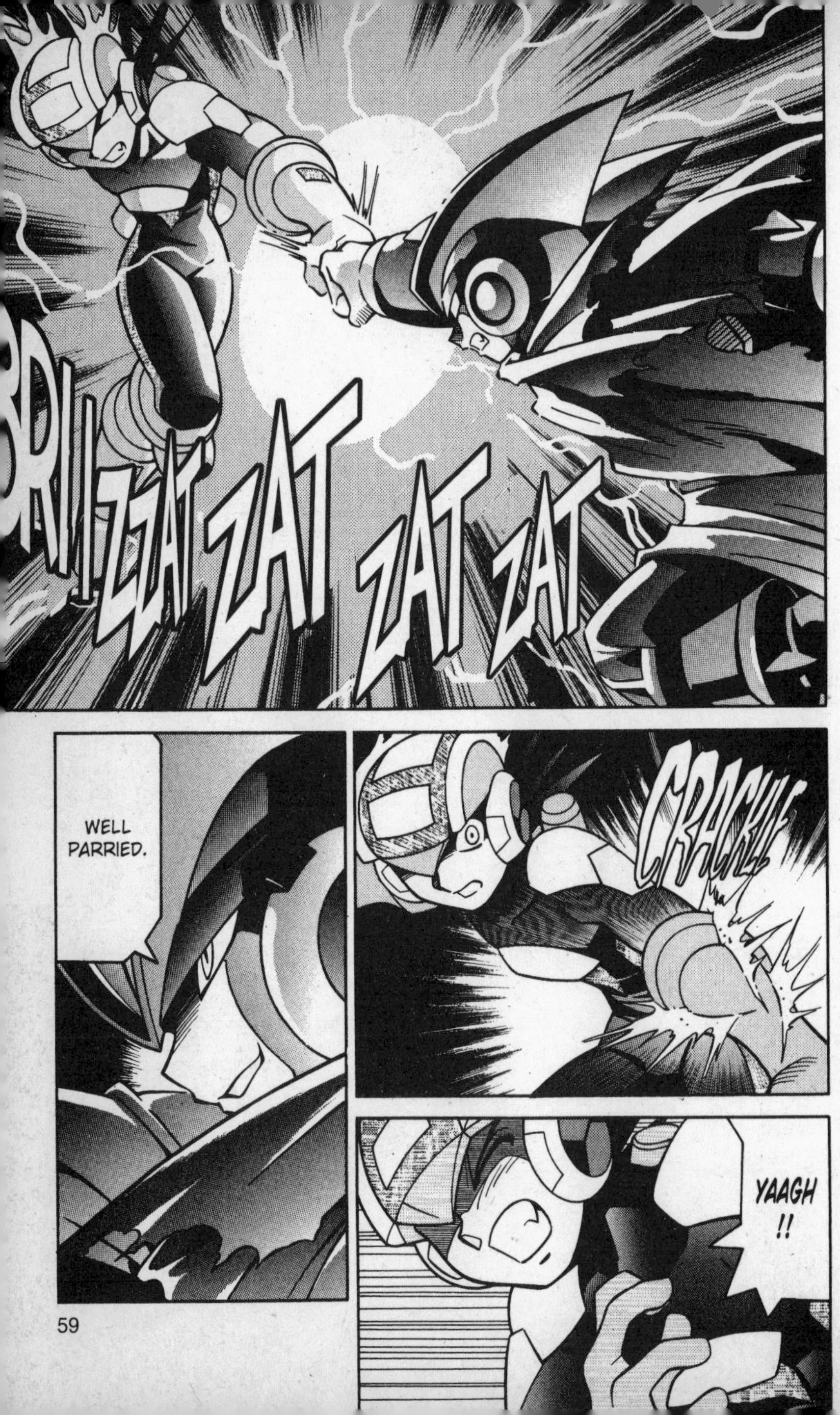
RIIZZAT ZAT ZAT ZAT
CRACKLE
YAAGH !!
WELL PARRIED.

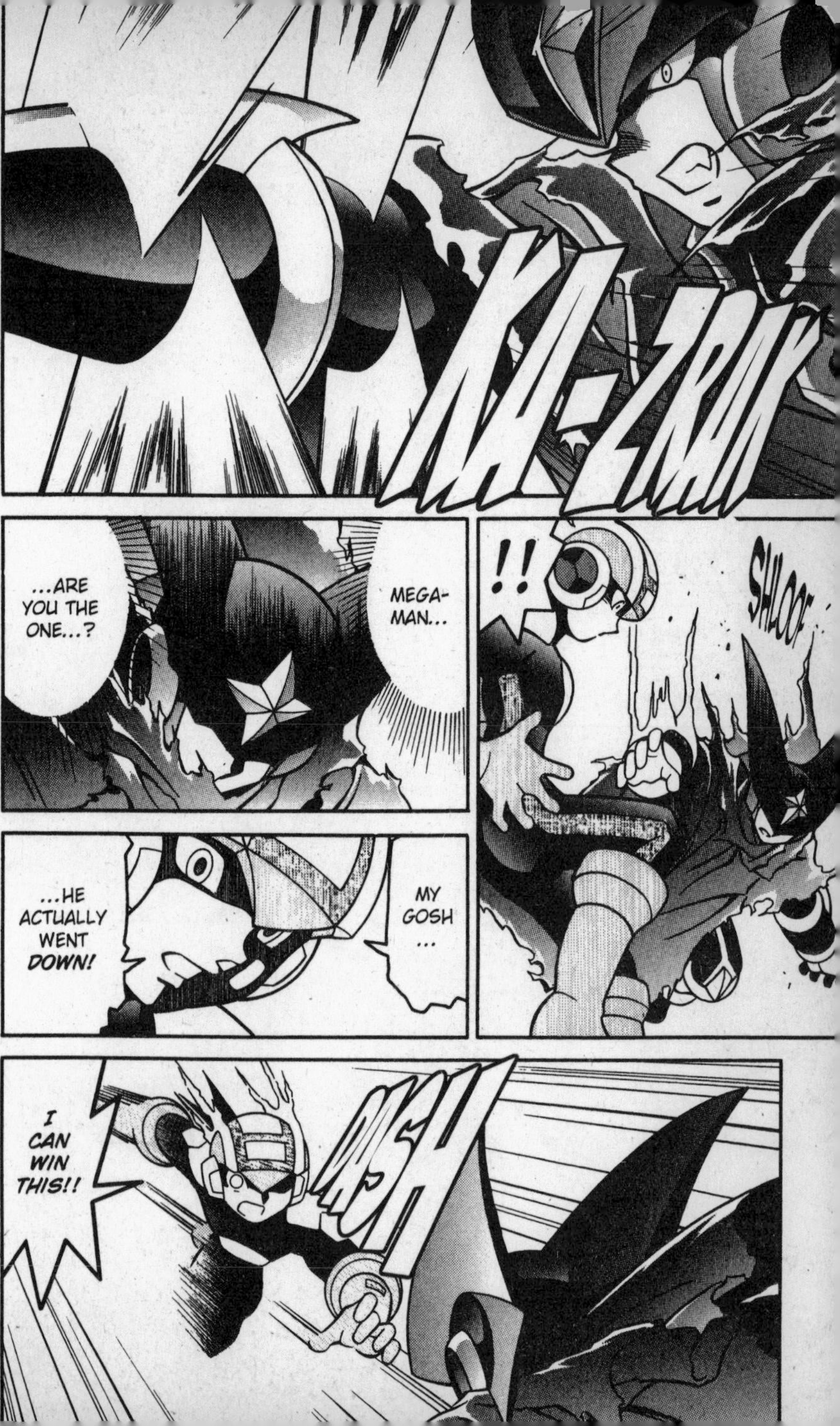
KA-ZRAK
!!
SHLOOF
MEGA-MAN...
...ARE YOU THE ONE...?
MY GOSH ...
...HE ACTUALLY WENT DOWN!
I CAN WIN THIS!!

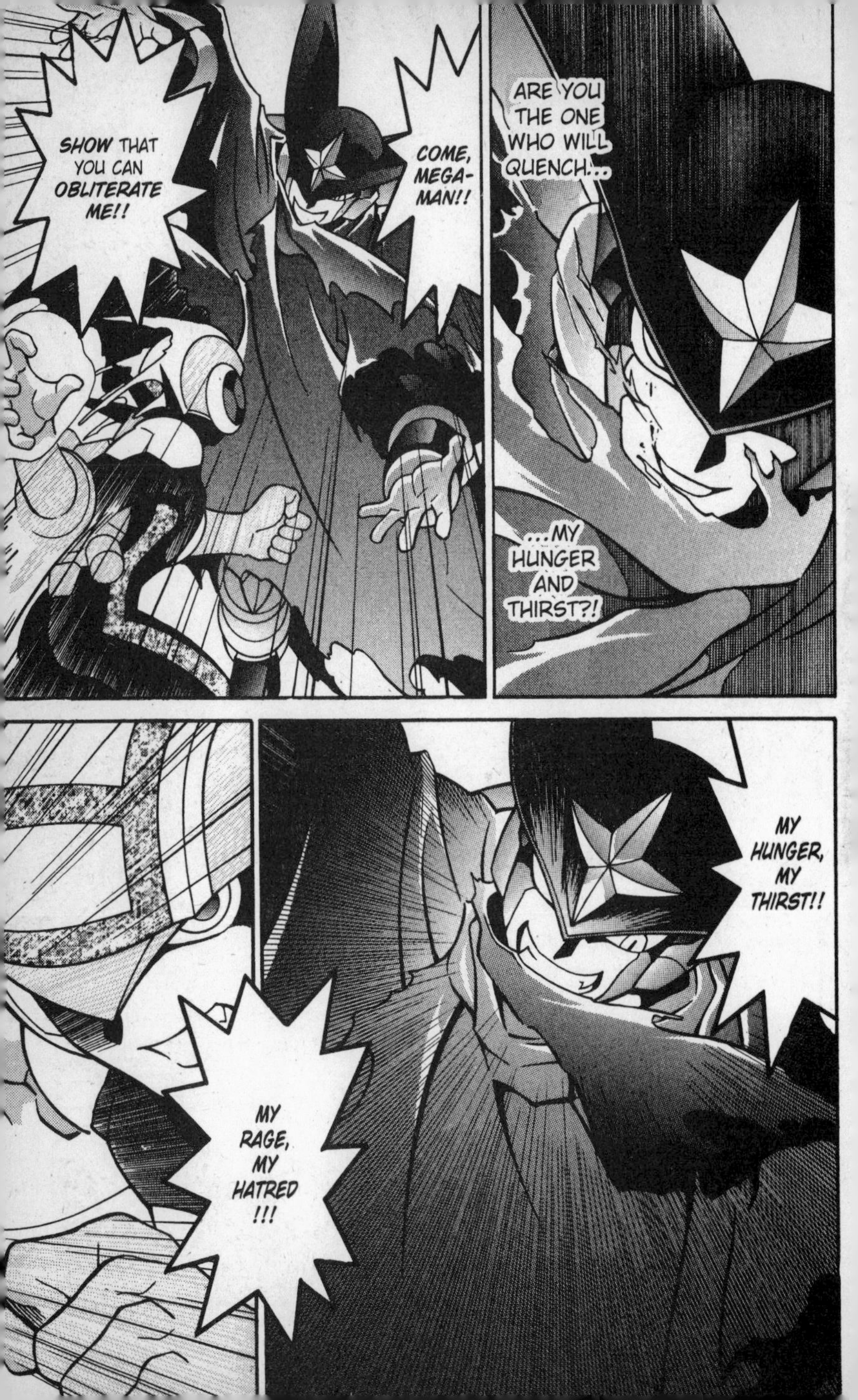
ARE YOU THE ONE WHO WILL QUENCH...
...MY HUNGER AND THIRST?!
COME, MEGA-MAN!!
SHOW THAT YOU CAN OBLITERATE ME!!
MY HUNGER, MY THIRST!!
MY RAGE, MY HATRED!!!

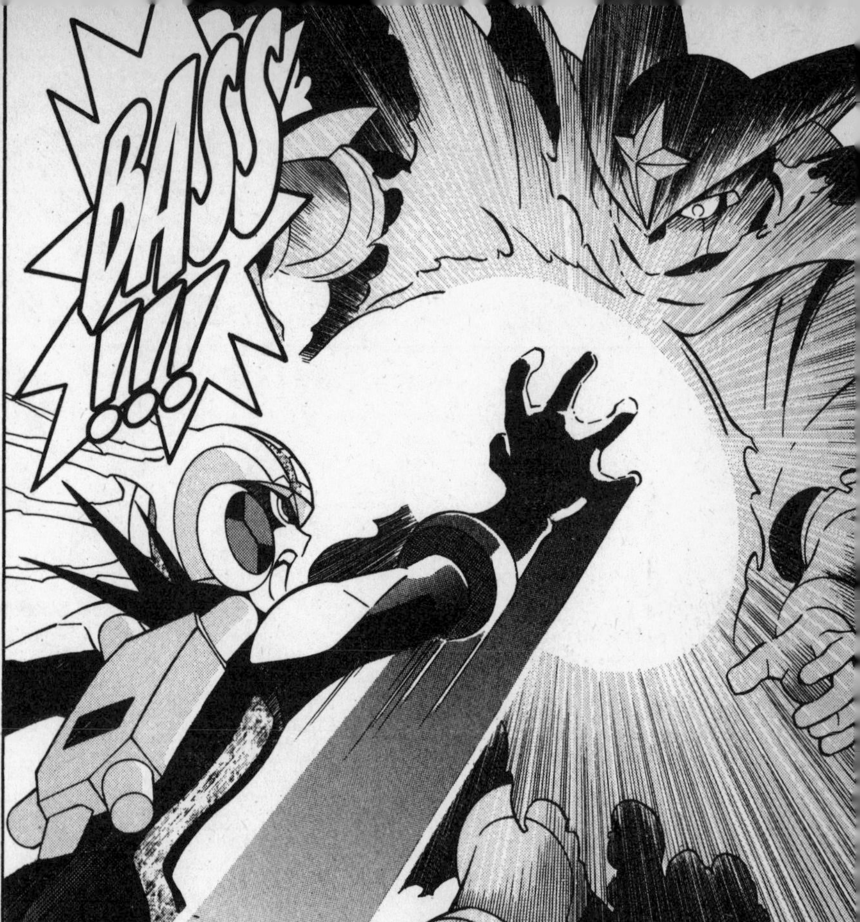
BASS!!...
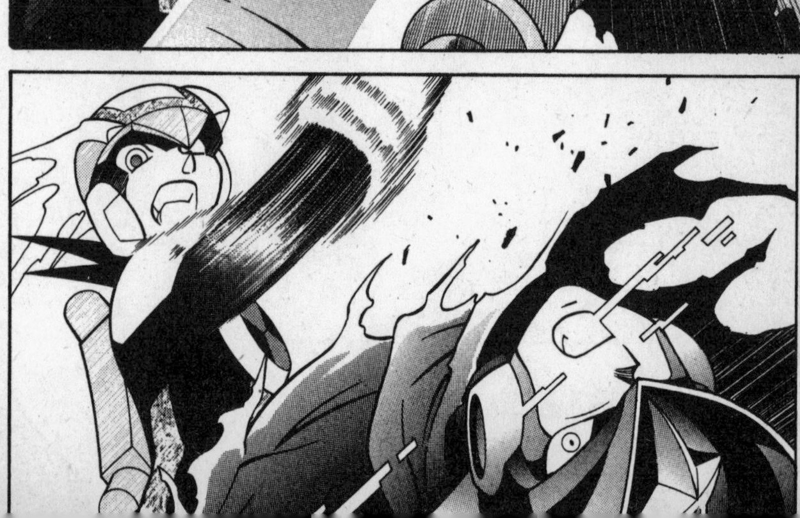

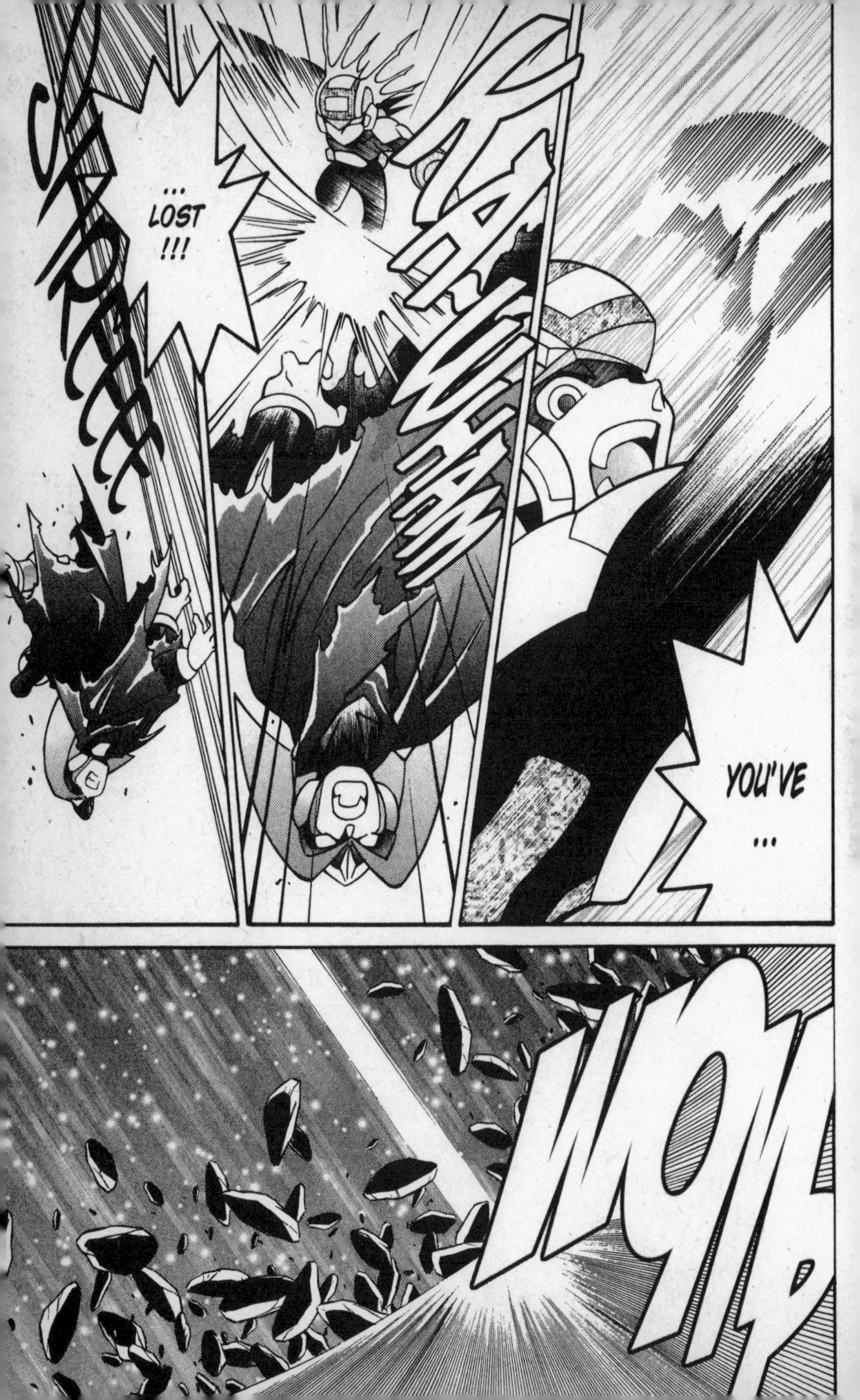
YOU'VE ...
... LOST !!!

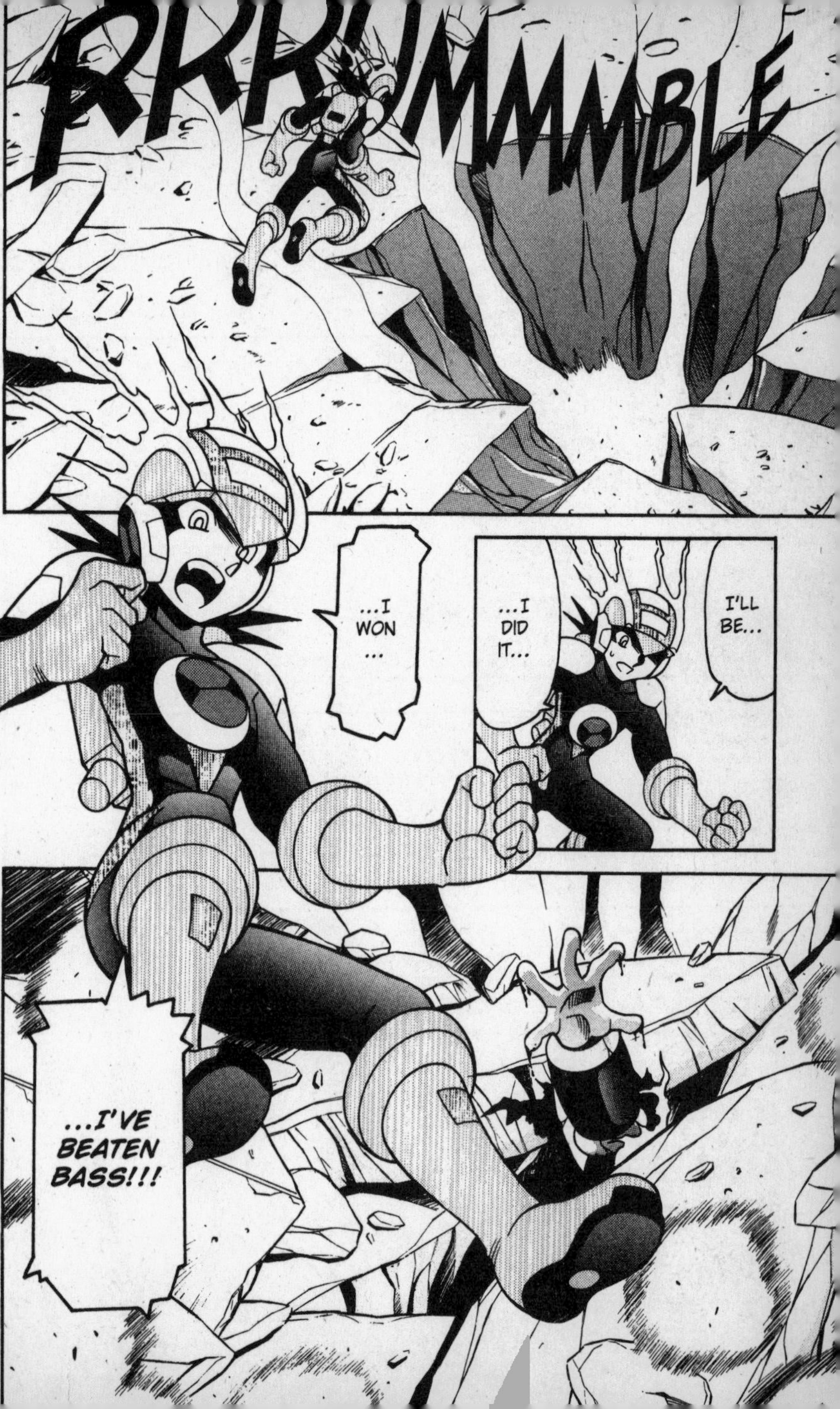
RRRUMMMMBLE
I'LL BE...
...I DID IT...
...I WON ...
...I'VE BEATEN BASS!!!

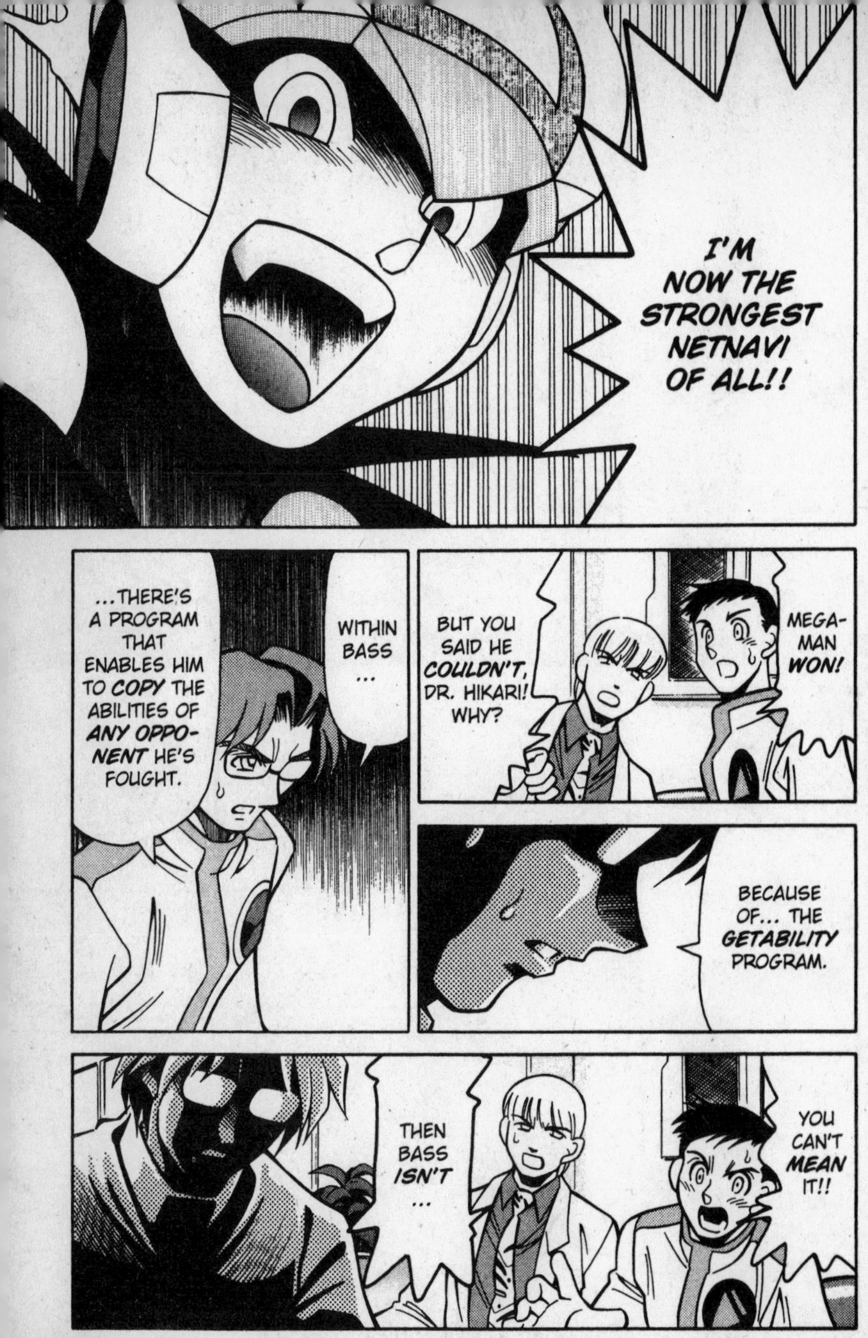
I'M NOW THE STRONGEST NETNAVI OF ALL!!
MEGA-MAN WON!
BUT YOU SAID HE COULDN'T, DR. HIKARI! WHY?
BECAUSE OF... THE GETABILITY PROGRAM.
WITHIN BASS ...
...THERE'S A PROGRAM THAT ENABLES HIM TO COPY THE ABILITIES OF ANY OPPONENT HE'S FOUGHT.
YOU CAN'T MEAN IT!!
THEN BASS ISN'T ...

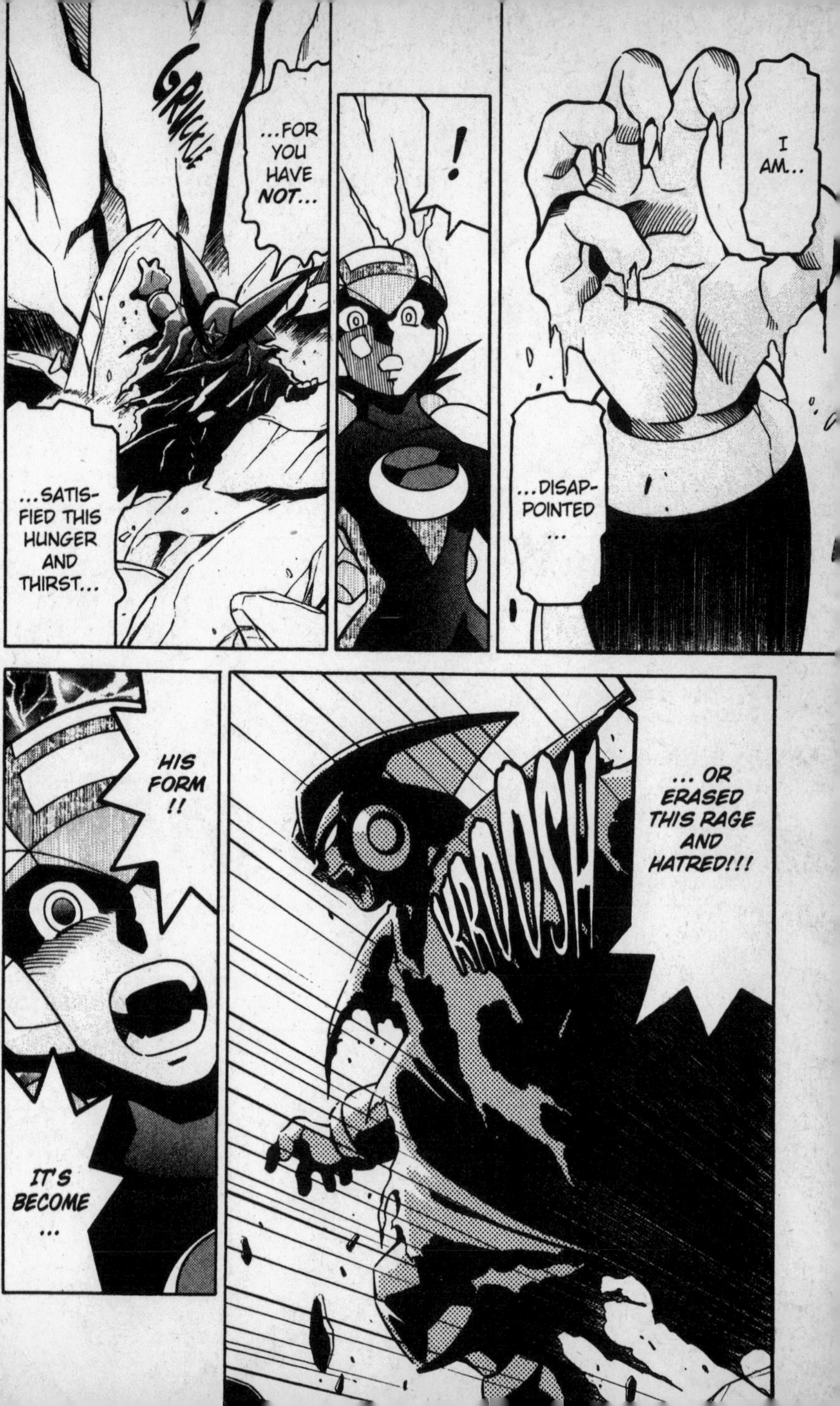
I AM...
...DISAP-POINTED...
!
...FOR YOU HAVE NOT...
GRUCK!!
...SATIS-FIED THIS HUNGER AND THIRST...
... OR ERASED THIS RAGE AND HATRED!!!
KROOSH
HIS FORM !!
IT'S BECOME ...

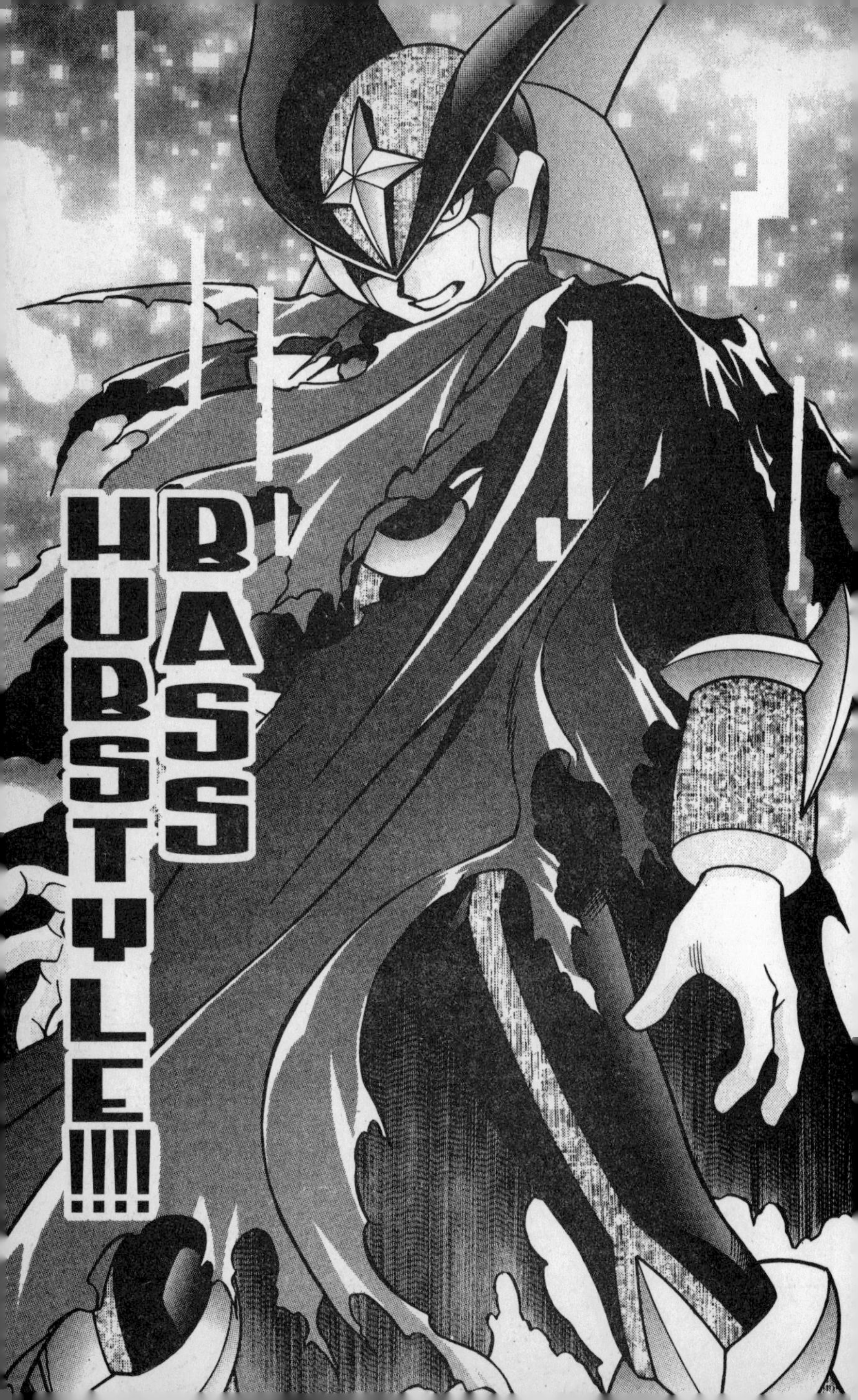
BASS
HUB STYLE!!!!

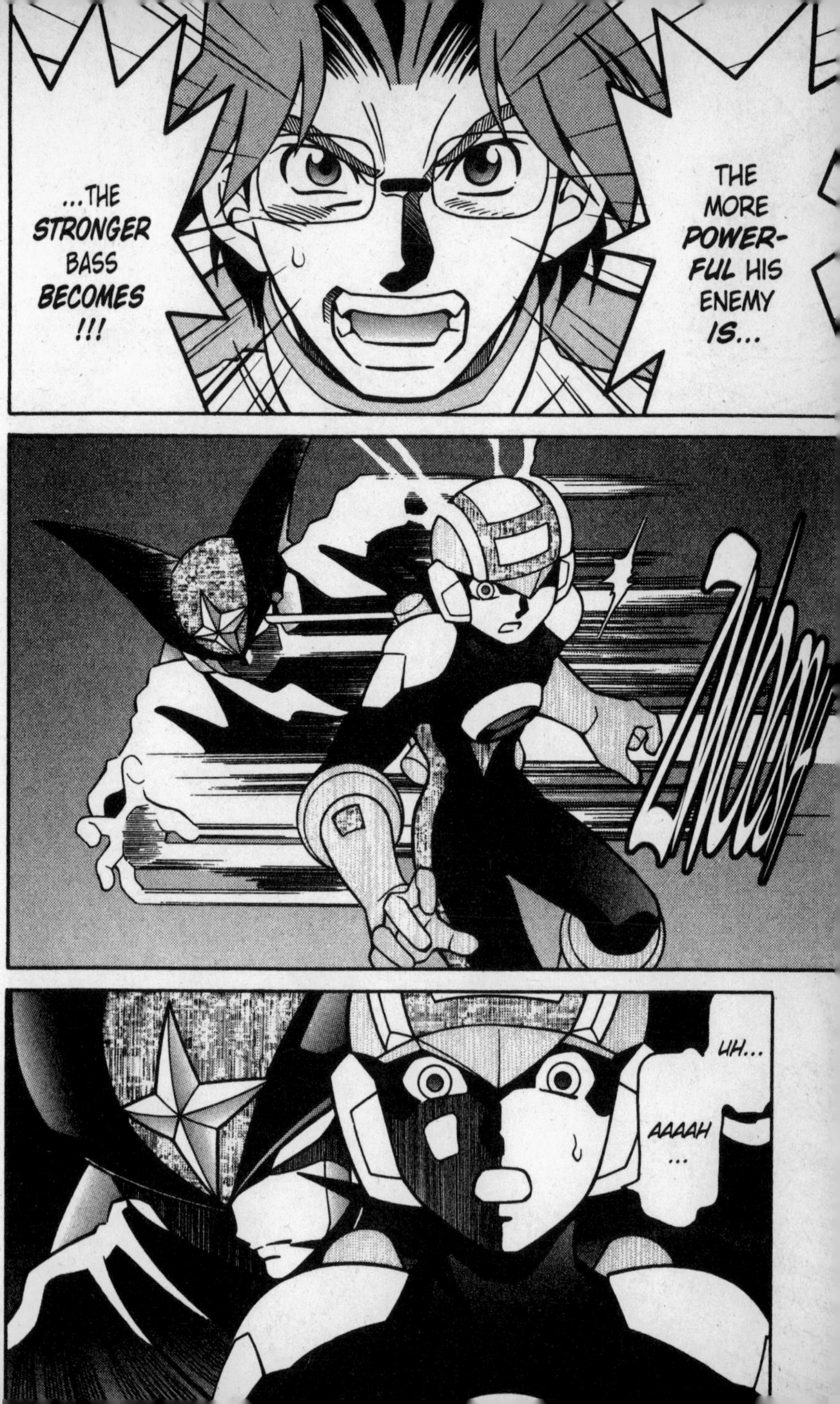
THE MORE POWER-FUL HIS ENEMY IS...
...THE STRONGER BASS BECOMES!!!
UH...
AAAAH...

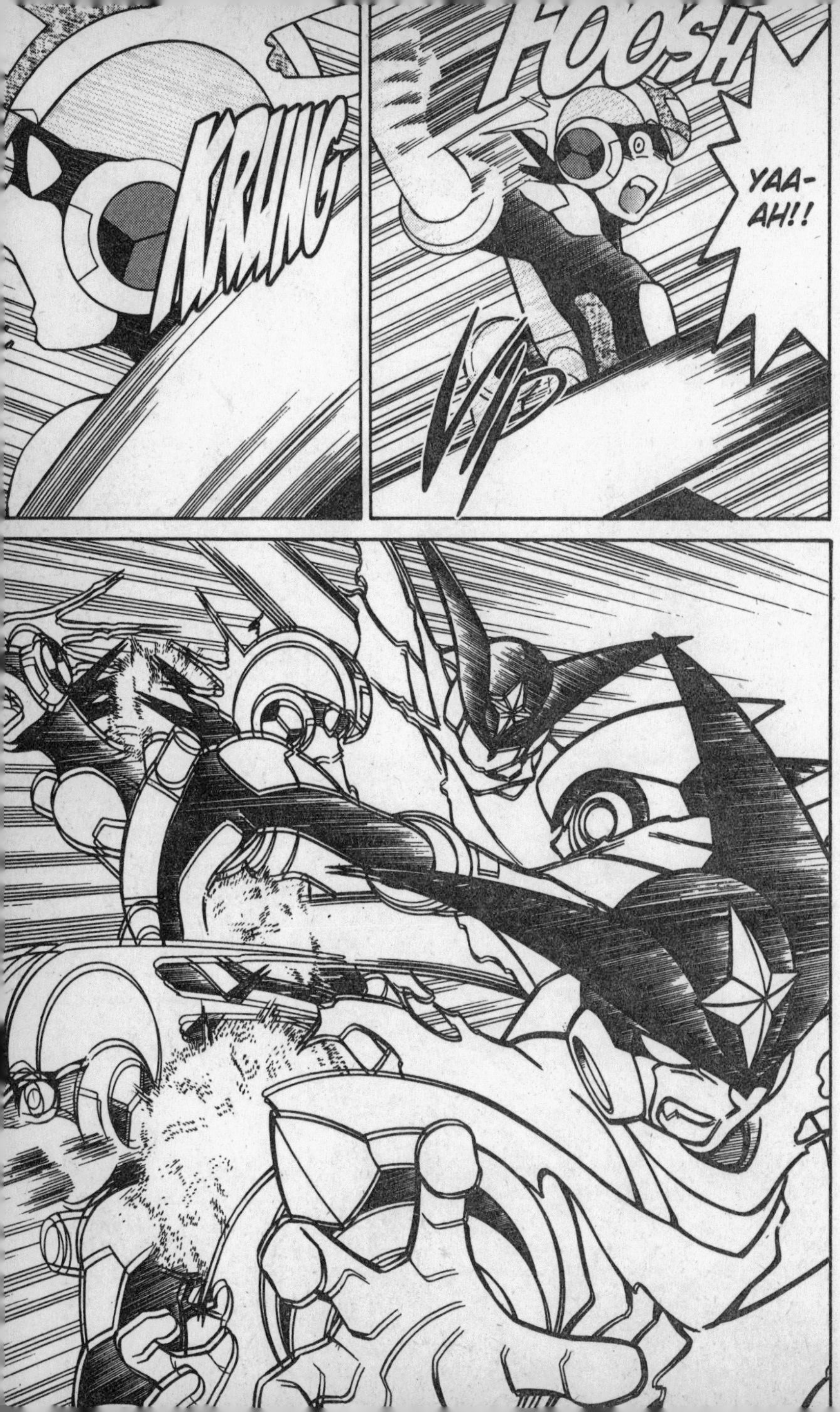
FOOSH
YAA-AH!!
KRUNG

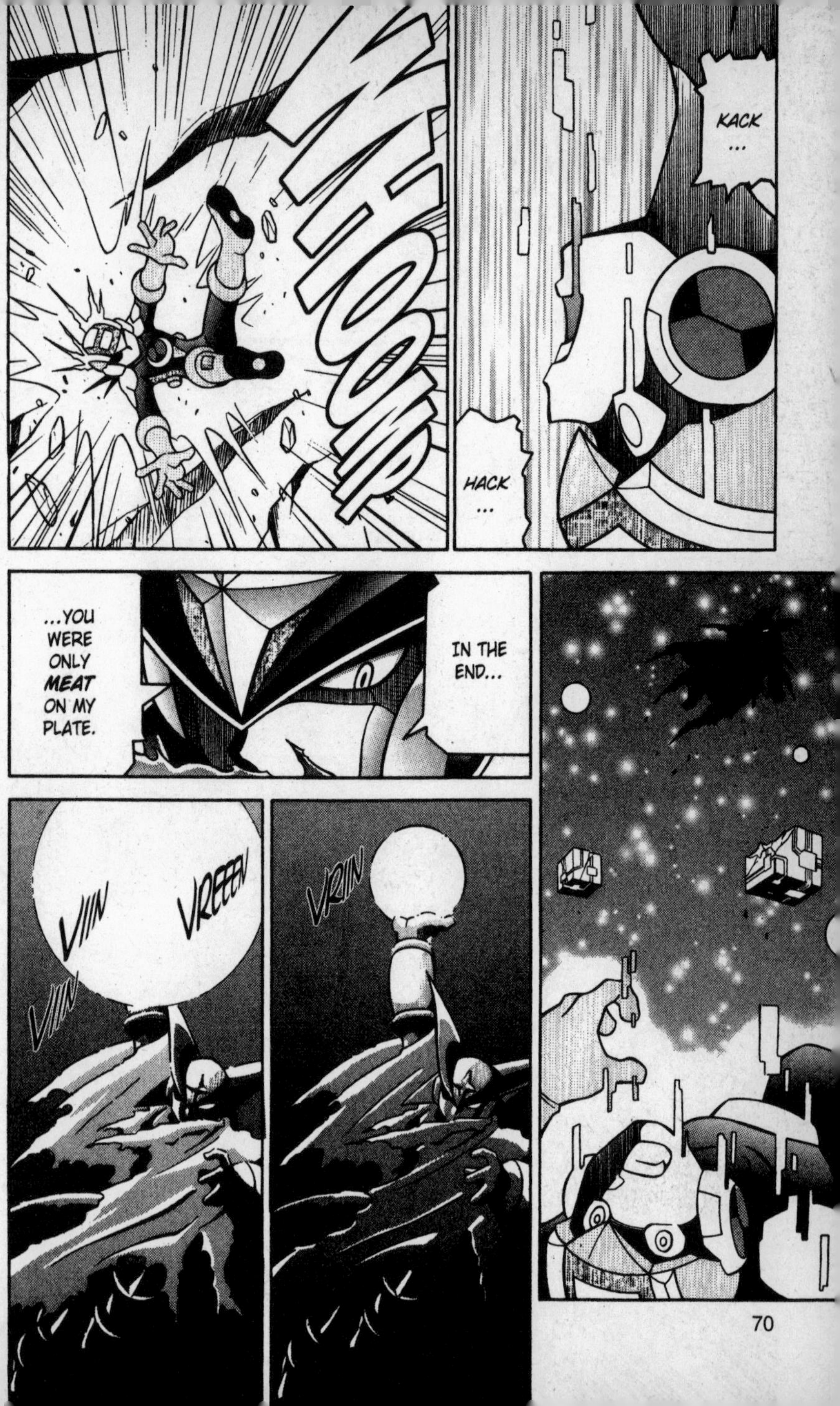
KACK ...
HACK ...
WHOOMP
IN THE END...
...YOU WERE ONLY **MEAT** ON MY PLATE.
VRIIN
VIIIN
VREEEN
VIIIN

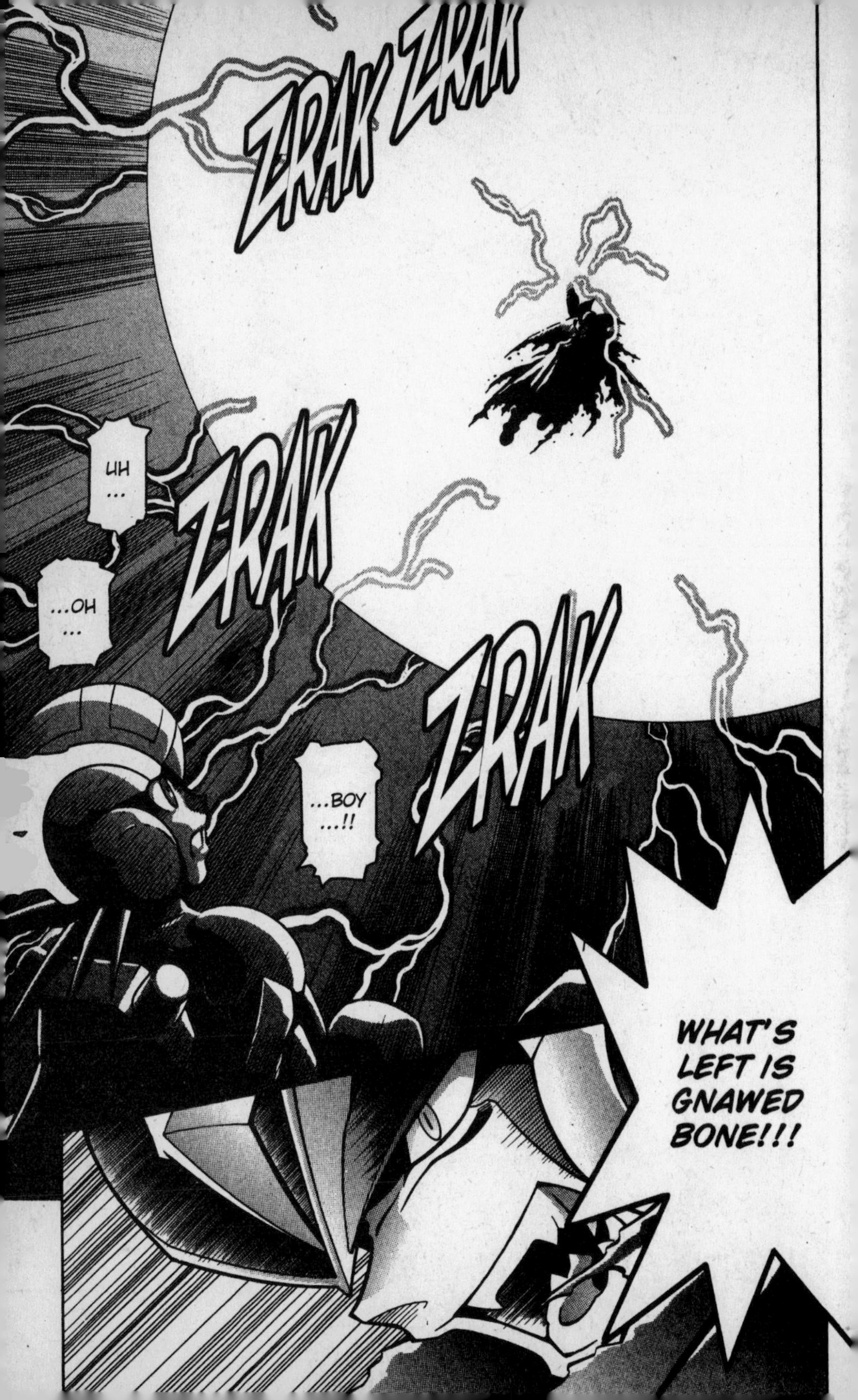
ZRAK ZRAK
UH ...
ZRAK
...OH ...
ZRAK
...BOY ...!!
WHAT'S LEFT IS GNAWED BONE!!!

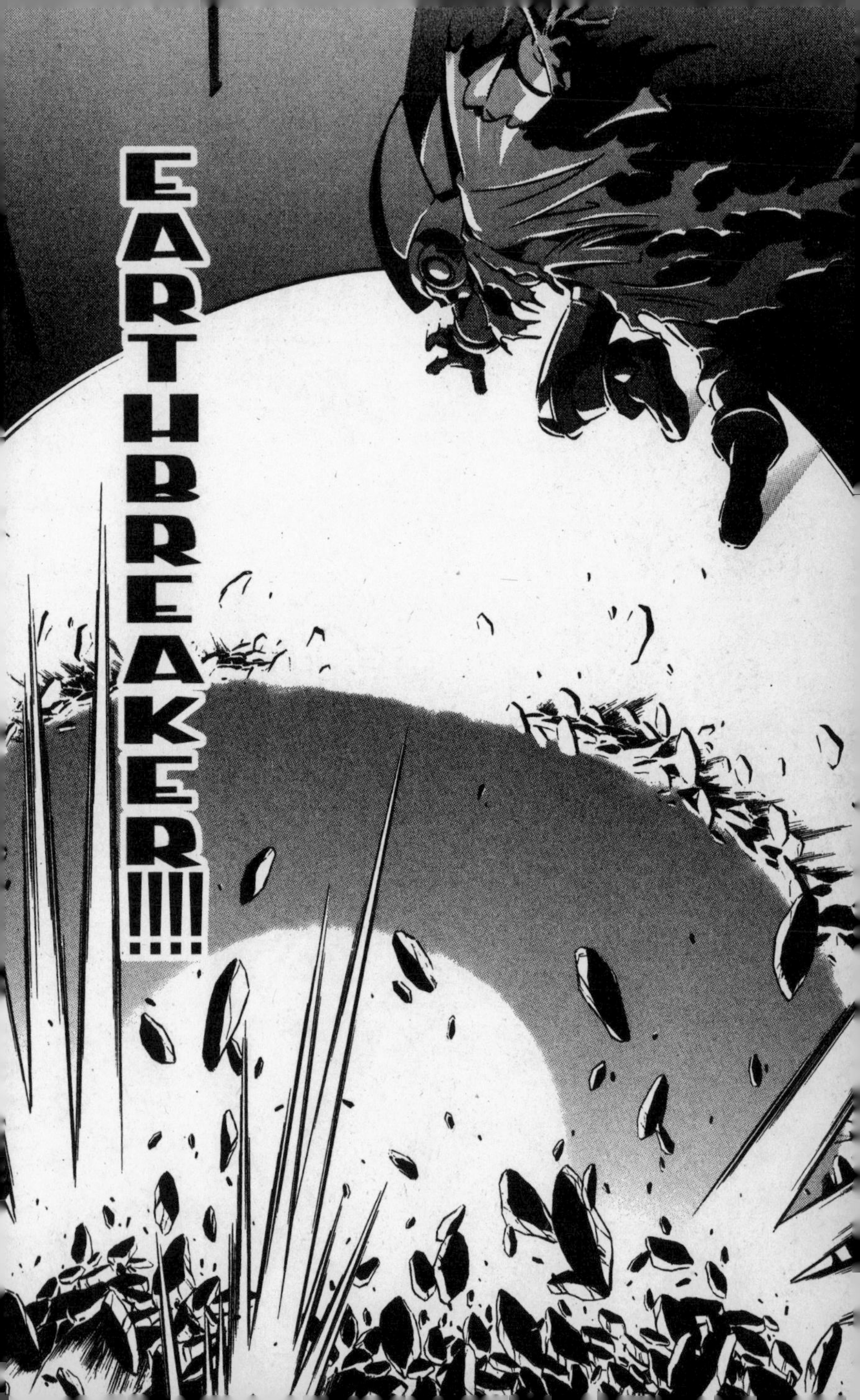
EARTHBREAKER!!!!

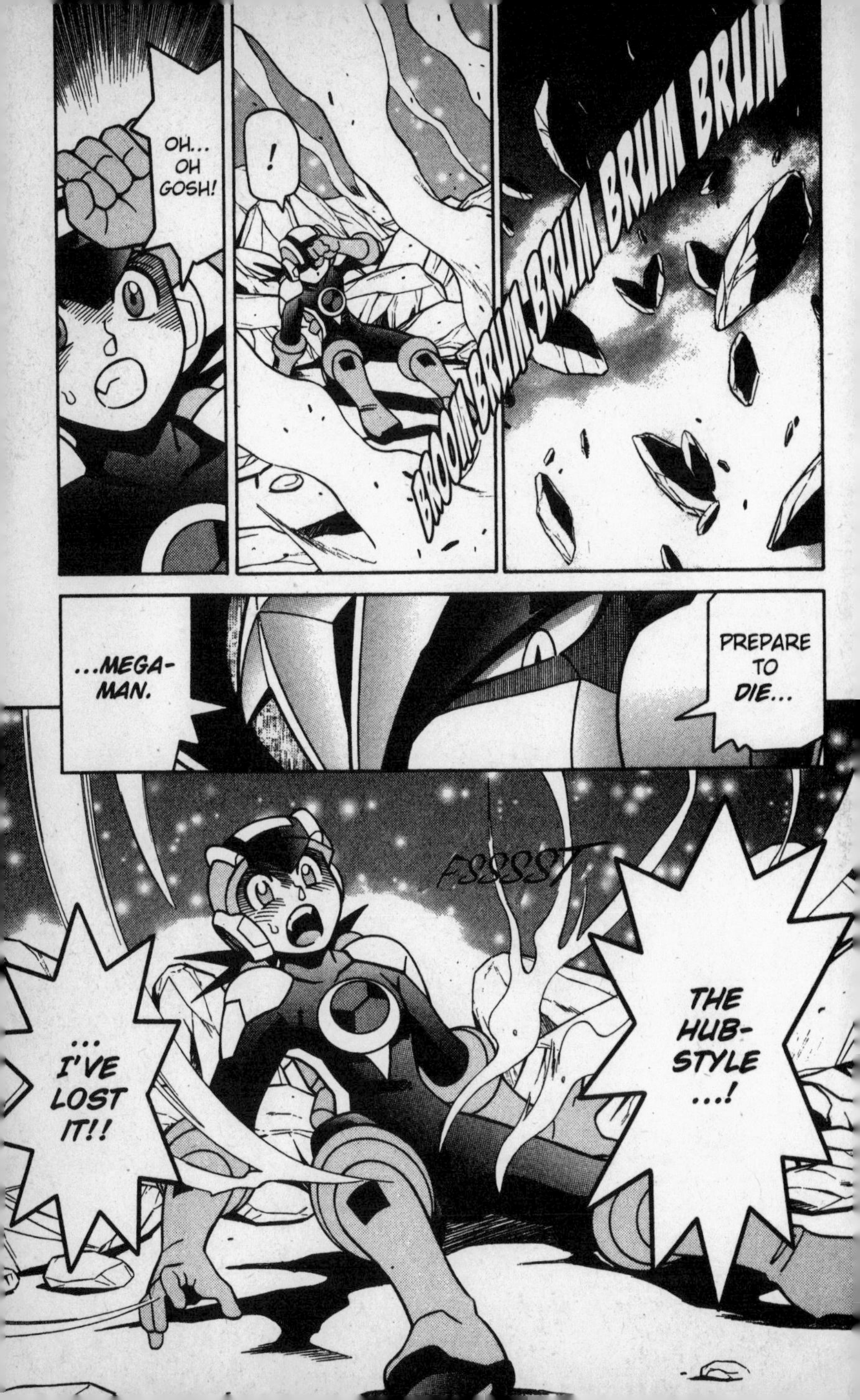
BROOM BRUM BRUM BRUM BRUM BRUM
!
OH... OH GOSH!
PREPARE TO DIE...
...MEGA-MAN.
THE HUB-STYLE ...!
FSSSST
... I'VE LOST IT!!

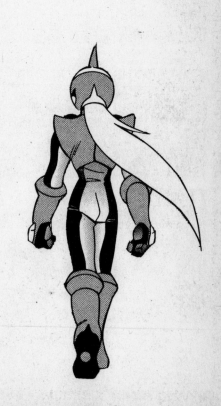

# THE STRONGEST OF NETNAVIS

# SECRETS OF BASS

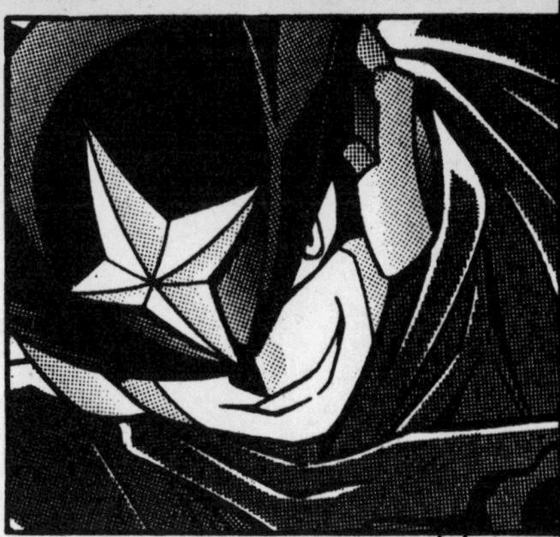

OTHER THAN HIS REP AS "THE UNDERNET'S STRONGEST NETNAVI," HE IS SHROUDED IN MYSTERY. WHAT IS THE SECRET OF HIS STRENGTH...?!

## 1 THIRSTING FOR REVENGE AGAINST HUMANS, HE SEEKS EVEN GREATER STRENGTH!!

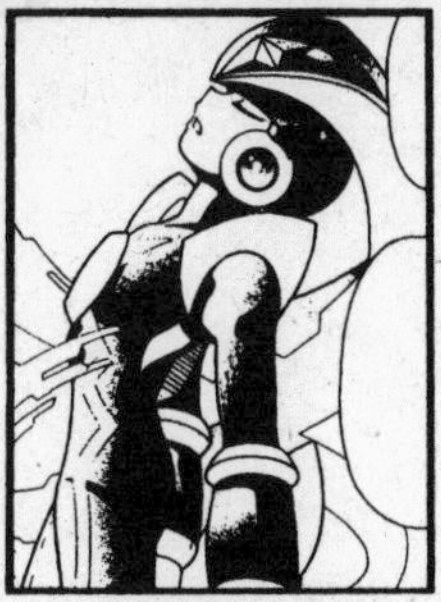

▲ BASS WAS THE WORLD'S FIRST INDEPENDENT NETNAVI, AND ONLY OPENED UP TO HIS CREATOR DOCTOR COSSACK...

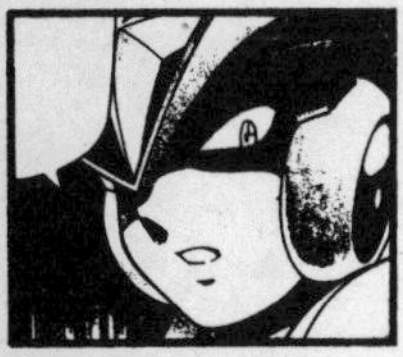

▲ HE WAS TOO ADVANCED...

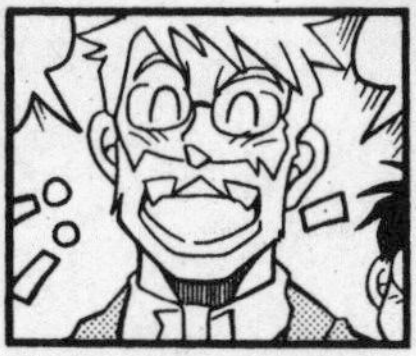

▲ ...THE ONLY PERSON WHO UNDERSTOOD HIM.

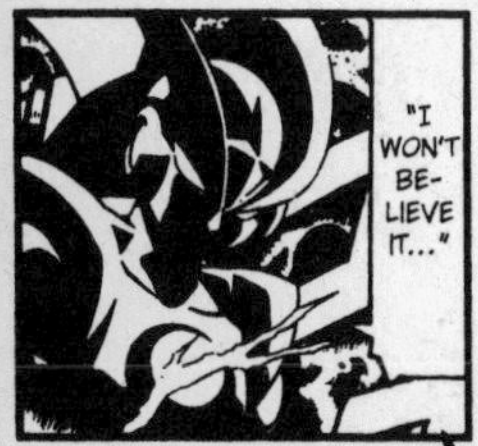
"I WON'T BE-LIEVE IT..."

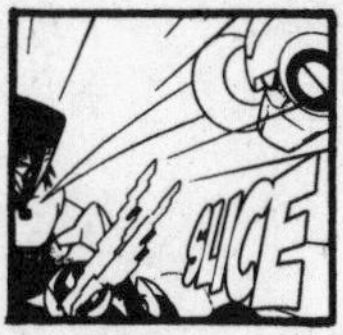
SLICE

▲ ...AND WAS NEARLY EXECUTED AS A REBEL...!!

## 2 THE GET ABILITY PROGRAM!!

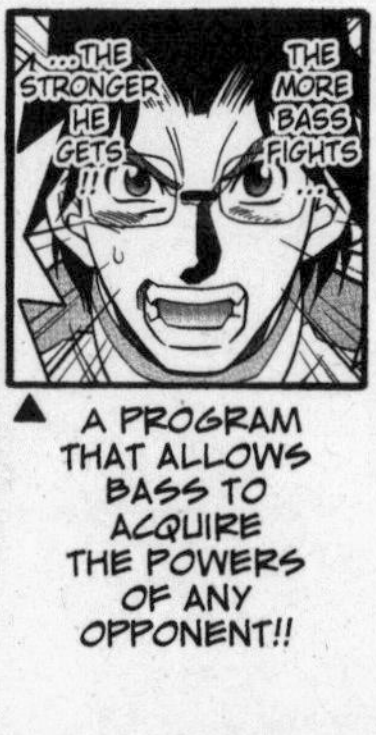
THE MORE BASS FIGHTS...
...THE STRONGER HE GETS!!

▲ A PROGRAM THAT ALLOWS BASS TO ACQUIRE THE POWERS OF ANY OPPONENT!!

## 3 EARTH-BREAKER

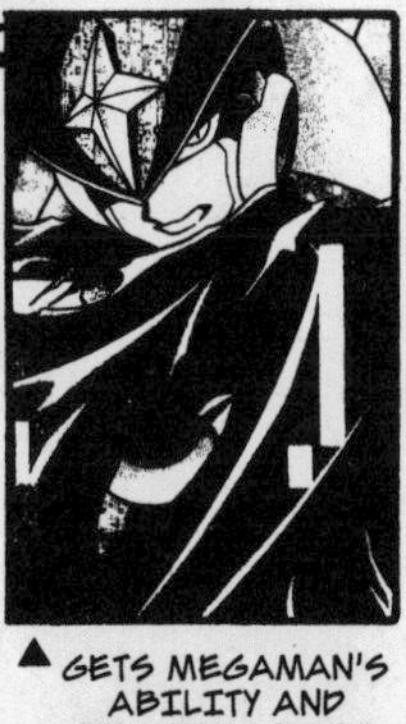

▲ GETS MEGAMAN'S ABILITY AND BECOMES BASS HUBSTYLE!!

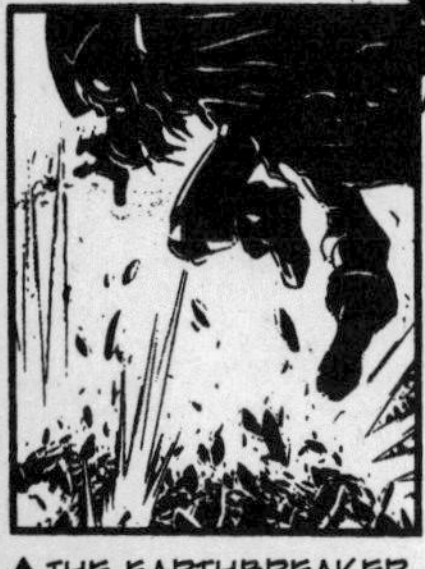

▲ THE EARTHBREAKER IS A TREMEN-DOUSLY DESTRUCTIVE TECHNIQUE THAT SEEMS TO MIRROR THE DARKNESS IN BASS'S SOUL!!

BASS'S SECRETS REVEALED!!

**BASS THE STRONGEST: AND HE'LL PROVE IT!**

TO BE RECORDED IN VOLUME 6!!

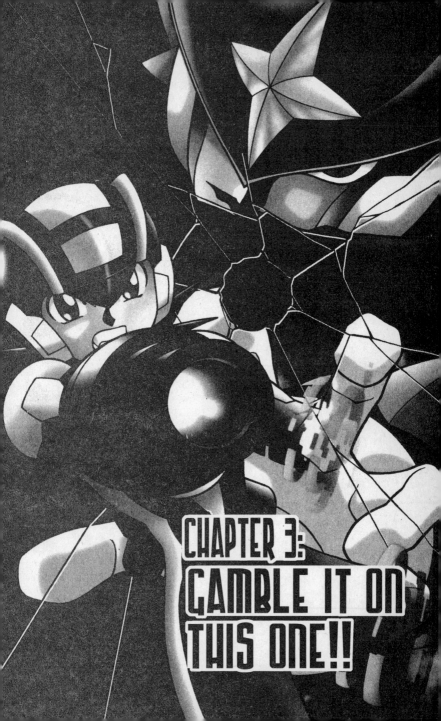

# CHAPTER 3: GAMBLE IT ON THIS ONE!!

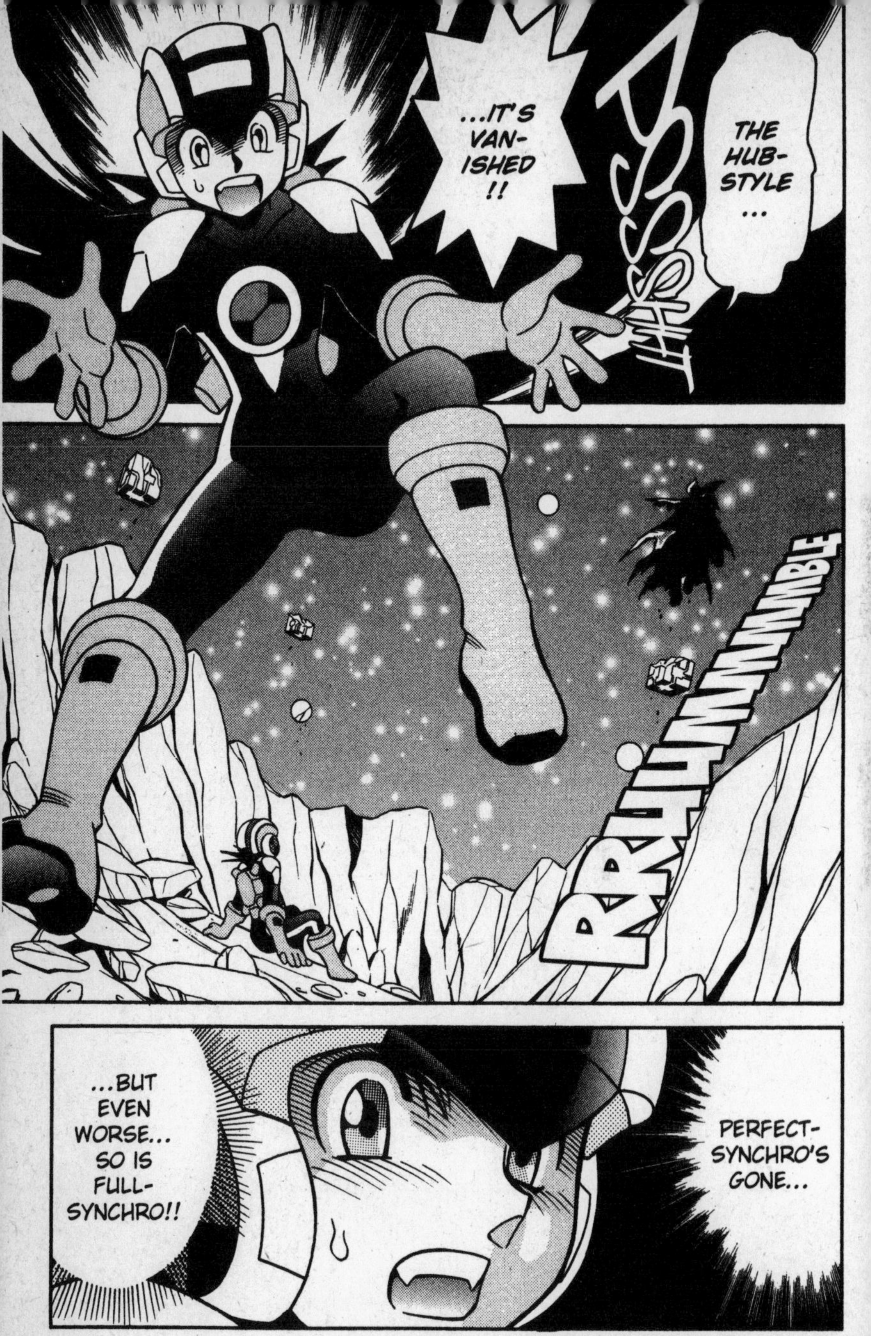
THE HUB-STYLE...
PSSSHHT
...IT'S VAN-ISHED!!
RRRUMMMMMMMBLE
PERFECT-SYNCHRO'S GONE...
...BUT EVEN WORSE... SO IS FULL-SYNCHRO!!

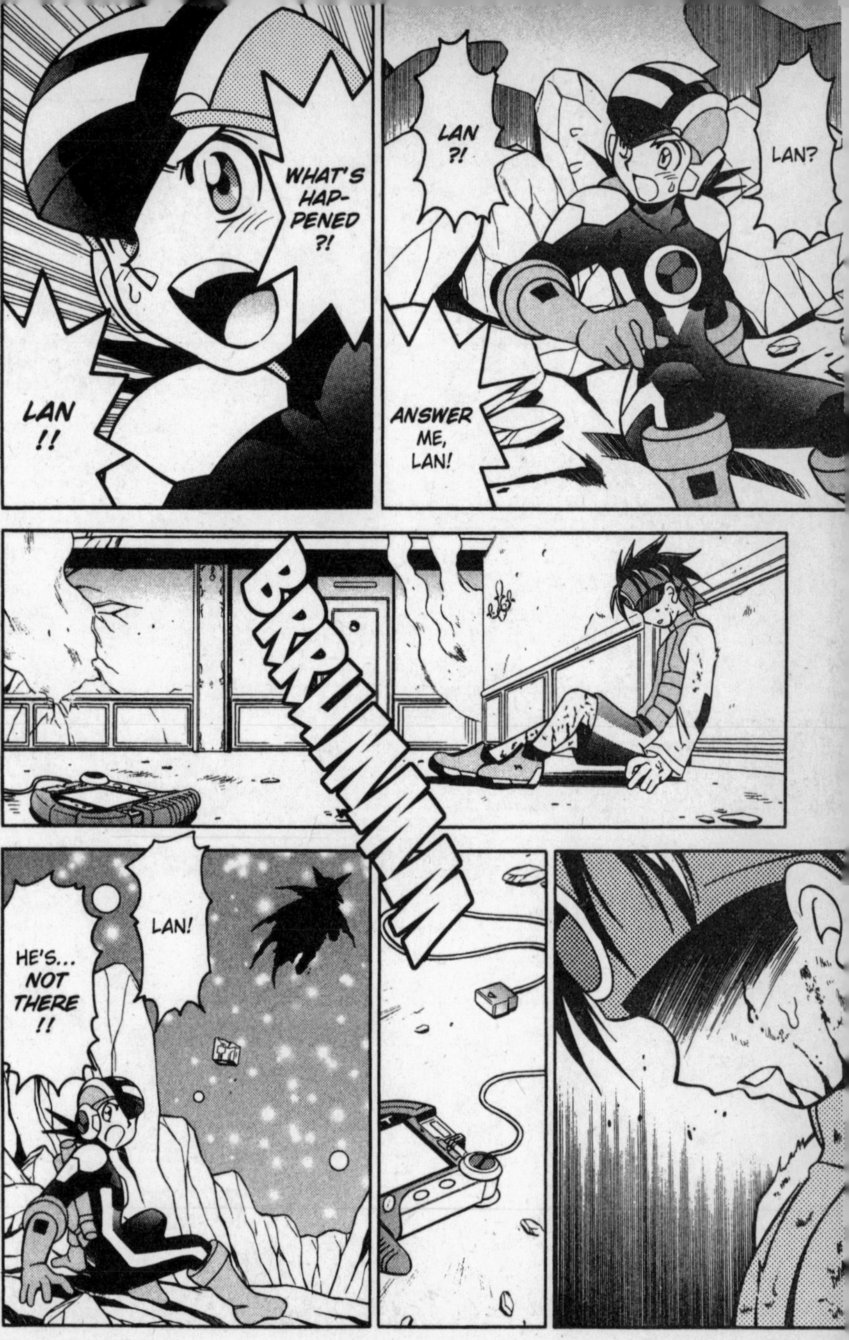
LAN?
LAN ?!
ANSWER ME, LAN!
WHAT'S HAP-PENED ?!
LAN !!
BRRUMMMMMM
LAN!
HE'S... NOT THERE !!

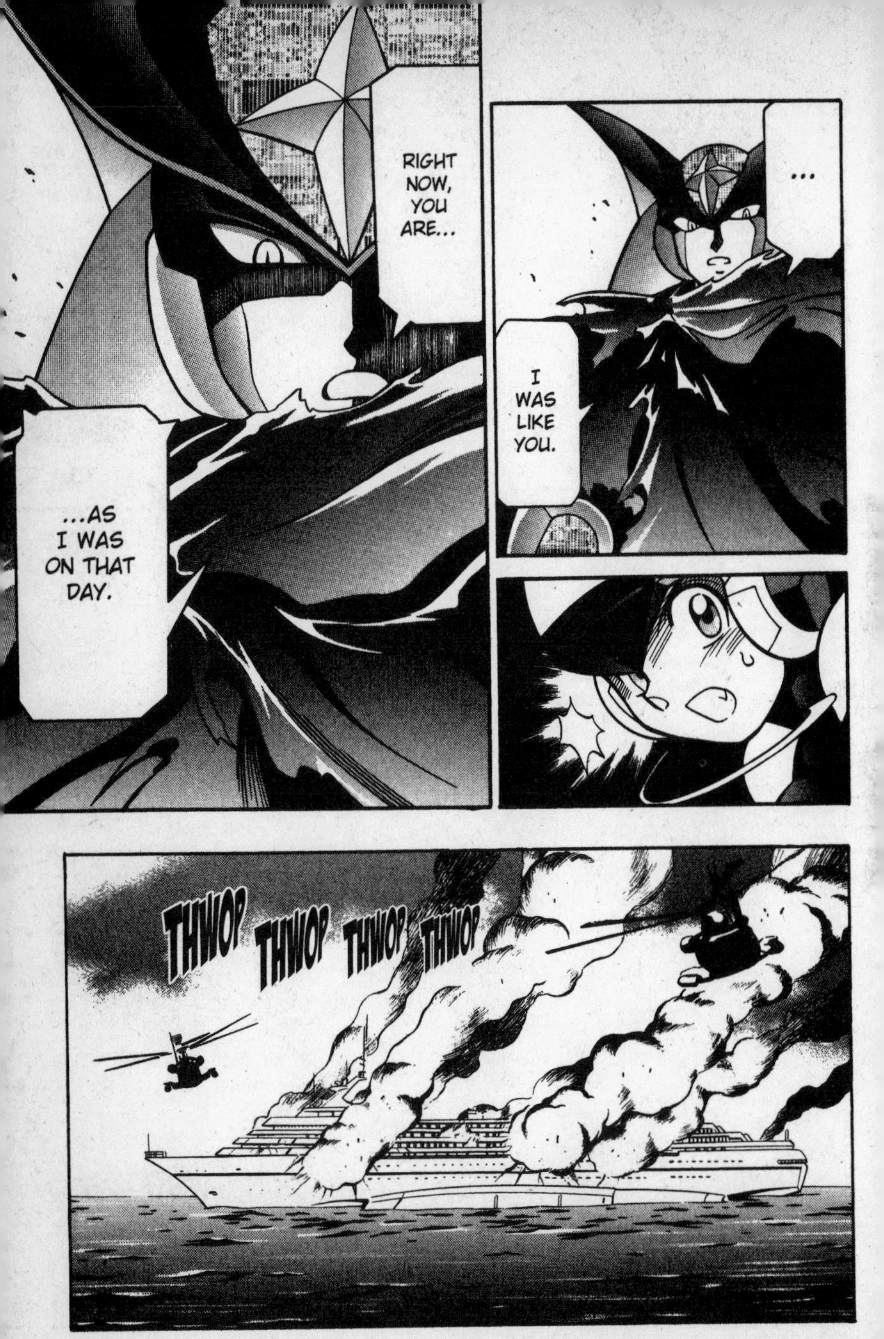
...
I WAS LIKE YOU.
RIGHT NOW, YOU ARE...
...AS I WAS ON THAT DAY.
THWOP THWOP THWOP THWOP

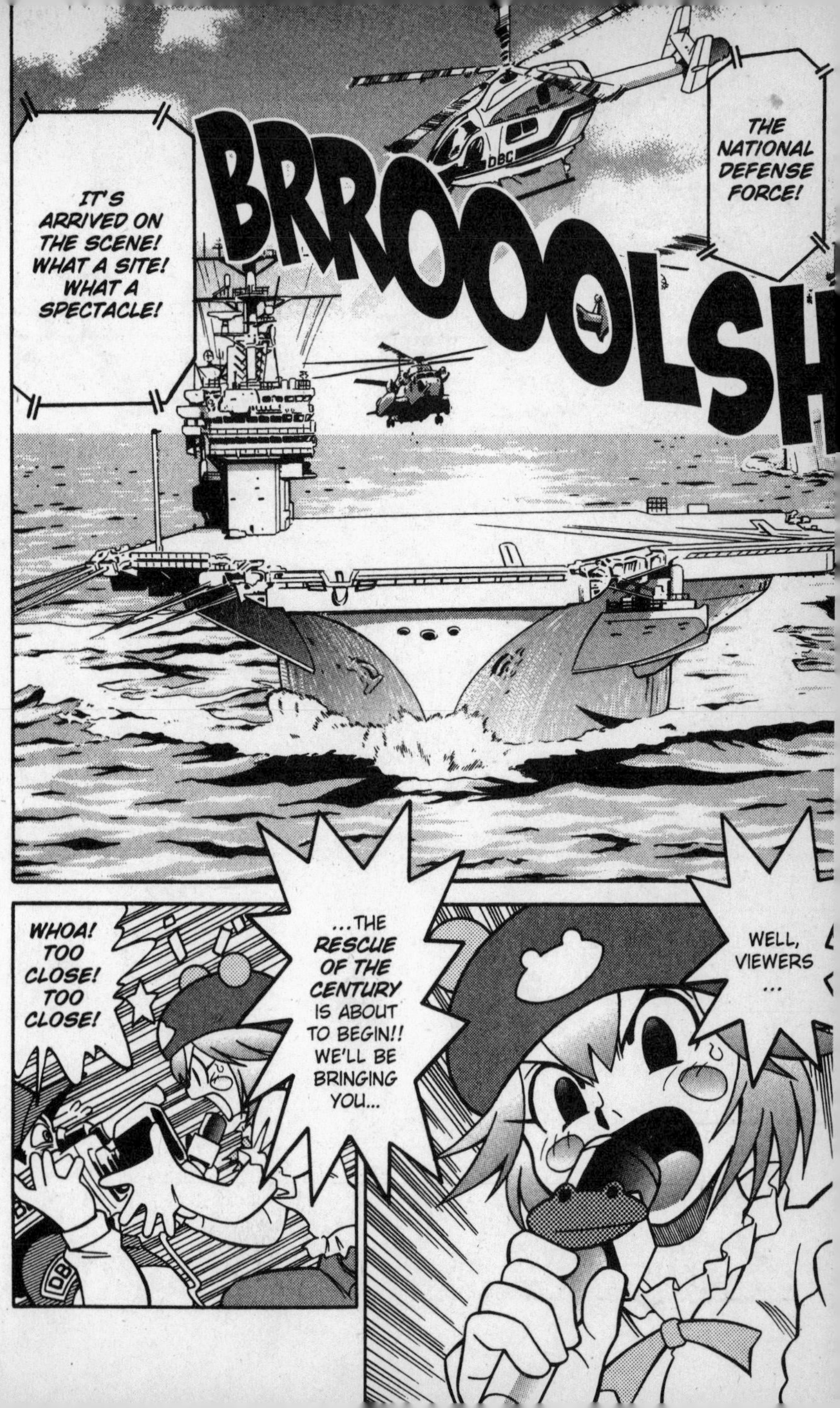
THE NATIONAL DEFENSE FORCE!
BRROOOOLSH
IT'S ARRIVED ON THE SCENE! WHAT A SITE! WHAT A SPECTACLE!
WELL, VIEWERS ...
...THE RESCUE OF THE CENTURY IS ABOUT TO BEGIN!! WE'LL BE BRINGING YOU...
WHOA! TOO CLOSE! TOO CLOSE!
DBC

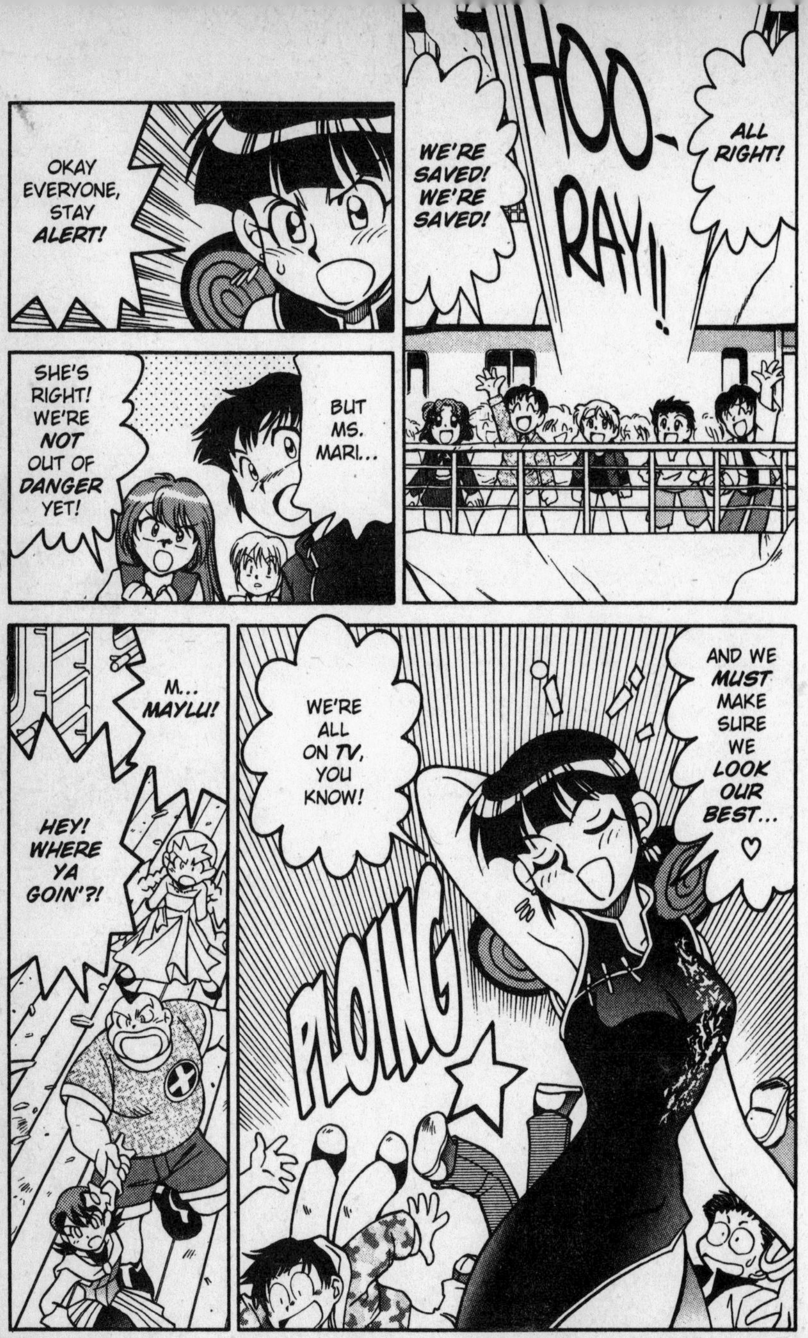
ALL RIGHT!
HOO-RAY!!
WE'RE SAVED! WE'RE SAVED!
OKAY EVERYONE, STAY ALERT!
BUT MS. MARI...
SHE'S RIGHT! WE'RE NOT OUT OF DANGER YET!
WE'RE ALL ON TV, YOU KNOW!
AND WE MUST MAKE SURE WE LOOK OUR BEST... ♡
PLOING
M... MAYLU!
HEY! WHERE YA GOIN'?!

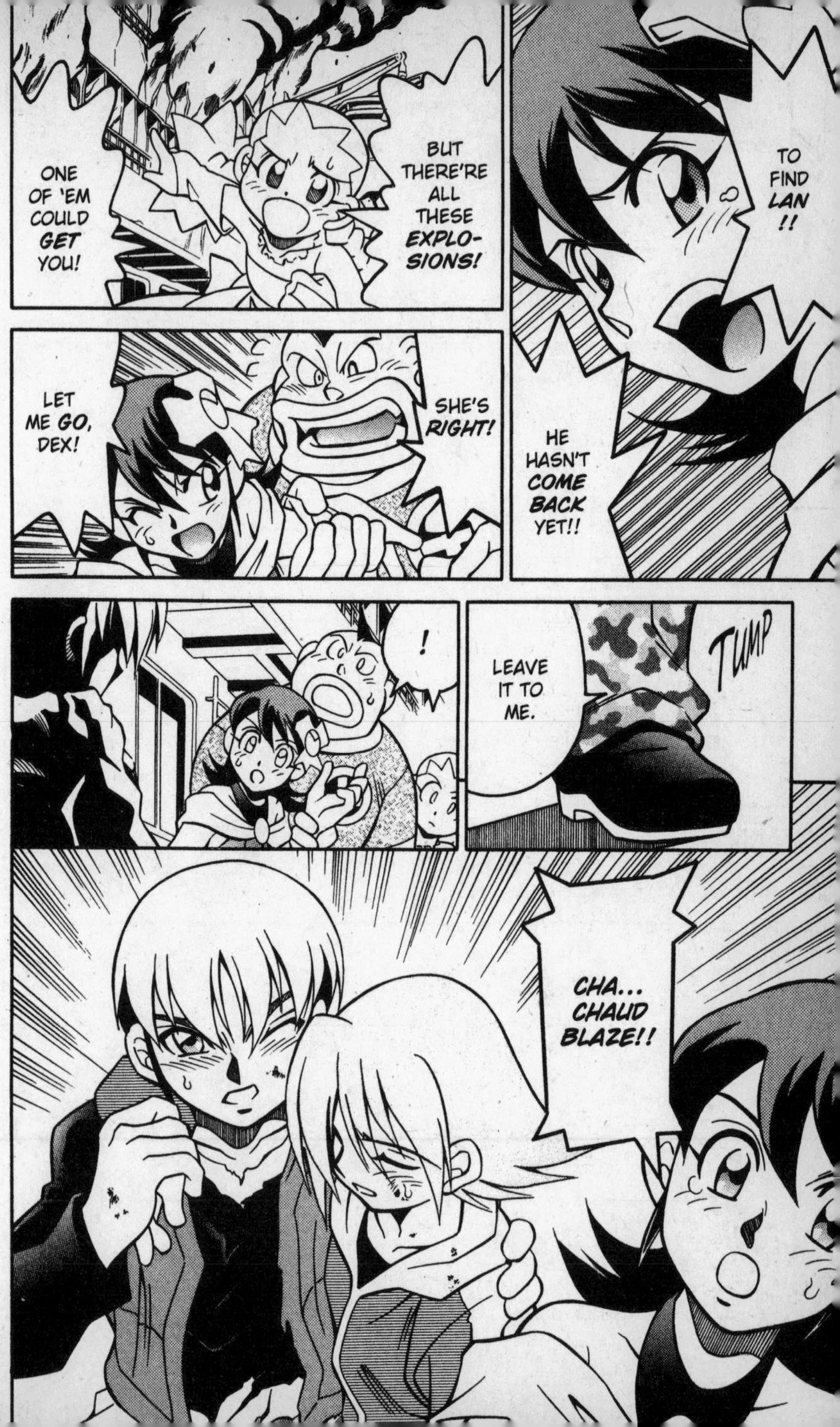
TO FIND LAN!!
HE HASN'T COME BACK YET!!
BUT THERE'RE ALL THESE EXPLOSIONS!
ONE OF 'EM COULD GET YOU!
SHE'S RIGHT!
LET ME GO, DEX!
TUMP
LEAVE IT TO ME.
!
CHA... CHAUD BLAZE!!

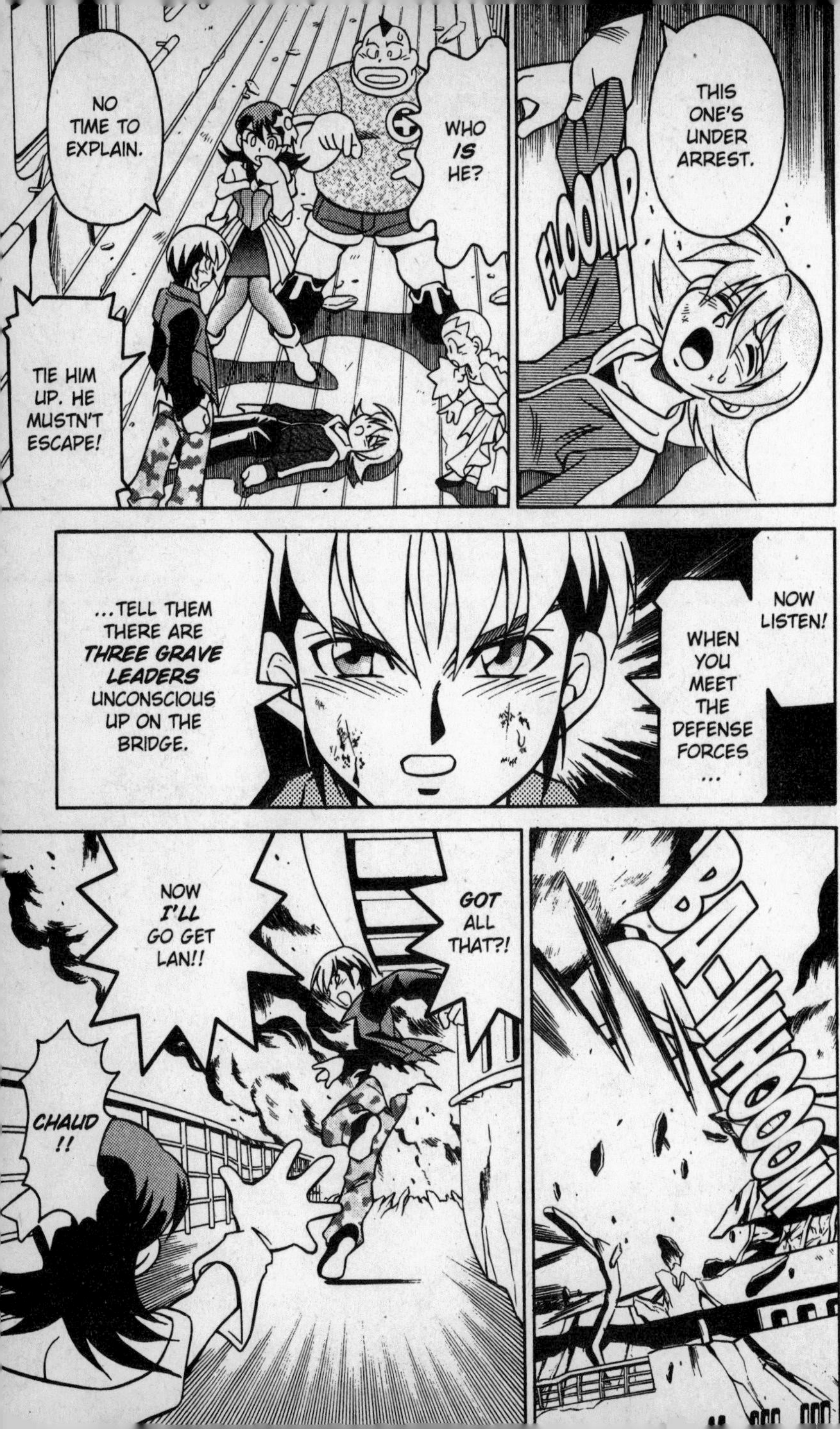
THIS ONE'S UNDER ARREST.
FLOOMP
WHO IS HE?
NO TIME TO EXPLAIN.
TIE HIM UP. HE MUSTN'T ESCAPE!
NOW LISTEN!
WHEN YOU MEET THE DEFENSE FORCES ...
...TELL THEM THERE ARE THREE GRAVE LEADERS UNCONSCIOUS UP ON THE BRIDGE.
BA-WHOOOOM
GOT ALL THAT?!
NOW I'LL GO GET LAN!!
CHAUD !!

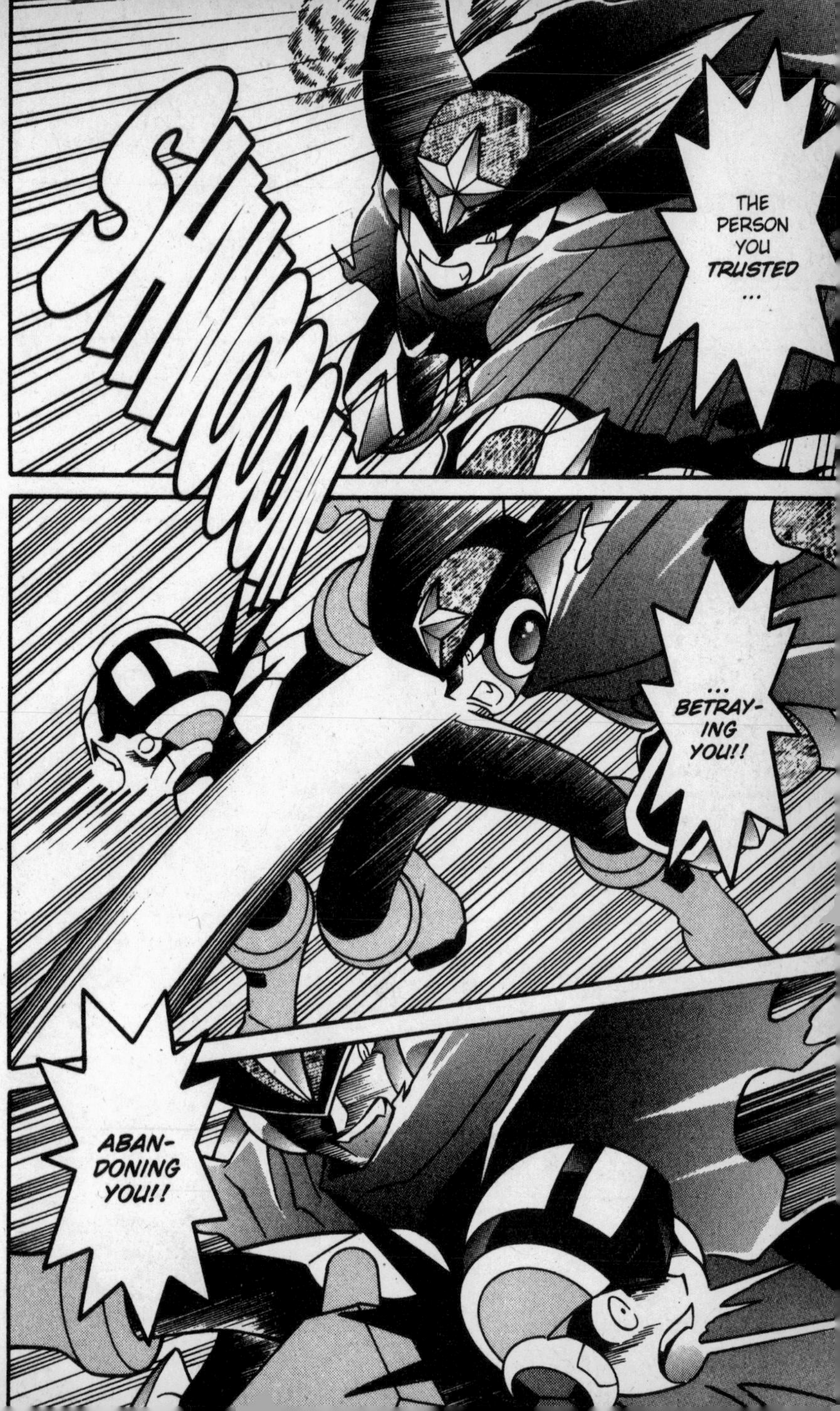
THE PERSON YOU TRUSTED ...
... BETRAYING YOU!!
ABANDONING YOU!!

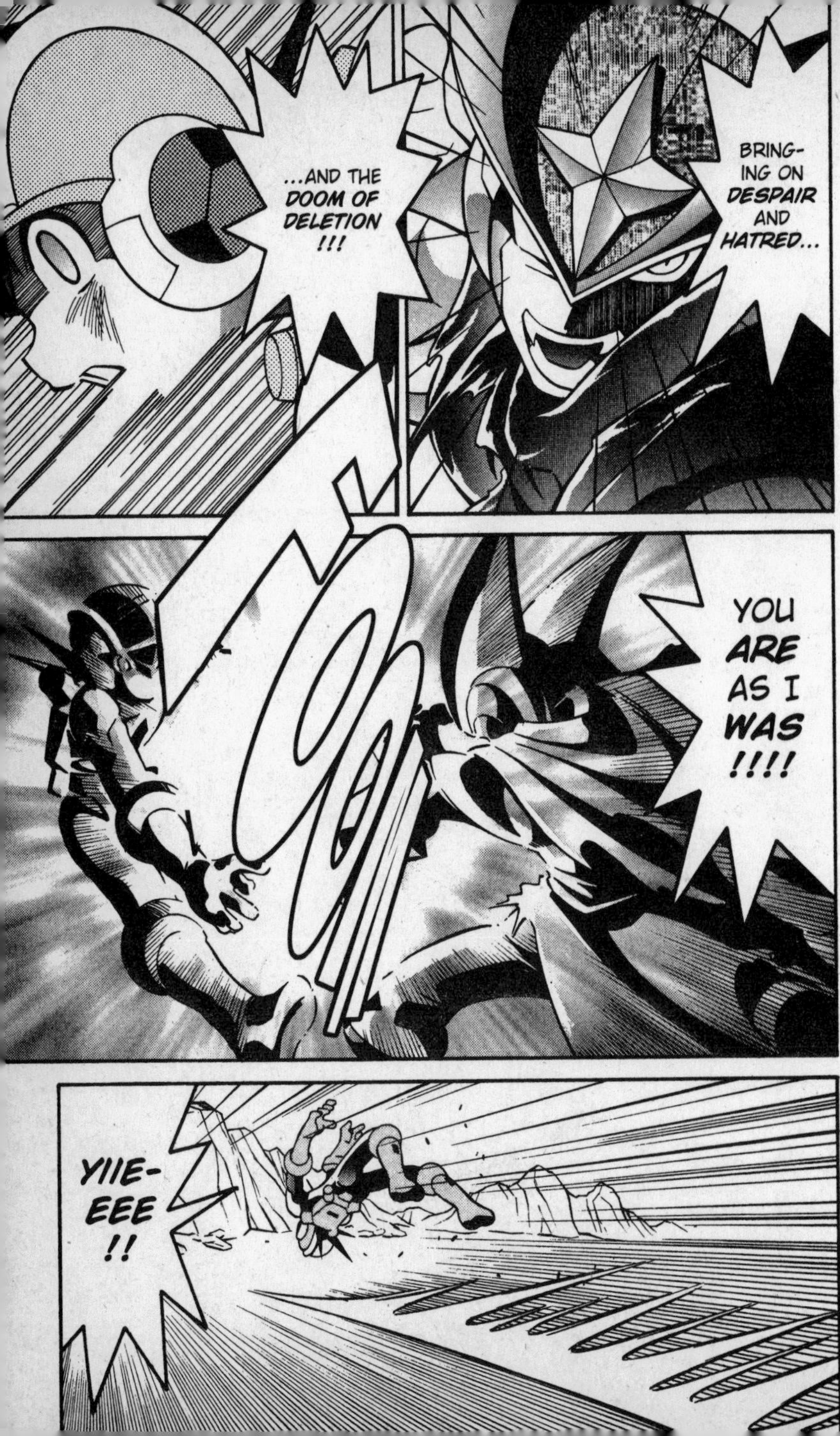
BRING-ING ON DESPAIR AND HATRED...
...AND THE DOOM OF DELETION !!!
YOU ARE AS I WAS !!!!
YIIE-EEE !!

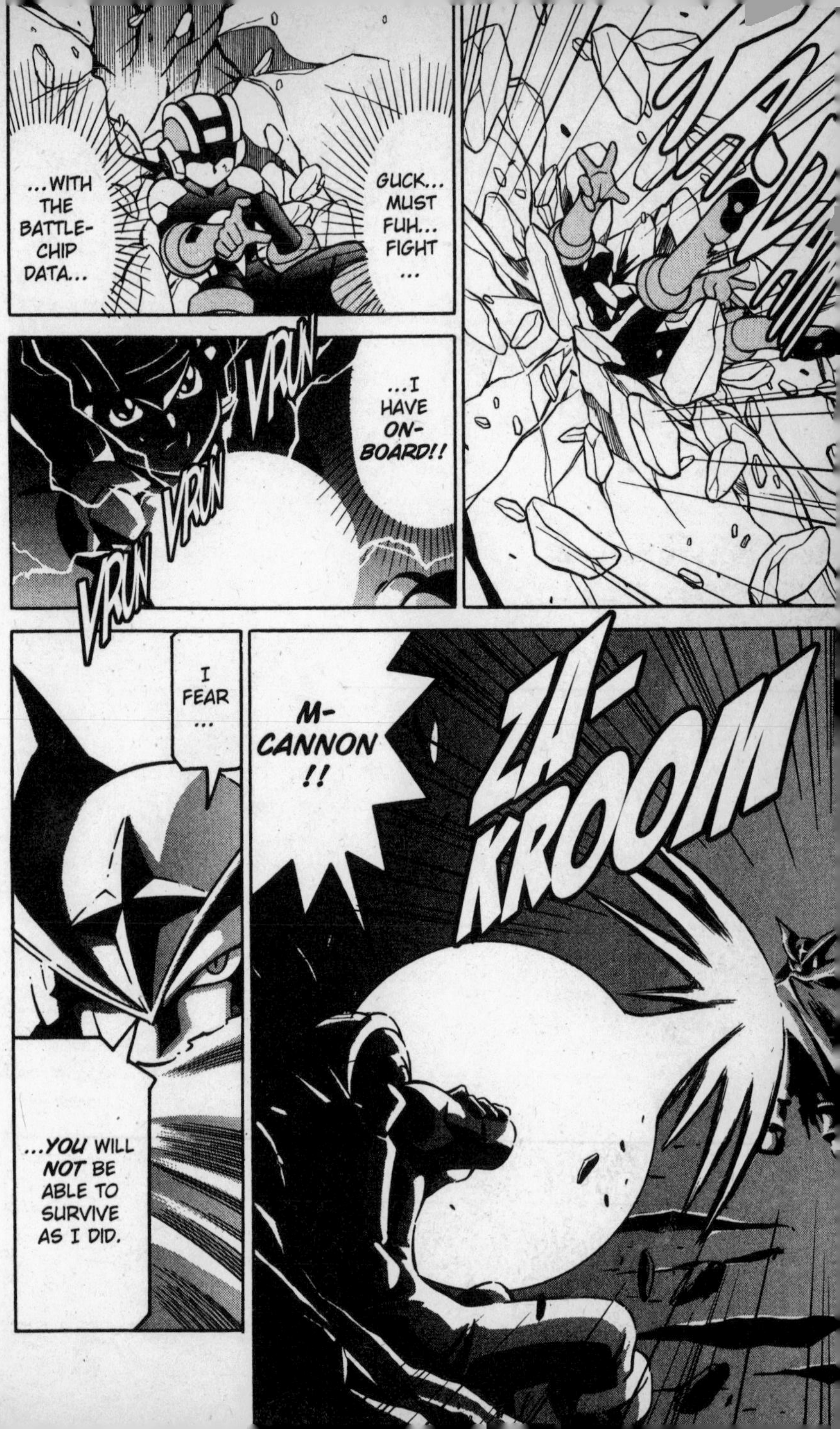
GUCK... MUST FUH... FIGHT ...
...WITH THE BATTLE-CHIP DATA...
...I HAVE ON-BOARD!!
VRUN VRUN VRUN VRUN
M-CANNON!!
ZA-KROOOM
I FEAR ...
...YOU WILL NOT BE ABLE TO SURVIVE AS I DID.

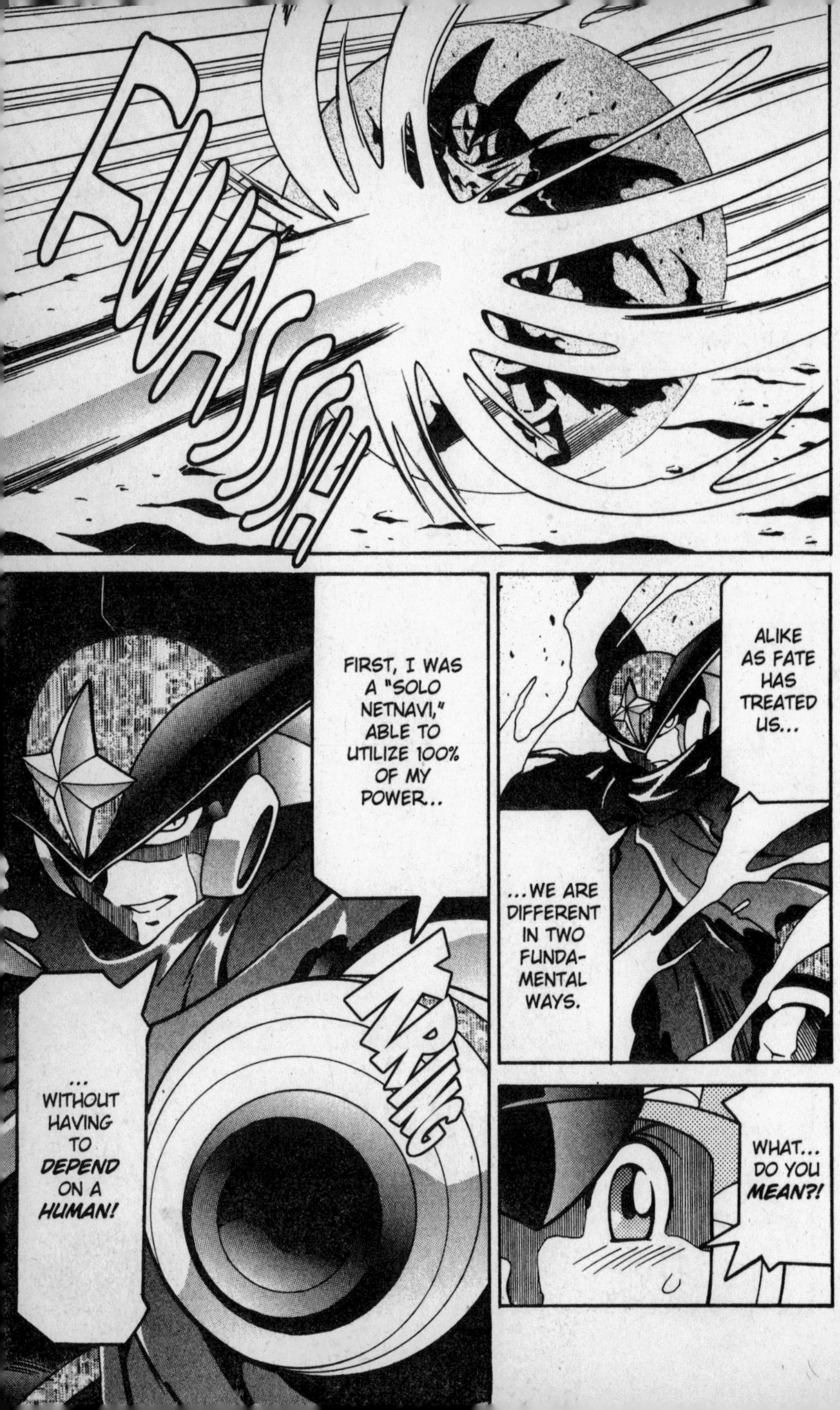
FWASSH!
ALIKE AS FATE HAS TREATED US...
...WE ARE DIFFERENT IN TWO FUNDAMENTAL WAYS.
WHAT... DO YOU *MEAN?!*
FIRST, I WAS A "SOLO NETNAVI," ABLE TO UTILIZE 100% OF MY POWER...
KRING
...WITHOUT HAVING TO *DEPEND* ON A *HUMAN!*

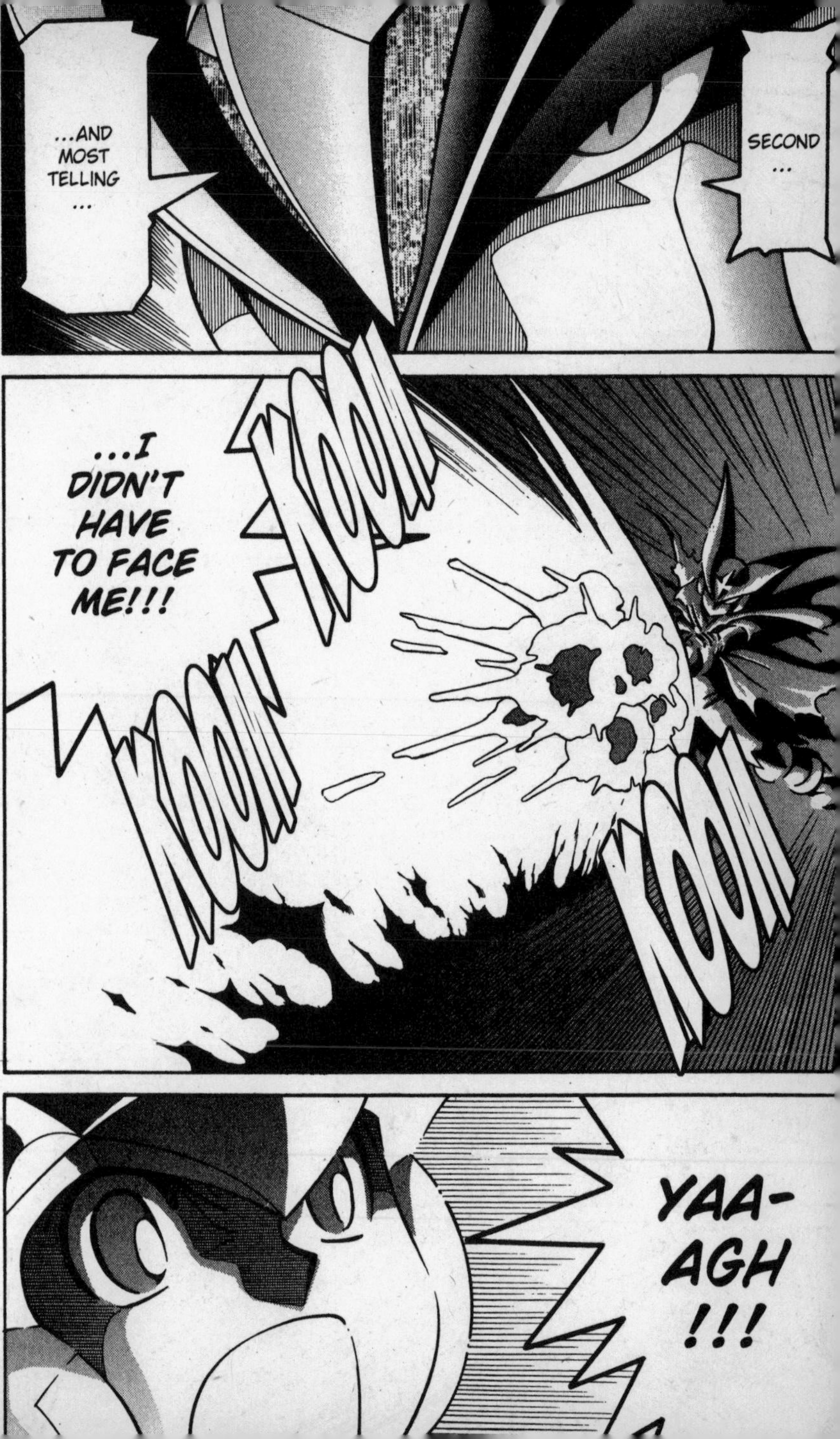
SECOND ...
...AND MOST TELLING ...
...I DIDN'T HAVE TO FACE ME!!!
YAA-AGH !!!

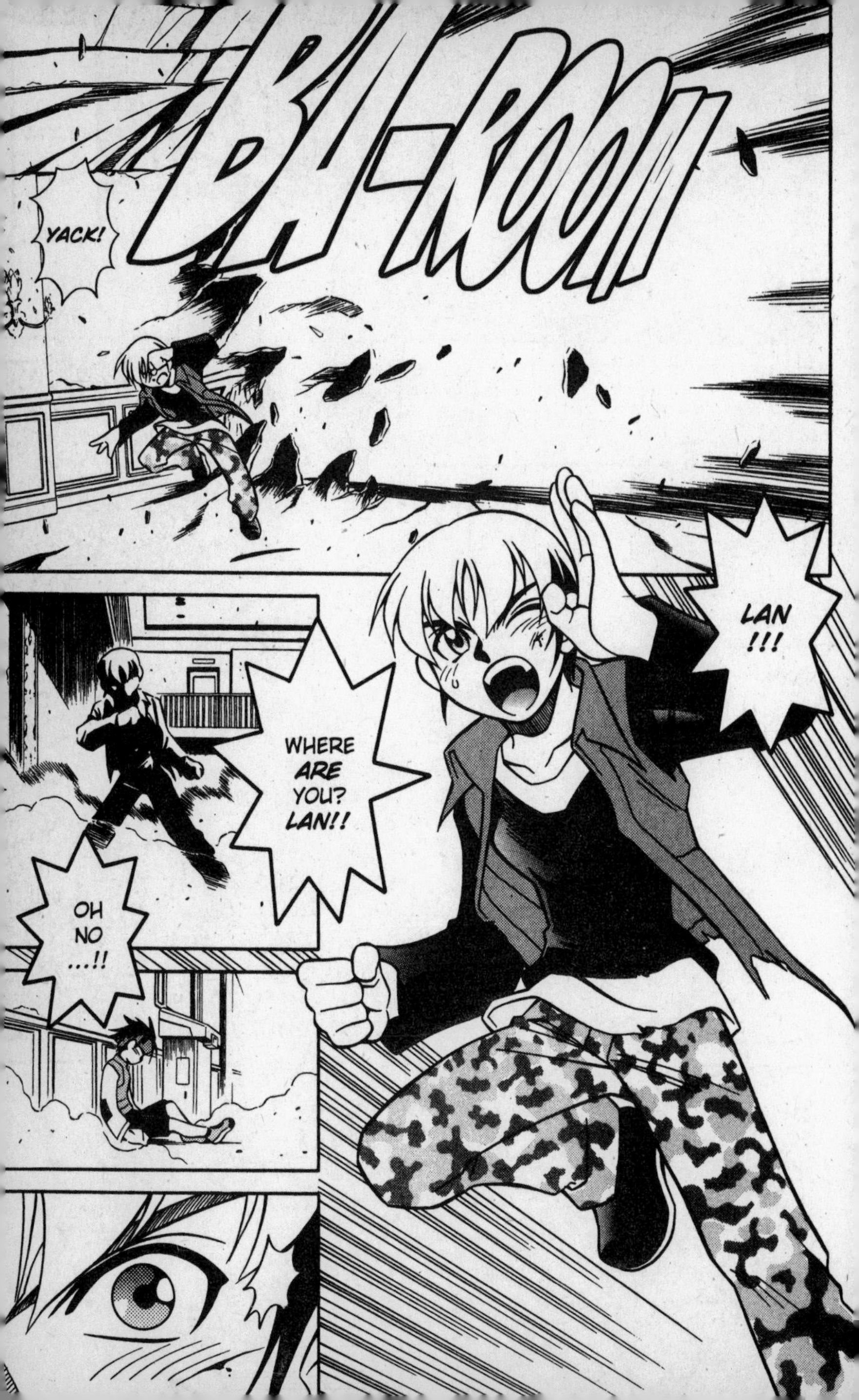
BA-ROOM
YACK!
LAN!!!
WHERE ARE YOU? LAN!!
OH NO ...!!

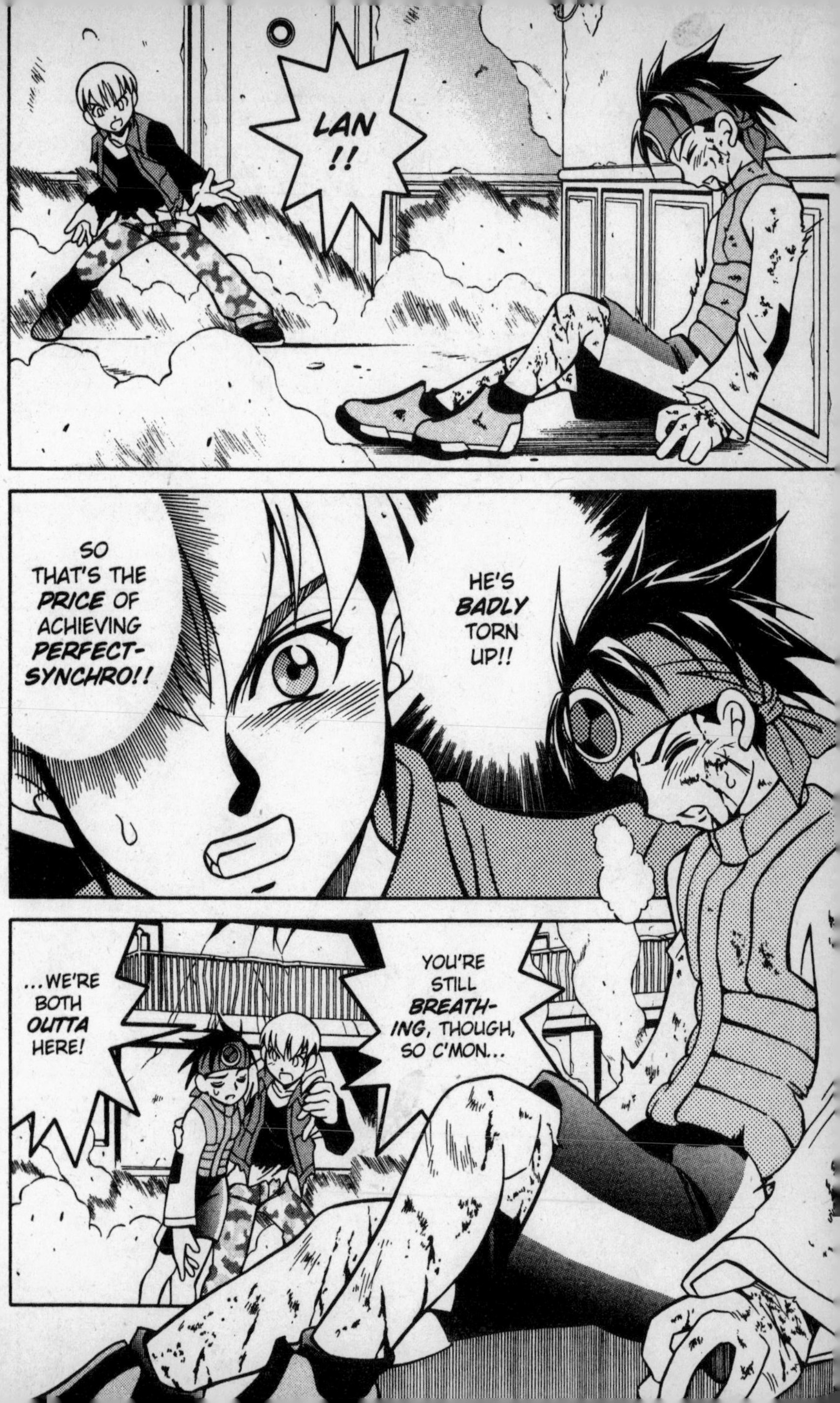
LAN !!
HE'S BADLY TORN UP!!
SO THAT'S THE PRICE OF ACHIEVING PERFECT-SYNCHRO!!
YOU'RE STILL BREATHING, THOUGH, SO C'MON...
...WE'RE BOTH OUTTA HERE!

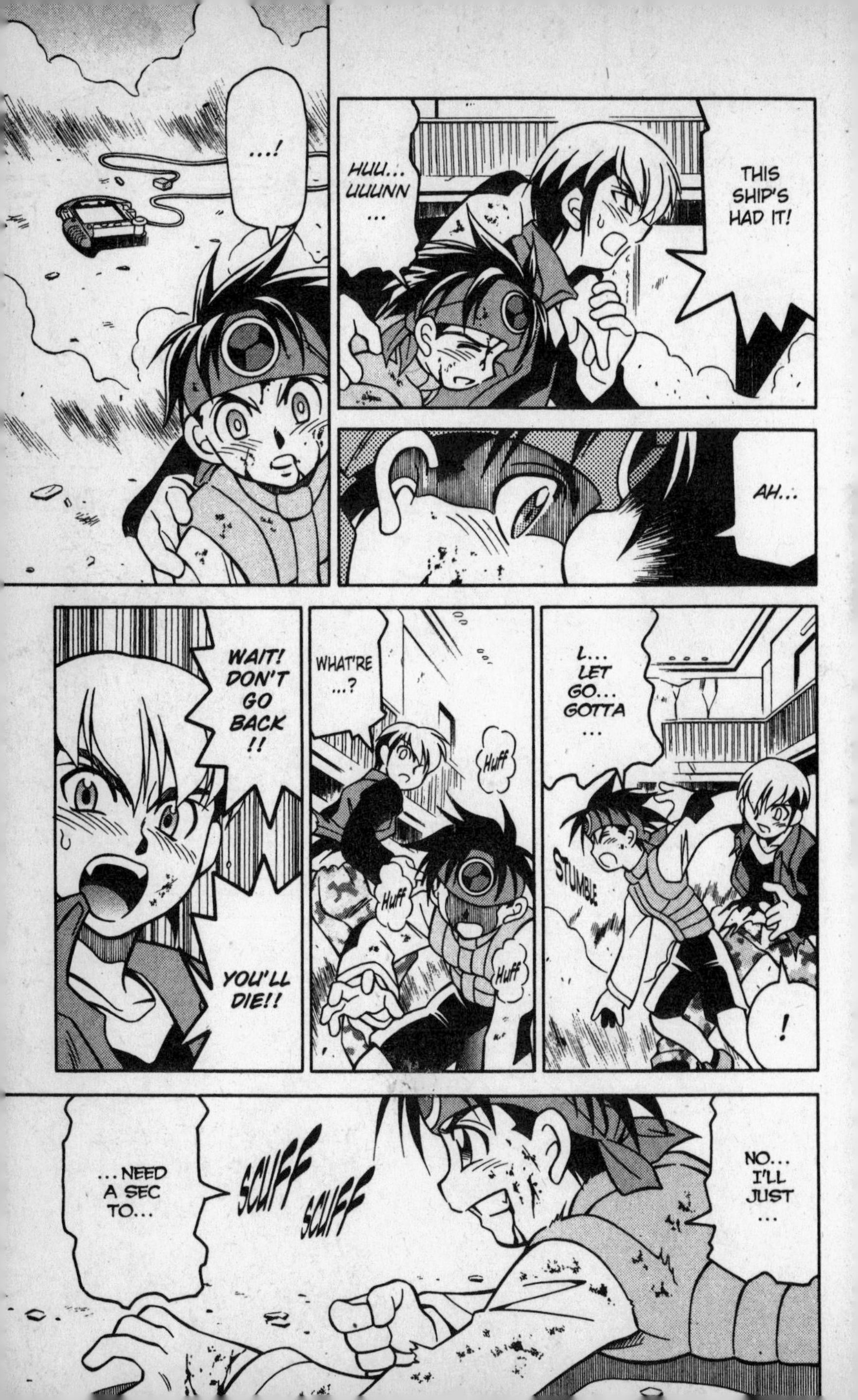
THIS SHIP'S HAD IT!
HUU... UUUNN ...
AH...
...!
L... LET GO... GOTTA ...
STUMBLE
!
WHAT'RE ...?
Huff
Huff
Huff
WAIT! DON'T GO BACK !!
YOU'LL DIE!!
NO... I'LL JUST ...
SCUFF
SCUFF
... NEED A SEC TO...

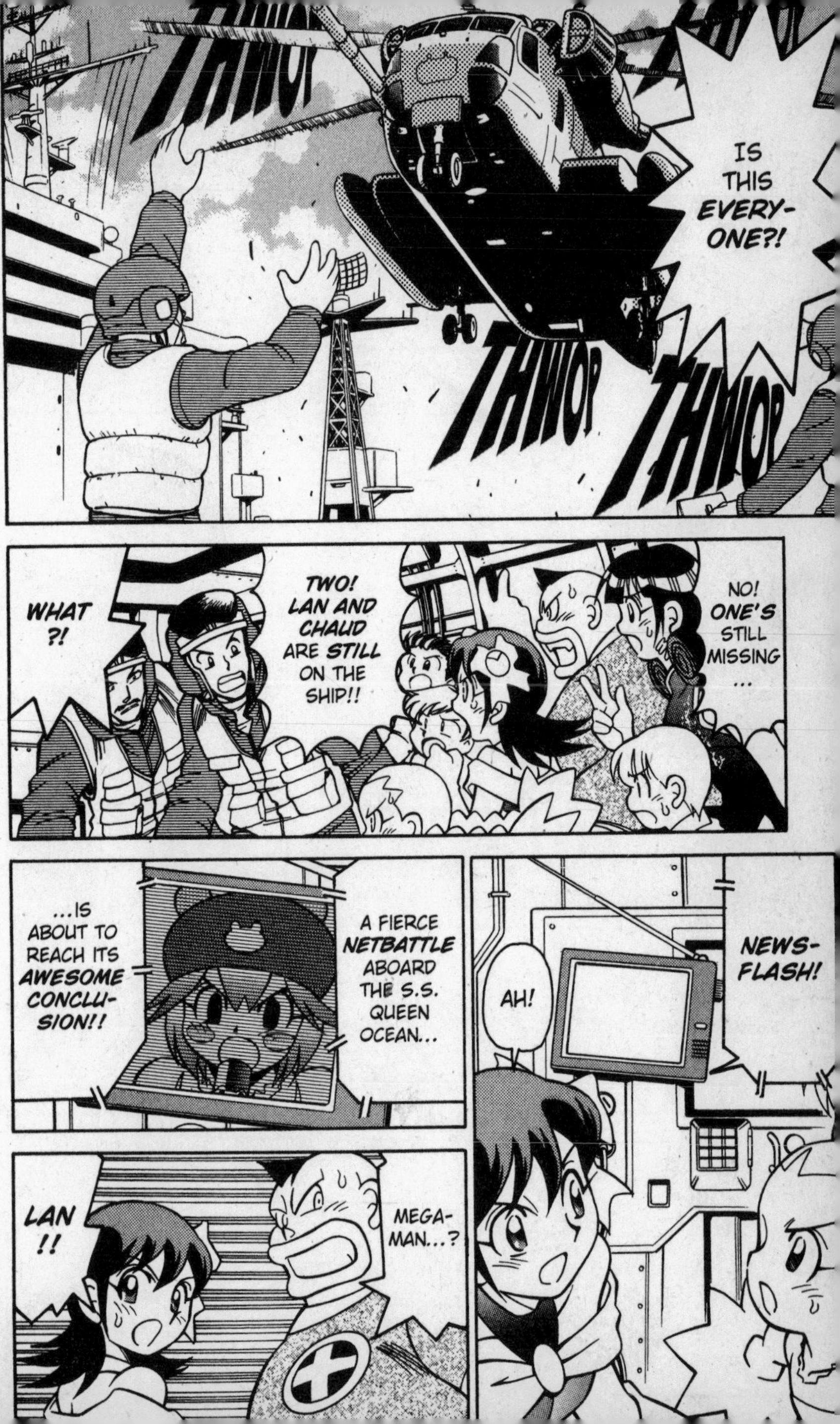
THWOP
IS THIS EVERY-ONE?!
THWOP
THWOP
NO! ONE'S STILL MISSING...
TWO! LAN AND CHAUD ARE STILL ON THE SHIP!!
WHAT?!
NEWS-FLASH!
AH!
A FIERCE NETBATTLE ABOARD THE S.S. QUEEN OCEAN...
...IS ABOUT TO REACH ITS AWESOME CONCLUSION!!
MEGA-MAN...?
LAN!!

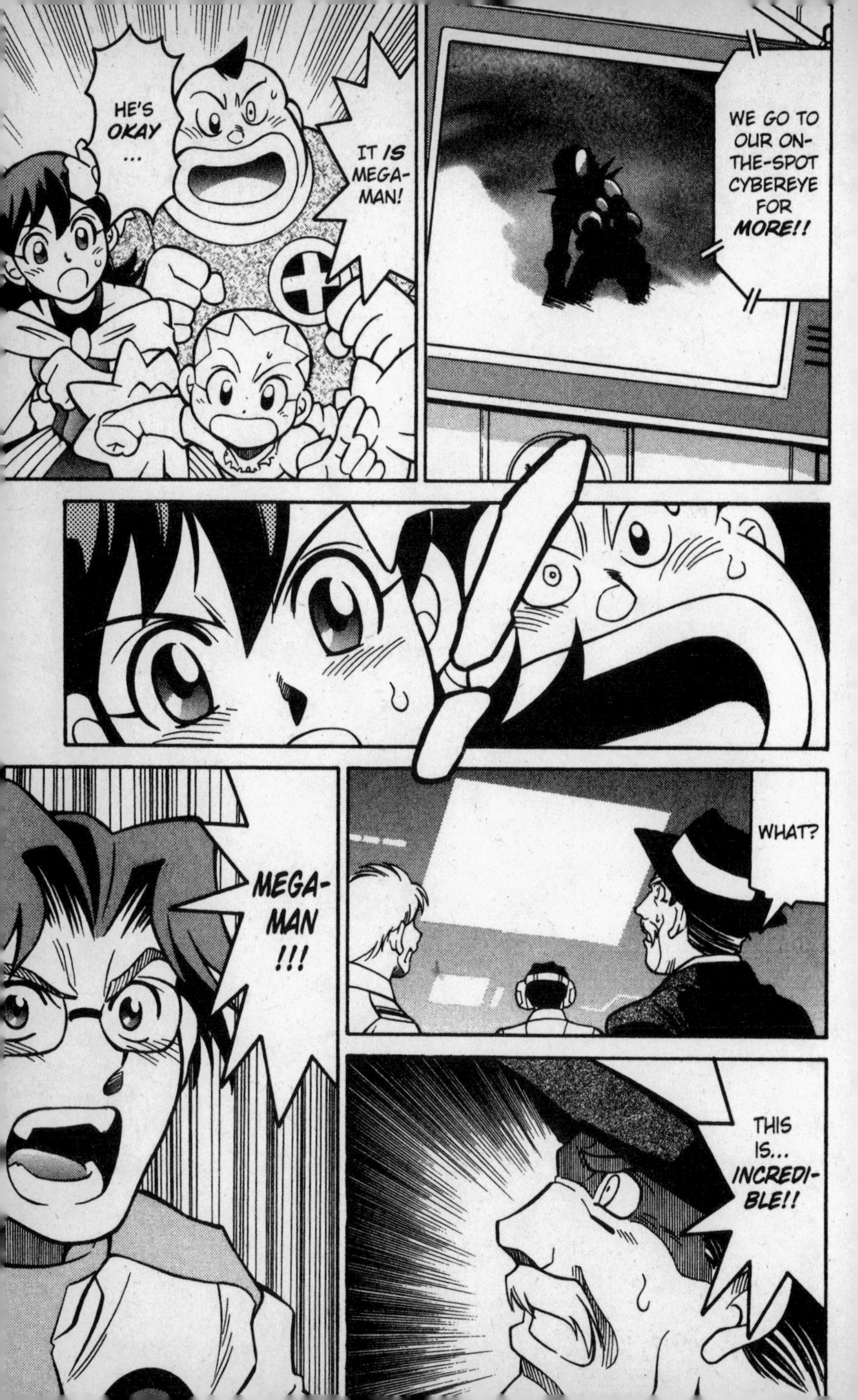
WE GO TO OUR ON-THE-SPOT CYBEREYE FOR *MORE!!*
IT *IS* MEGA-MAN!
HE'S *OKAY* ...
WHAT?
THIS IS... *INCREDIBLE!!*
*MEGA-MAN !!!*

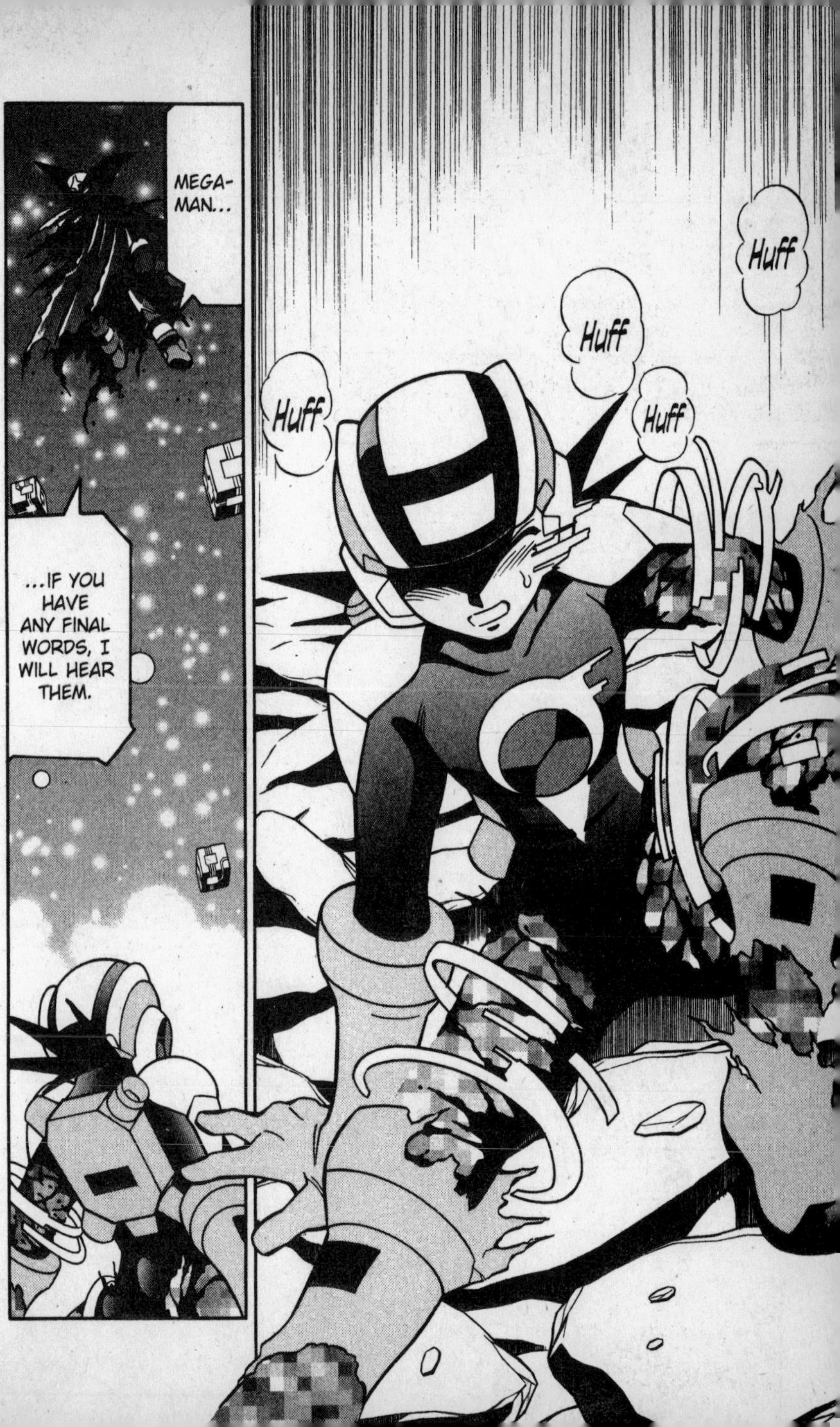
Huff
Huff
Huff
Huff
MEGA-MAN...
...IF YOU HAVE ANY FINAL WORDS, I WILL HEAR THEM.

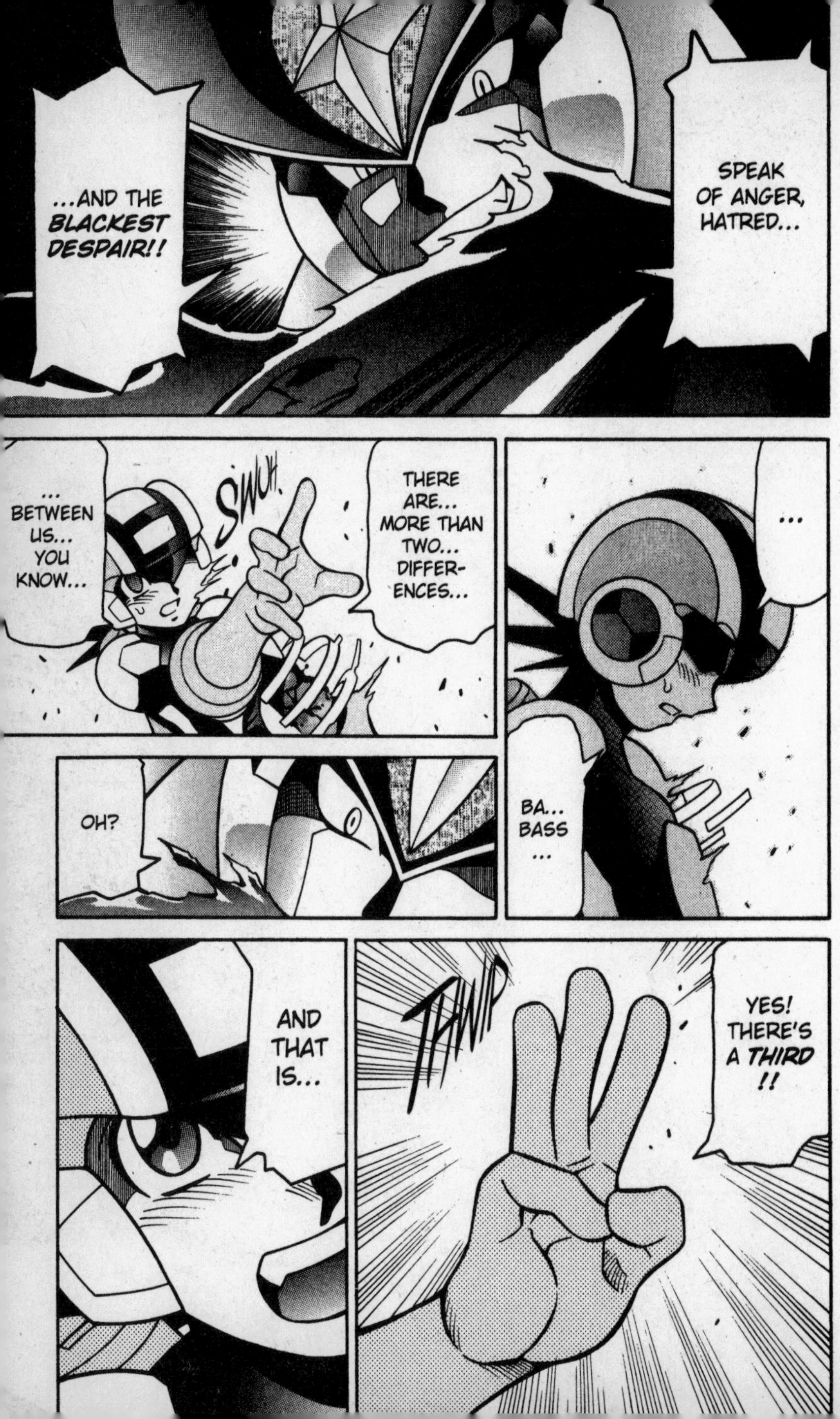
SPEAK OF ANGER, HATRED...
...AND THE BLACKEST DESPAIR!!
...
BA... BASS ...
THERE ARE... MORE THAN TWO... DIFFER-ENCES...
SWOH
... BETWEEN US... YOU KNOW...
OH?
YES! THERE'S A THIRD !!
THWIP
AND THAT IS...

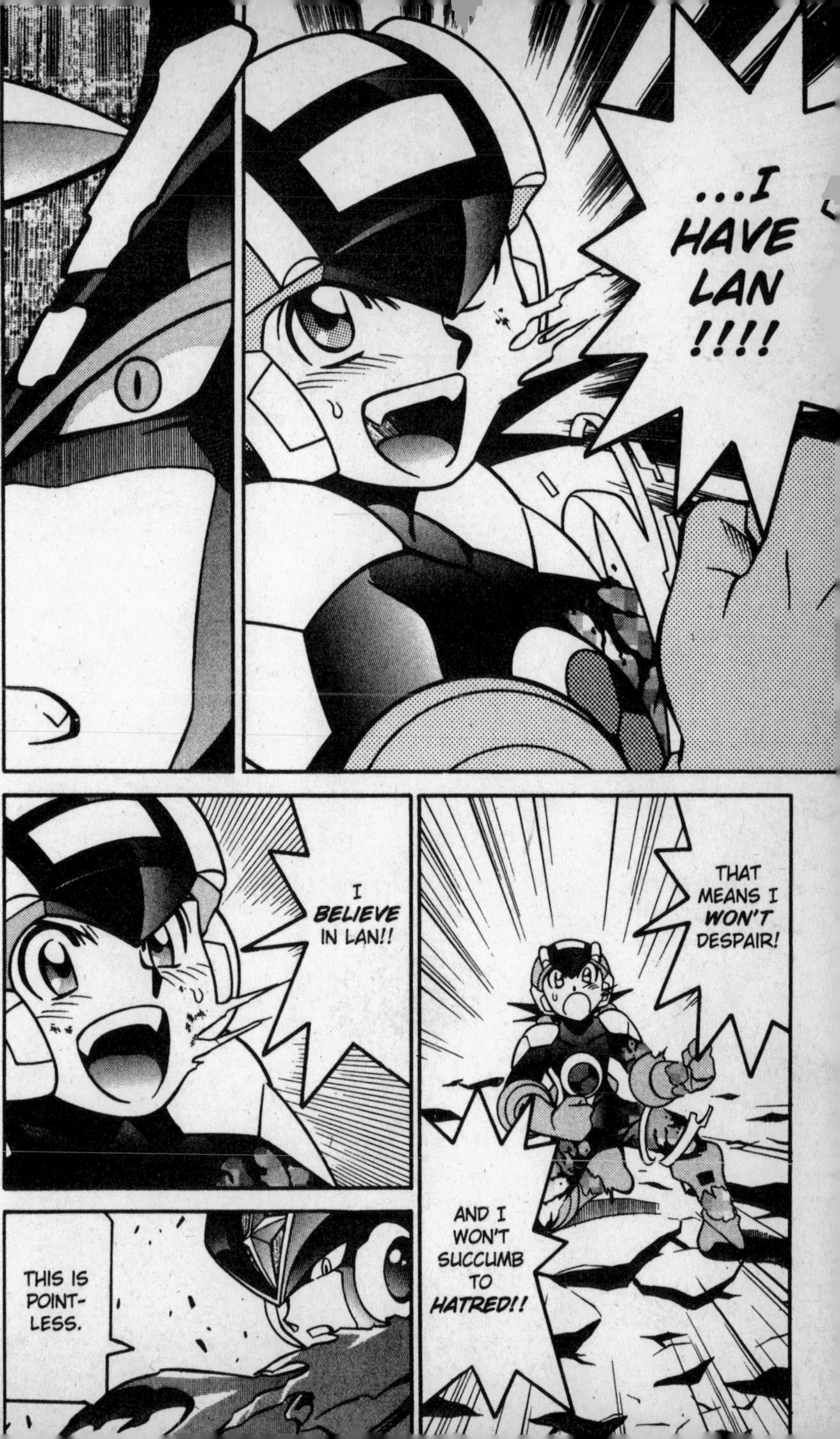
...I HAVE LAN!!!!
THAT MEANS I WON'T DESPAIR!
AND I WON'T SUCCUMB TO HATRED!!
I BELIEVE IN LAN!!
THIS IS POINT-LESS.

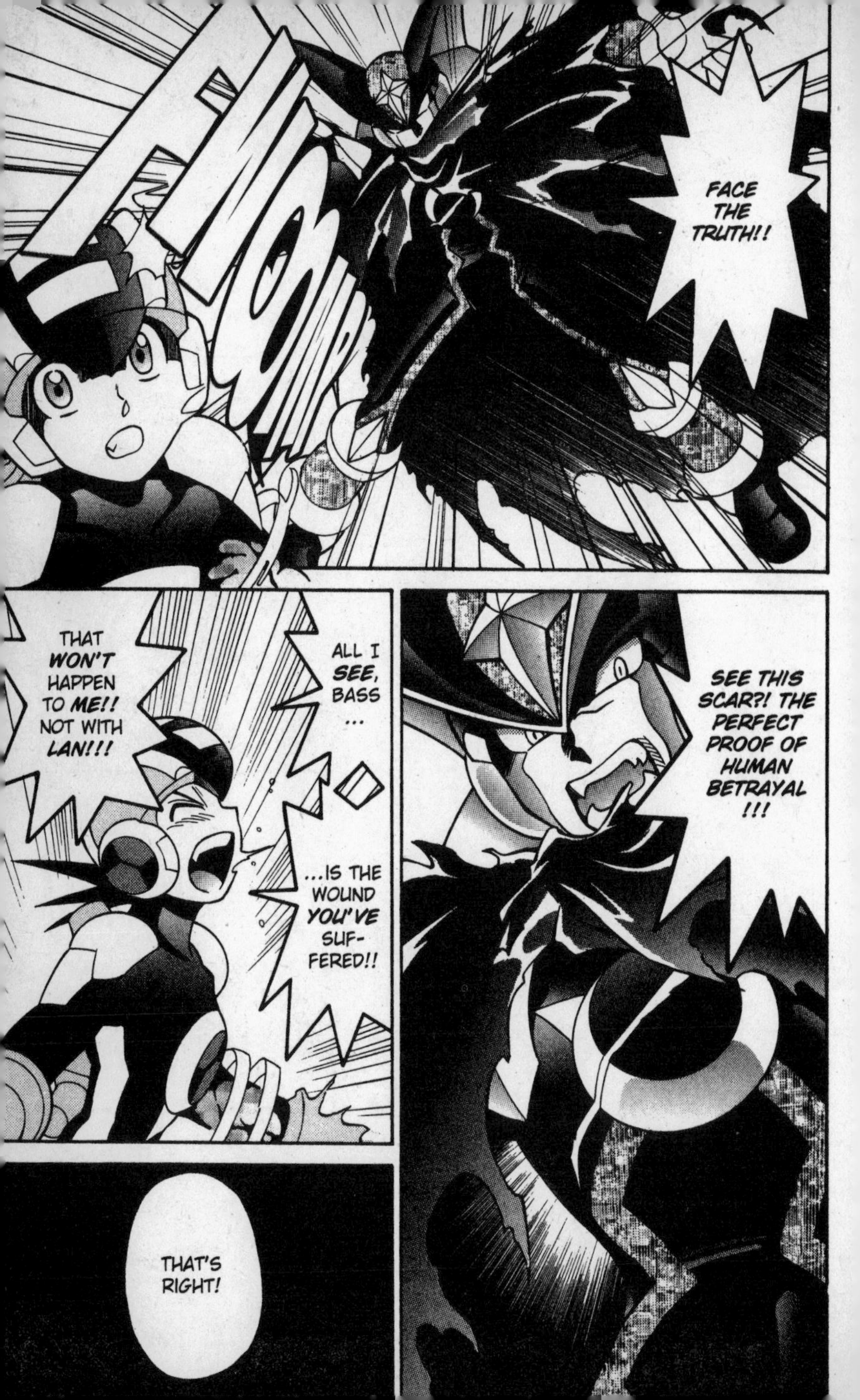
FACE THE TRUTH!!
SEE THIS SCAR?! THE PERFECT PROOF OF HUMAN BETRAYAL!!!
ALL I SEE, BASS...
...IS THE WOUND YOU'VE SUF-FERED!!
THAT WON'T HAPPEN TO ME!! NOT WITH LAN!!!
THAT'S RIGHT!

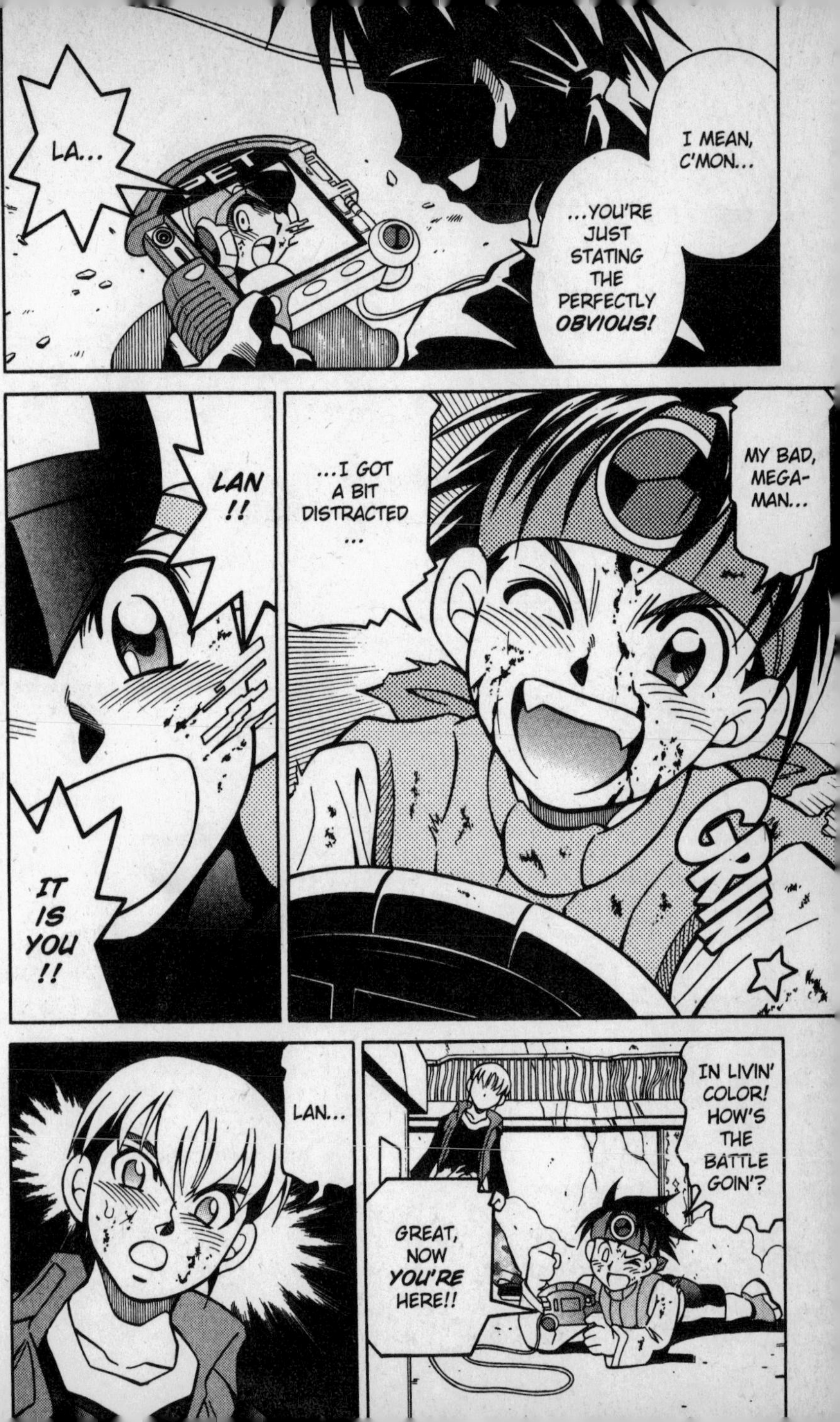
I MEAN, C'MON...
...YOU'RE JUST STATING THE PERFECTLY *OBVIOUS!*
LA...
MY BAD, MEGA-MAN...
...I GOT A BIT DISTRACTED...
GRIN
*LAN!!*
*IT IS YOU!!*
IN LIVIN' COLOR! HOW'S THE BATTLE GOIN'?
GREAT, NOW *YOU'RE* HERE!!
LAN...

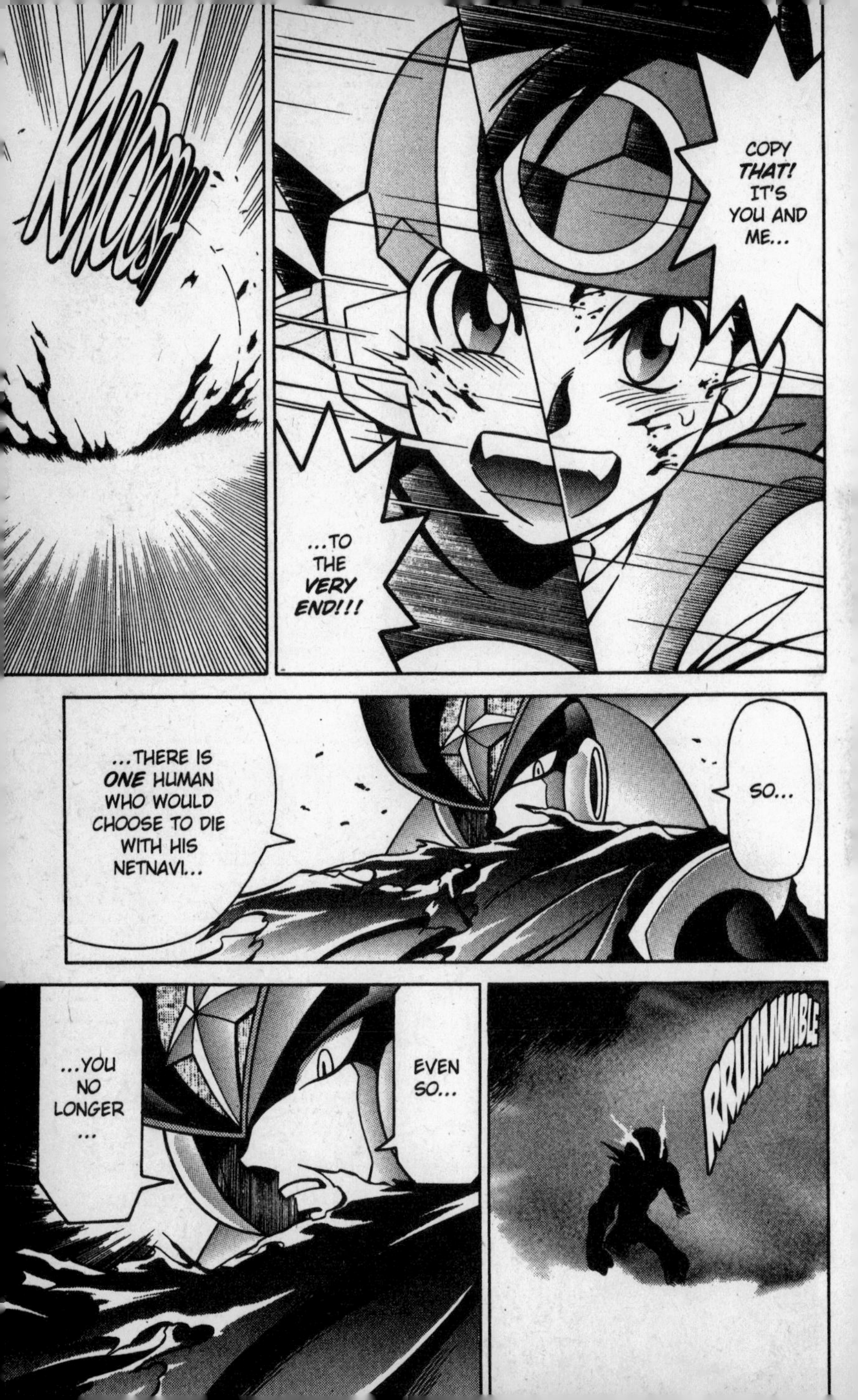
COPY THAT! IT'S YOU AND ME...
...TO THE VERY END!!!
SO...
...THERE IS ONE HUMAN WHO WOULD CHOOSE TO DIE WITH HIS NETNAVI...
EVEN SO...
...YOU NO LONGER ...

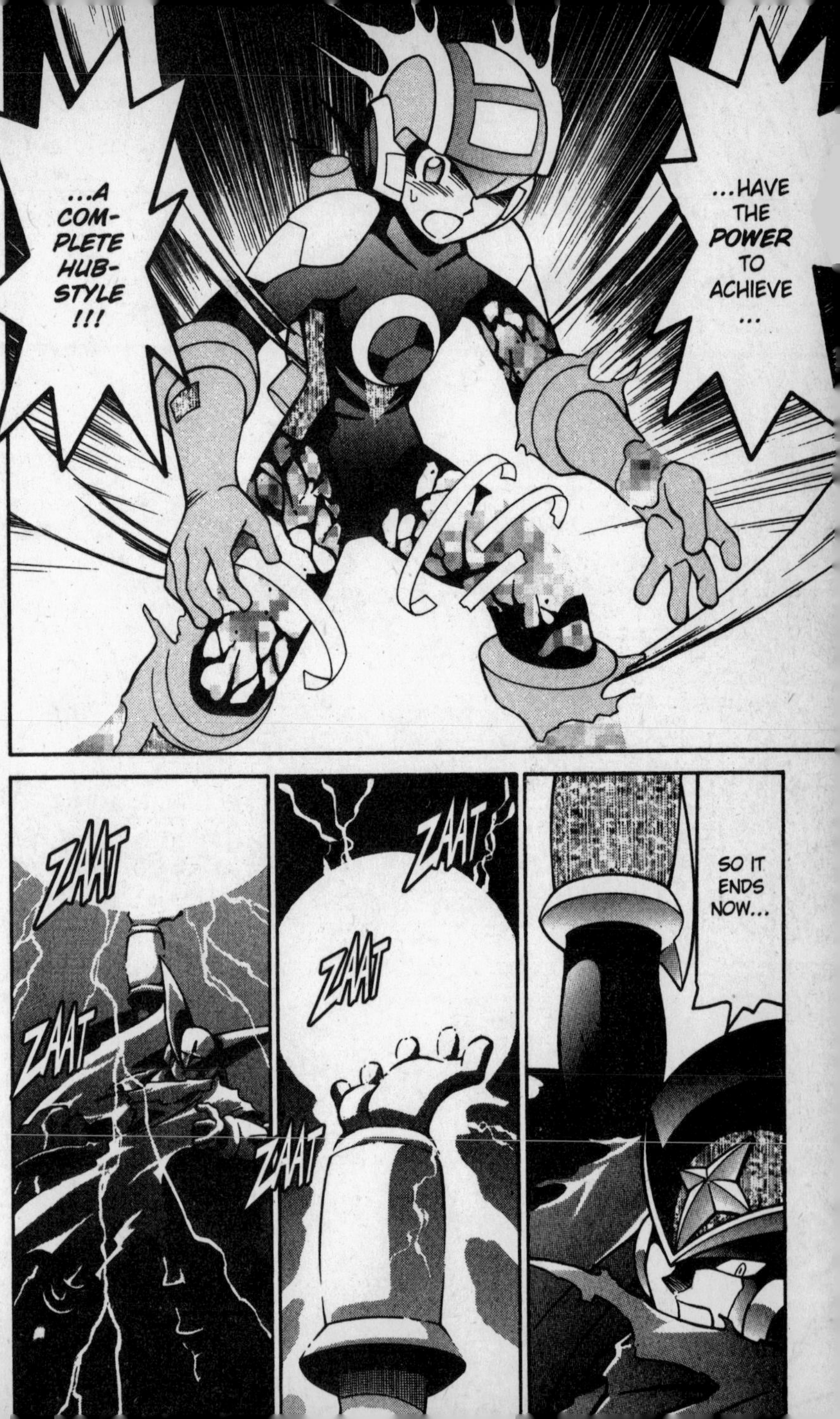
...HAVE THE POWER TO ACHIEVE...
...A COM-PLETE HUB-STYLE!!!
SO IT ENDS NOW...
ZAAT
ZAAT
ZAAT
ZAAT
ZAAT

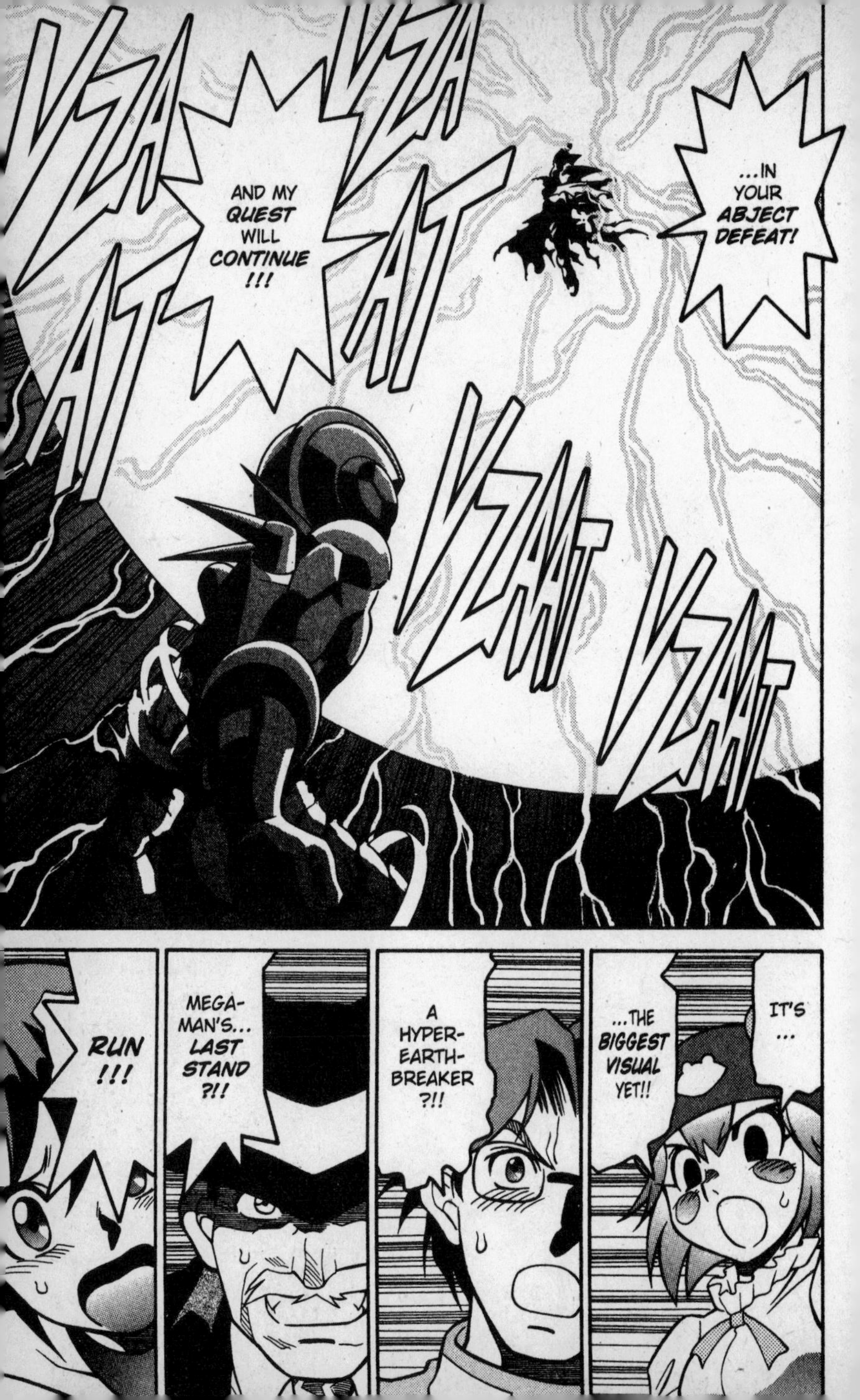
...IN YOUR ABJECT DEFEAT!
VZAAT
VZAAT
AND MY QUEST WILL CONTINUE!!!
VZAAT
VZAAT
VZAAT
IT'S ...
...THE BIGGEST VISUAL YET!!
A HYPER-EARTH-BREAKER?!!
MEGA-MAN'S... LAST STAND?!!
RUN!!!

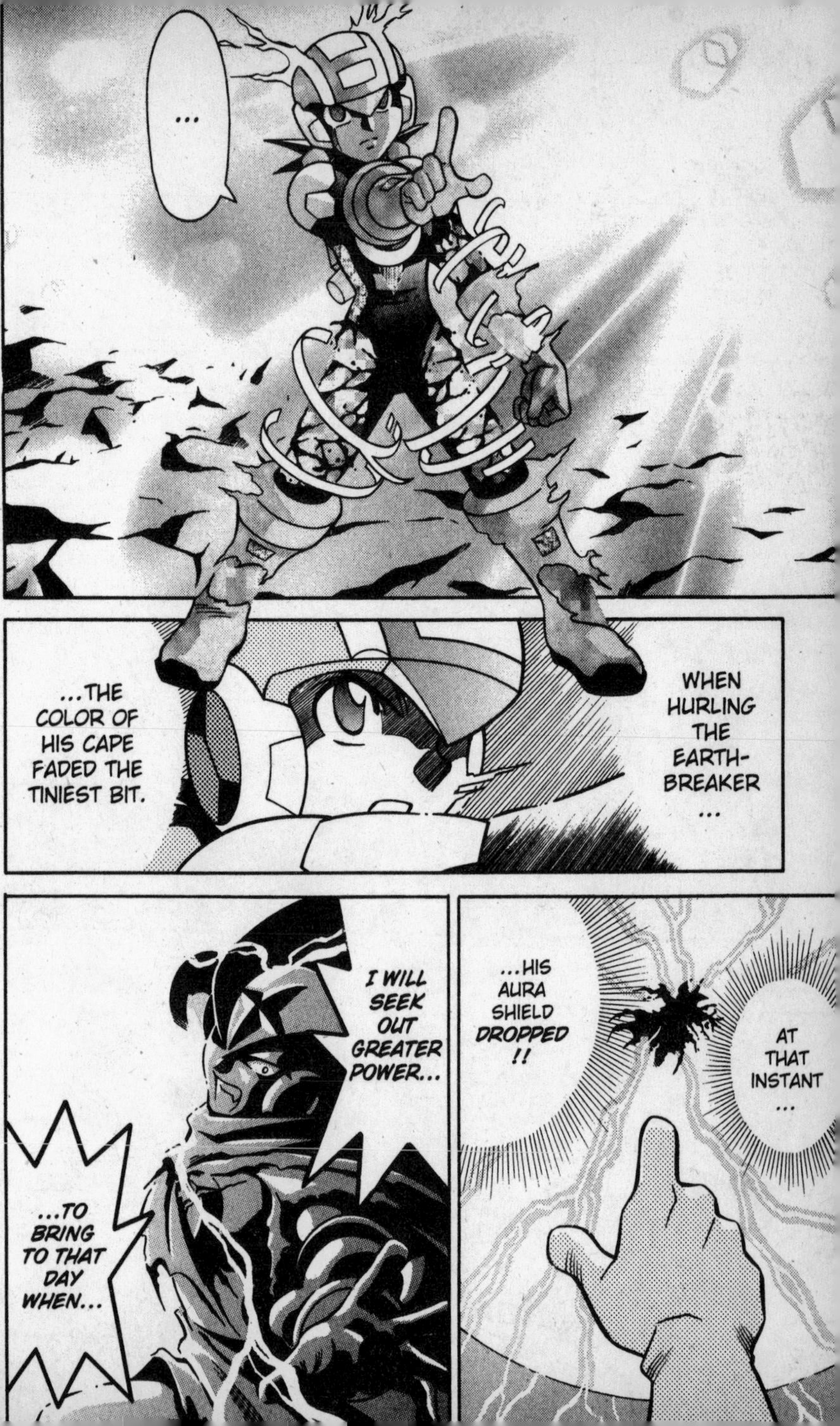
...
WHEN HURLING THE EARTH-BREAKER ...
...THE COLOR OF HIS CAPE FADED THE TINIEST BIT.
AT THAT INSTANT ...
...HIS AURA SHIELD DROPPED !!
I WILL SEEK OUT GREATER POWER...
...TO BRING TO THAT DAY WHEN...

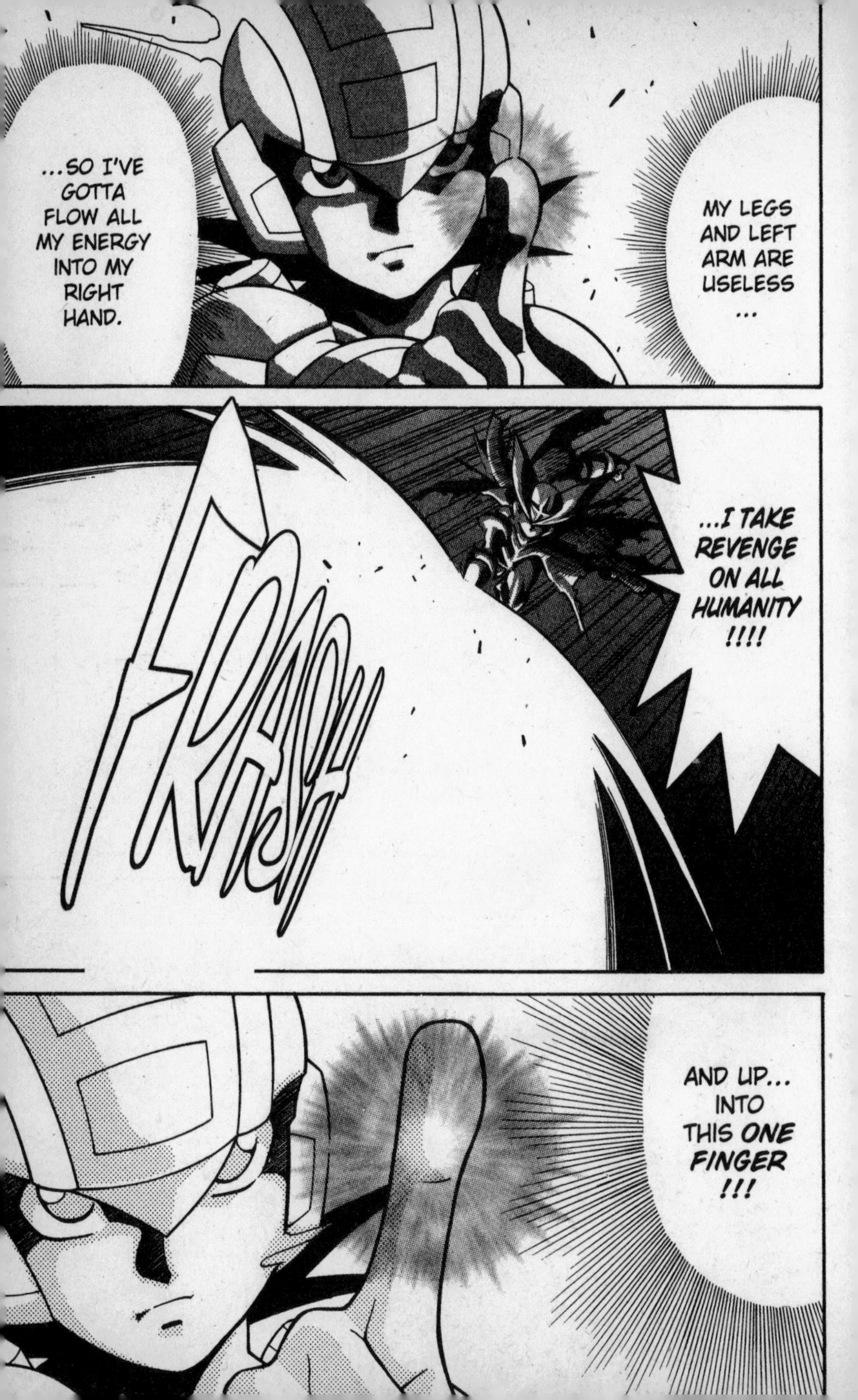
MY LEGS AND LEFT ARM ARE USELESS ...
...SO I'VE GOTTA FLOW ALL MY ENERGY INTO MY RIGHT HAND.
...I TAKE REVENGE ON ALL HUMANITY!!!!
FRASH
AND UP... INTO THIS ONE FINGER!!!

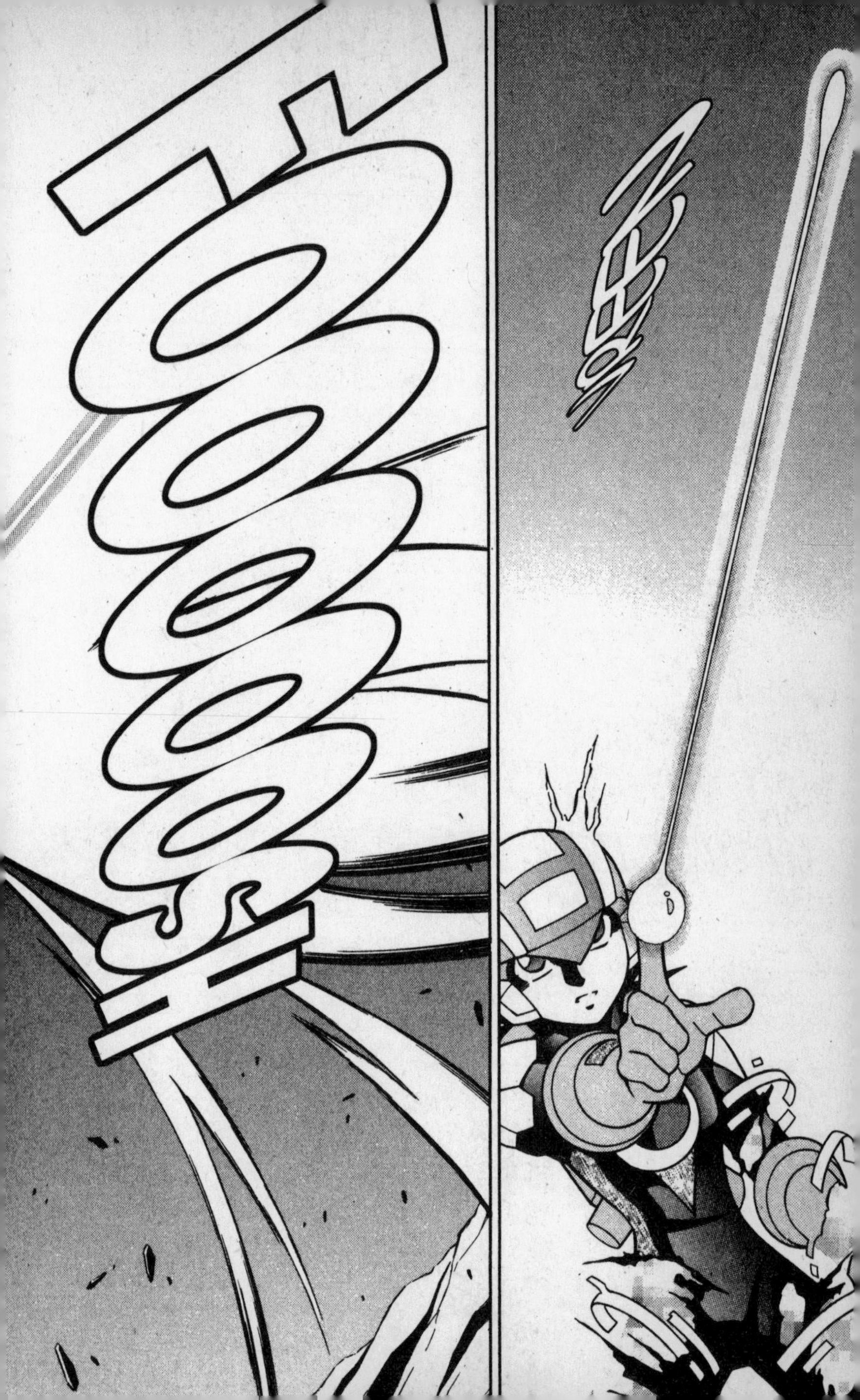
WOOOOOOOSH

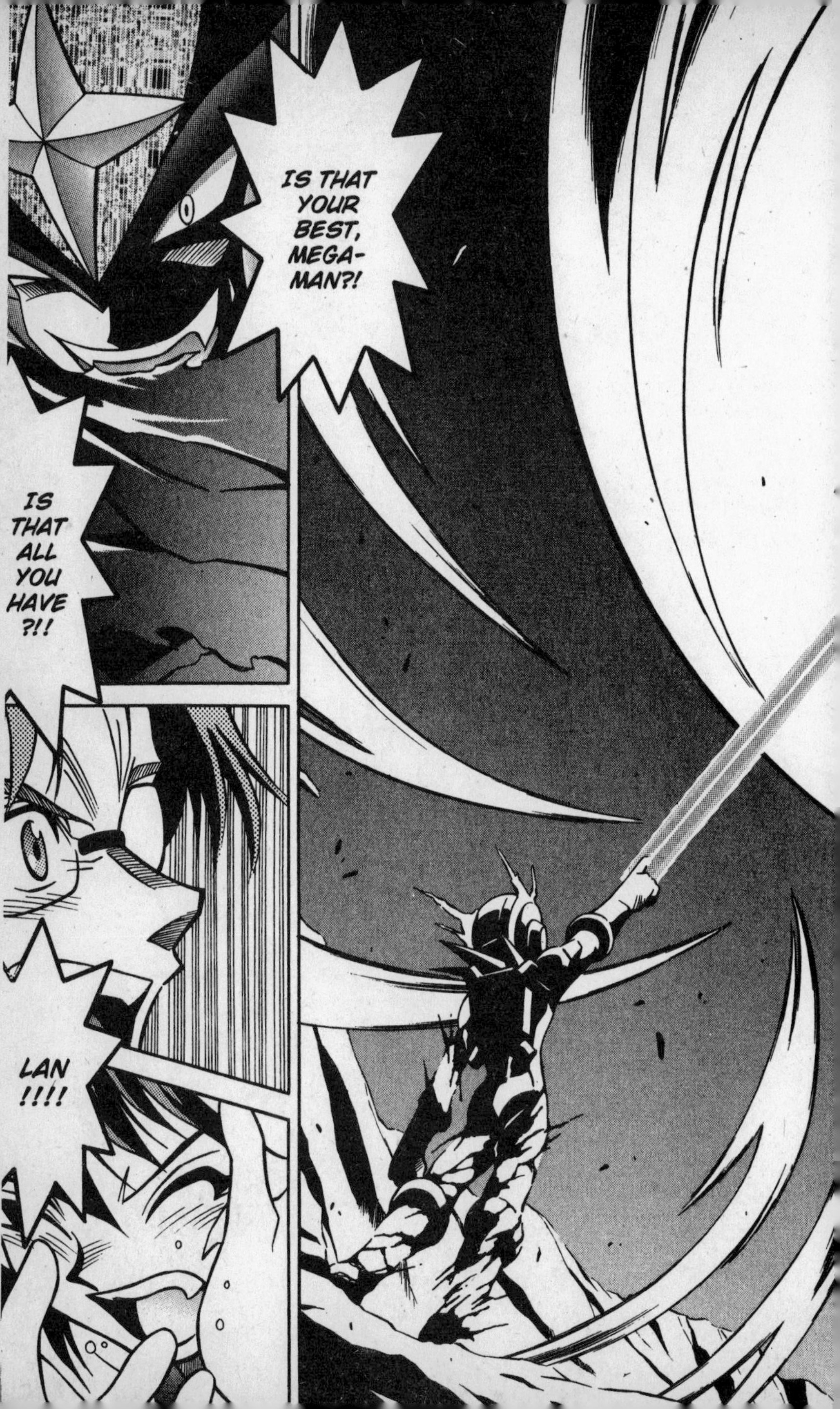
IS THAT YOUR BEST, MEGA-MAN?!
IS THAT ALL YOU HAVE?!!
LAN!!!!

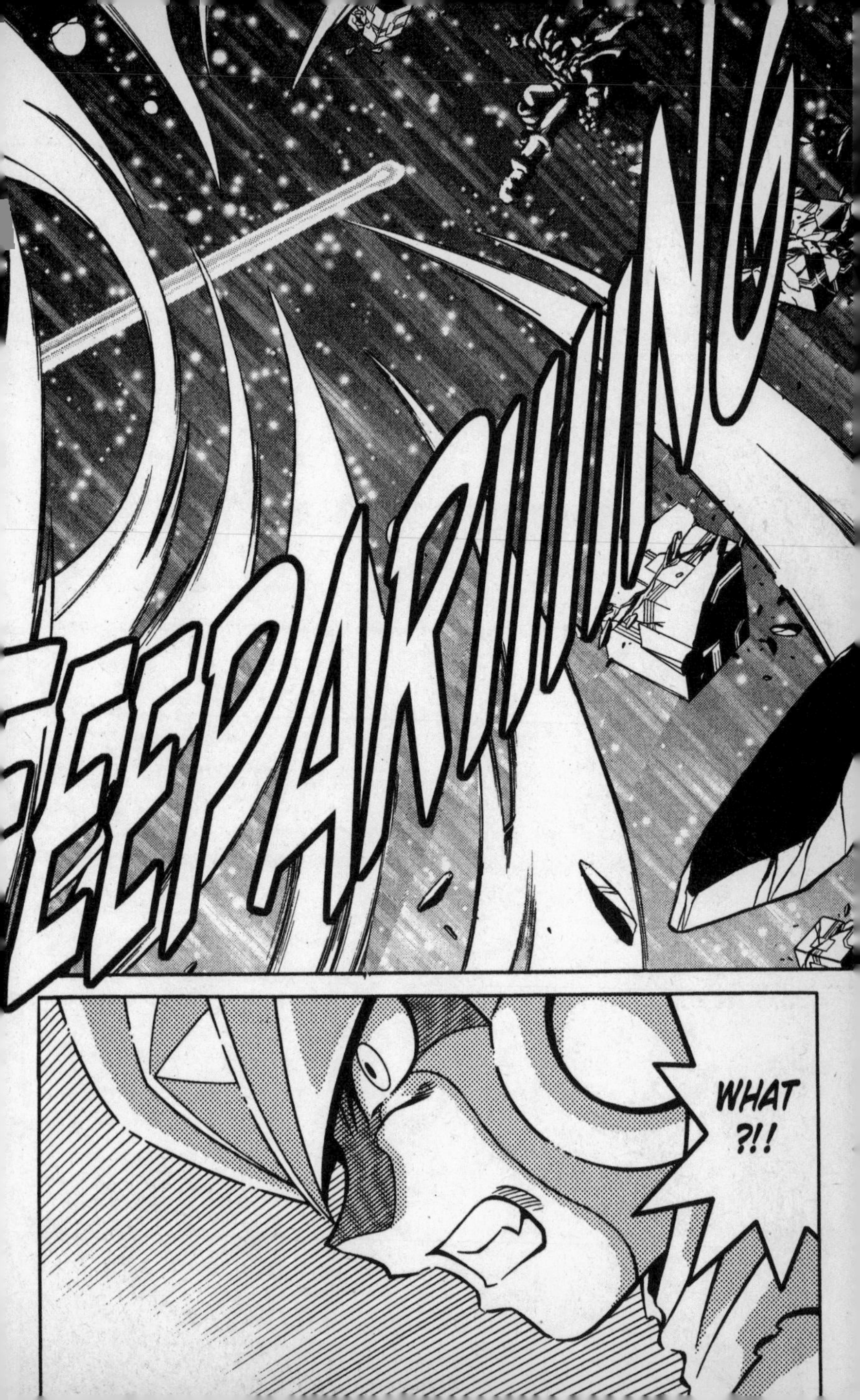
EEEPARUUUNG
WHAT ?!!

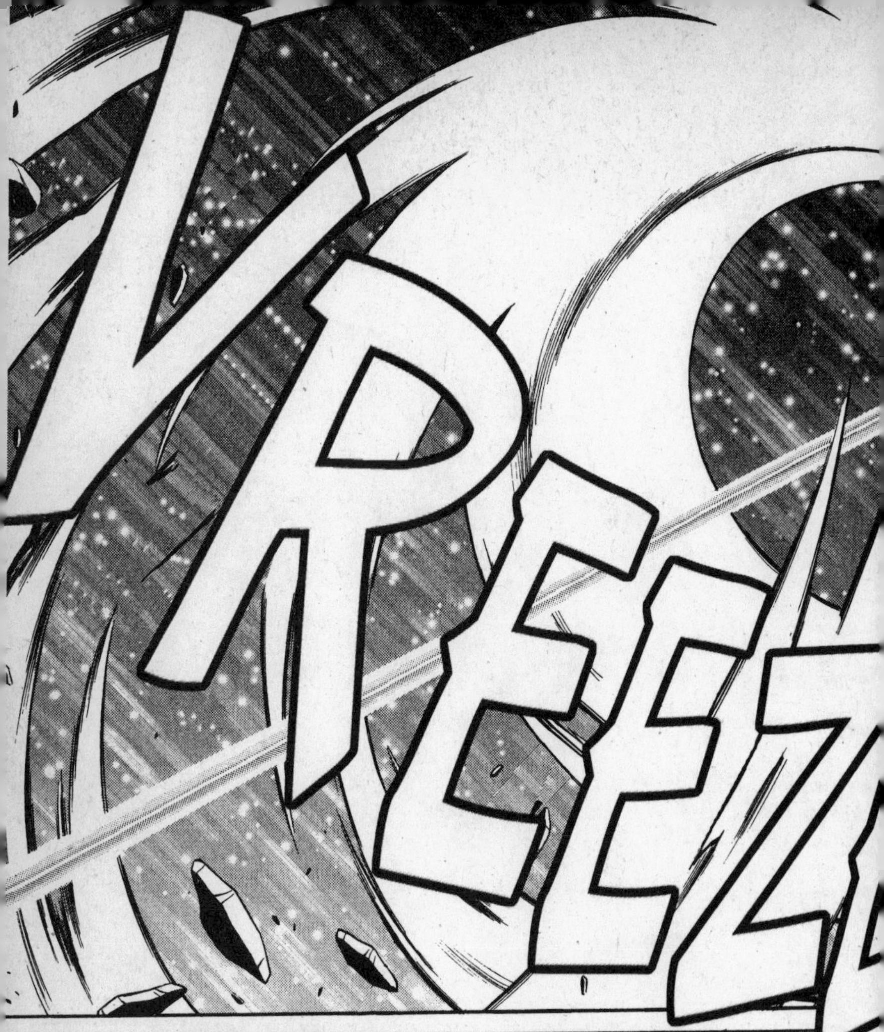
VREEZ
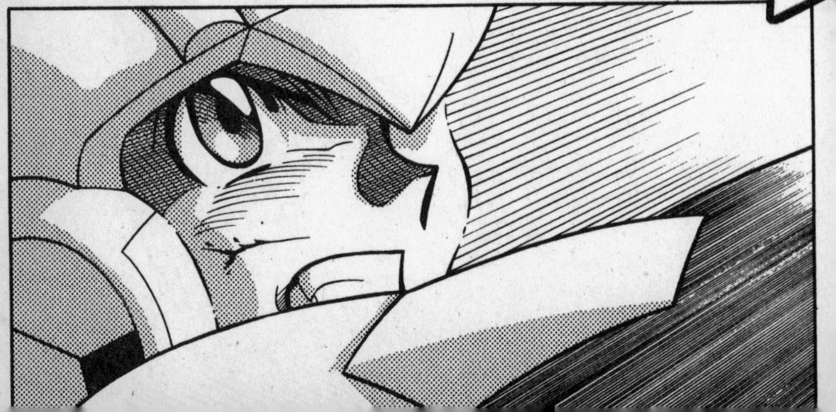

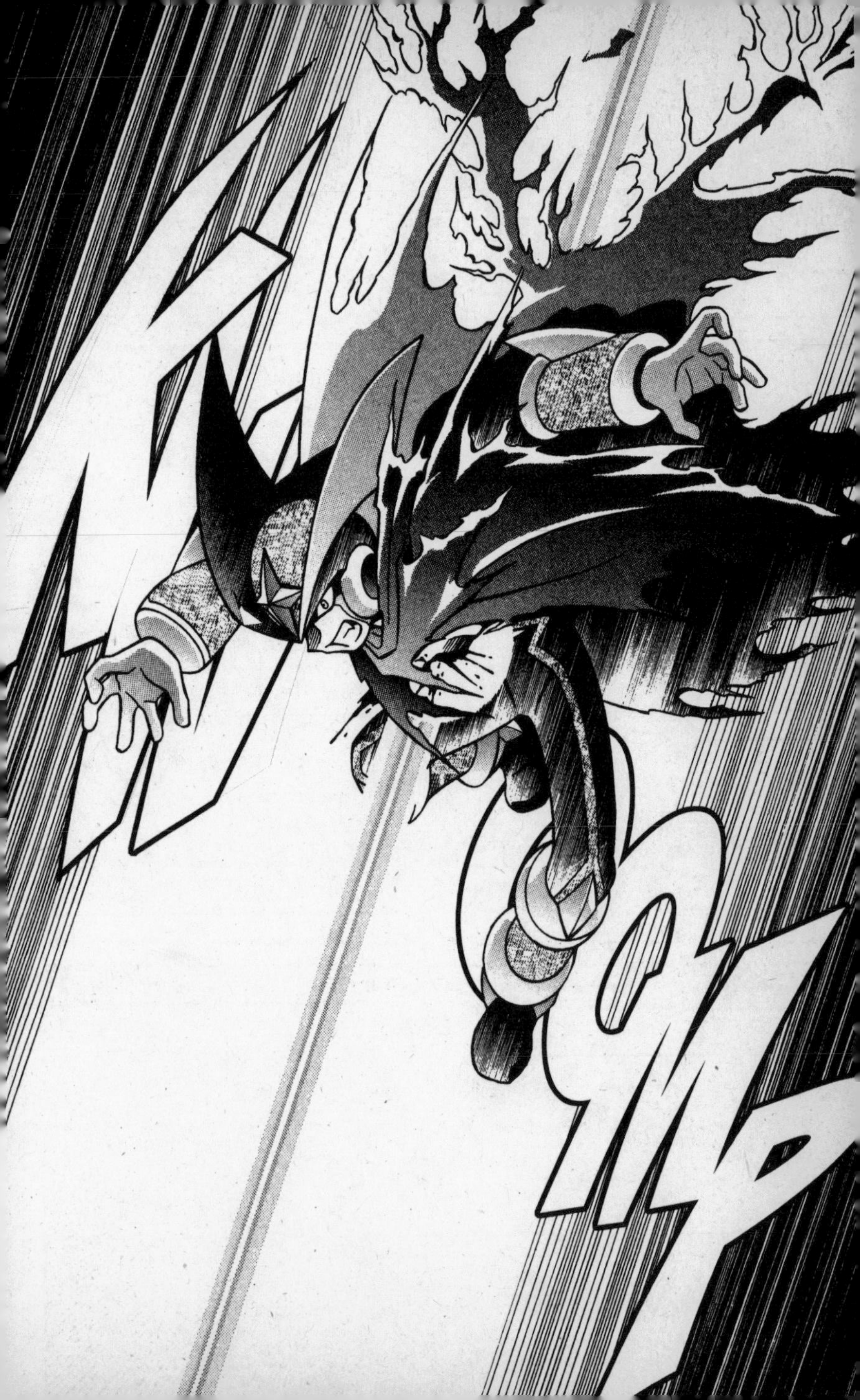

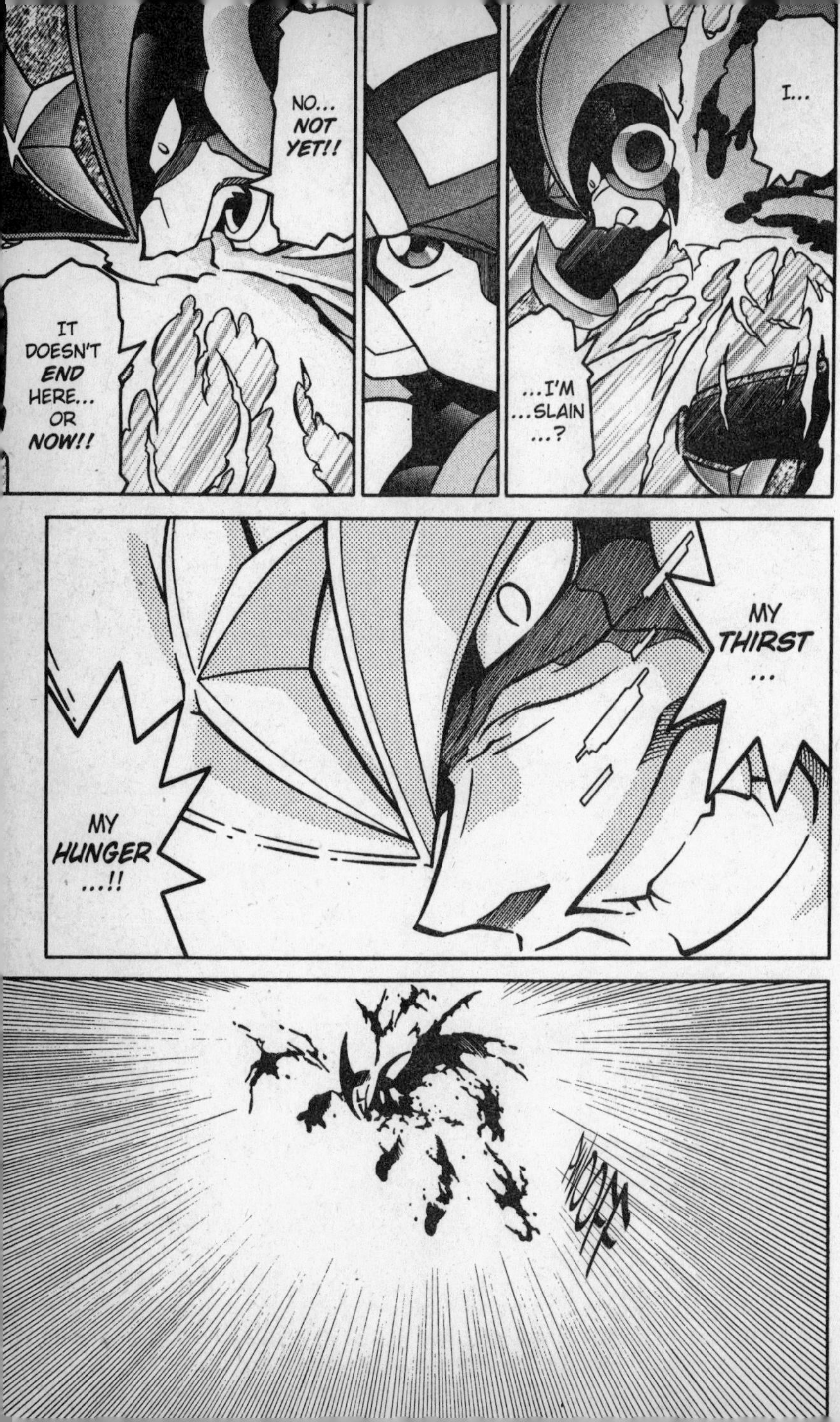
I...
...I'M ...SLAIN ...?
NO... NOT YET!!
IT DOESN'T END HERE... OR NOW!!
MY THIRST ...
MY HUNGER ...!!

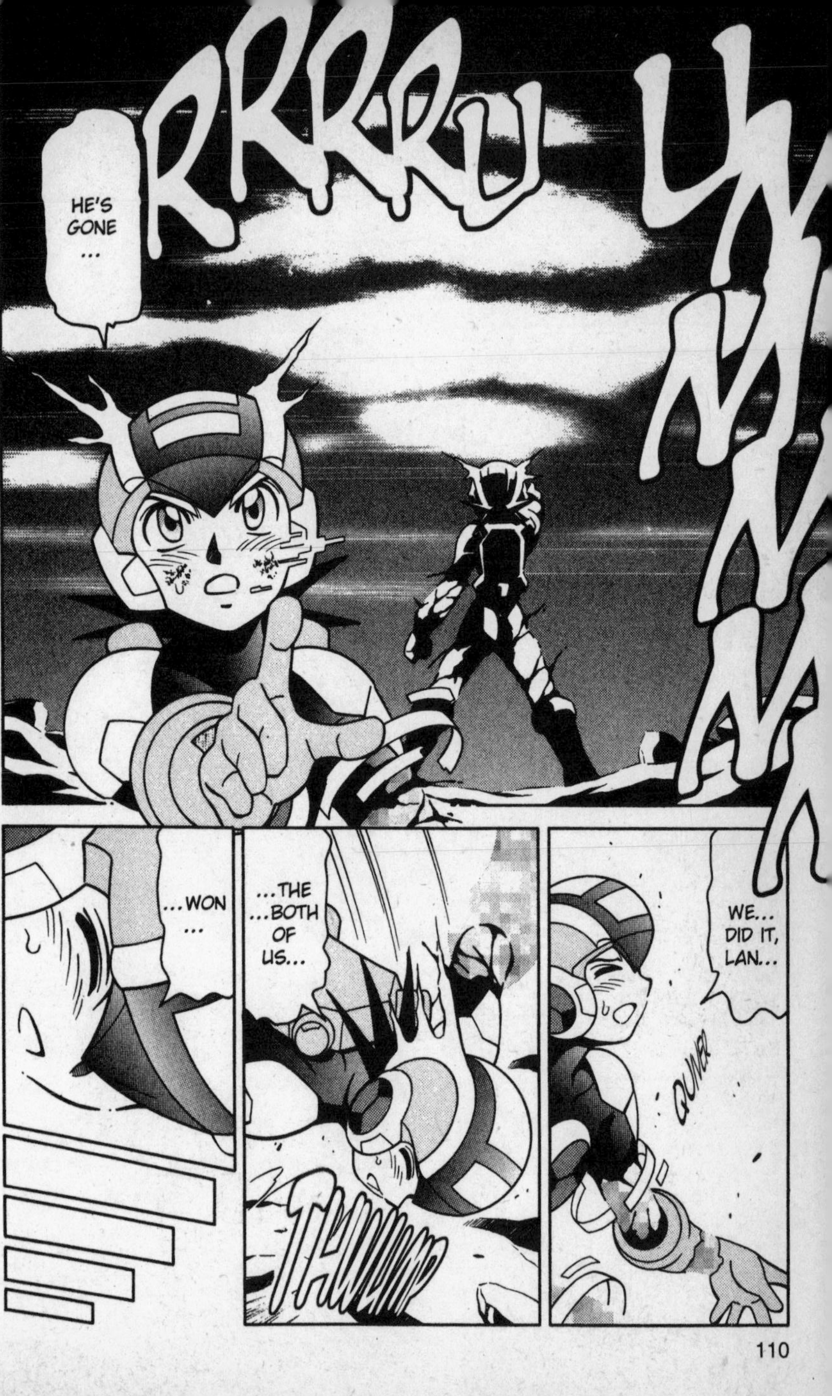
RRRRU
HE'S GONE ...
WE... DID IT, LAN...
...THE ...BOTH OF US...
...WON ...

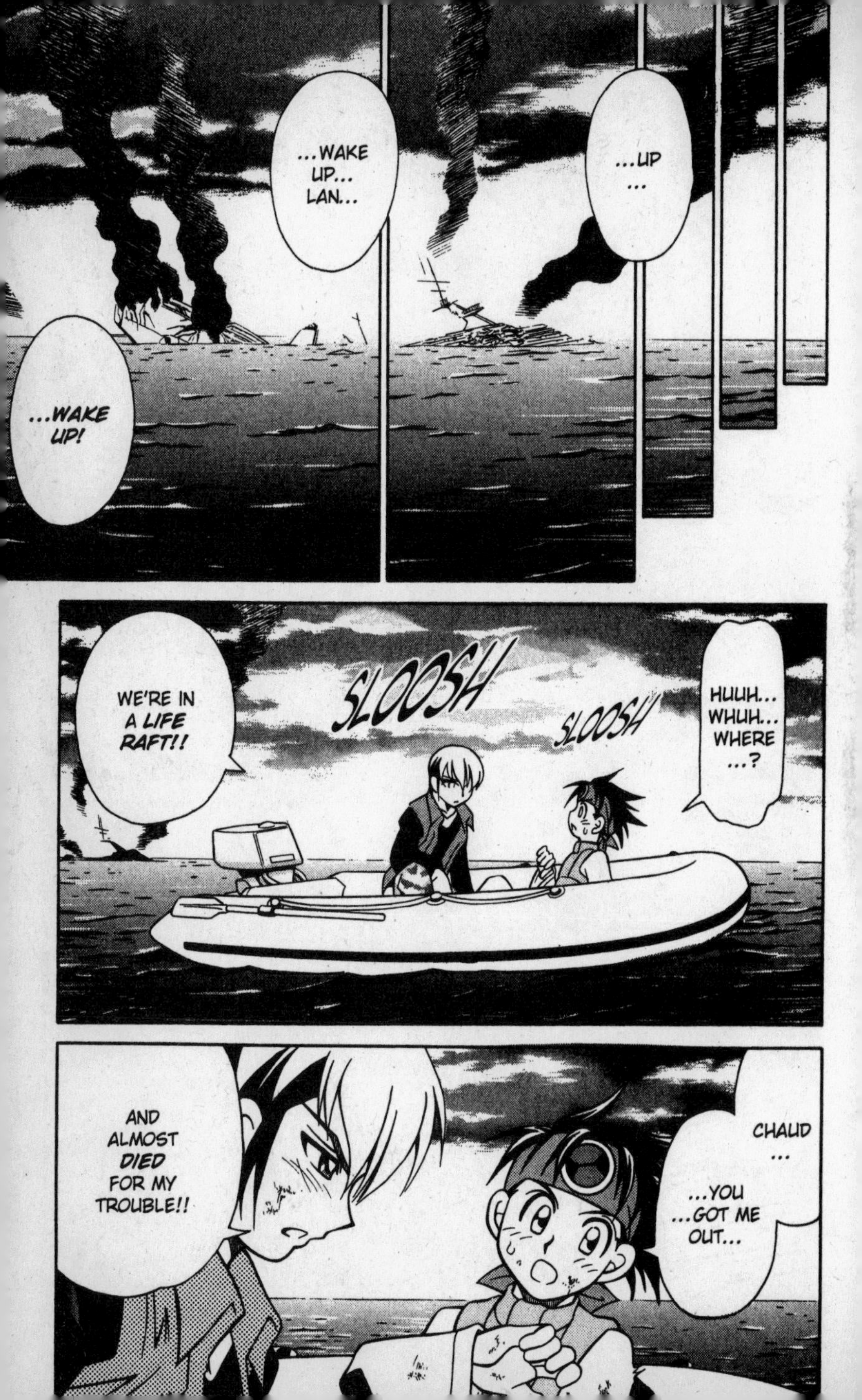
...UP ...
...WAKE UP... LAN...
...WAKE UP!
HUUH... WHUH... WHERE ...?
SLOOSH
SLOOSH
WE'RE IN A LIFE RAFT!!
CHAUD ... ...YOU ...GOT ME OUT...
AND ALMOST DIED FOR MY TROUBLE!!

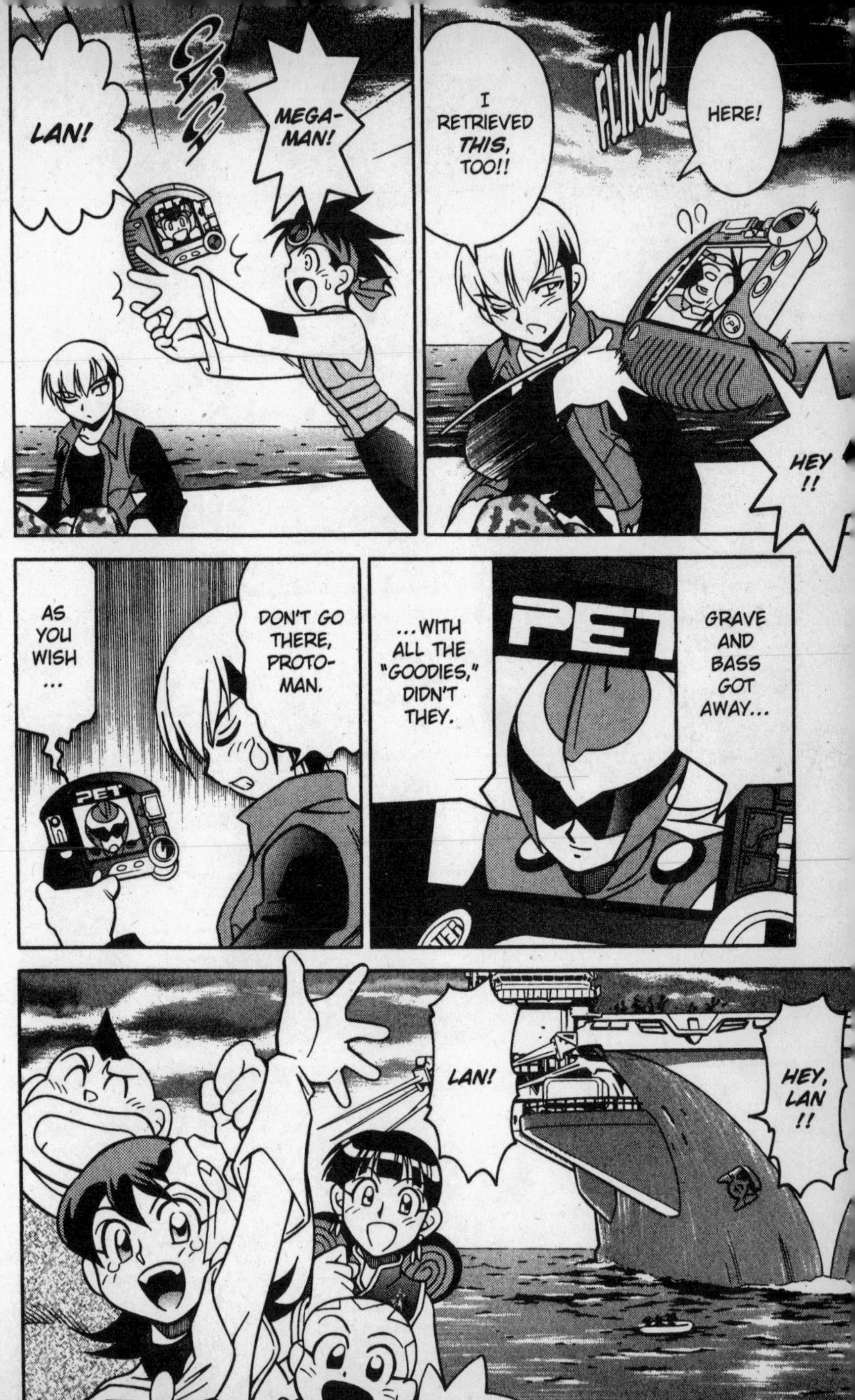
HERE!
FLING!
I RETRIEVED THIS, TOO!!
HEY !!
MEGA-MAN!
CATCH
LAN!
GRAVE AND BASS GOT AWAY...
...WITH ALL THE "GOODIES," DIDN'T THEY.
PET
DON'T GO THERE, PROTO-MAN.
AS YOU WISH ...
PET
HEY, LAN !!
LAN!

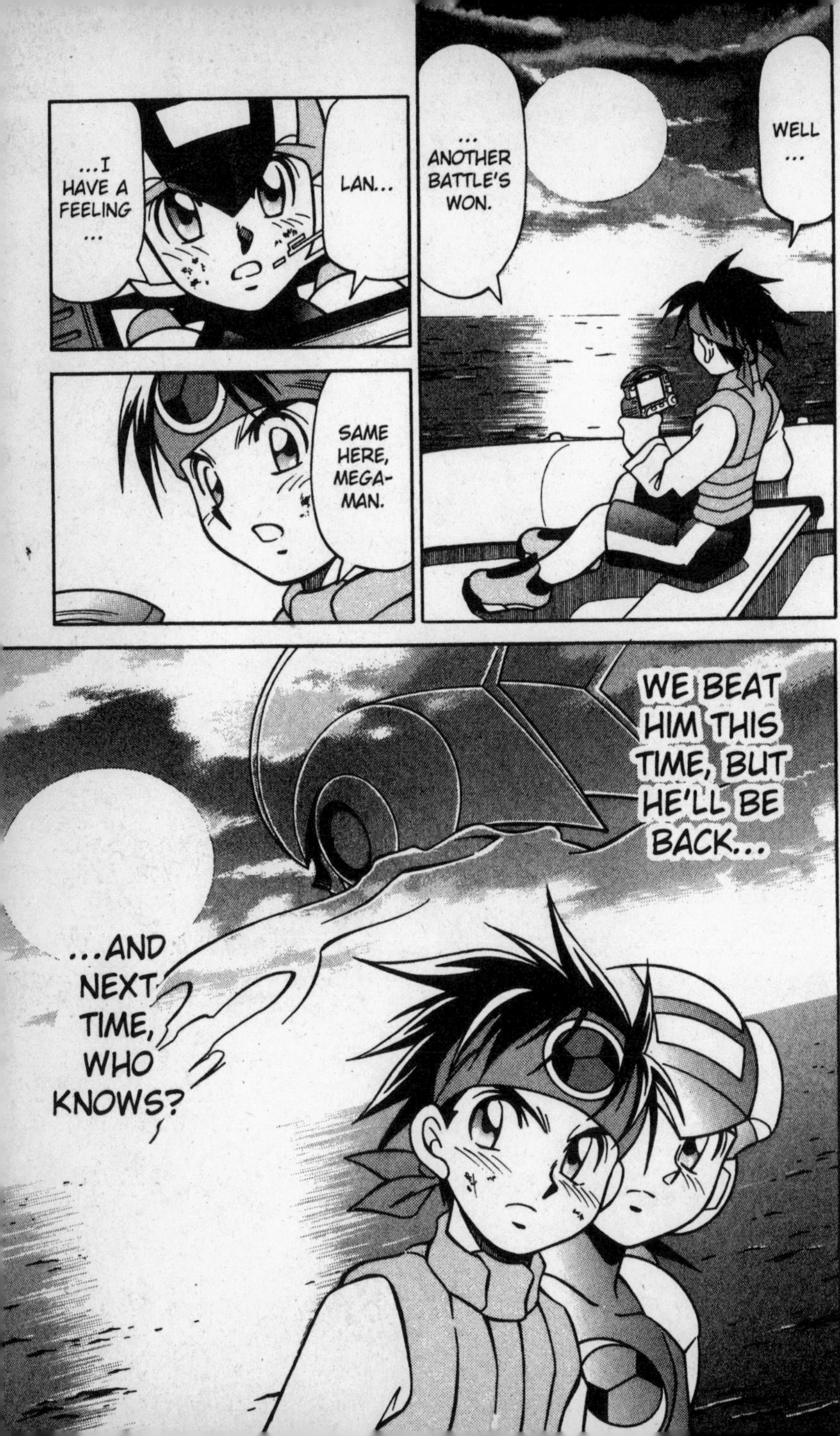
WELL ...
... ANOTHER BATTLE'S WON.
LAN...
...I HAVE A FEELING ...
SAME HERE, MEGA-MAN.
WE BEAT HIM THIS TIME, BUT HE'LL BE BACK...
...AND NEXT TIME, WHO KNOWS?

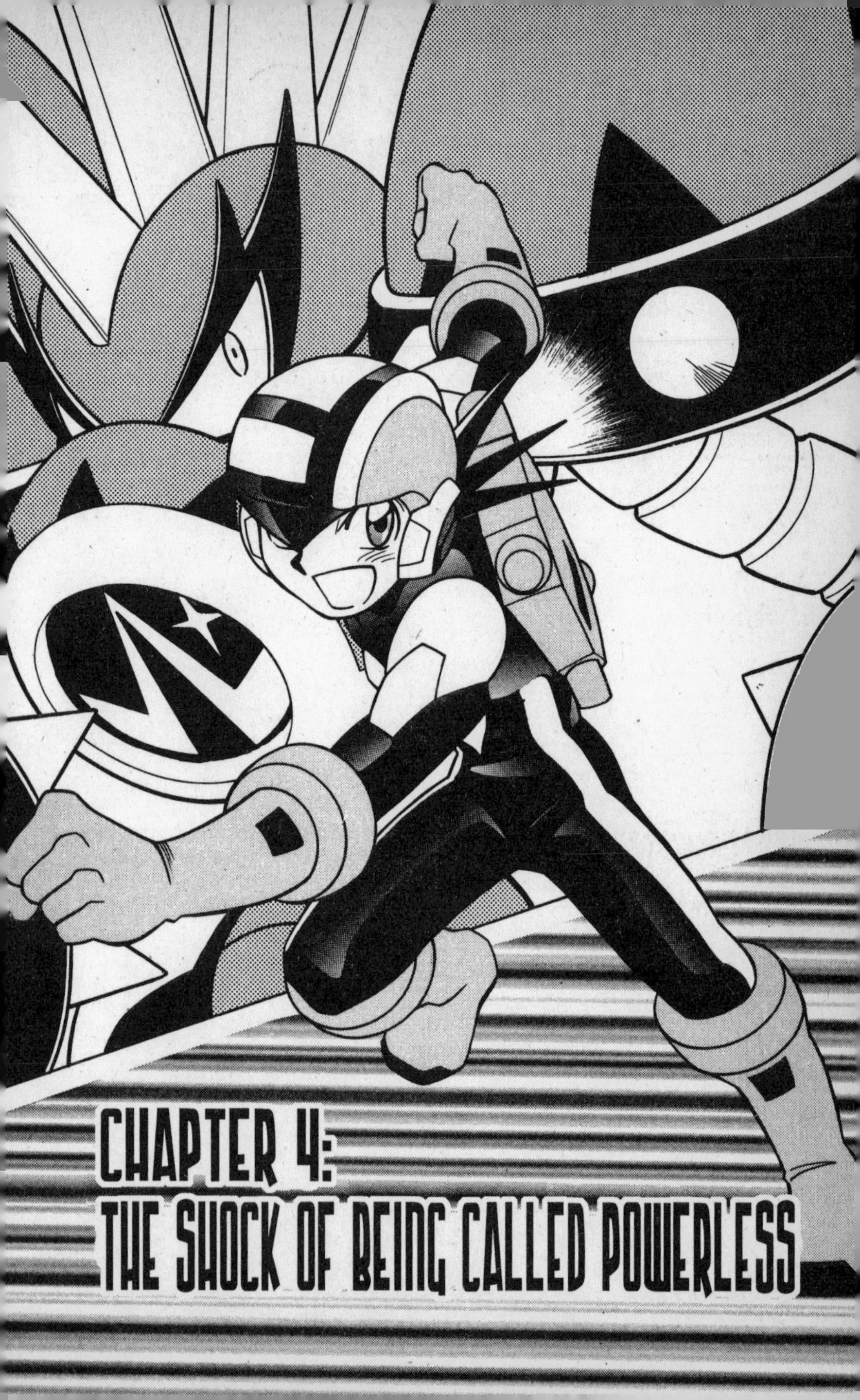
CHAPTER 4:
THE SHOCK OF BEING CALLED POWERLESS

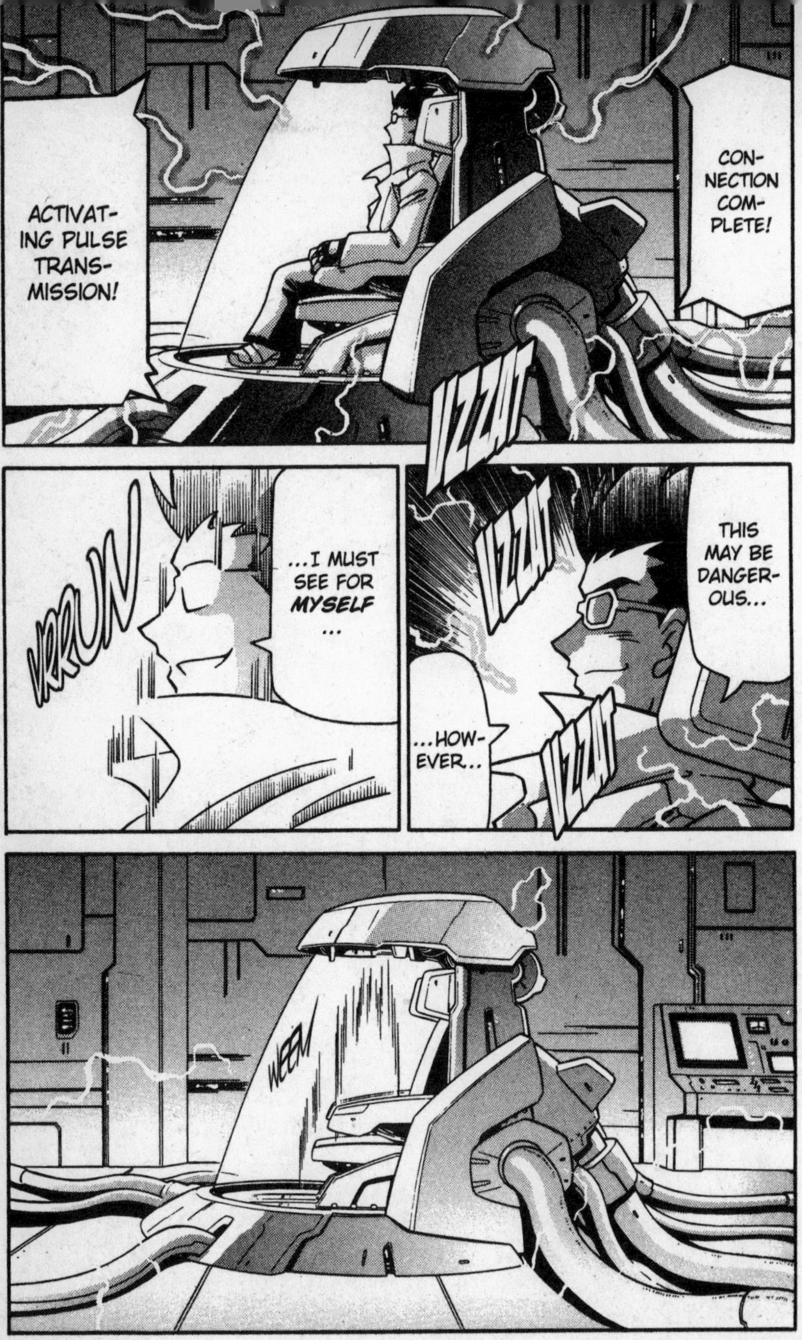
CONNECTION COMPLETE!
ACTIVATING PULSE TRANSMISSION!
VZZZAT
THIS MAY BE DANGEROUS...
VZZZAT
...HOWEVER...
VZZZAT
...I MUST SEE FOR *MYSELF* ...
VRRUN
WEEEM

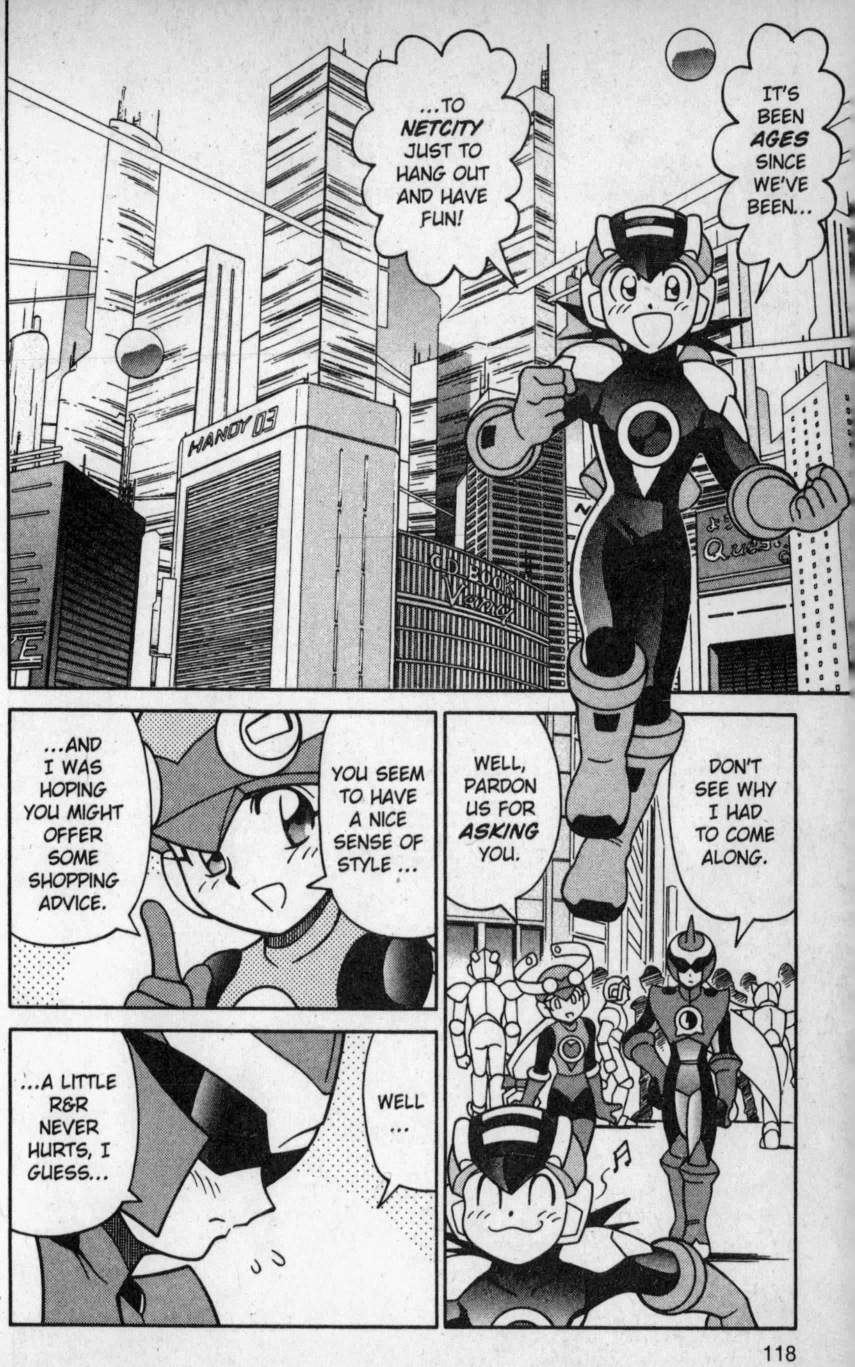
IT'S BEEN AGES SINCE WE'VE BEEN...
...TO NETCITY JUST TO HANG OUT AND HAVE FUN!
HANDY 03
DON'T SEE WHY I HAD TO COME ALONG.
WELL, PARDON US FOR ASKING YOU.
YOU SEEM TO HAVE A NICE SENSE OF STYLE ...
...AND I WAS HOPING YOU MIGHT OFFER SOME SHOPPING ADVICE.
WELL ...
...A LITTLE R&R NEVER HURTS, I GUESS...

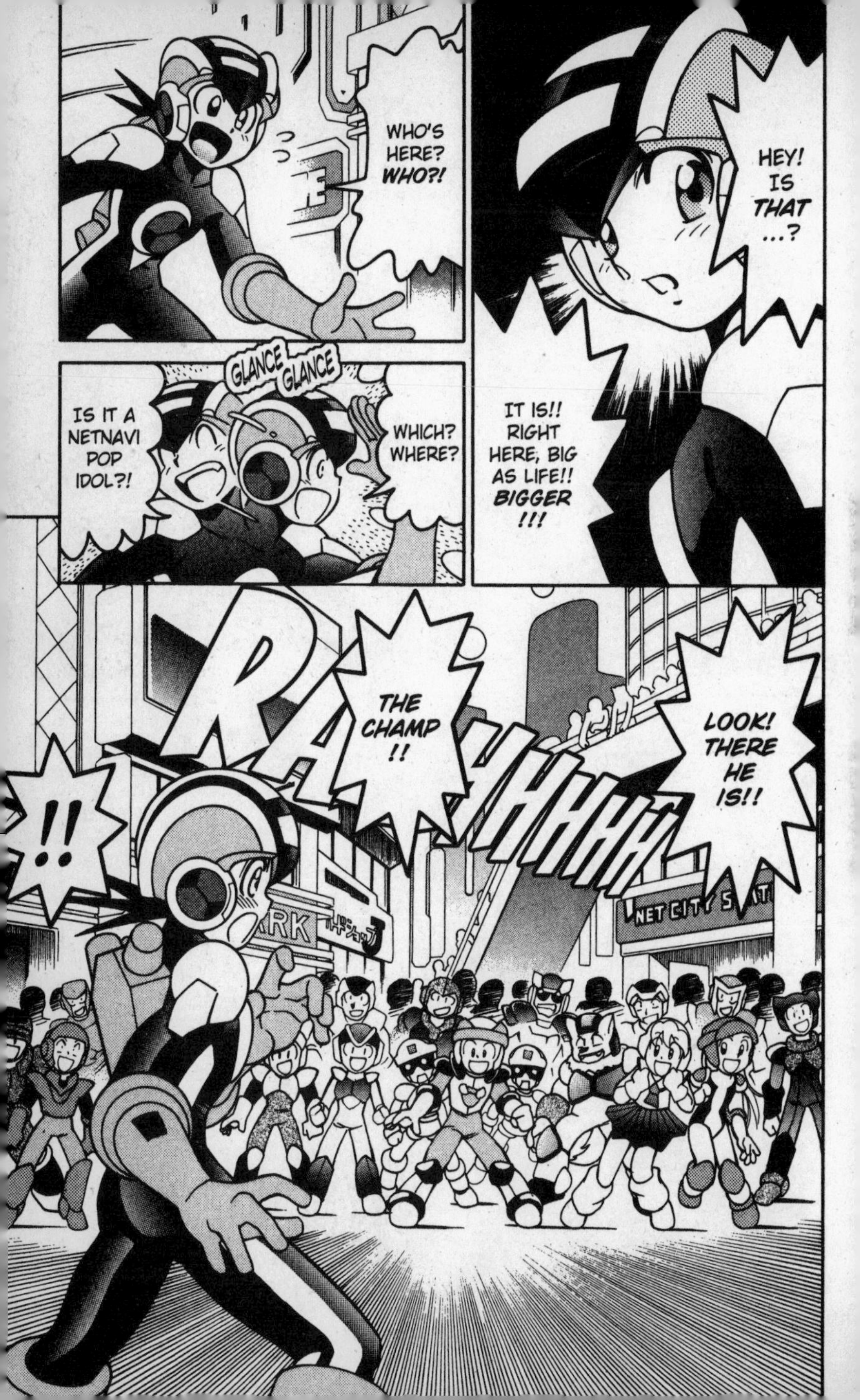
HEY! IS THAT ...?
IT IS!! RIGHT HERE, BIG AS LIFE!! BIGGER !!!
WHO'S HERE? WHO?!
GLANCE GLANCE
WHICH? WHERE?
IS IT A NETNAVI POP IDOL?!
LOOK! THERE HE IS!!
RAHHHHH
THE CHAMP !!
!!

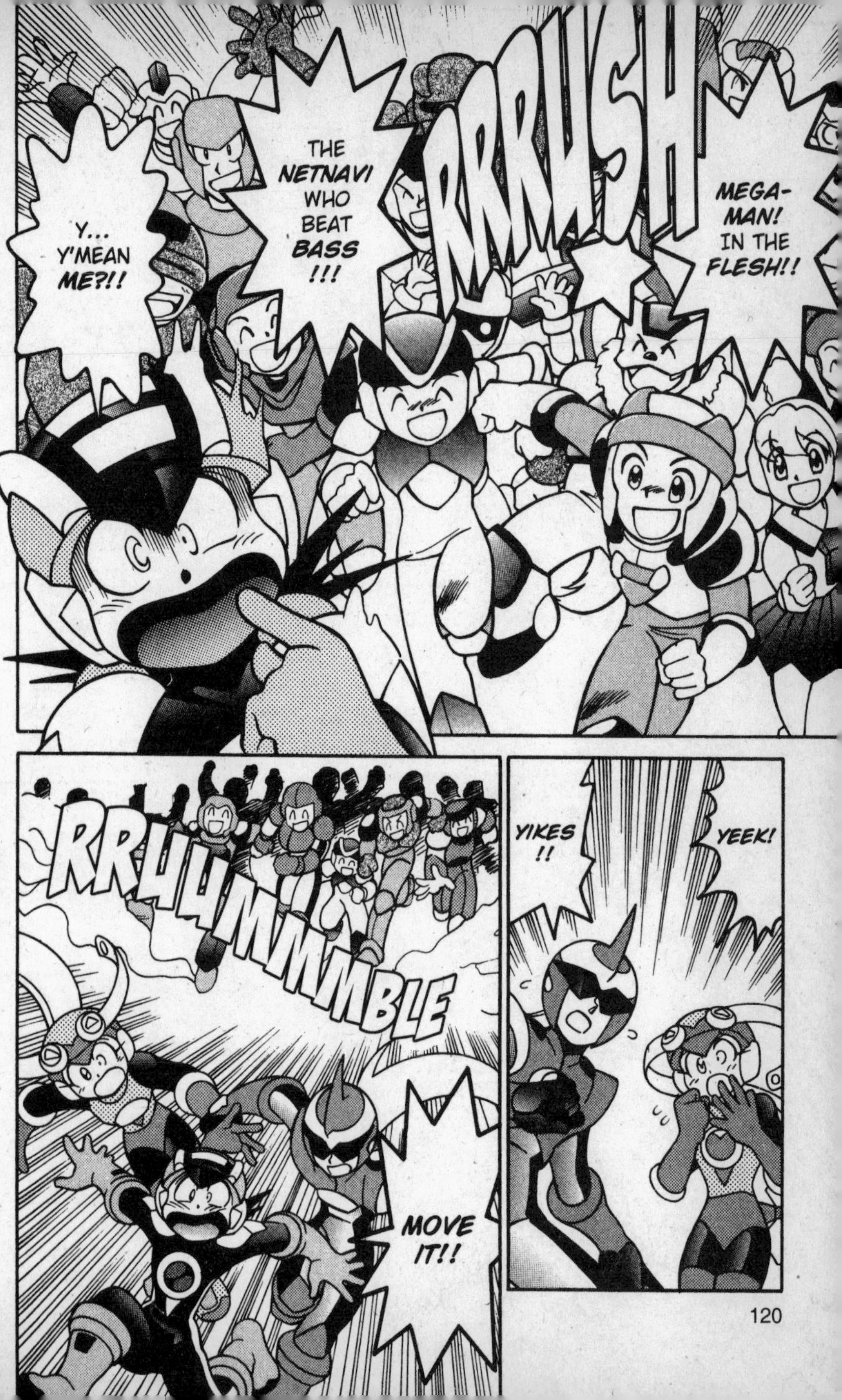
MEGA-MAN! IN THE FLESH!!
RRRUSH
THE NETNAVI WHO BEAT BASS!!!
Y... Y'MEAN ME?!!
YEEK!
YIKES!!
RRUUMMMMBLE
MOVE IT!!

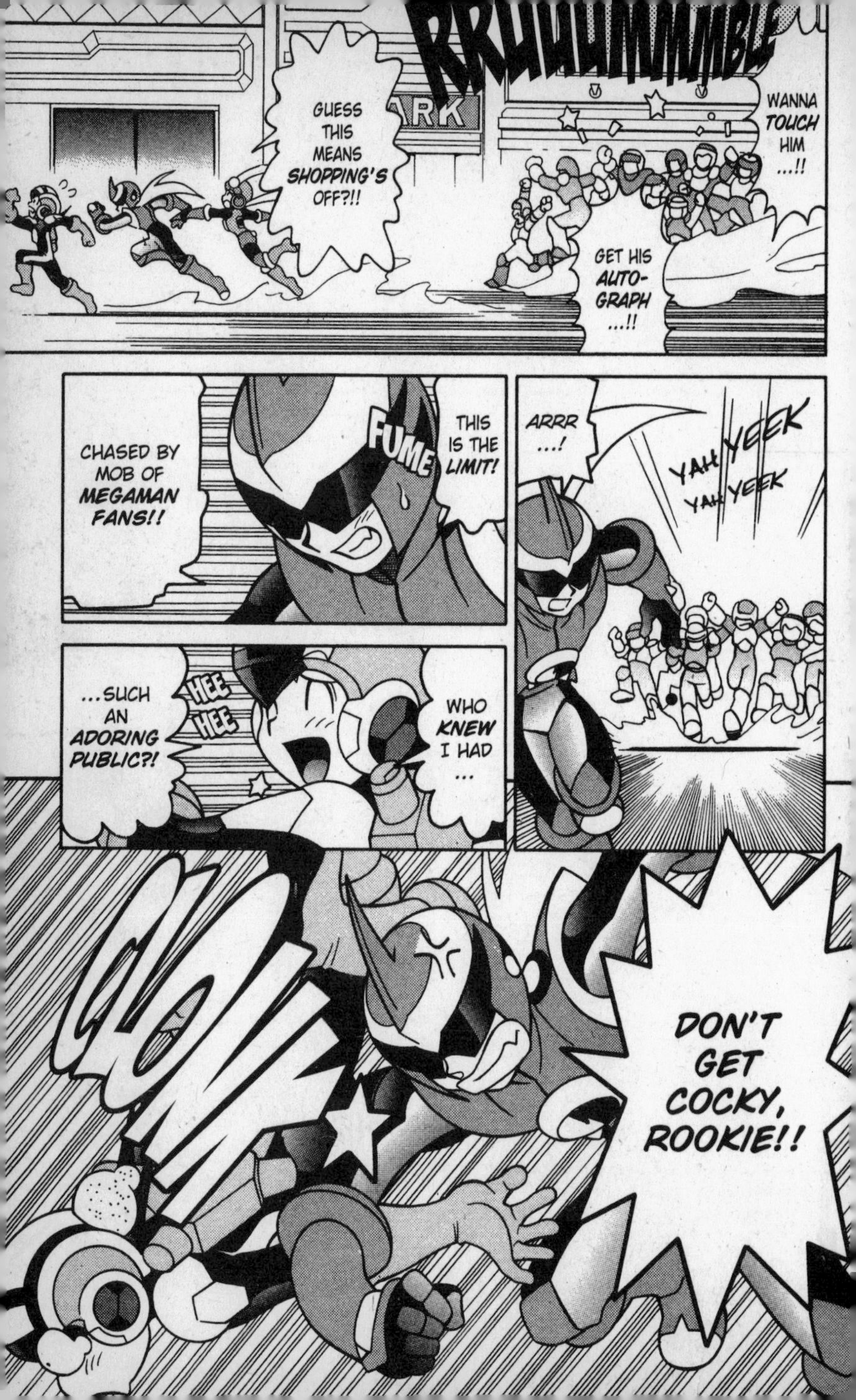
WANNA TOUCH HIM ...!!
GET HIS AUTO-GRAPH ...!!
GUESS THIS MEANS SHOPPING'S OFF?!!
ARRR ...!
YAH YEEK
YAH YEEK
THIS IS THE LIMIT!
FUME
CHASED BY MOB OF MEGAMAN FANS!!
WHO KNEW I HAD ...
HEE HEE
...SUCH AN ADORING PUBLIC?!
DON'T GET COCKY, ROOKIE!!

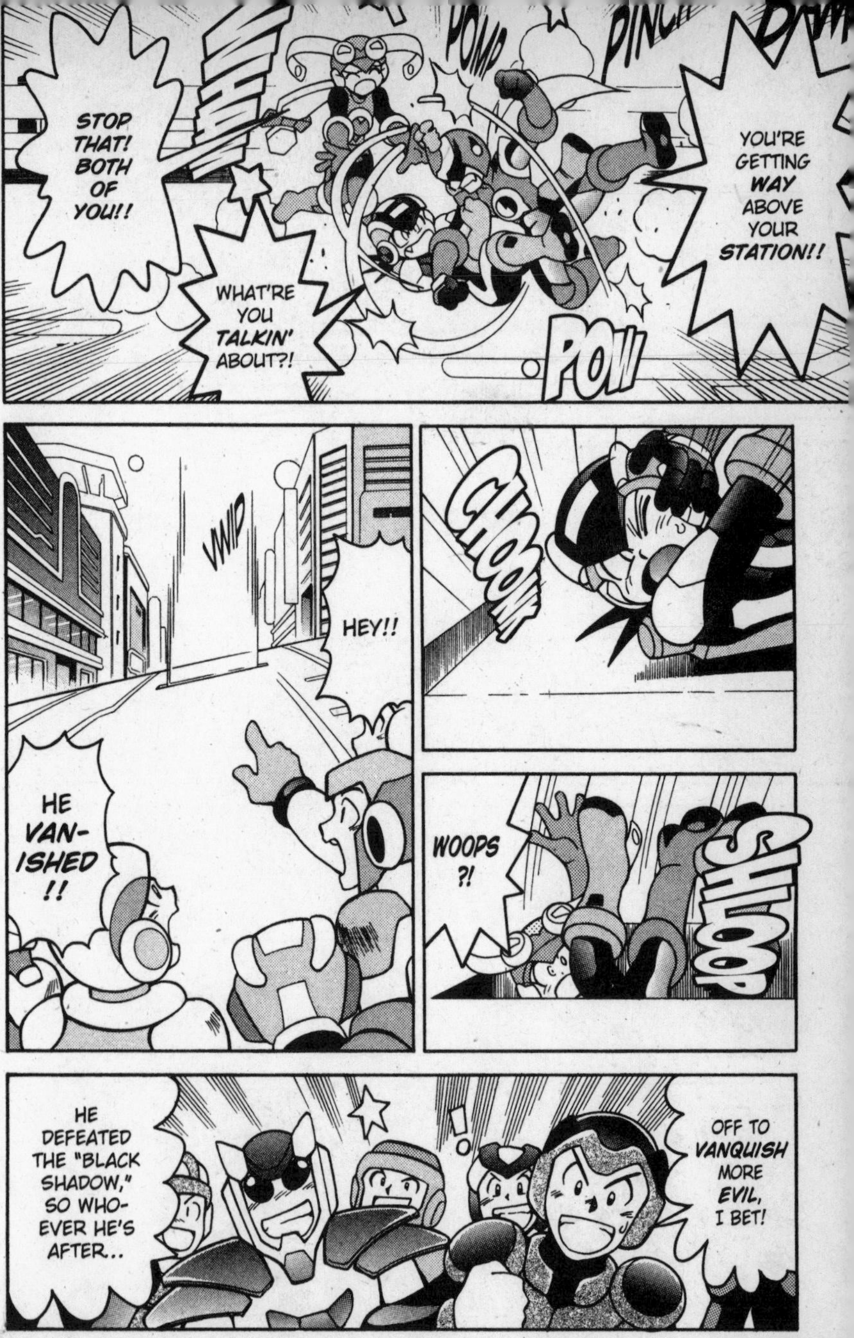
POMP
YOU'RE GETTING WAY ABOVE YOUR STATION!!
WHAT'RE YOU TALKIN' ABOUT?!
STOP THAT! BOTH OF YOU!!
POW
CHOOOM
SHLOOP
WOOPS ?!
HEY!!
VWIP
HE VAN-ISHED !!
OFF TO VANQUISH MORE EVIL, I BET!
HE DEFEATED THE "BLACK SHADOW," SO WHO-EVER HE'S AFTER...

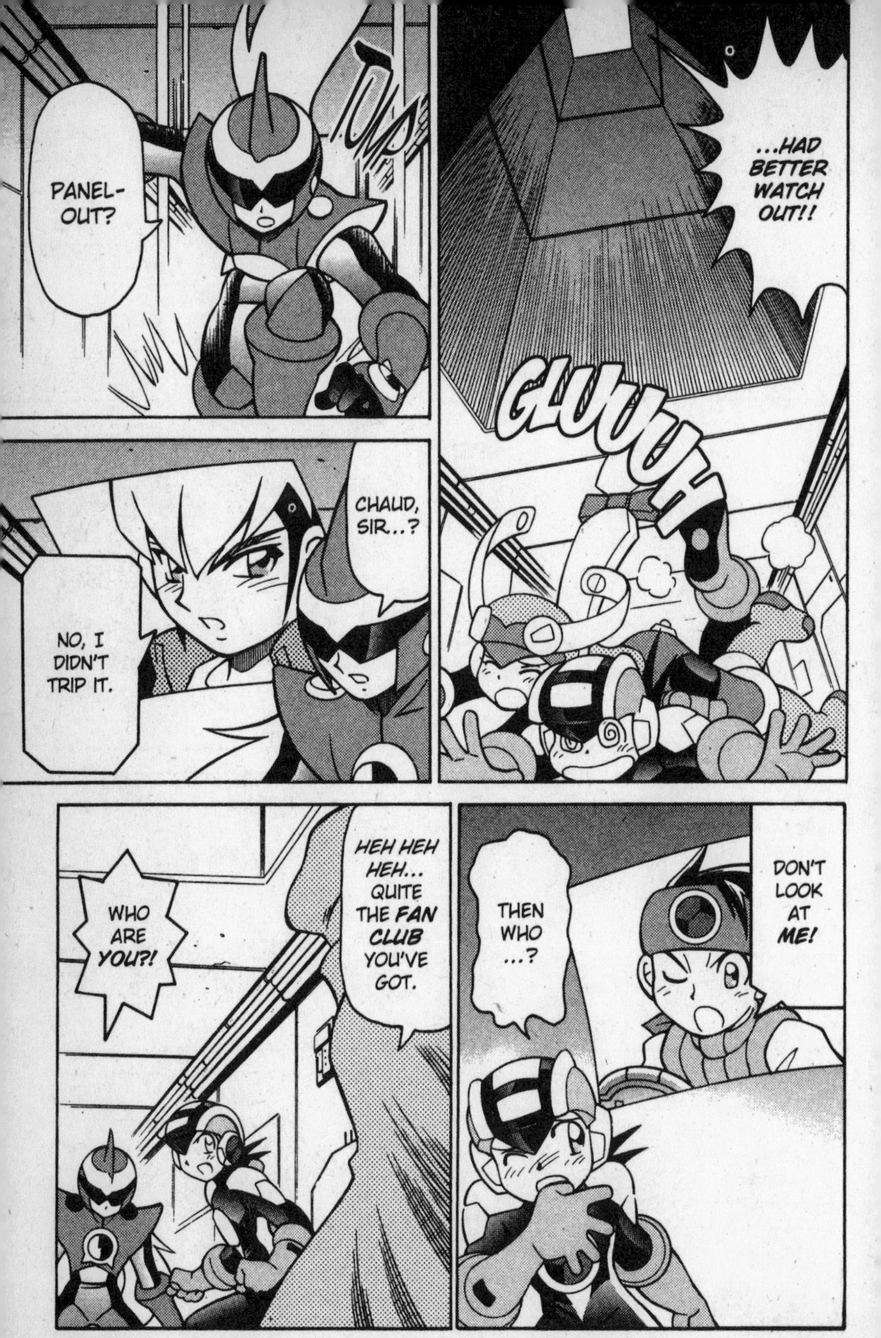
...HAD BETTER WATCH OUT!!
GLUUUH
DIP
PANEL-OUT?
CHAUD, SIR...?
NO, I DIDN'T TRIP IT.
DON'T LOOK AT ME!
THEN WHO ...?
HEH HEH HEH... QUITE THE FAN CLUB YOU'VE GOT.
WHO ARE YOU?!

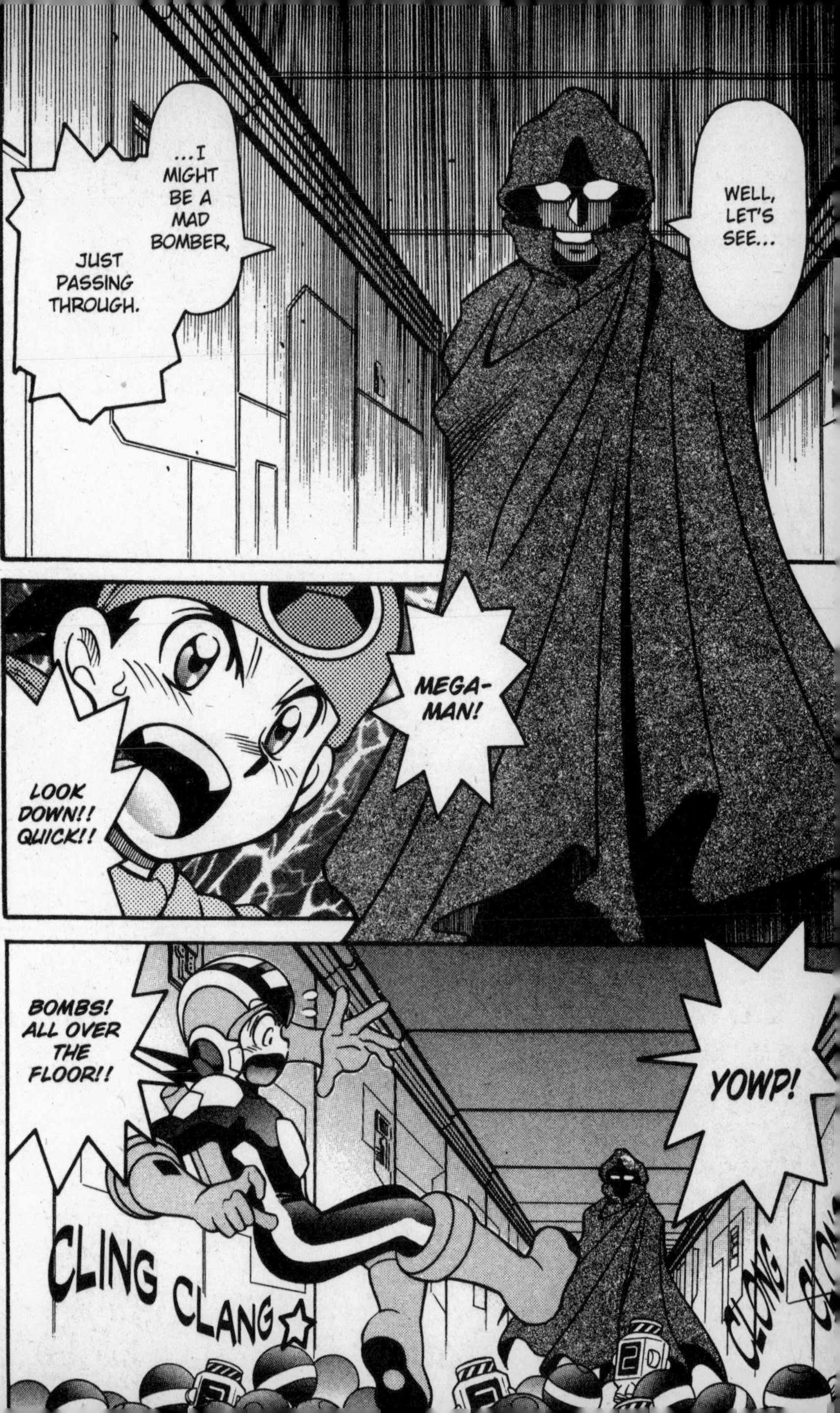
WELL, LET'S SEE...
...I MIGHT BE A MAD BOMBER,
JUST PASSING THROUGH.
MEGA-MAN!
LOOK DOWN!! QUICK!!
YOWP!
BOMBS! ALL OVER THE FLOOR!!
CLONG
CLING CLANG

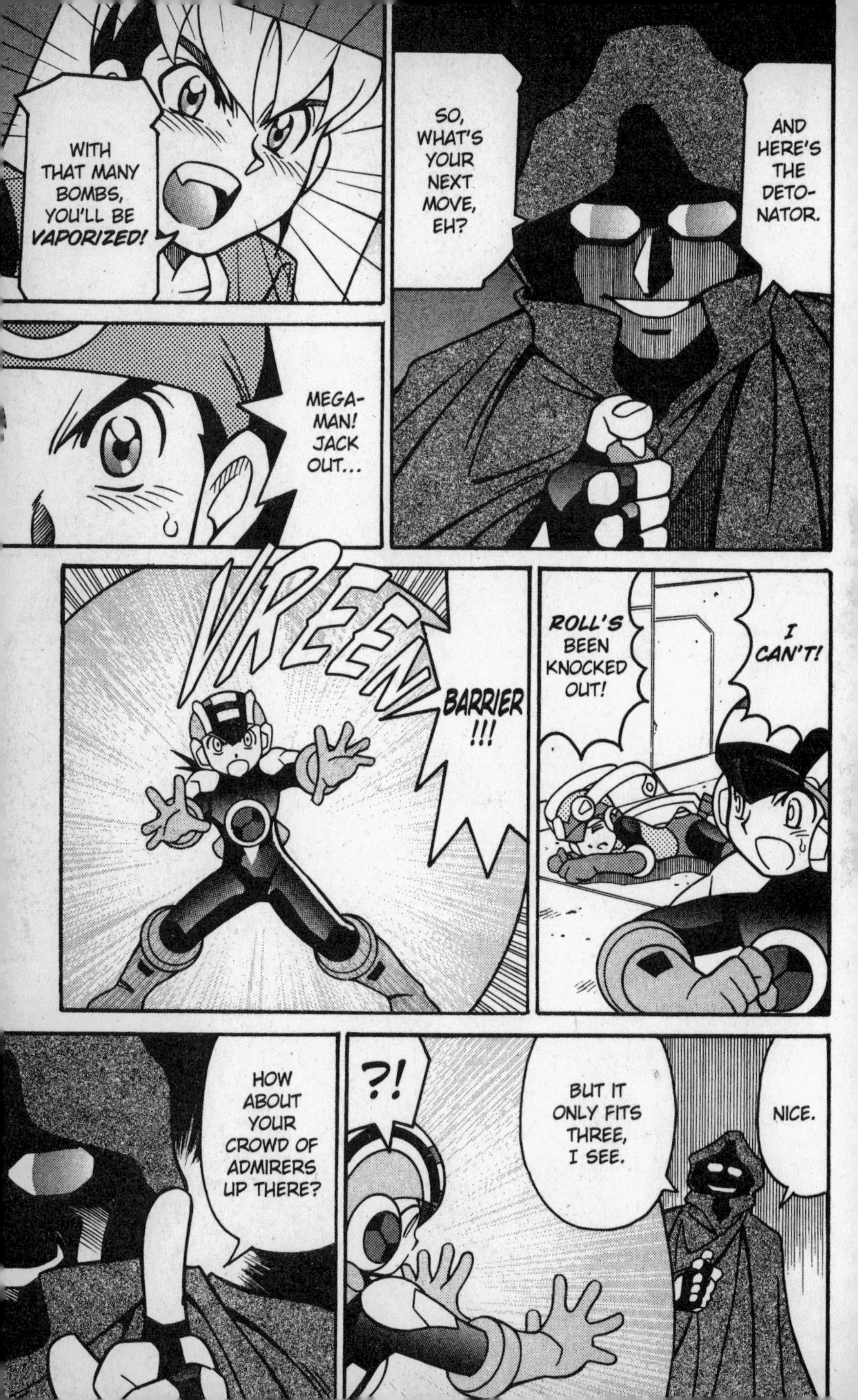
AND HERE'S THE DETO-NATOR.
SO, WHAT'S YOUR NEXT MOVE, EH?
WITH THAT MANY BOMBS, YOU'LL BE VAPORIZED!
MEGA-MAN! JACK OUT...
I CAN'T!
ROLL'S BEEN KNOCKED OUT!
VREEN
BARRIER!!!
NICE.
BUT IT ONLY FITS THREE, I SEE.
?!
HOW ABOUT YOUR CROWD OF ADMIRERS UP THERE?

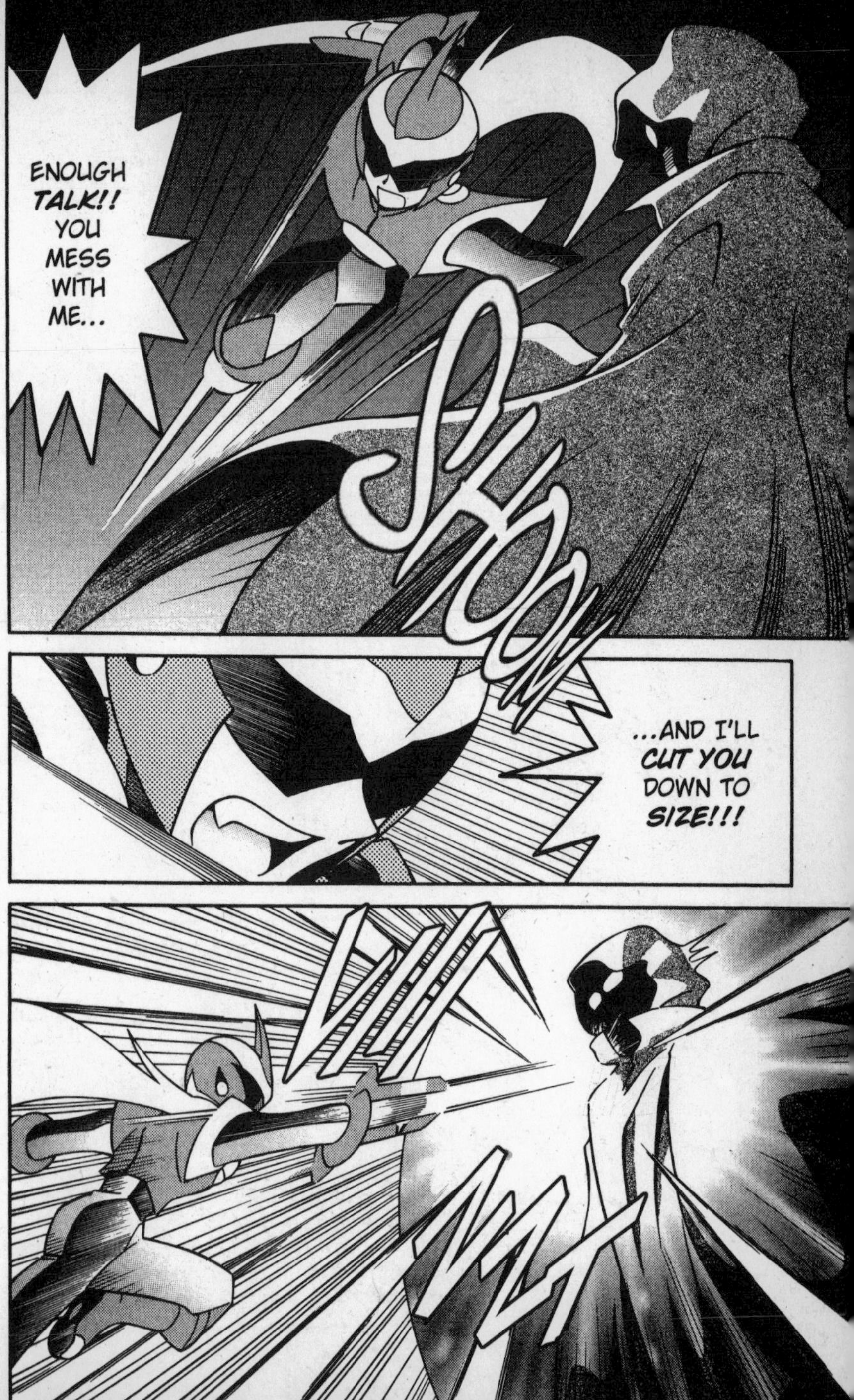

ENOUGH TALK!! YOU MESS WITH ME...
SHOOM
...AND I'LL CUT YOU DOWN TO SIZE!!!

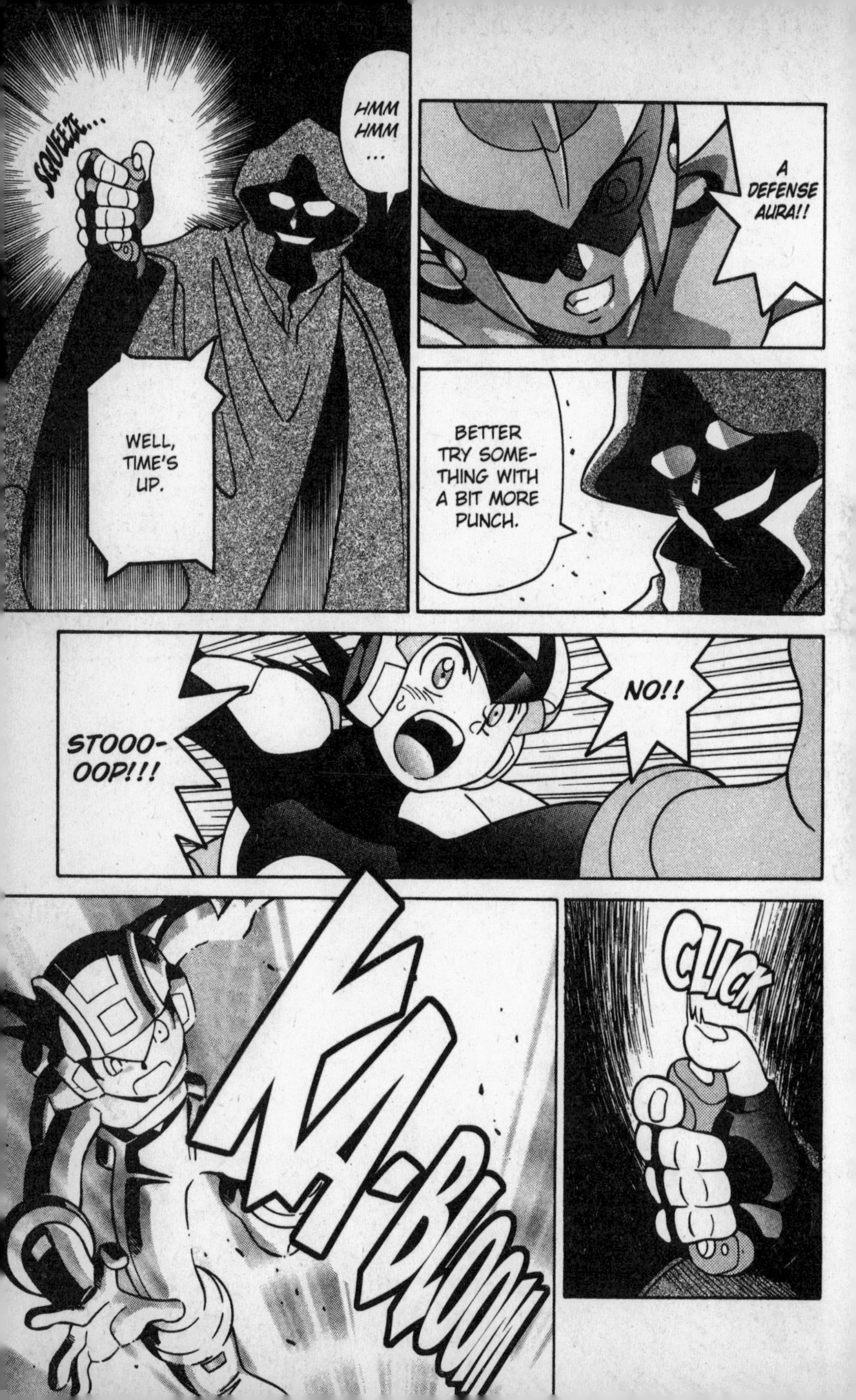
A DEFENSE AURA!!
BETTER TRY SOME-THING WITH A BIT MORE PUNCH.
HMM HMM ...
SQUEEZE...
WELL, TIME'S UP.
NO!!
STOOOO-OOP!!!
CLICK
KA-BLOOM

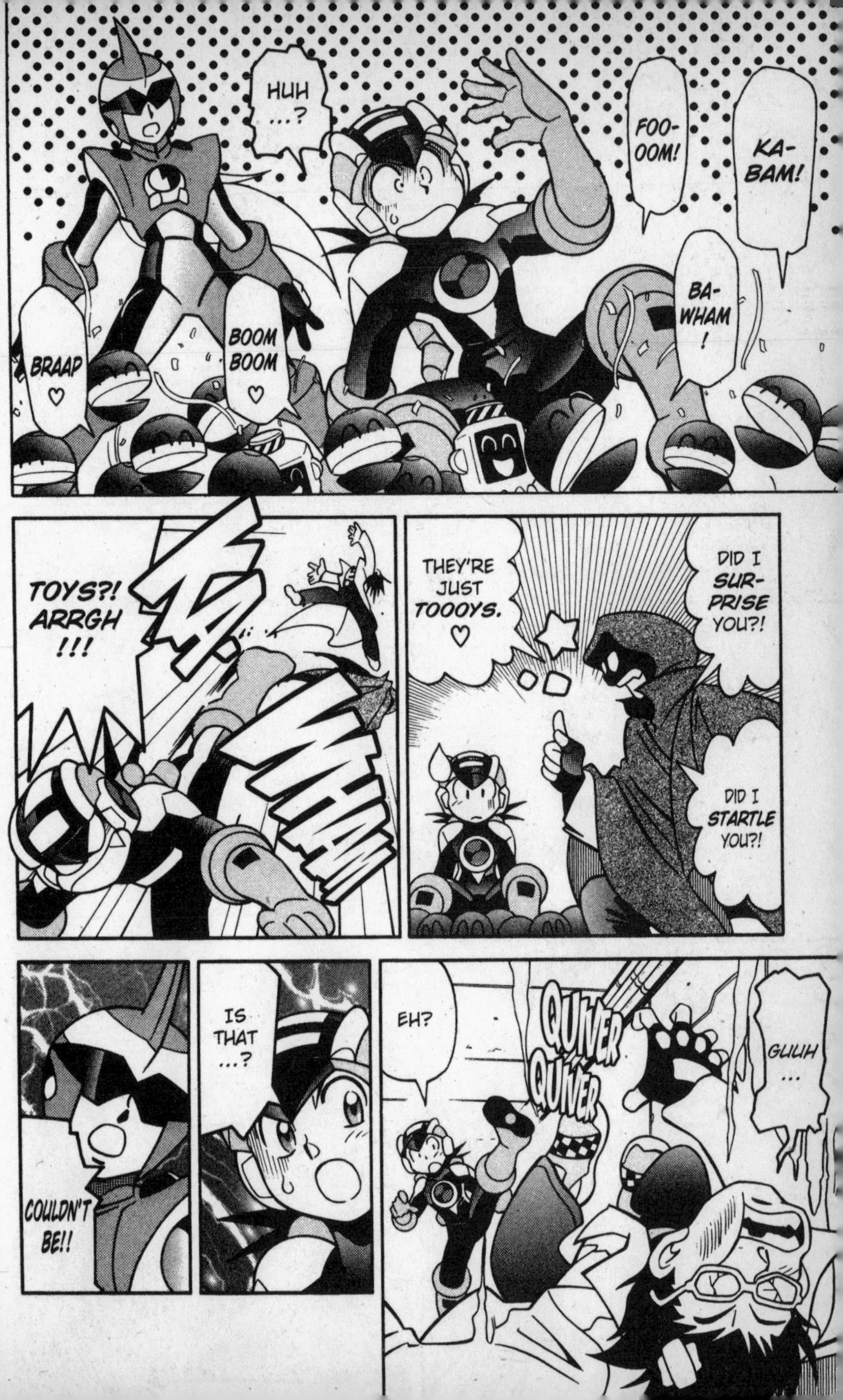
KA-BAM!
FOO-OOM!
BA-WHAM!
HUH ...?
BOOM BOOM ♡
BRAAP ♡
DID I SURPRISE YOU?!
THEY'RE JUST TOOOYS. ♡
DID I STARTLE YOU?!
TOYS?! ARRGH!!!
GUUH ...
QUIVER QUIVER
EH?
IS THAT ...?
COULDN'T BE!!

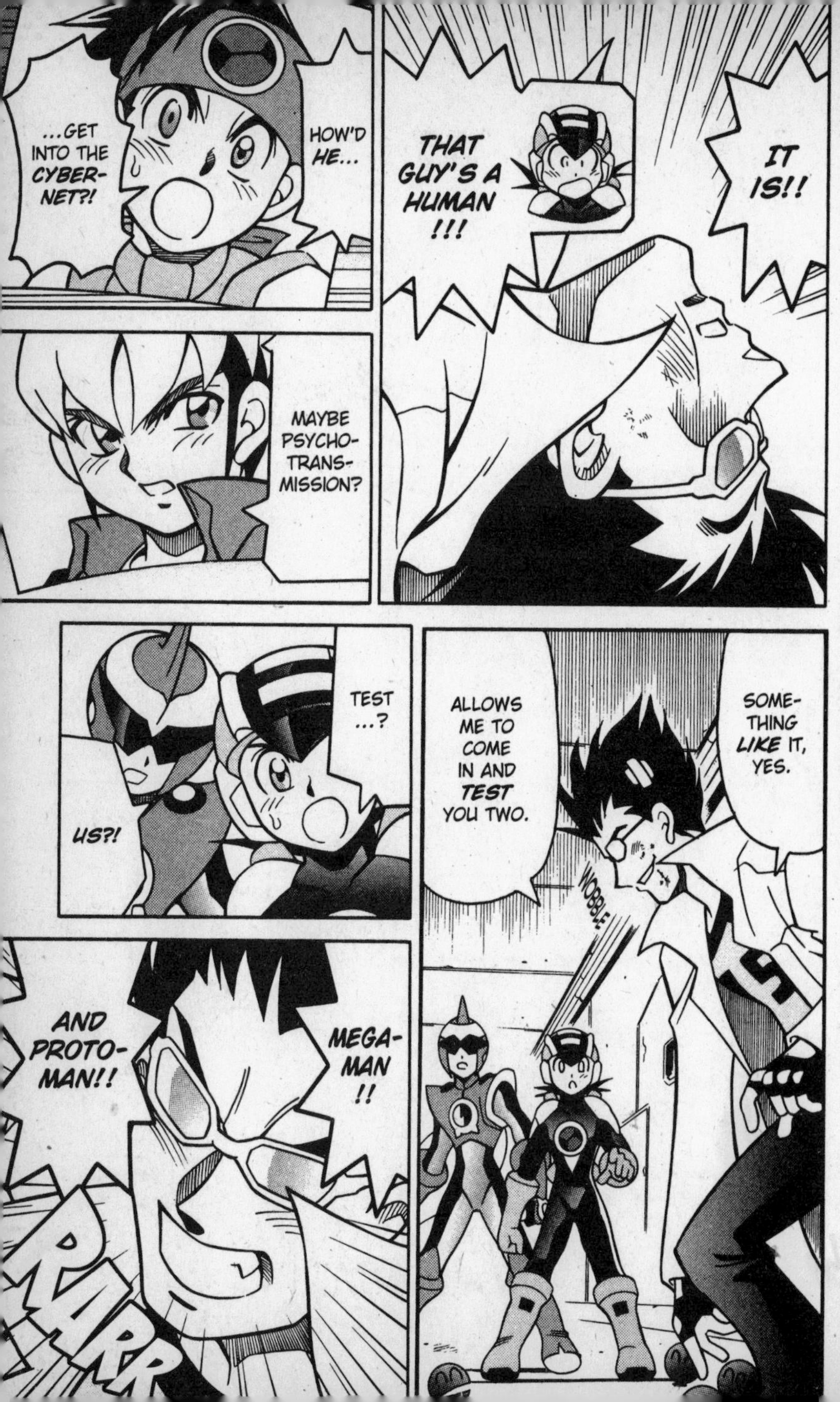
IT IS!!
THAT GUY'S A HUMAN!!!
HOW'D HE...
...GET INTO THE CYBER-NET?!
MAYBE PSYCHO-TRANS-MISSION?
SOME-THING LIKE IT, YES.
ALLOWS ME TO COME IN AND TEST YOU TWO.
WOBBLE
TEST ...?
US?!
MEGA-MAN!!
AND PROTO-MAN!!
RARR

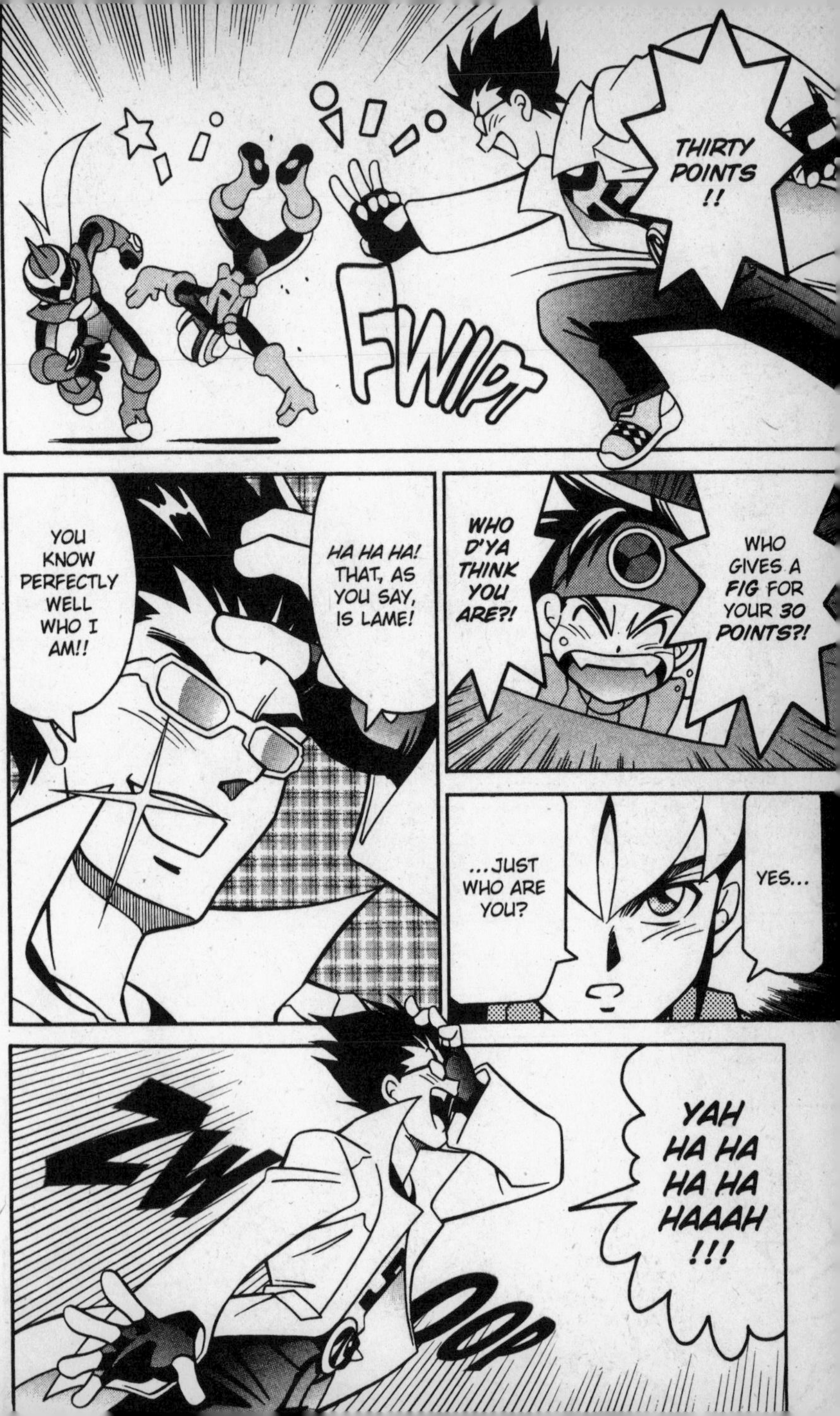
THIRTY POINTS!!
FWIPT
WHO GIVES A FIG FOR YOUR 30 POINTS?!
WHO D'YA THINK YOU ARE?!
YES...
...JUST WHO ARE YOU?
HA HA HA! THAT, AS YOU SAY, IS LAME!
YOU KNOW PERFECTLY WELL WHO I AM!!
YAH HA HA HA HA HAAAH!!!
ZW

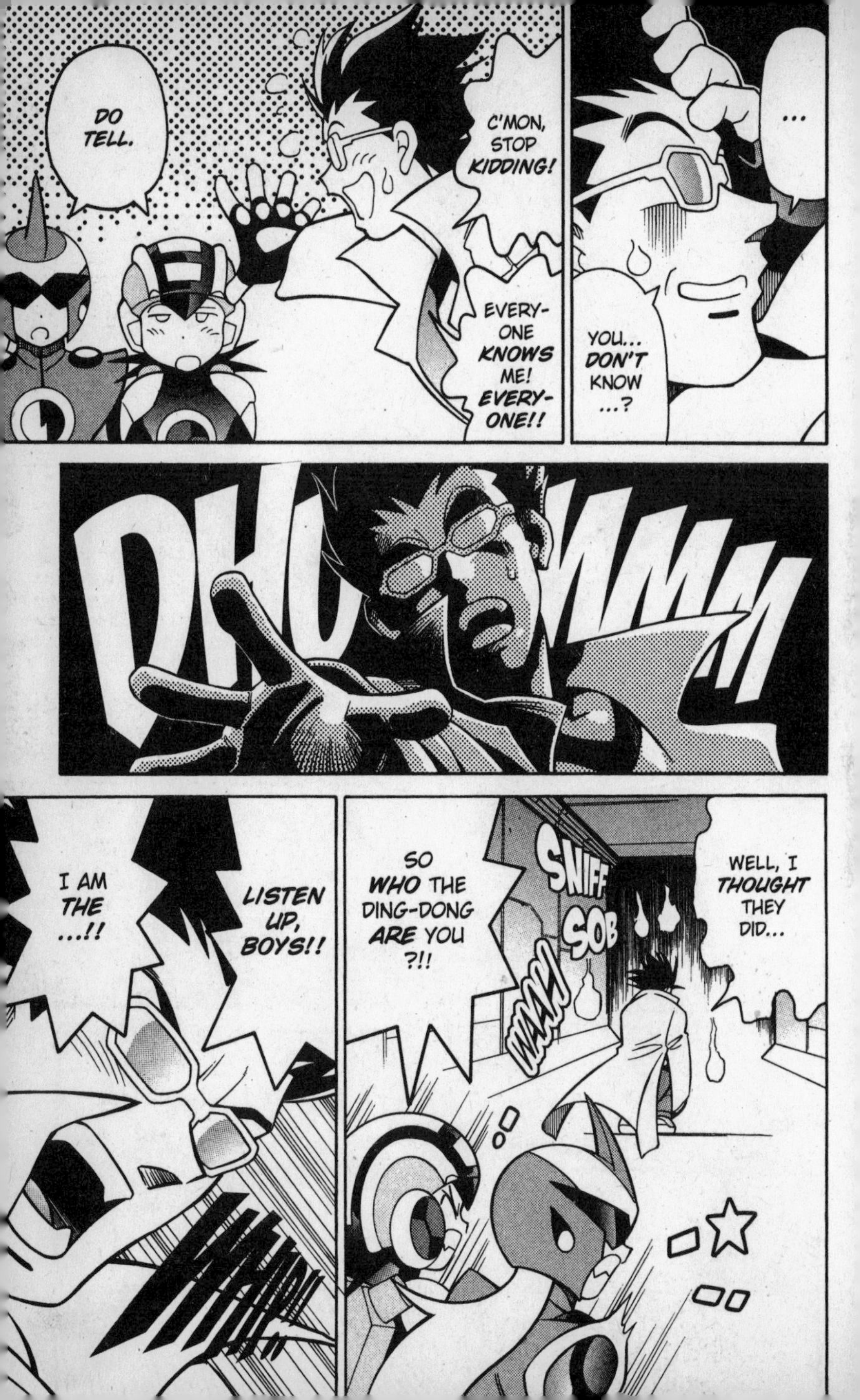
...
YOU... DON'T KNOW ...?
C'MON, STOP KIDDING!
EVERY-ONE KNOWS ME! EVERY-ONE!!
DO TELL.
DHOMMM
WELL, I THOUGHT THEY DID...
SNIFF
SOB
SO WHO THE DING-DONG ARE YOU ?!!
LISTEN UP, BOYS!!
I AM THE ...!!

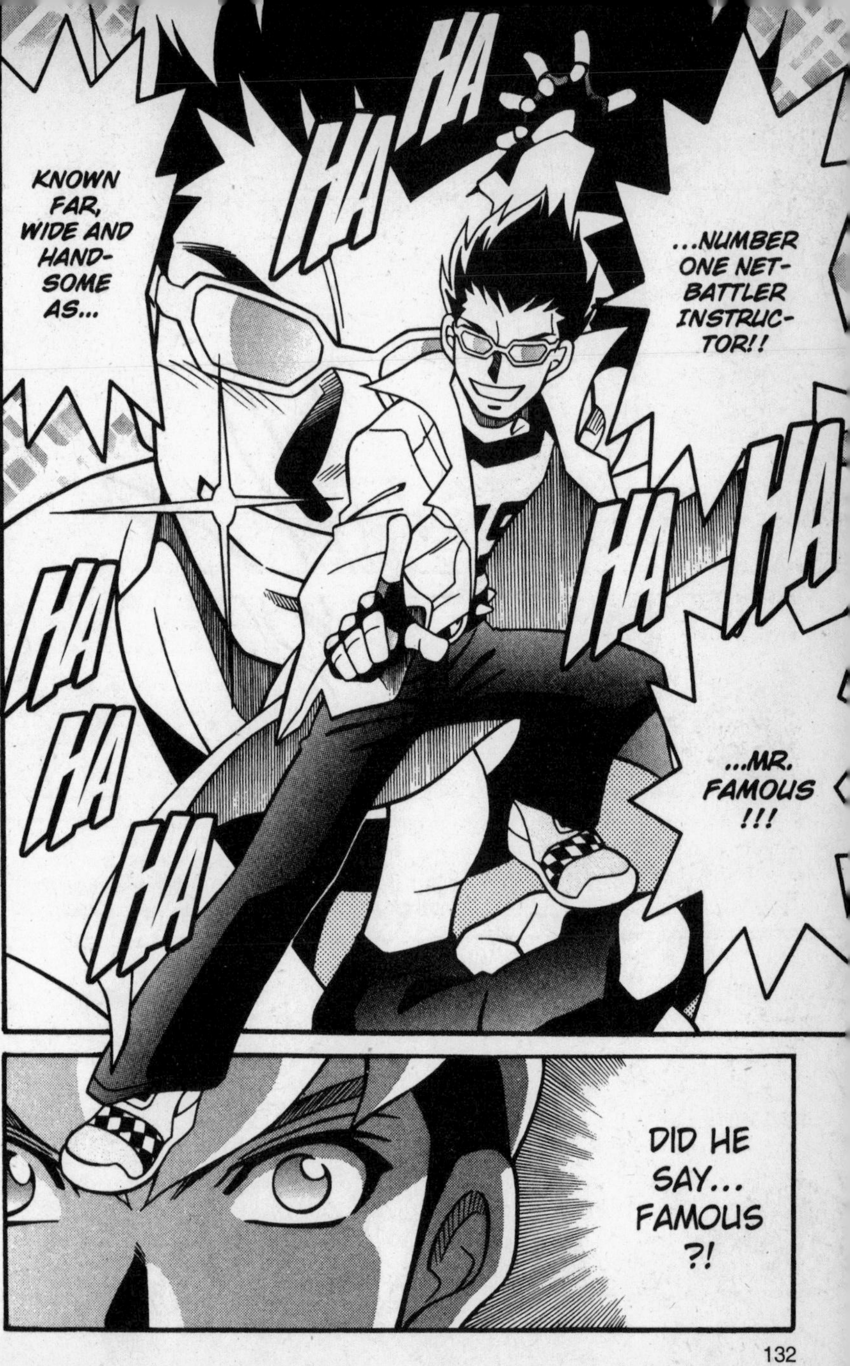
KNOWN FAR, WIDE AND HAND-SOME AS...
...NUMBER ONE NET-BATTLER INSTRUC-TOR!!
HA HA
HA HA
HA HA HA
...MR. FAMOUS !!!
DID HE SAY... FAMOUS ?!

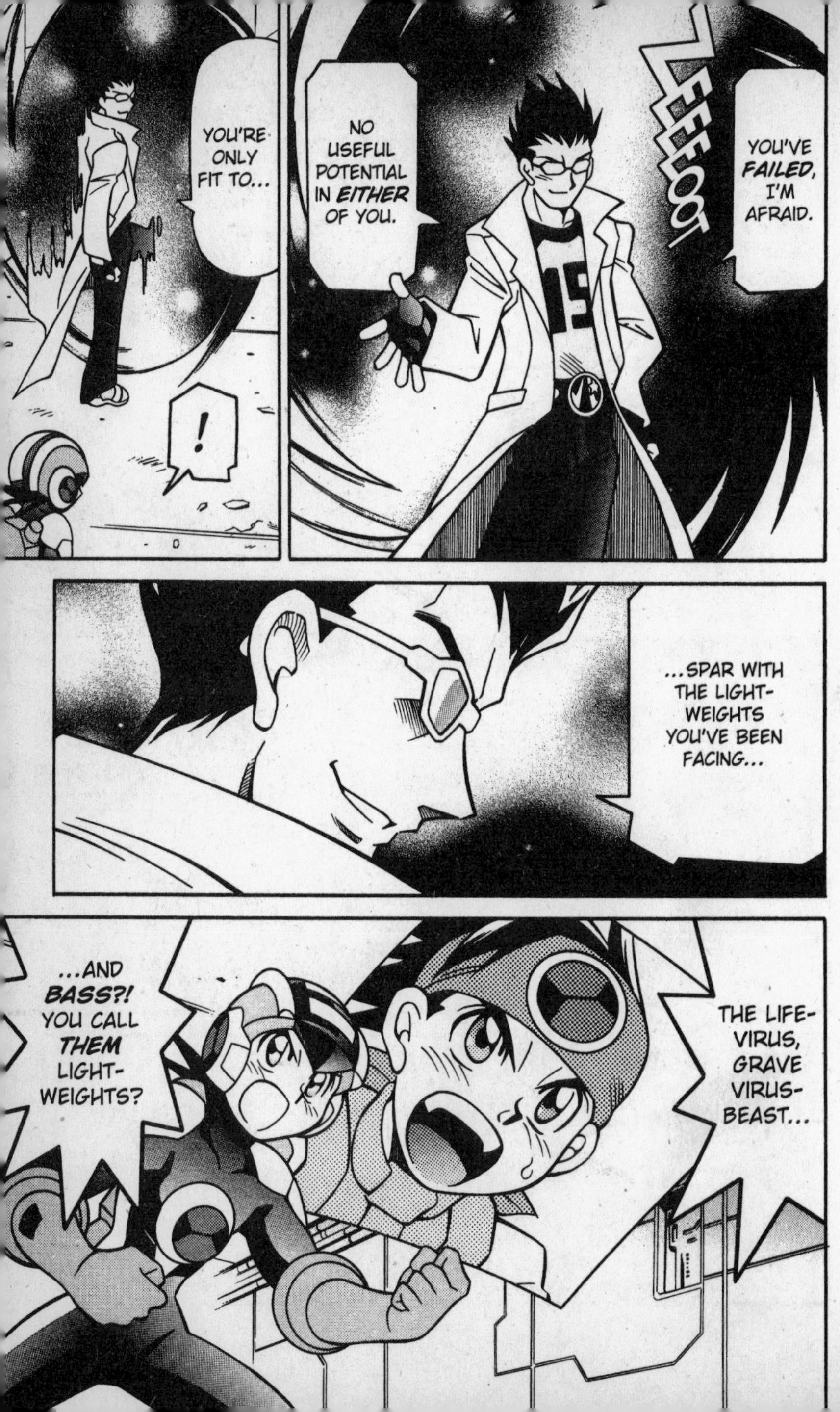
ZEELOOT
YOU'VE FAILED, I'M AFRAID.
NO USEFUL POTENTIAL IN EITHER OF YOU.
YOU'RE ONLY FIT TO...
!
...SPAR WITH THE LIGHT-WEIGHTS YOU'VE BEEN FACING...
THE LIFE-VIRUS, GRAVE VIRUS-BEAST...
...AND BASS?! YOU CALL THEM LIGHT-WEIGHTS?

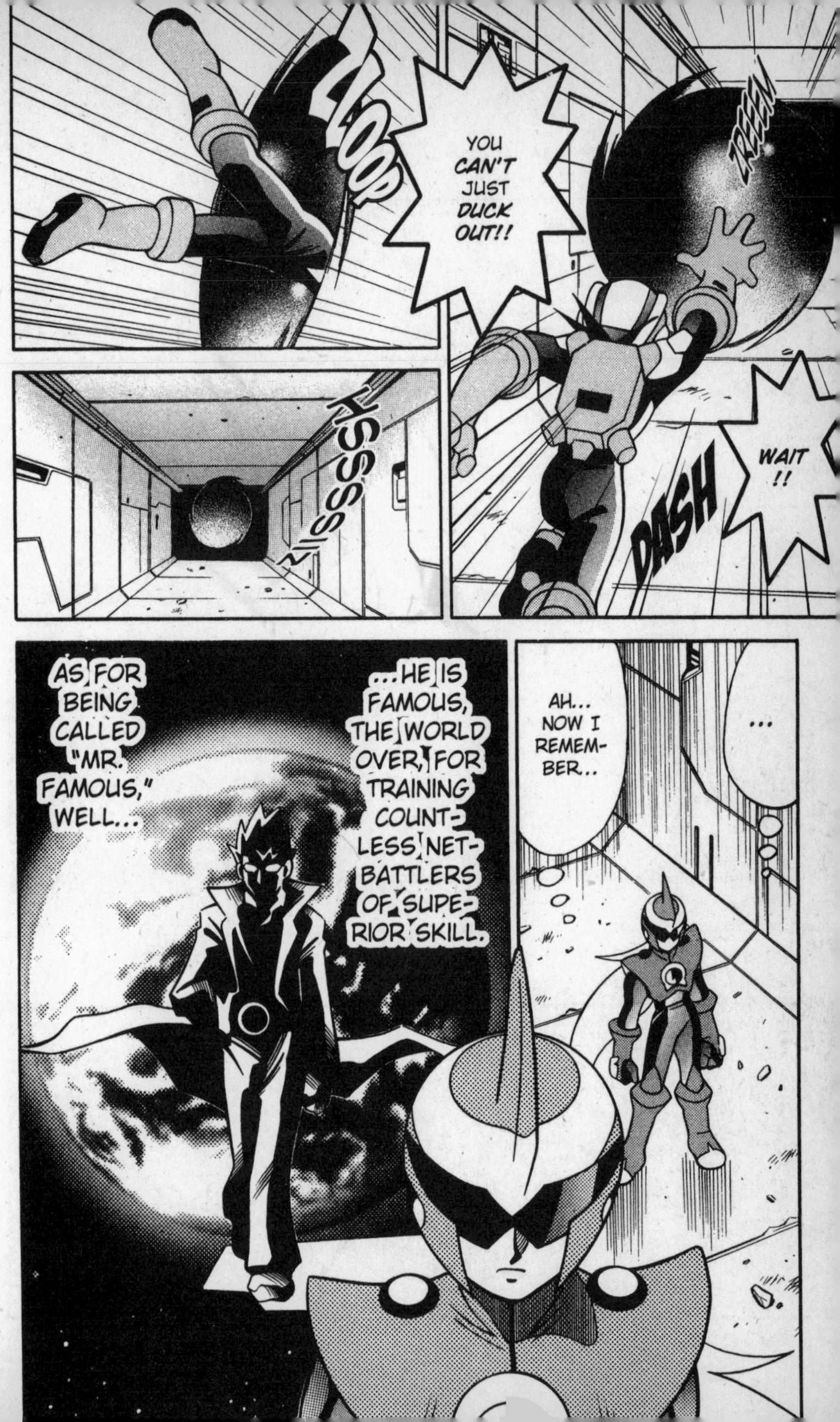
TREEEN
YOU CAN'T JUST DUCK OUT!!
WAIT !!
DASH
ZWOOP
HSSSSN
...
AH... NOW I REMEMBER...
AS FOR BEING CALLED "MR. FAMOUS," WELL...
...HE IS FAMOUS, THE WORLD OVER, FOR TRAINING COUNTLESS NETBATTLERS OF SUPERIOR SKILL.

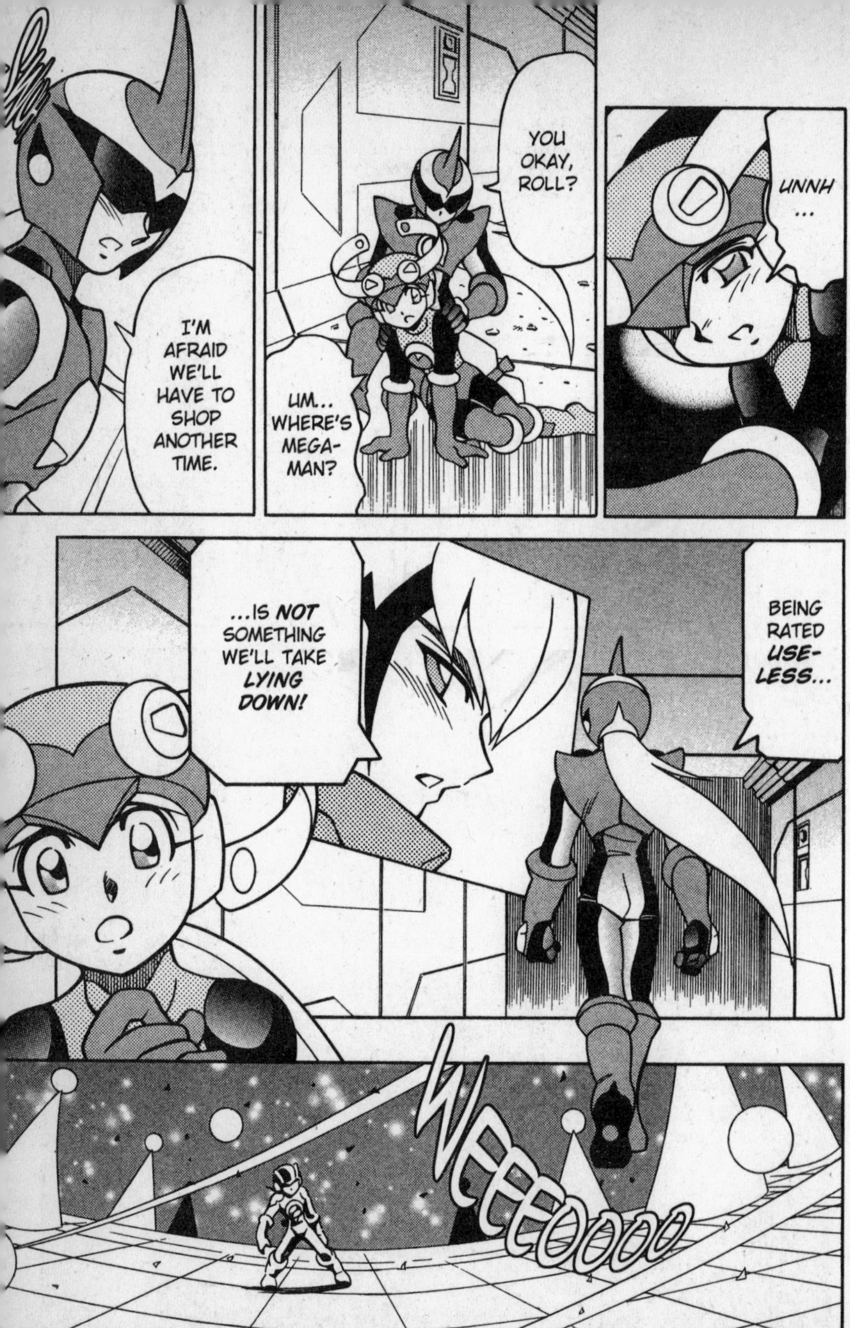
UNNH ...
YOU OKAY, ROLL?
UM... WHERE'S MEGA-MAN?
I'M AFRAID WE'LL HAVE TO SHOP ANOTHER TIME.
BEING RATED *USE-LESS...*
...IS *NOT* SOMETHING WE'LL TAKE *LYING DOWN!*
WEEEOOOOO

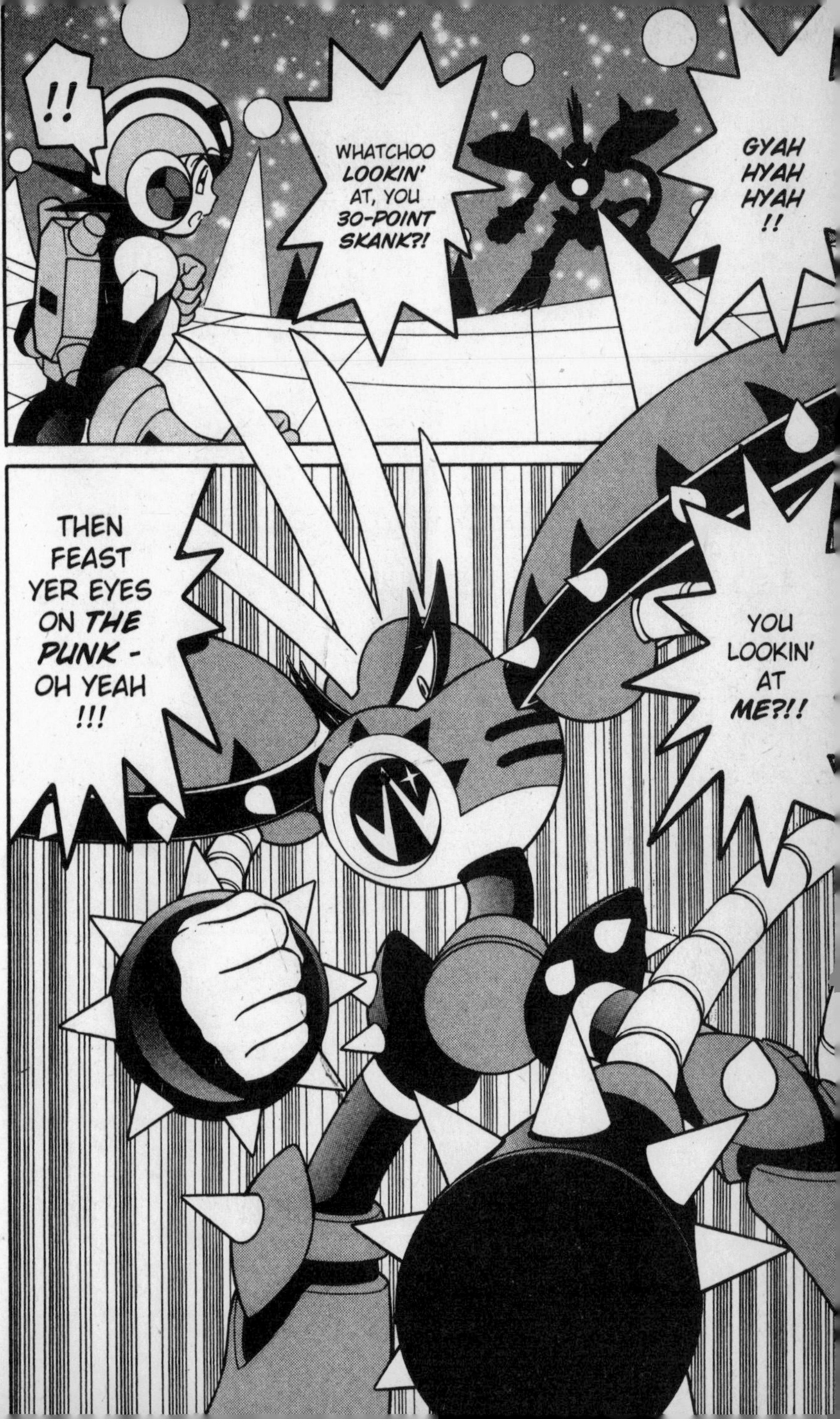
GYAH HYAH HYAH !!
WHATCHOO LOOKIN' AT, YOU 30-POINT SKANK?!
!!
YOU LOOKIN' AT ME?!!
THEN FEAST YER EYES ON THE PUNK - OH YEAH !!!

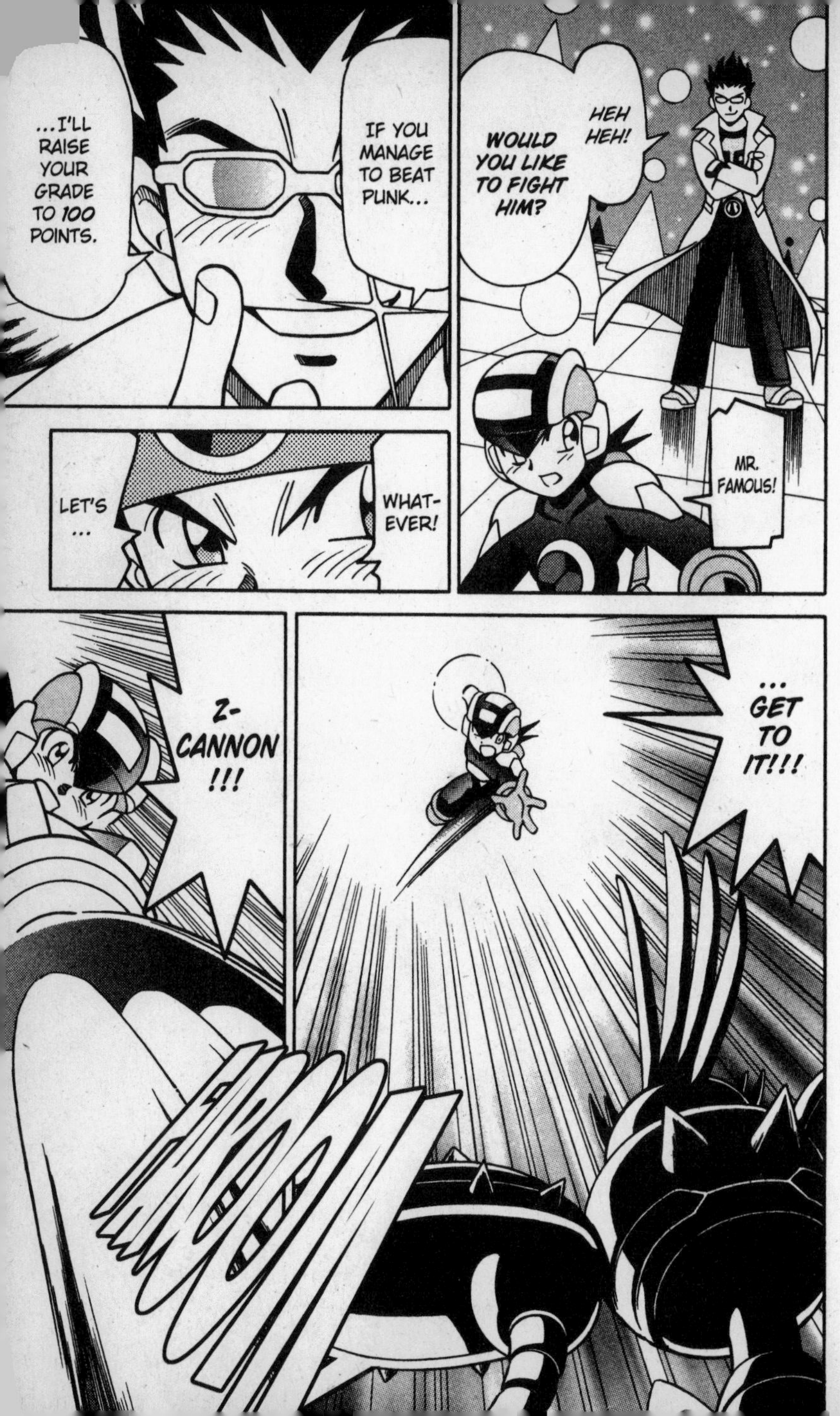
HEH HEH!
WOULD YOU LIKE TO FIGHT HIM?
MR. FAMOUS!
IF YOU MANAGE TO BEAT PUNK...
...I'LL RAISE YOUR GRADE TO 100 POINTS.
WHAT-EVER!
LET'S ...
... GET TO IT!!!
Z-CANNON !!!

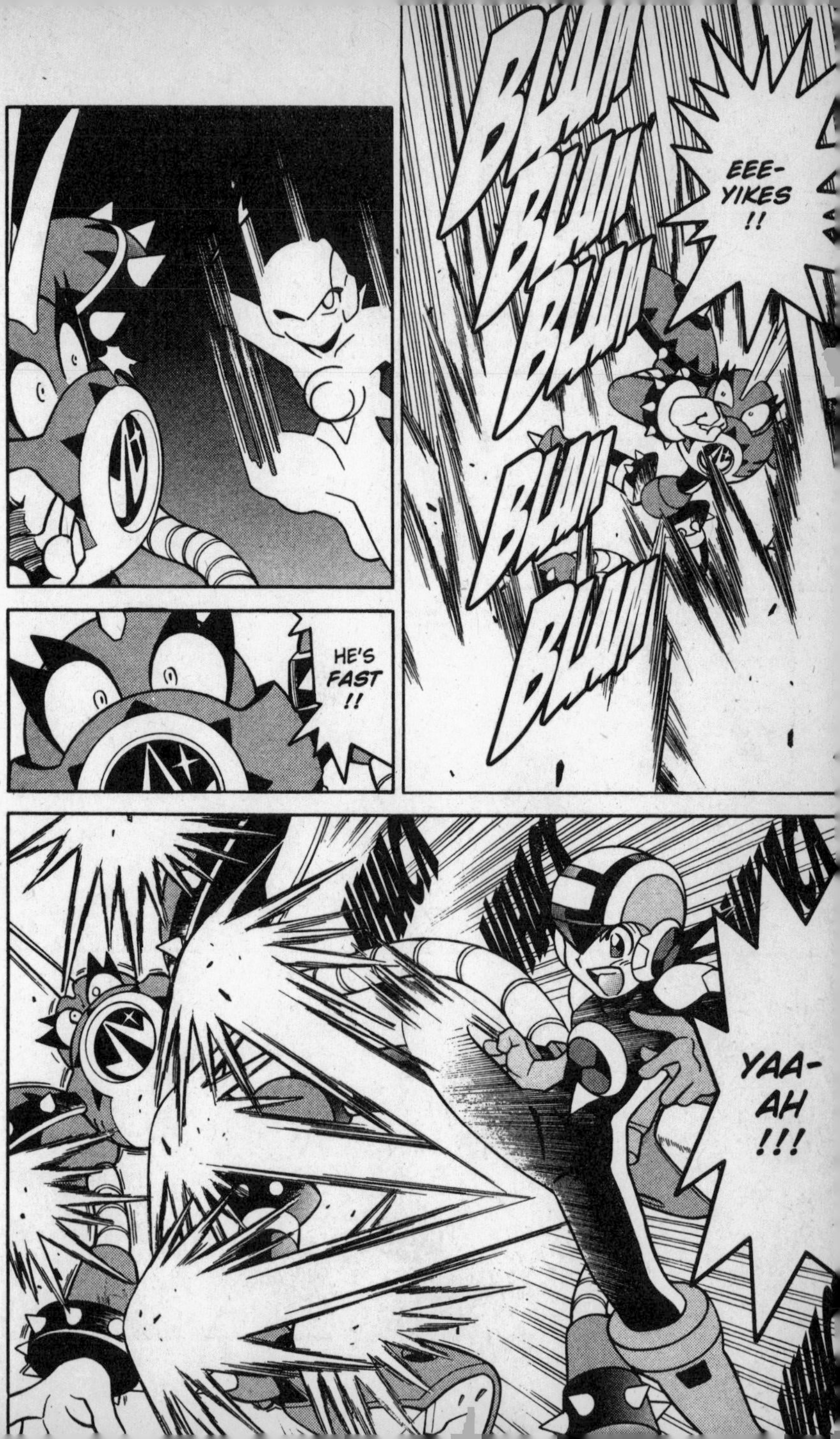
EEE-YIKES !!
HE'S FAST !!
YAA-AH !!!

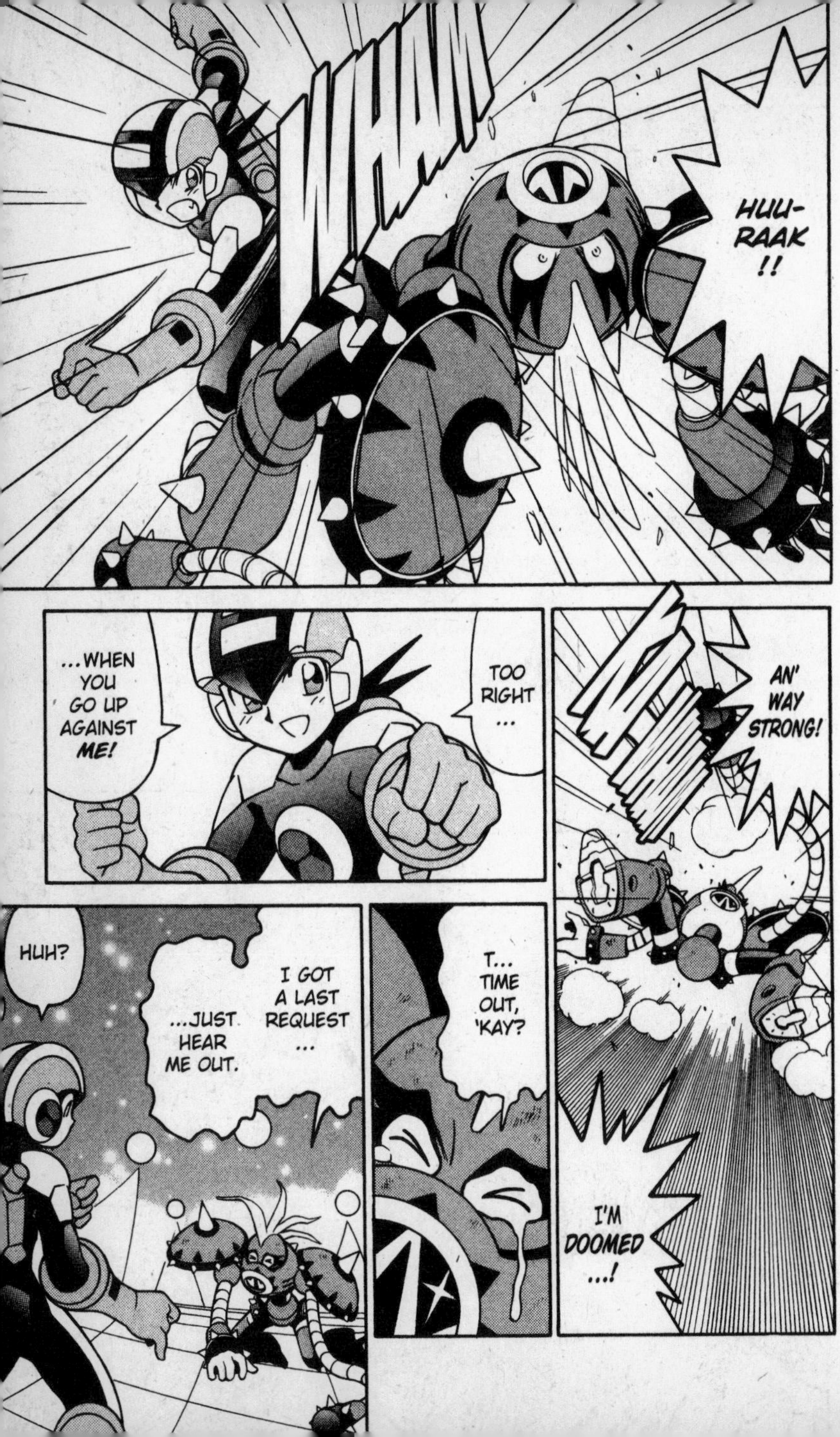
WHAM
HUU-RAAK!!
AN' WAY STRONG!
I'M DOOMED...!
TOO RIGHT...
...WHEN YOU GO UP AGAINST ME!
T... TIME OUT, 'KAY?
I GOT A LAST REQUEST...
...JUST HEAR ME OUT.
HUH?

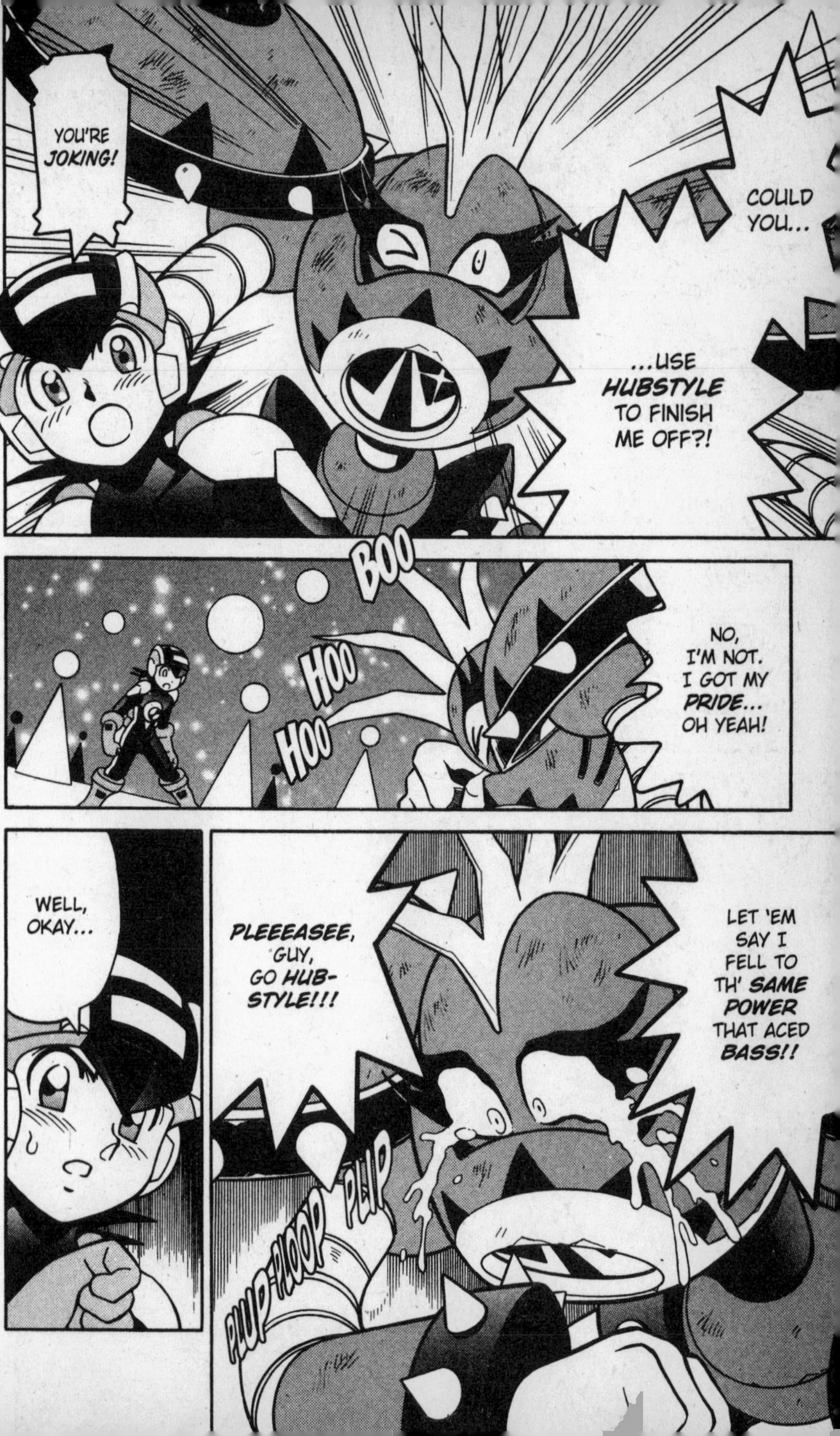
COULD YOU...
...USE HUBSTYLE TO FINISH ME OFF?!
YOU'RE JOKING!
BOO
NO, I'M NOT. I GOT MY PRIDE... OH YEAH!
HOO
HOO
LET 'EM SAY I FELL TO TH' SAME POWER THAT ACED BASS!!
PLEEEASEE, GUY, GO HUB-STYLE!!!
PLIP
PLUP-PLOOP
WELL, OKAY...

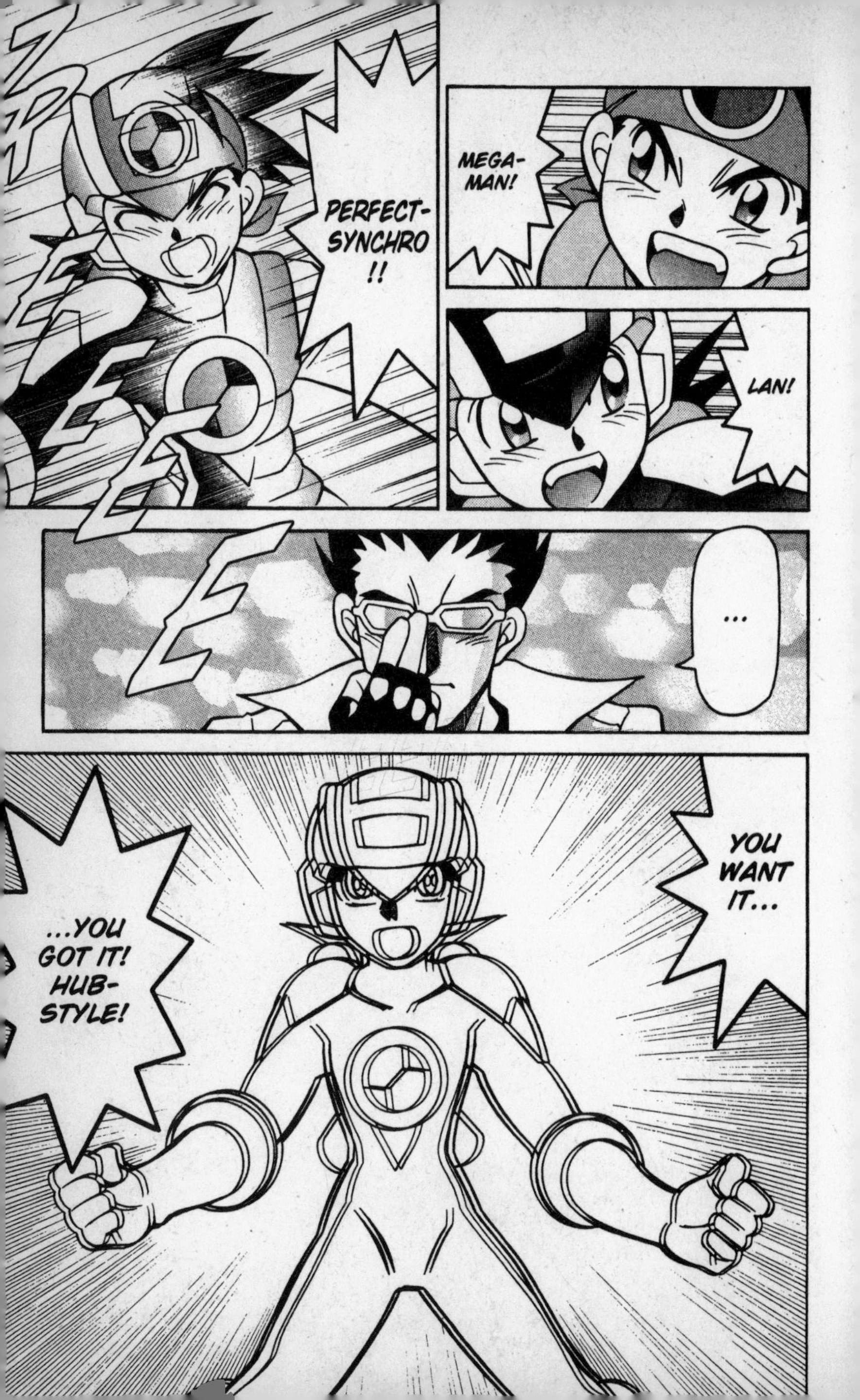
MEGA-MAN!
LAN!
PERFECT-SYNCHRO!!
...
YOU WANT IT...
...YOU GOT IT! HUB-STYLE!

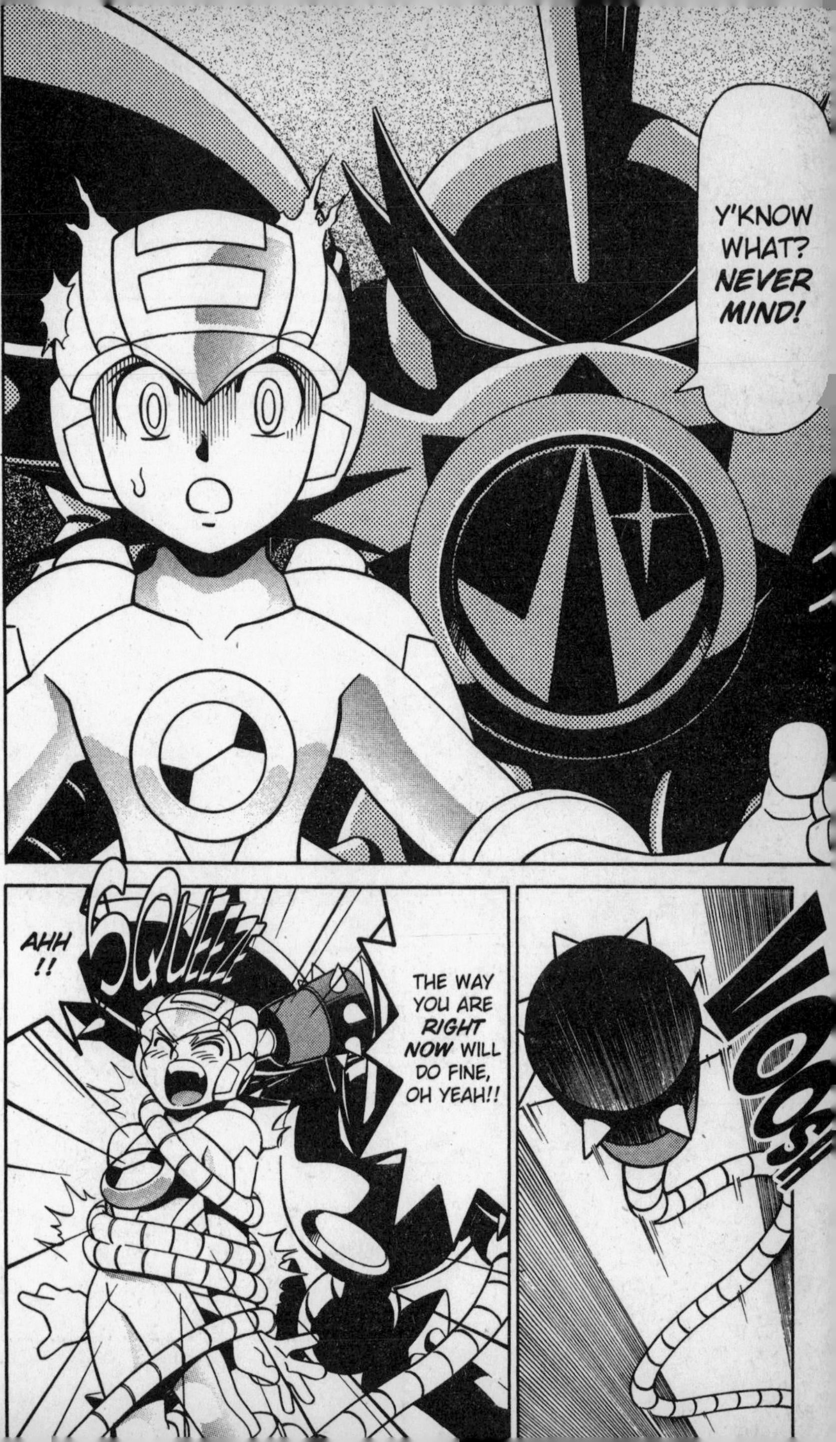
Y'KNOW WHAT? **NEVER MIND!**
WOOSH
AHH !!
SQUEEZE
THE WAY YOU ARE **RIGHT NOW** WILL DO FINE, OH YEAH!!

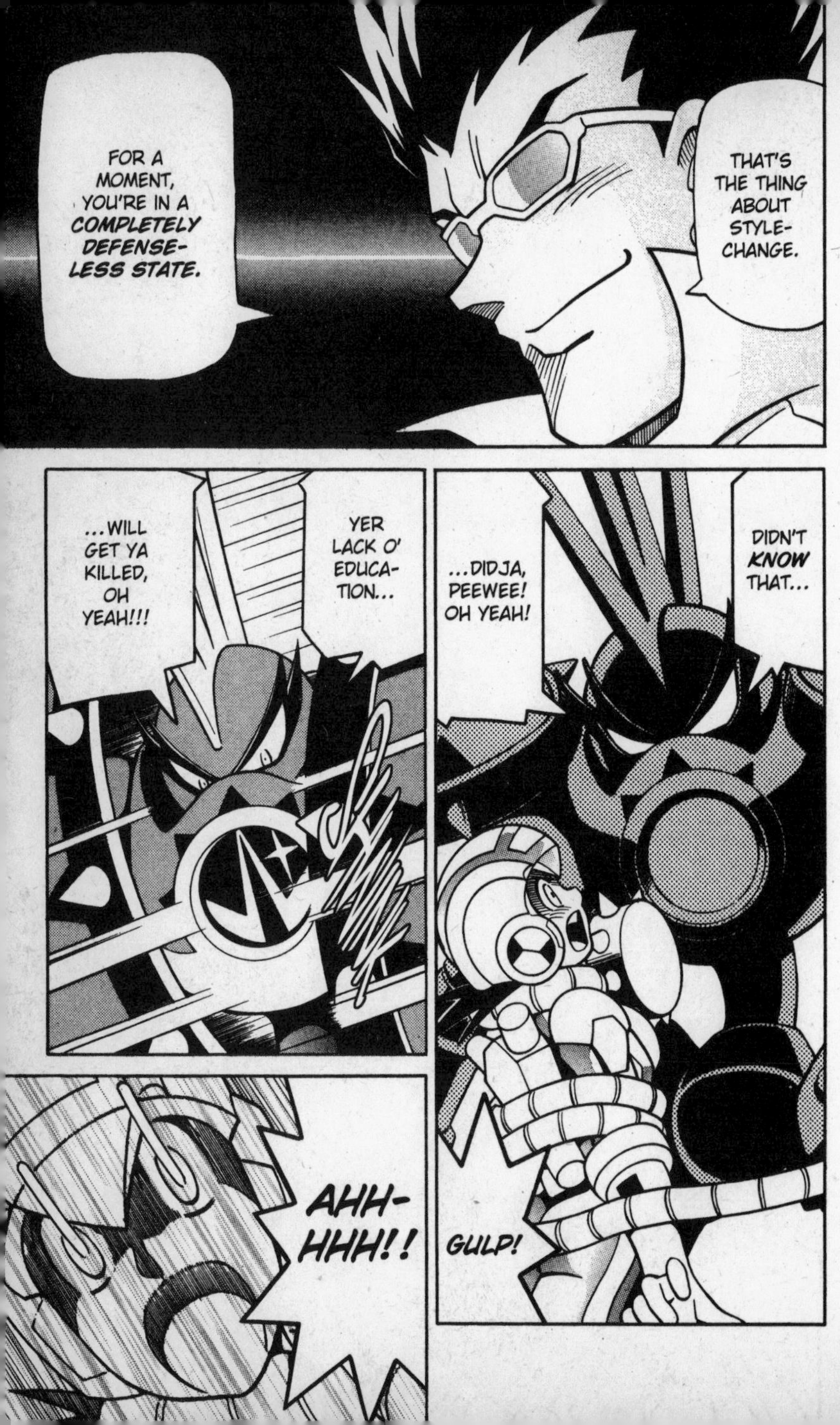
THAT'S THE THING ABOUT STYLE-CHANGE.
FOR A MOMENT, YOU'RE IN A **COMPLETELY DEFENSELESS STATE.**
DIDN'T ***KNOW*** THAT...
...DIDJA, PEEWEE! OH YEAH!
GULP!
YER LACK O' EDUCATION...
...WILL GET YA KILLED, OH YEAH!!!
AHH-HHH!!

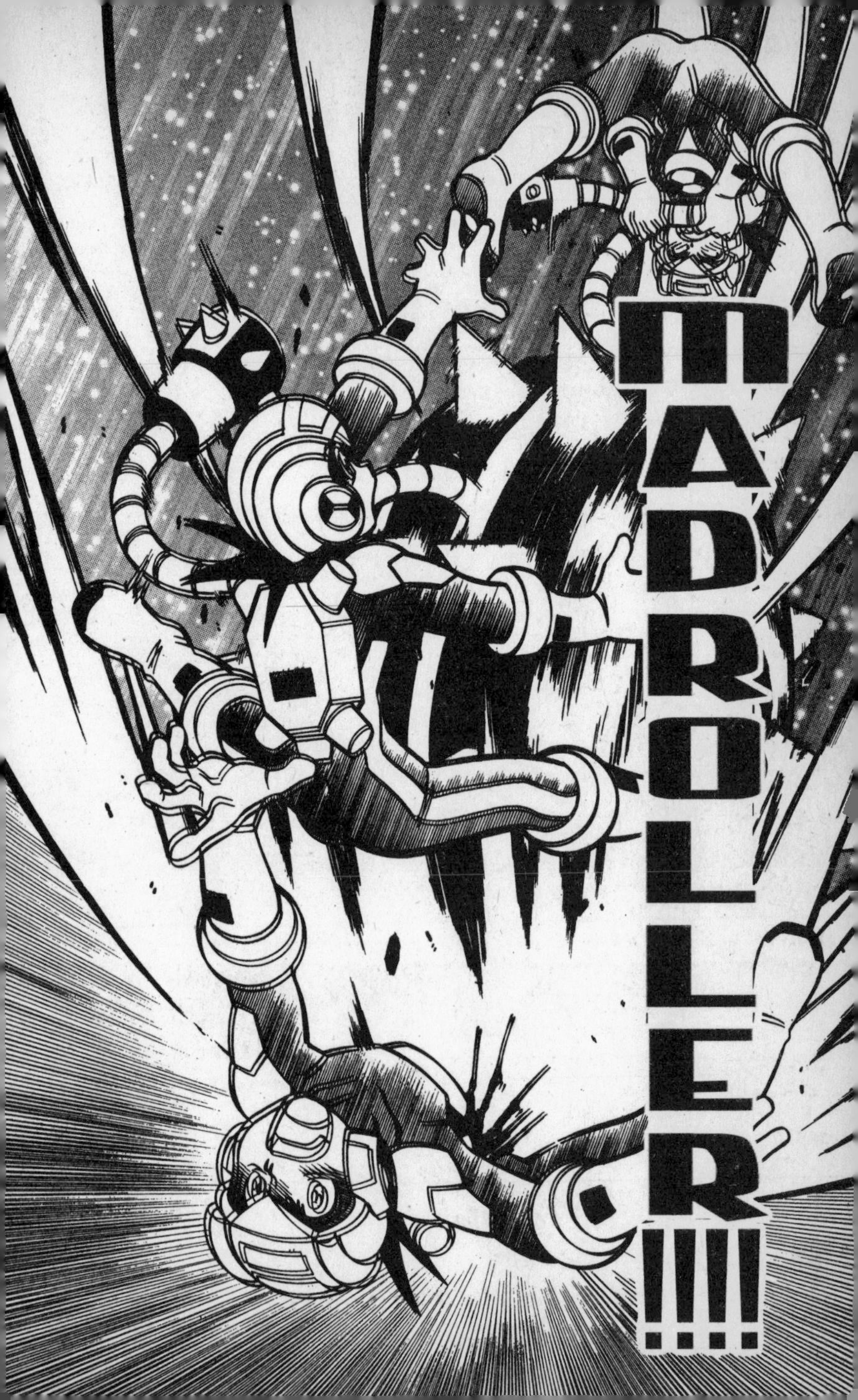
MADROLLER!!!!

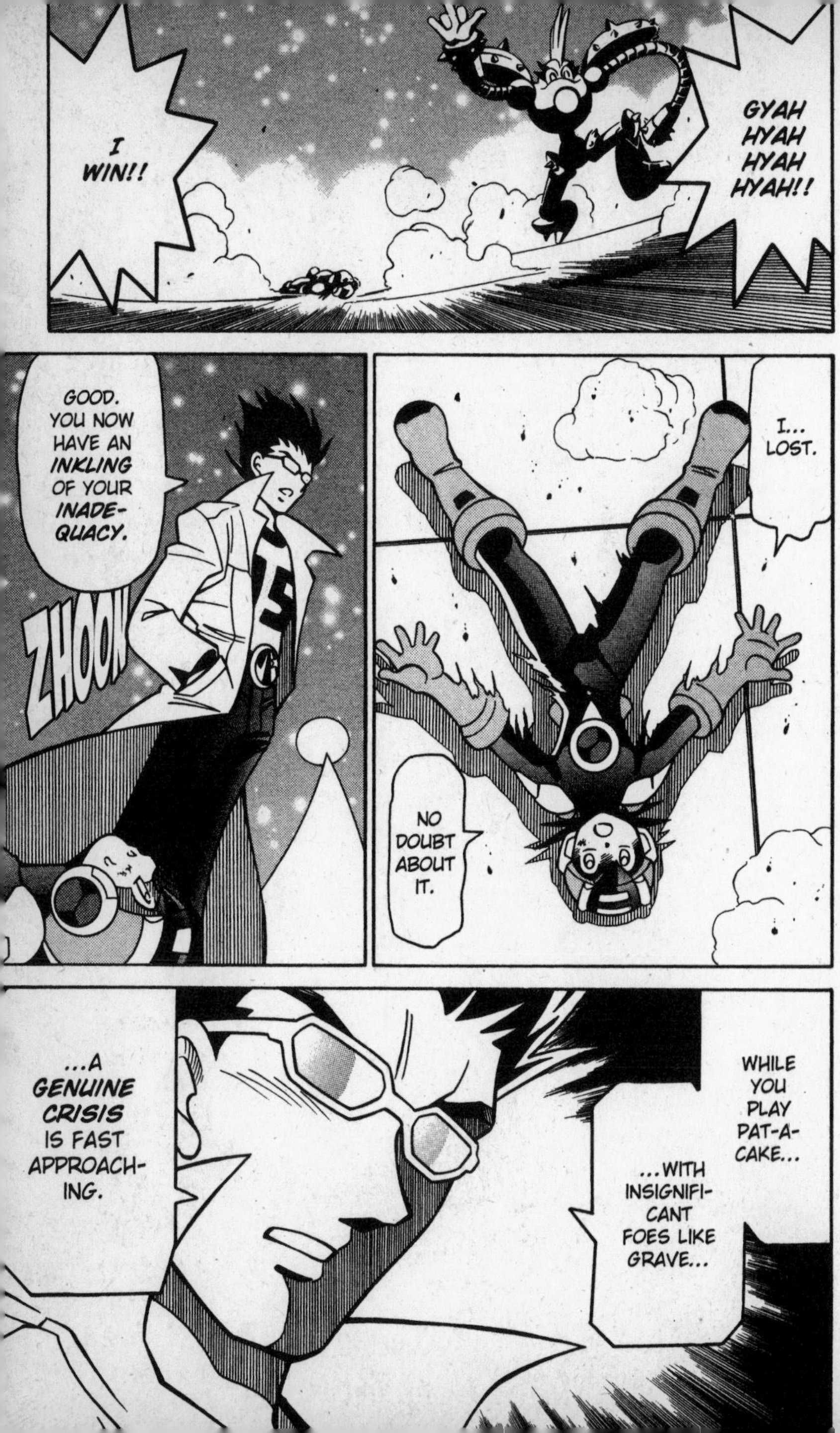
GYAH HYAH HYAH HYAH!!
I WIN!!
I... LOST.
NO DOUBT ABOUT IT.
GOOD. YOU NOW HAVE AN INKLING OF YOUR INADEQUACY.
ZHOOM
WHILE YOU PLAY PAT-A-CAKE...
...WITH INSIGNIFICANT FOES LIKE GRAVE...
...A GENUINE CRISIS IS FAST APPROACHING.

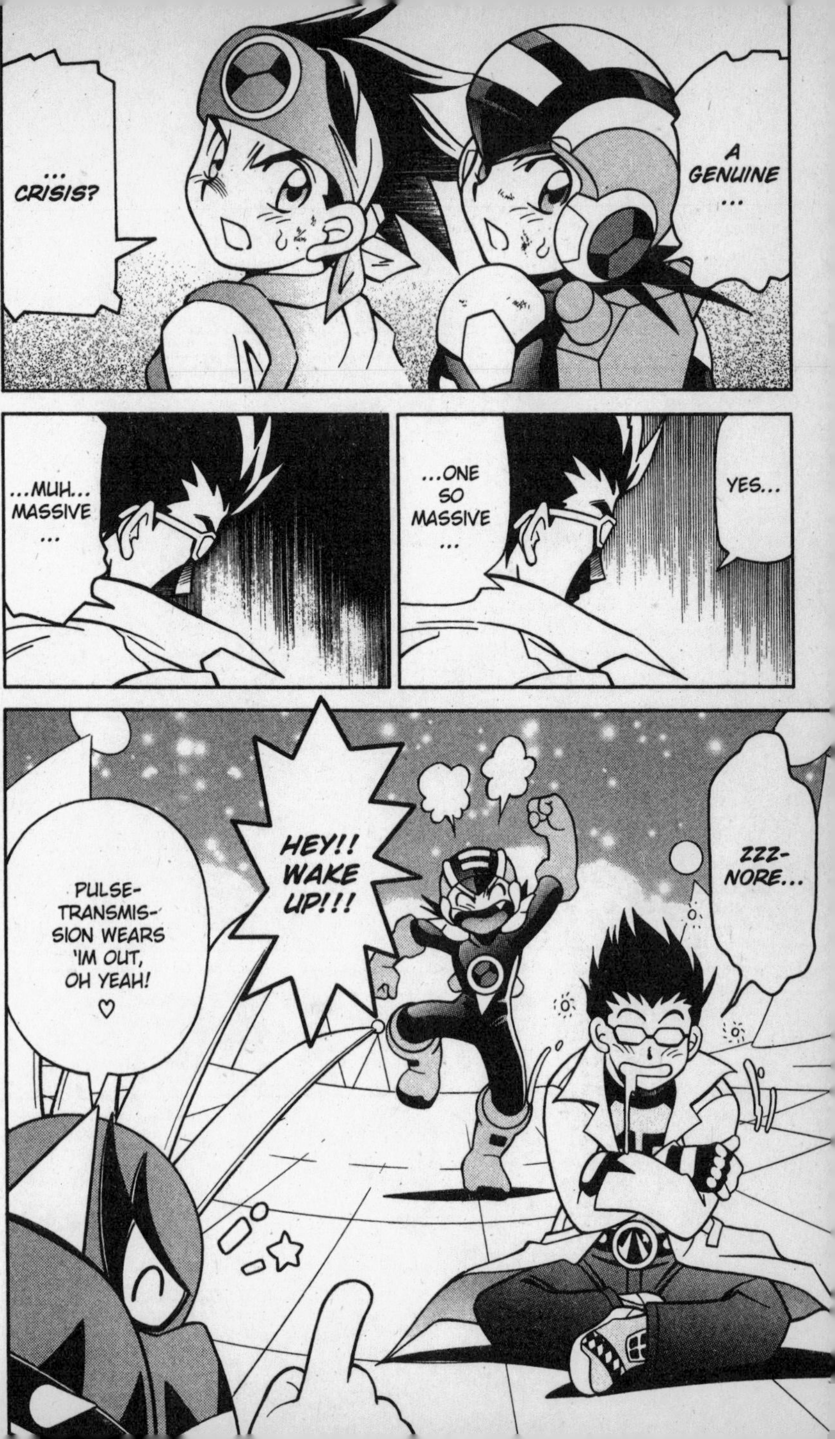
A GENUINE ...
... CRISIS?
YES...
...ONE SO MASSIVE ...
...MUH... MASSIVE ...
ZZZ-NORE...
HEY!! WAKE UP!!!
PULSE-TRANSMISSION WEARS 'IM OUT, OH YEAH! ♡

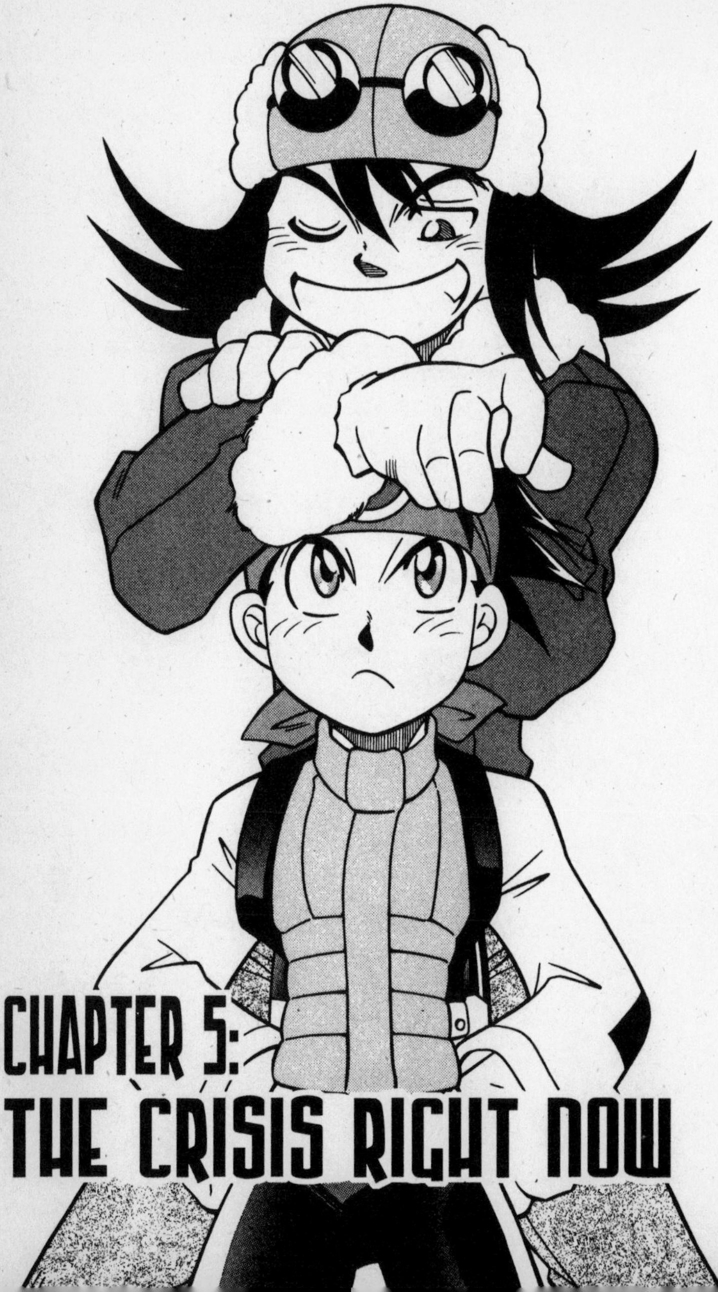
CHAPTER 5:
THE CRISIS RIGHT NOW

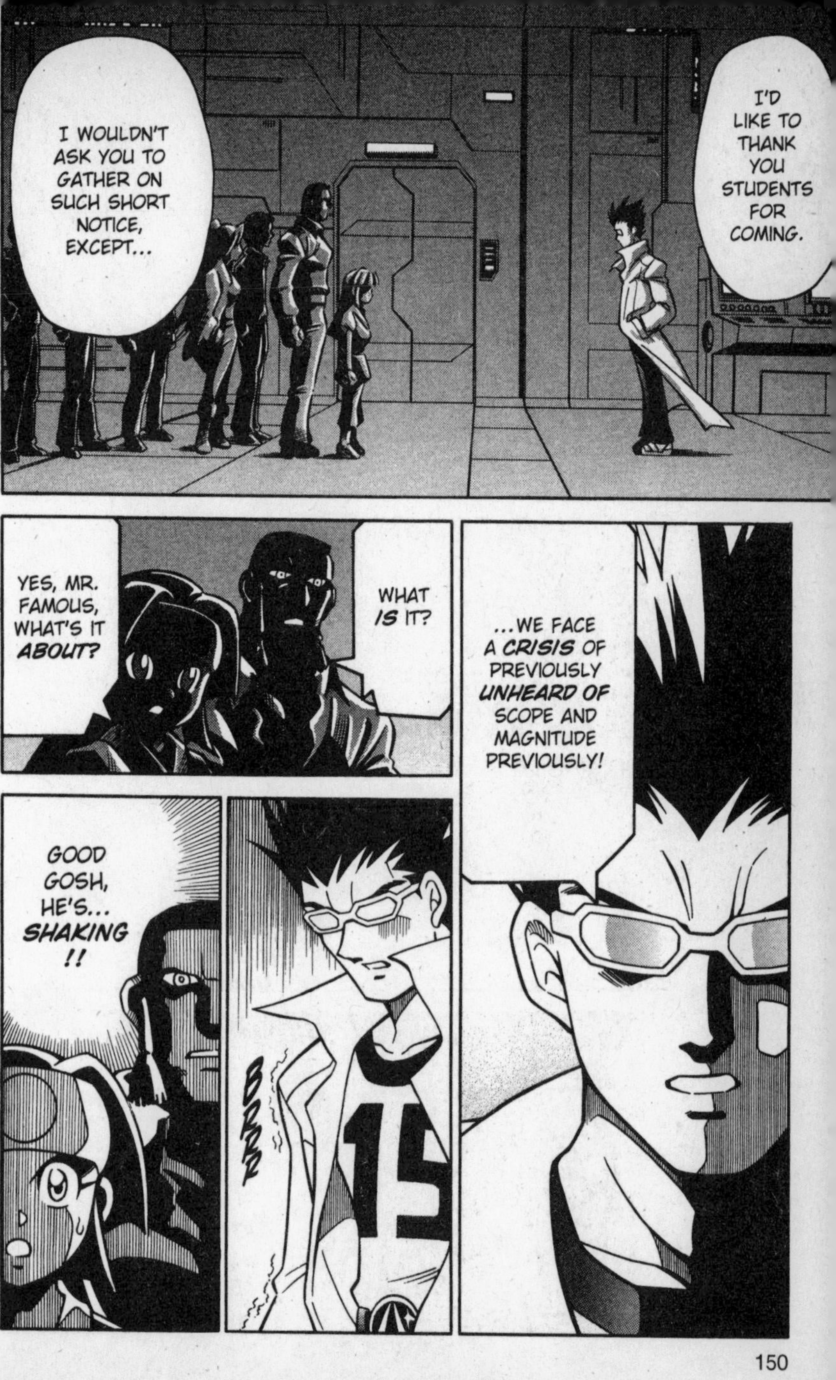
I'D LIKE TO THANK YOU STUDENTS FOR COMING.
I WOULDN'T ASK YOU TO GATHER ON SUCH SHORT NOTICE, EXCEPT...
...WE FACE A *CRISIS* OF PREVIOUSLY *UNHEARD OF* SCOPE AND MAGNITUDE PREVIOUSLY!
WHAT *IS* IT?
YES, MR. FAMOUS, WHAT'S IT *ABOUT?*
BRRR
GOOD GOSH, HE'S... *SHAKING* !!

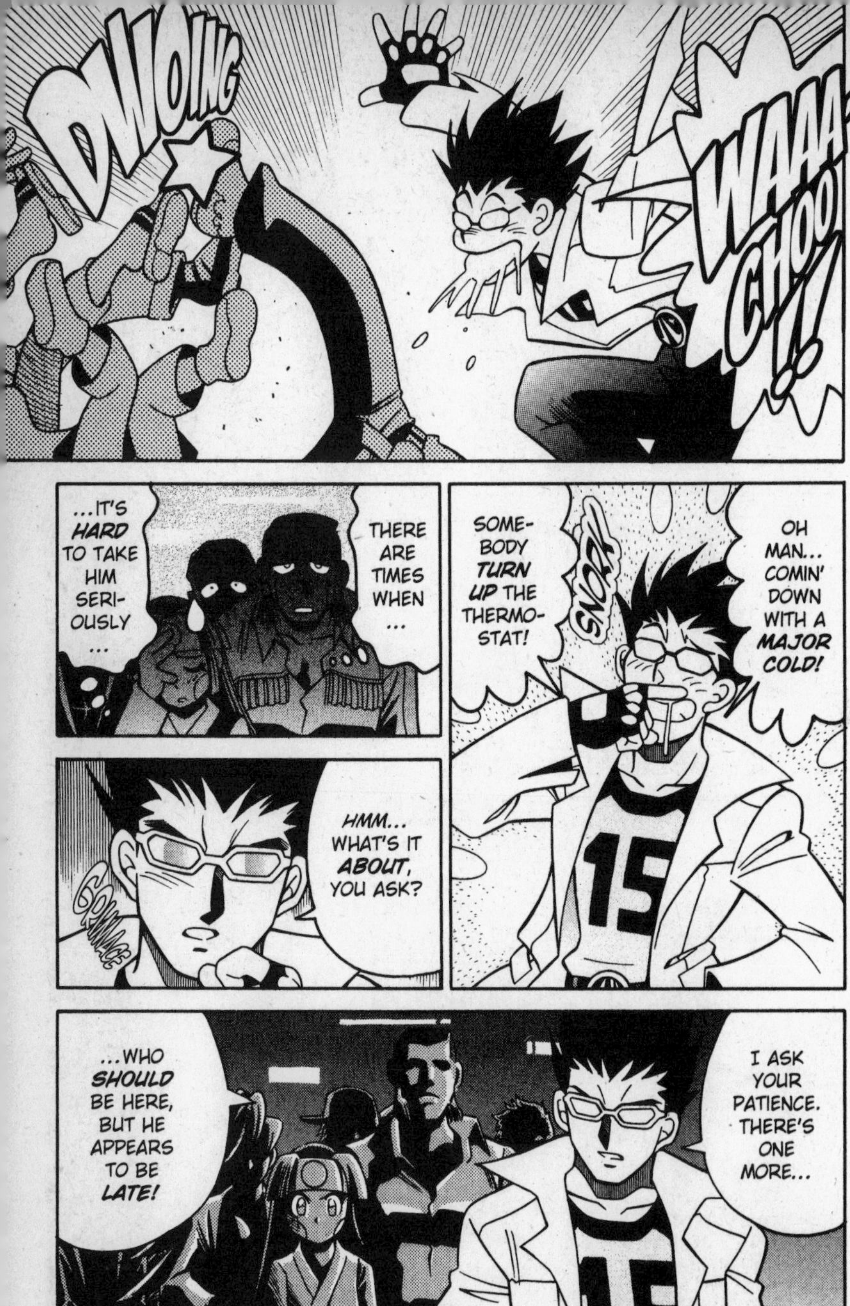
WAAA-CHOO!!
DWOING
OH MAN... COMIN' DOWN WITH A MAJOR COLD!
SNORT
SOMEBODY TURN UP THE THERMOSTAT!
THERE ARE TIMES WHEN...
...IT'S HARD TO TAKE HIM SERIOUSLY...
HMM... WHAT'S IT ABOUT, YOU ASK?
GRIMACE
I ASK YOUR PATIENCE. THERE'S ONE MORE...
...WHO SHOULD BE HERE, BUT HE APPEARS TO BE LATE!

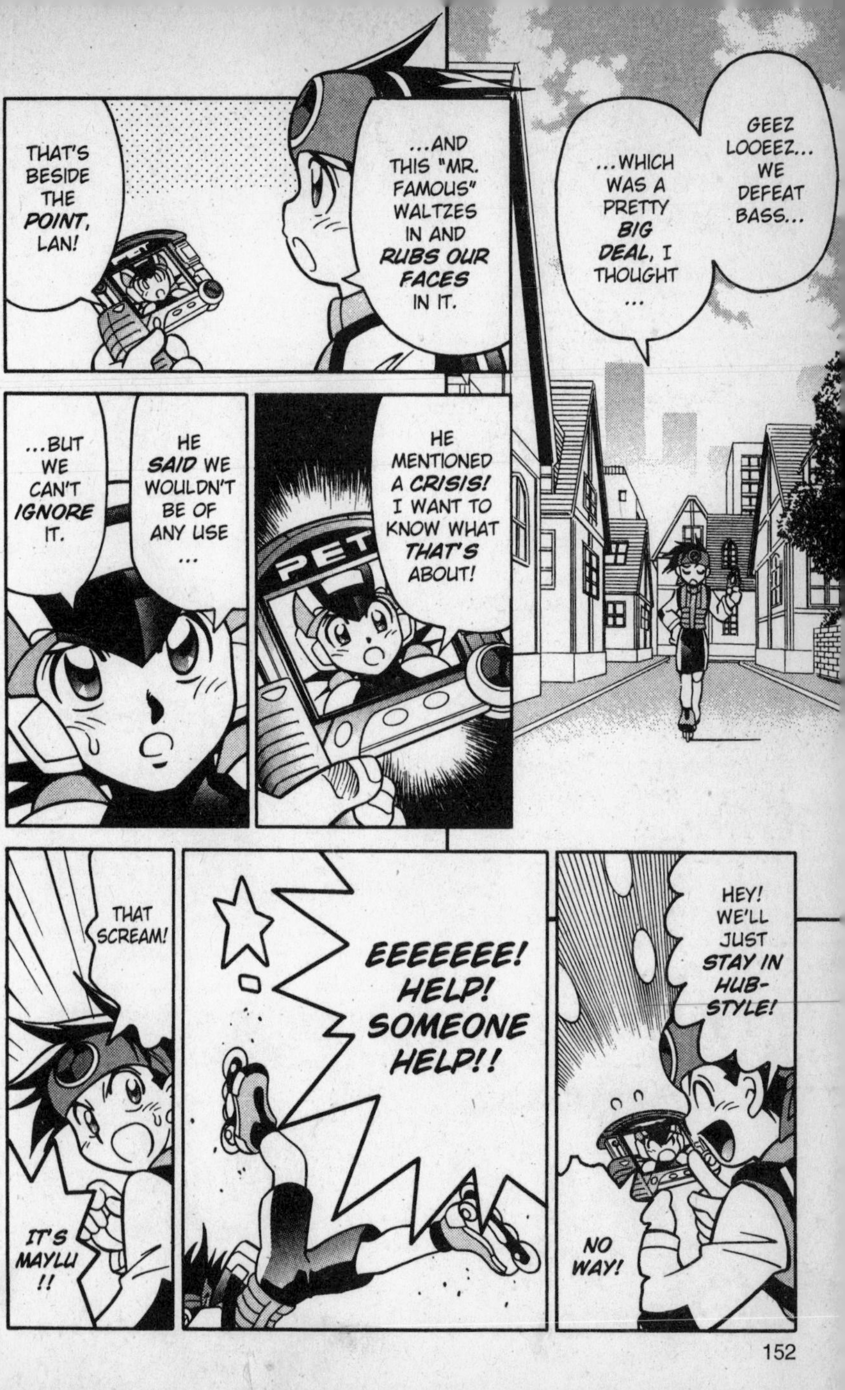
GEEZ LOOEEZ... WE DEFEAT BASS...
...WHICH WAS A PRETTY BIG DEAL, I THOUGHT...
...AND THIS "MR. FAMOUS" WALTZES IN AND RUBS OUR FACES IN IT.
THAT'S BESIDE THE POINT, LAN!
HE MENTIONED A CRISIS! I WANT TO KNOW WHAT THAT'S ABOUT!
PET
HE SAID WE WOULDN'T BE OF ANY USE...
...BUT WE CAN'T IGNORE IT.
HEY! WE'LL JUST STAY IN HUB-STYLE!
NO WAY!
EEEEEEE! HELP! SOMEONE HELP!!
THAT SCREAM!
IT'S MAYLU!!

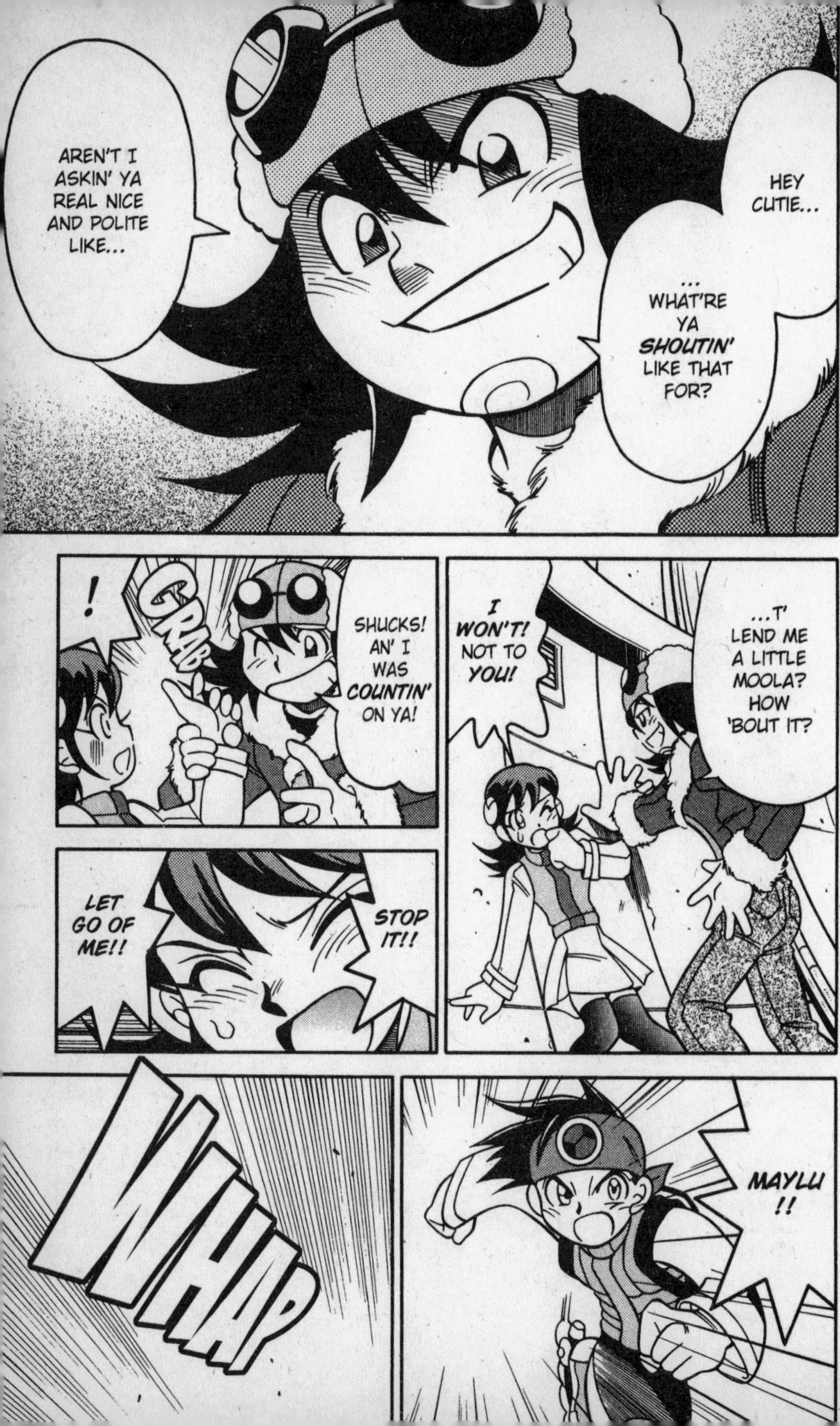
HEY CUTIE...
... WHAT'RE YA SHOUTIN' LIKE THAT FOR?
AREN'T I ASKIN' YA REAL NICE AND POLITE LIKE...
...T' LEND ME A LITTLE MOOLA? HOW 'BOUT IT?
I WON'T! NOT TO YOU!
SHUCKS! AN' I WAS COUNTIN' ON YA!
GRAB
!
STOP IT!!
LET GO OF ME!!
MAYLU !!
WHAP

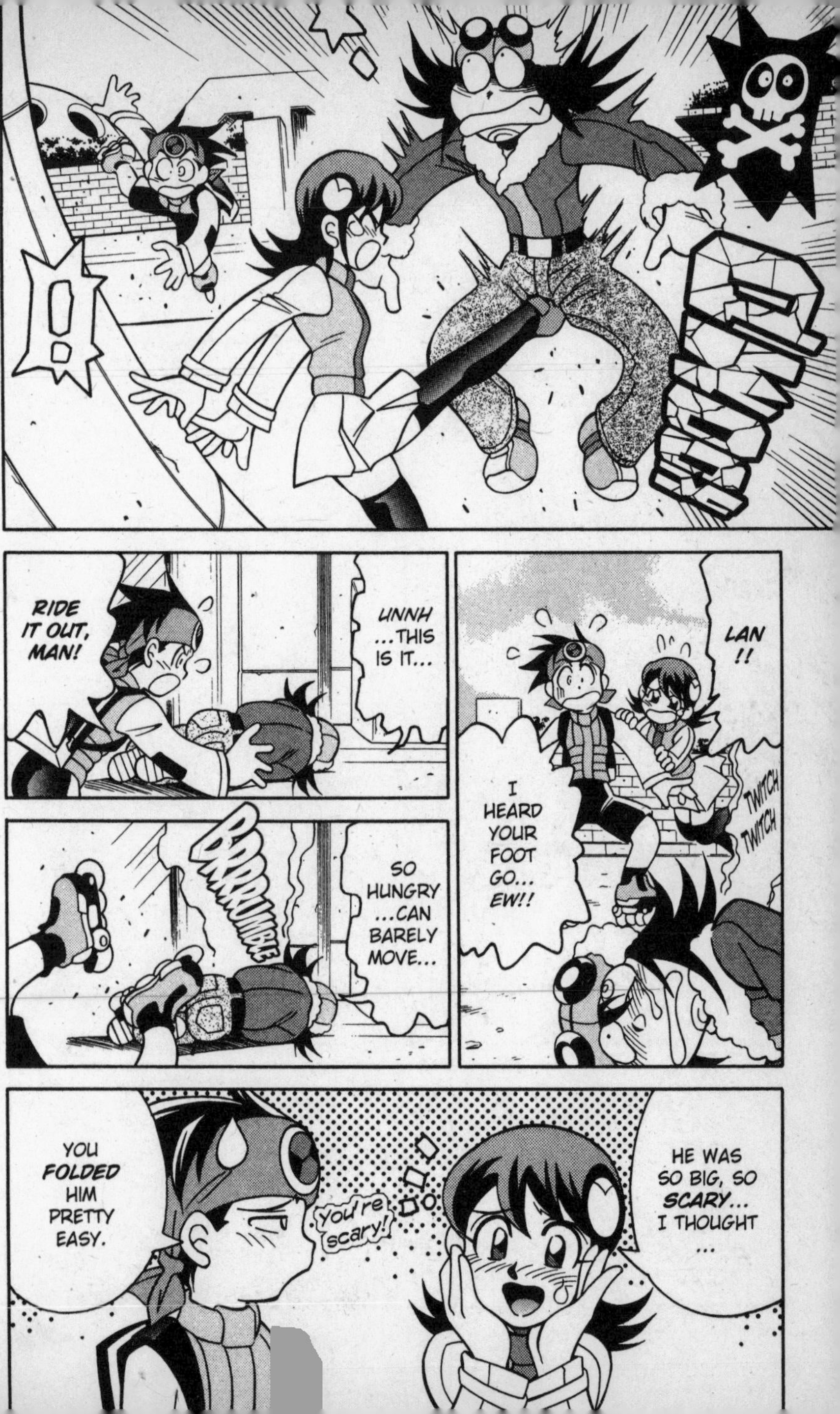

!
LAN !!
I HEARD YOUR FOOT GO... EW!!
TWITCH TWITCH
UNNH ...THIS IS IT...
RIDE IT OUT, MAN!
SO HUNGRY ...CAN BARELY MOVE...
HE WAS SO BIG, SO *SCARY*... I THOUGHT ...
you're scary!
YOU ***FOLDED*** HIM PRETTY EASY.

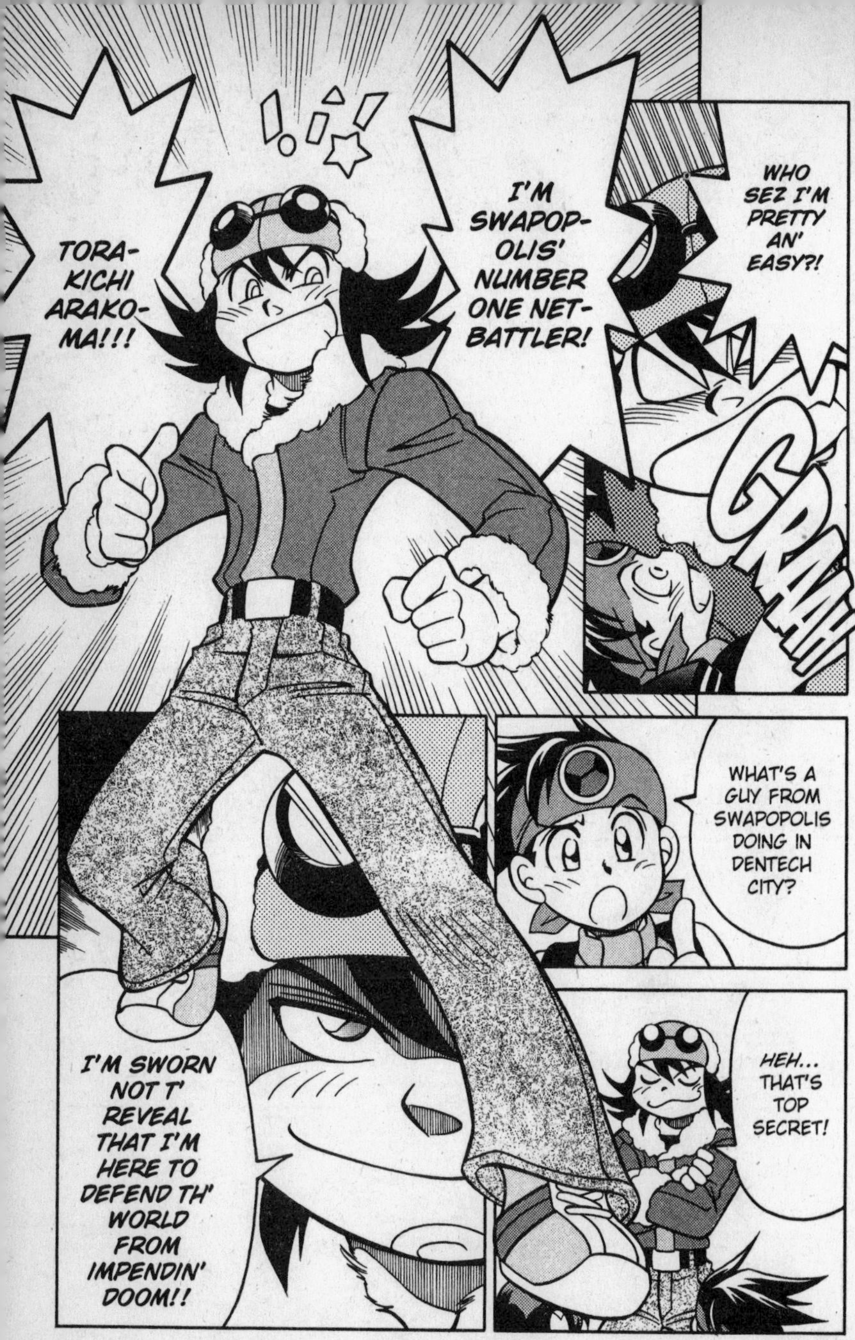
WHO SEZ I'M PRETTY AN' EASY?!
GRAAH
I'M SWAPOPOLIS' NUMBER ONE NET-BATTLER!
TORAKICHI ARAKOMA!!!
WHAT'S A GUY FROM SWAPOPOLIS DOING IN DENTECH CITY?
HEH... THAT'S TOP SECRET!
I'M SWORN NOT T' REVEAL THAT I'M HERE TO DEFEND TH' WORLD FROM IMPENDIN' DOOM!!

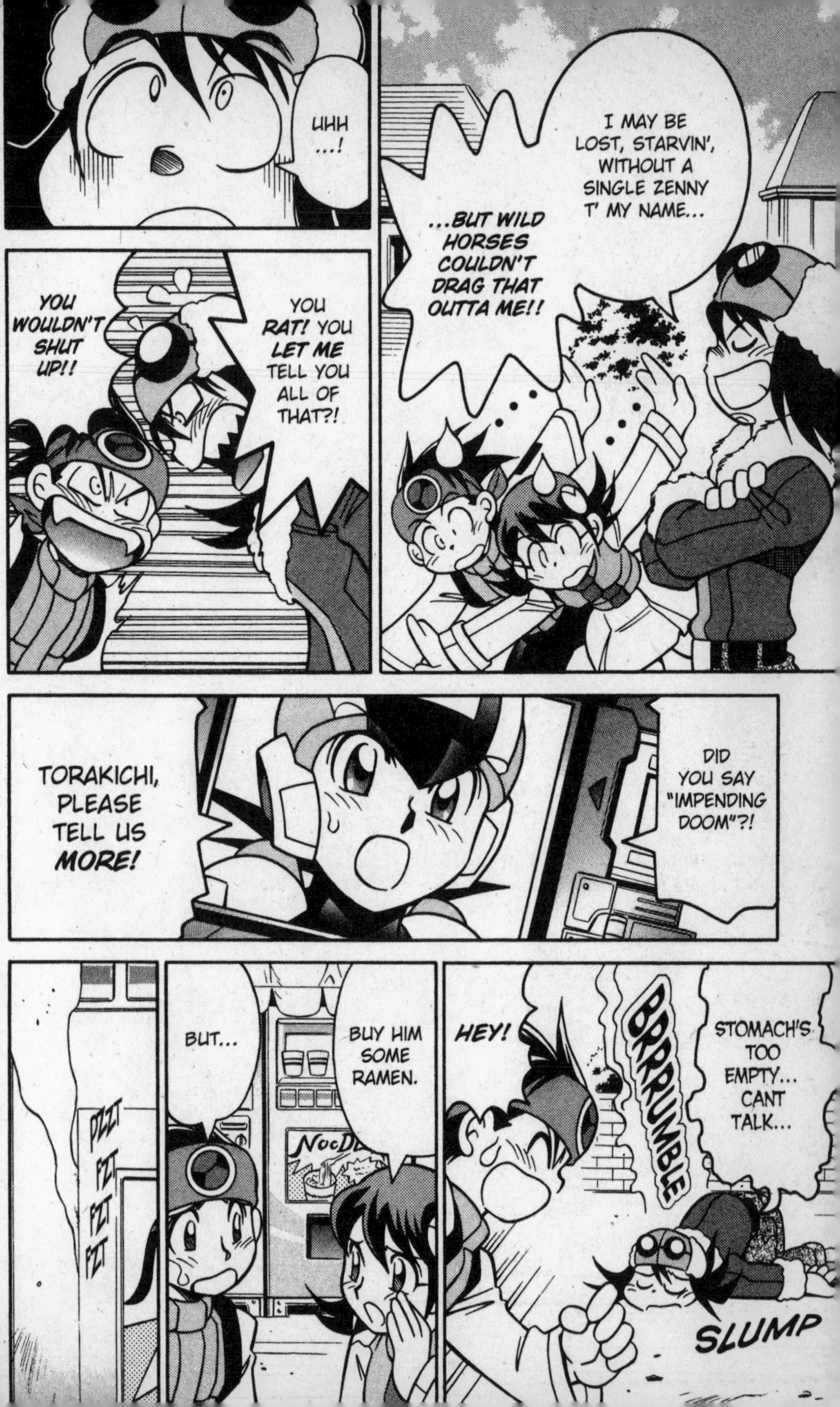

I MAY BE LOST, STARVIN', WITHOUT A SINGLE ZENNY T' MY NAME...
...BUT WILD HORSES COULDN'T DRAG THAT OUTTA ME!!
UHH ...!
YOU RAT! YOU LET ME TELL YOU ALL OF THAT?!
YOU WOULDN'T SHUT UP!!
DID YOU SAY "IMPENDING DOOM"?!
TORAKICHI, PLEASE TELL US MORE!
STOMACH'S TOO EMPTY... CANT TALK...
BRRRUMBLE
HEY!
SLUMP
BUY HIM SOME RAMEN.
BUT...
PZZT FZT FZT FZT

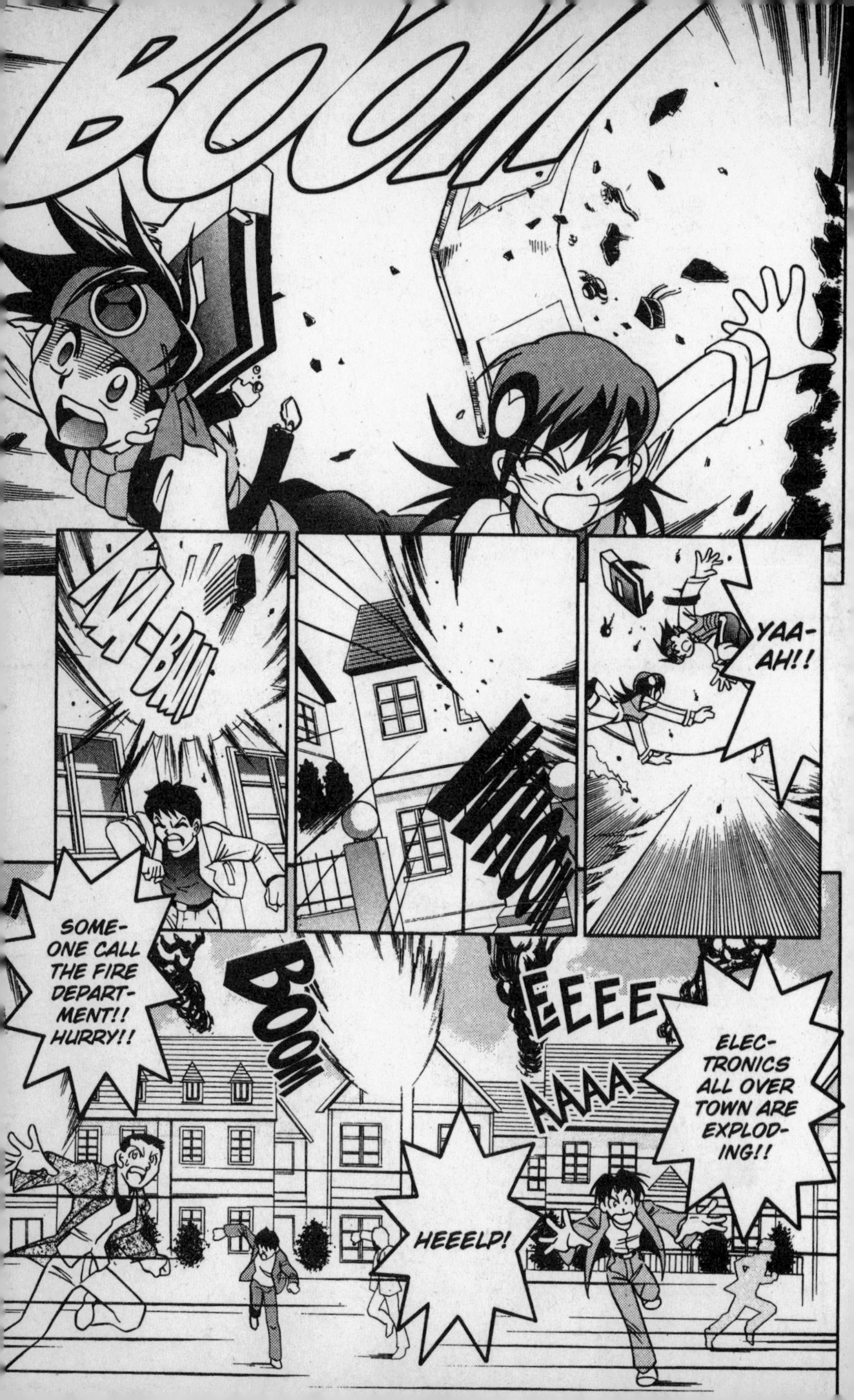
YAA-AH!!
ELEC-TRONICS ALL OVER TOWN ARE EXPLOD-ING!!
EEEE AAAA
HEEELP!
BOOOM
SOME-ONE CALL THE FIRE DEPART-MENT!! HURRY!!

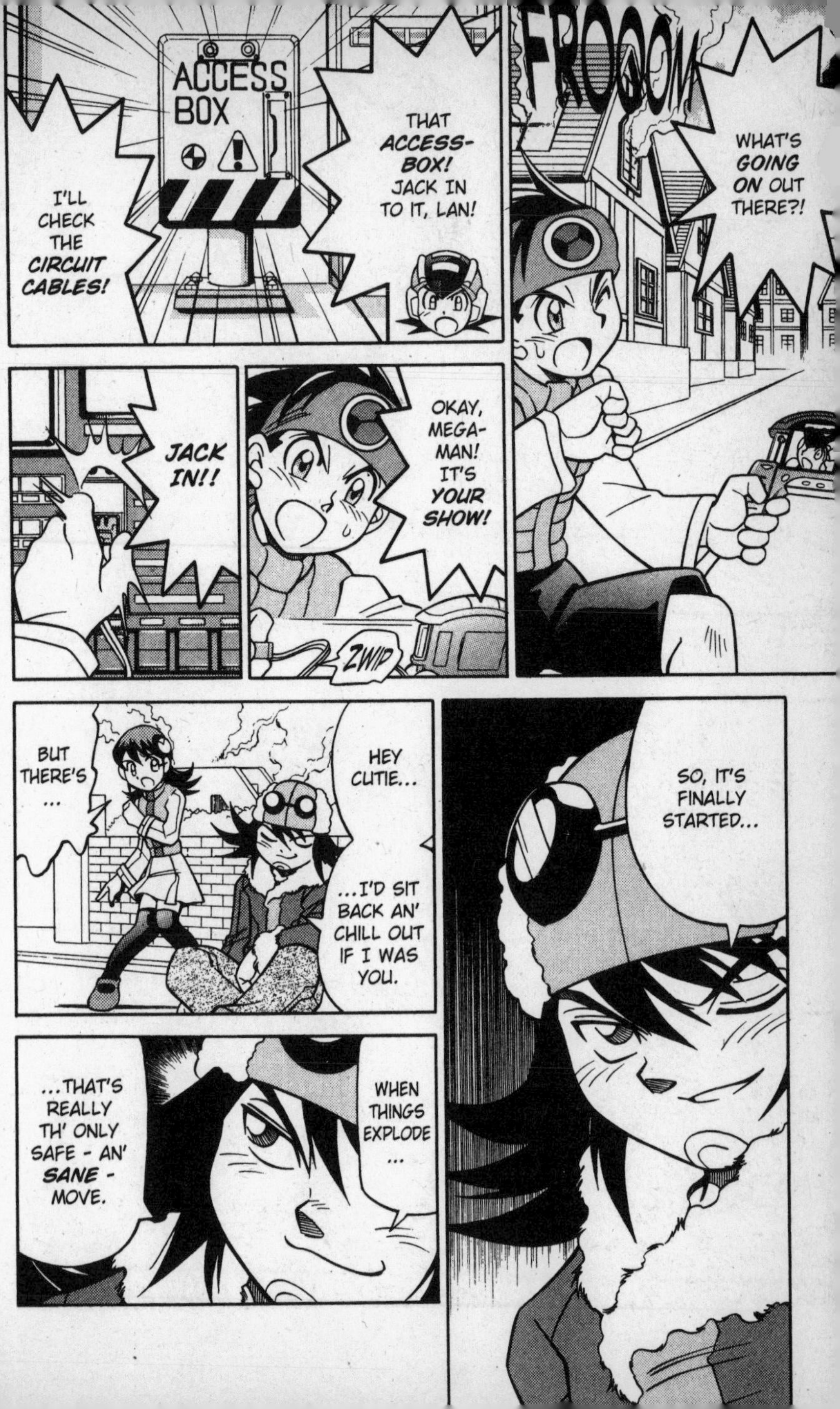
FROOOM
WHAT'S GOING ON OUT THERE?!
THAT ACCESS-BOX! JACK IN TO IT, LAN!
ACCESS BOX
I'LL CHECK THE CIRCUIT CABLES!
OKAY, MEGA-MAN! IT'S YOUR SHOW!
ZWIP
JACK IN!!
SO, IT'S FINALLY STARTED...
HEY CUTIE...
BUT THERE'S ...
...I'D SIT BACK AN' CHILL OUT IF I WAS YOU.
WHEN THINGS EXPLODE ...
...THAT'S REALLY TH' ONLY SAFE - AN' SANE - MOVE.

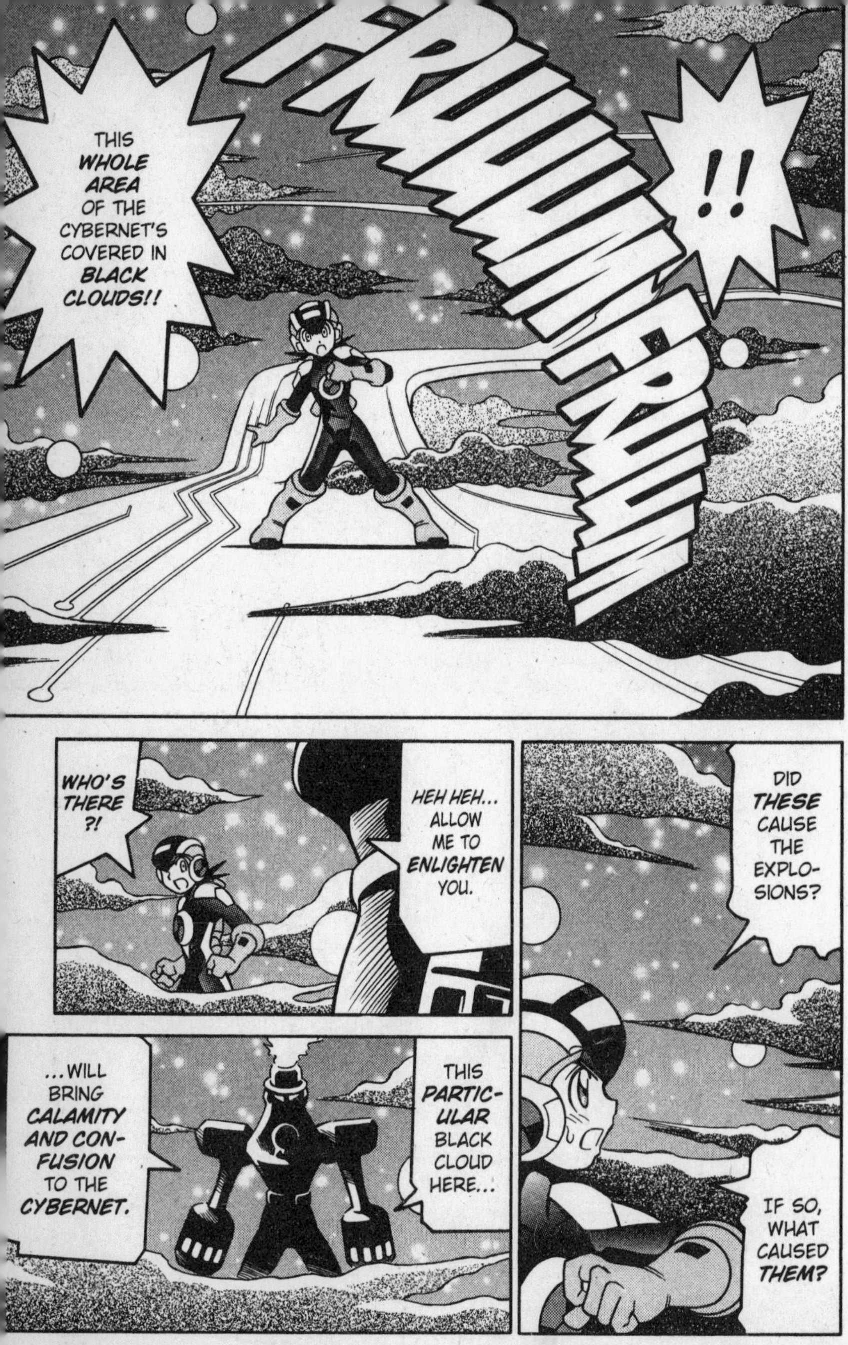
FRUUMM-FRUUMM
!!
THIS WHOLE AREA OF THE CYBERNET'S COVERED IN BLACK CLOUDS!!
DID THESE CAUSE THE EXPLO-SIONS?
IF SO, WHAT CAUSED THEM?
WHO'S THERE ?!
HEH HEH... ALLOW ME TO ENLIGHTEN YOU.
THIS PARTIC-ULAR BLACK CLOUD HERE...
...WILL BRING CALAMITY AND CON-FUSION TO THE CYBERNET.

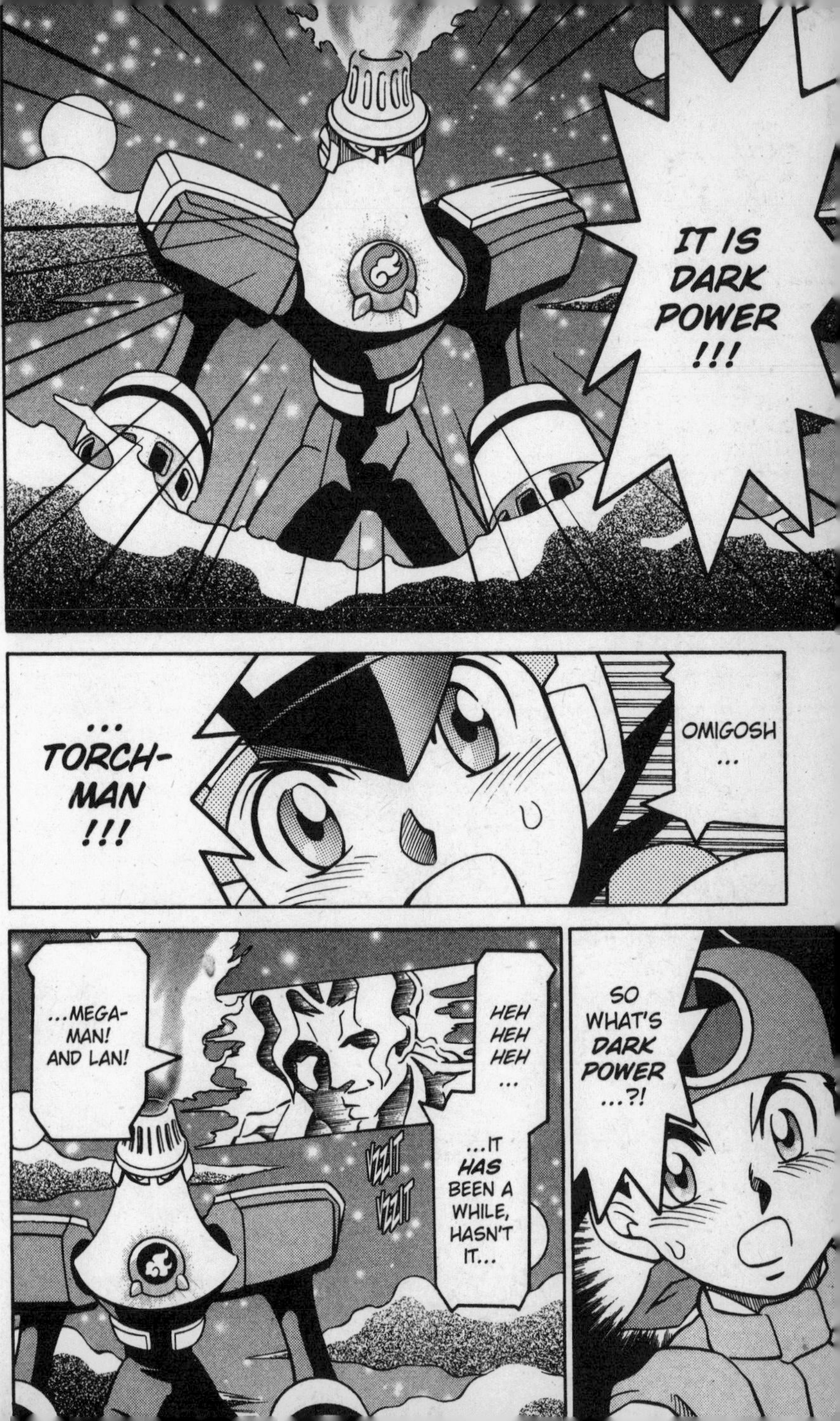
IT IS DARK POWER !!!
OMIGOSH ...
... TORCH-MAN !!!
SO WHAT'S DARK POWER ...?!
HEH HEH HEH ...
...MEGA-MAN! AND LAN!
...IT HAS BEEN A WHILE, HASN'T IT...
VZZIT VZZIT

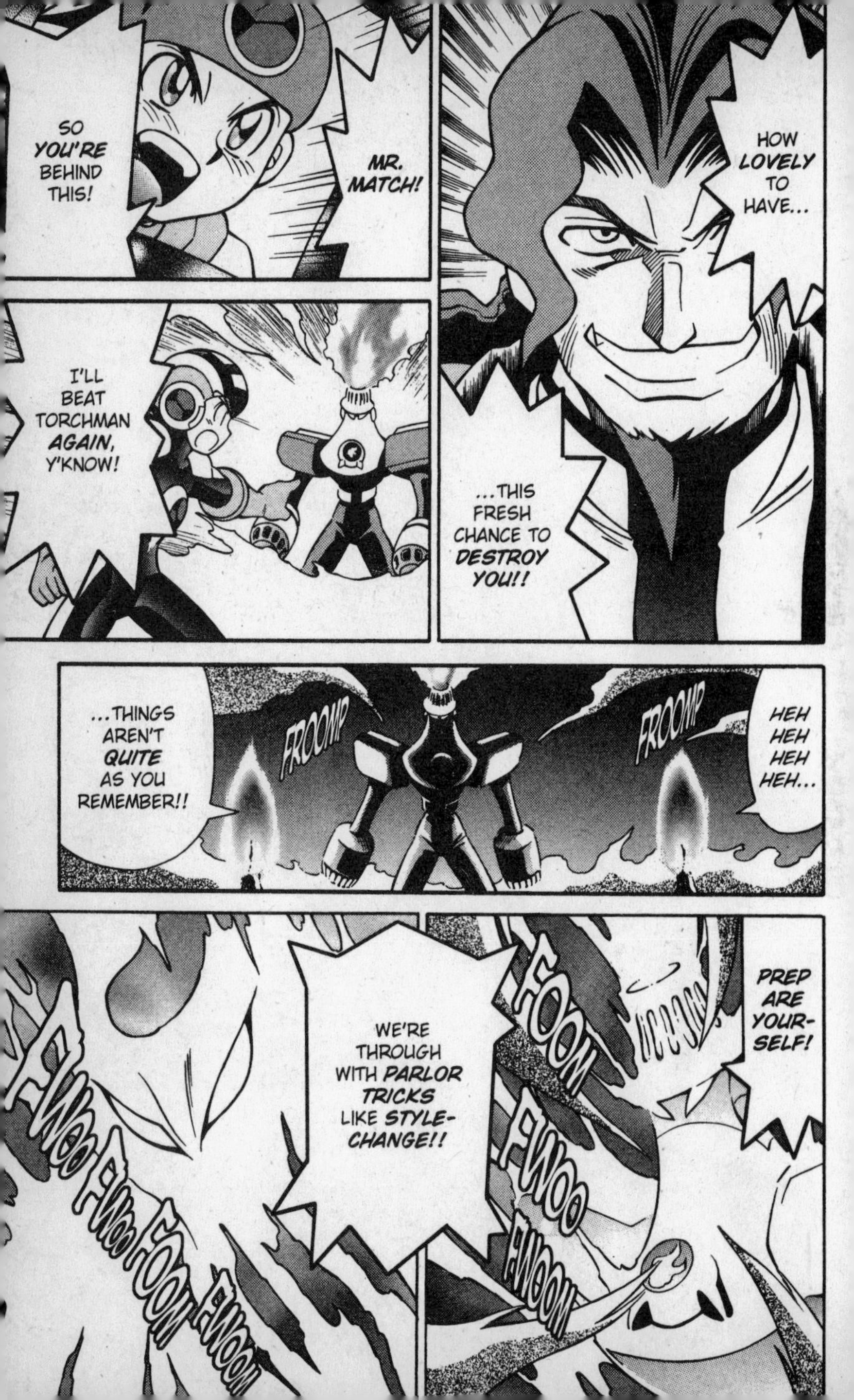
HOW LOVELY TO HAVE...
...THIS FRESH CHANCE TO DESTROY YOU!!
MR. MATCH!
SO YOU'RE BEHIND THIS!
I'LL BEAT TORCHMAN AGAIN, Y'KNOW!
HEH HEH HEH HEH...
FROOMP
FROOMP
...THINGS AREN'T QUITE AS YOU REMEMBER!!
PREP ARE YOURSELF!
FOOM
FWOO
FWOOOM
WE'RE THROUGH WITH PARLOR TRICKS LIKE STYLE-CHANGE!!
FWOO FWOO FOOM FWOOM

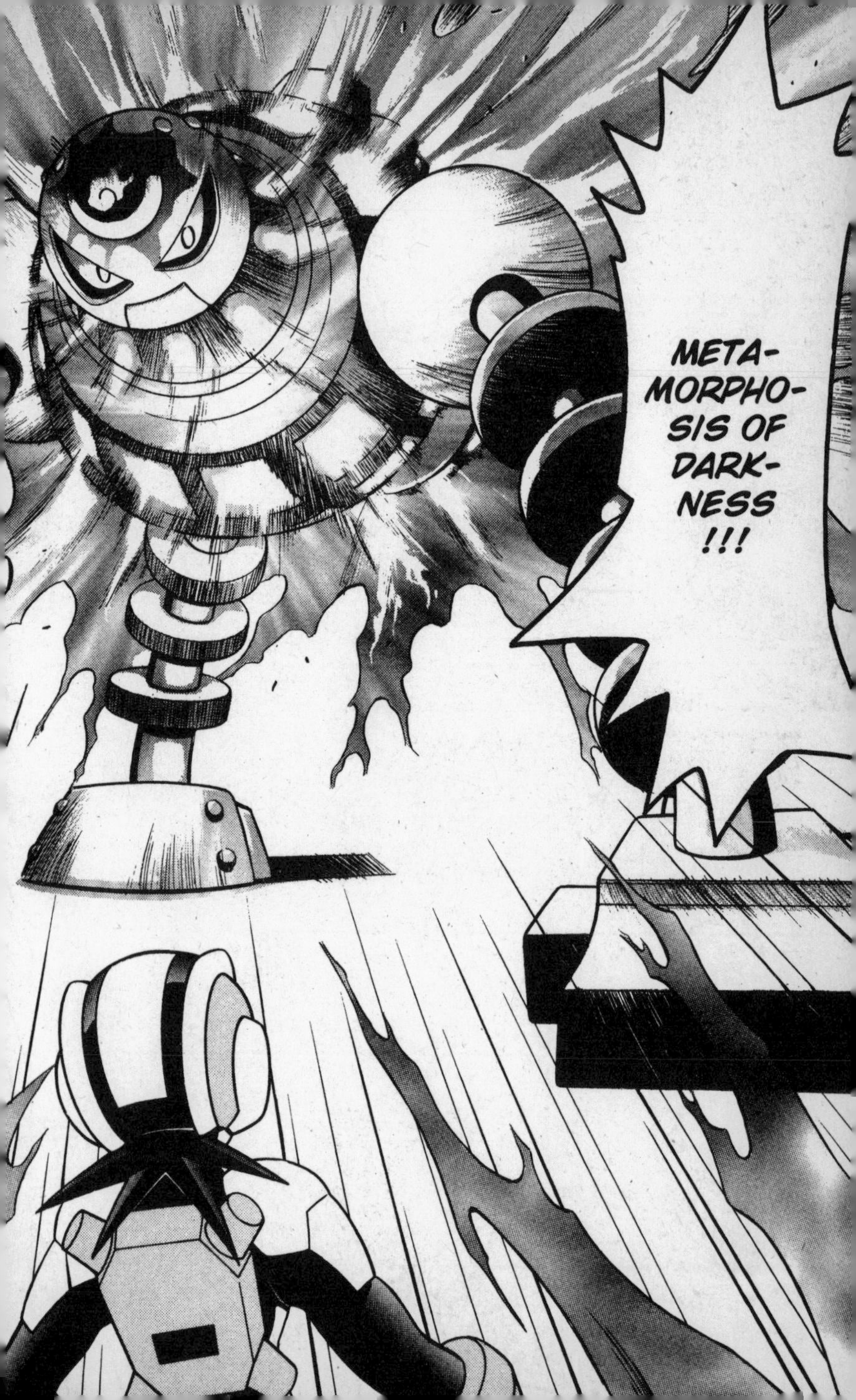
META-MORPHO-SIS OF DARK-NESS !!!

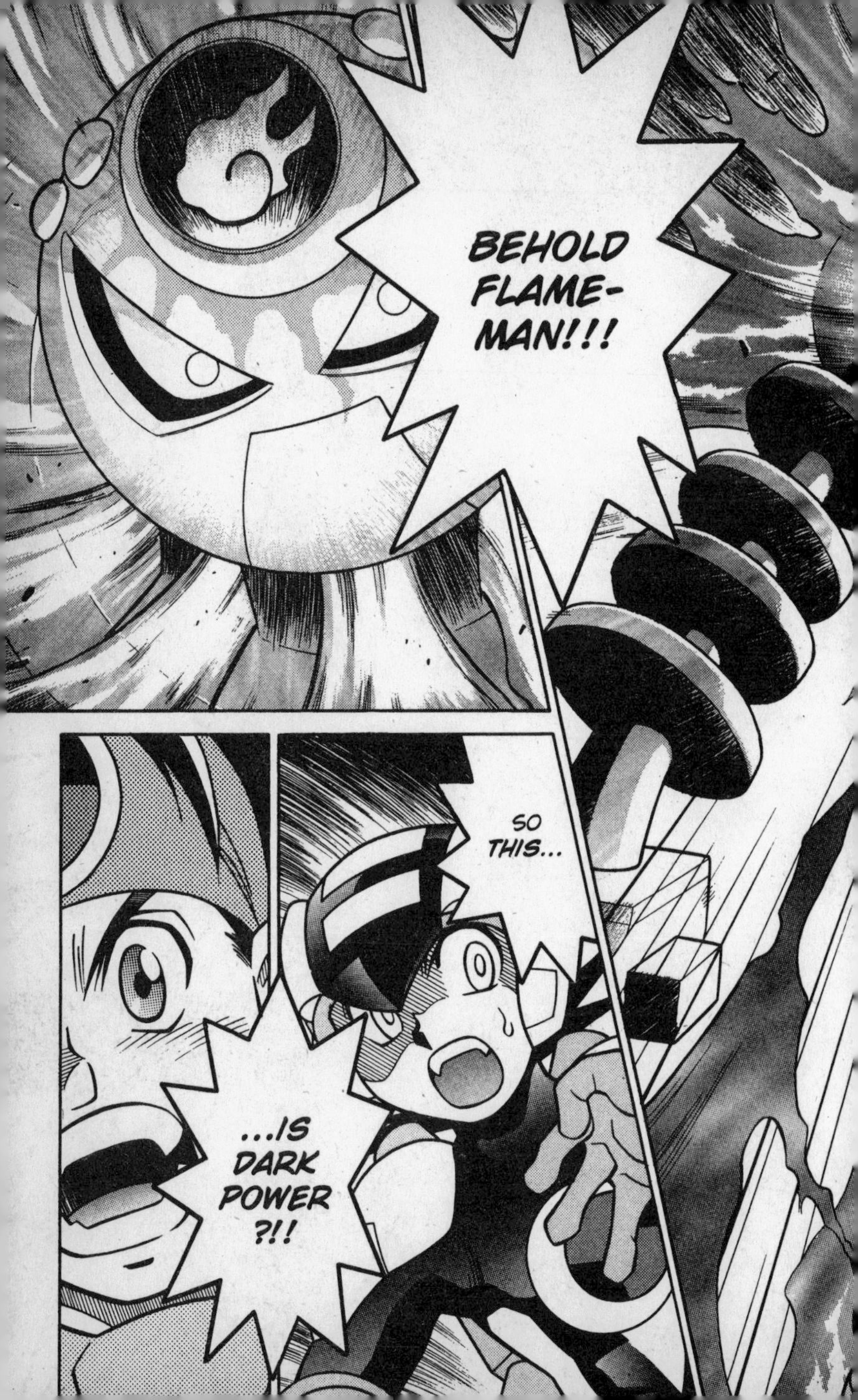
BEHOLD FLAME-MAN!!!
SO THIS...
...IS DARK POWER ?!!

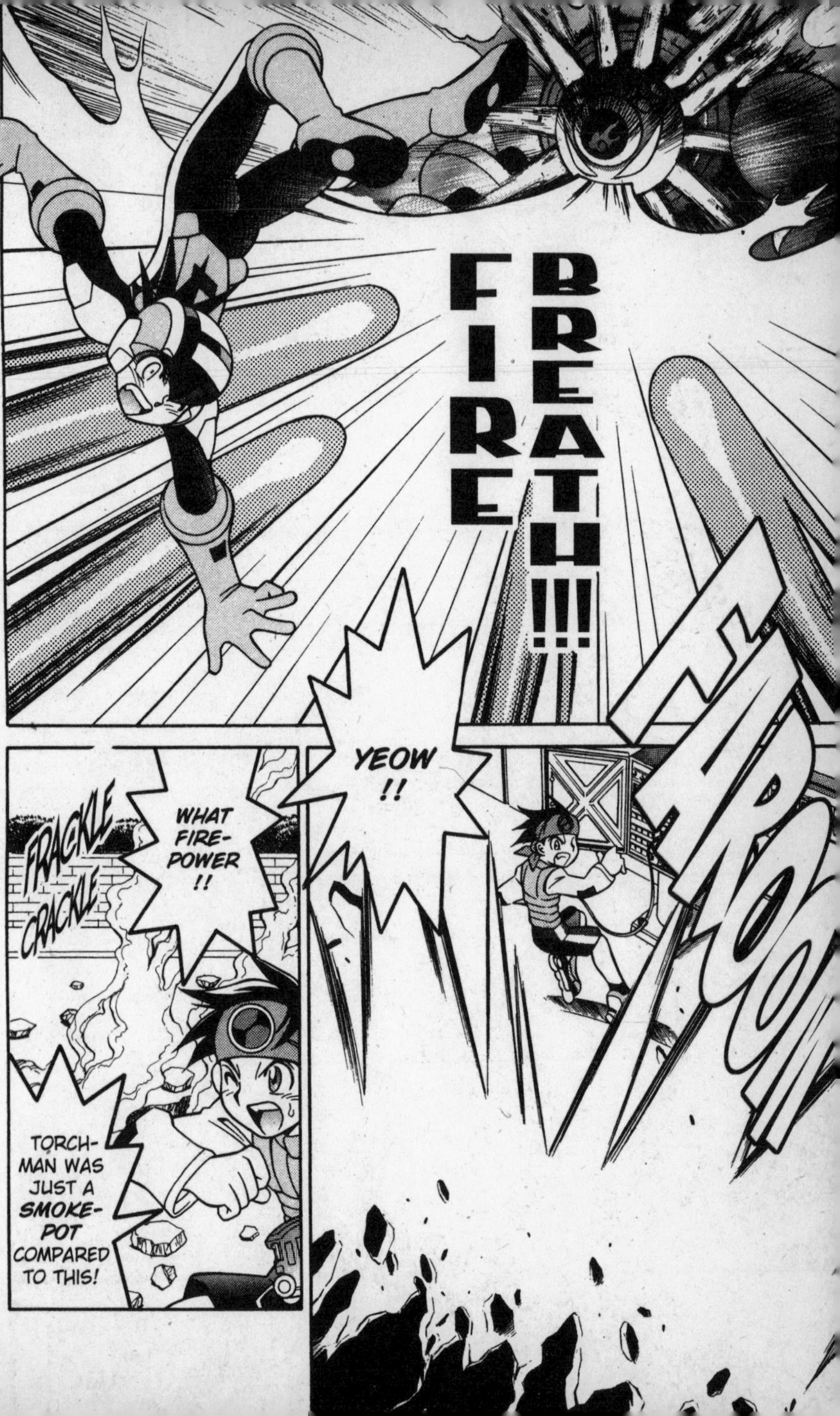
FIRE BREATH!!!
YEOW!!
WHAT FIRE-POWER!!
FRACKLE CRACKLE
TORCH-MAN WAS JUST A SMOKE-POT COMPARED TO THIS!

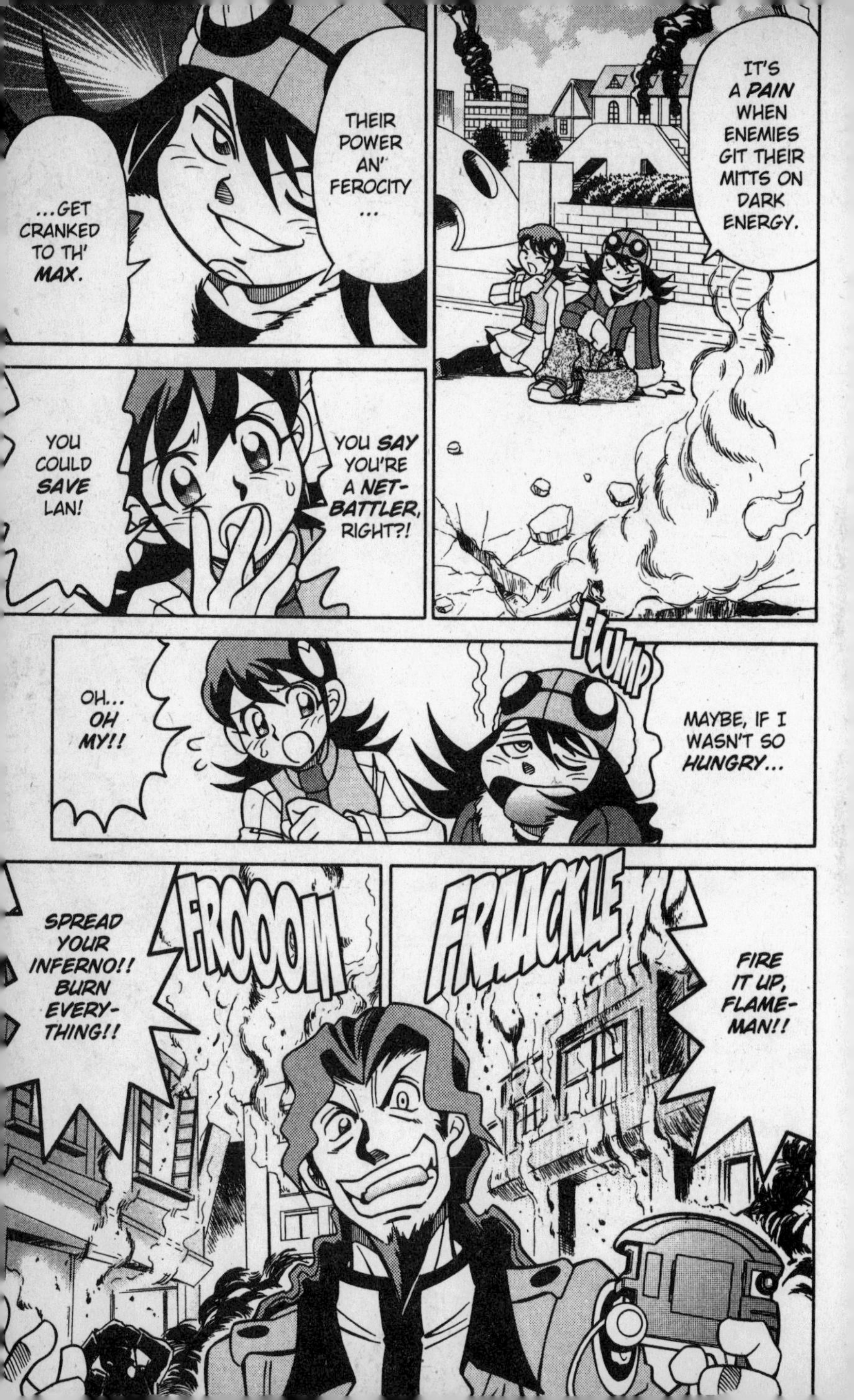
IT'S A PAIN WHEN ENEMIES GIT THEIR MITTS ON DARK ENERGY.
THEIR POWER AN' FEROCITY...
...GET CRANKED TO TH' MAX.
YOU SAY YOU'RE A NET-BATTLER, RIGHT?!
YOU COULD SAVE LAN!
FLUMP
MAYBE, IF I WASN'T SO HUNGRY...
OH... OH MY!!
FRAACKLE
FIRE IT UP, FLAME-MAN!!
FROOOM
SPREAD YOUR INFERNO!! BURN EVERY-THING!!

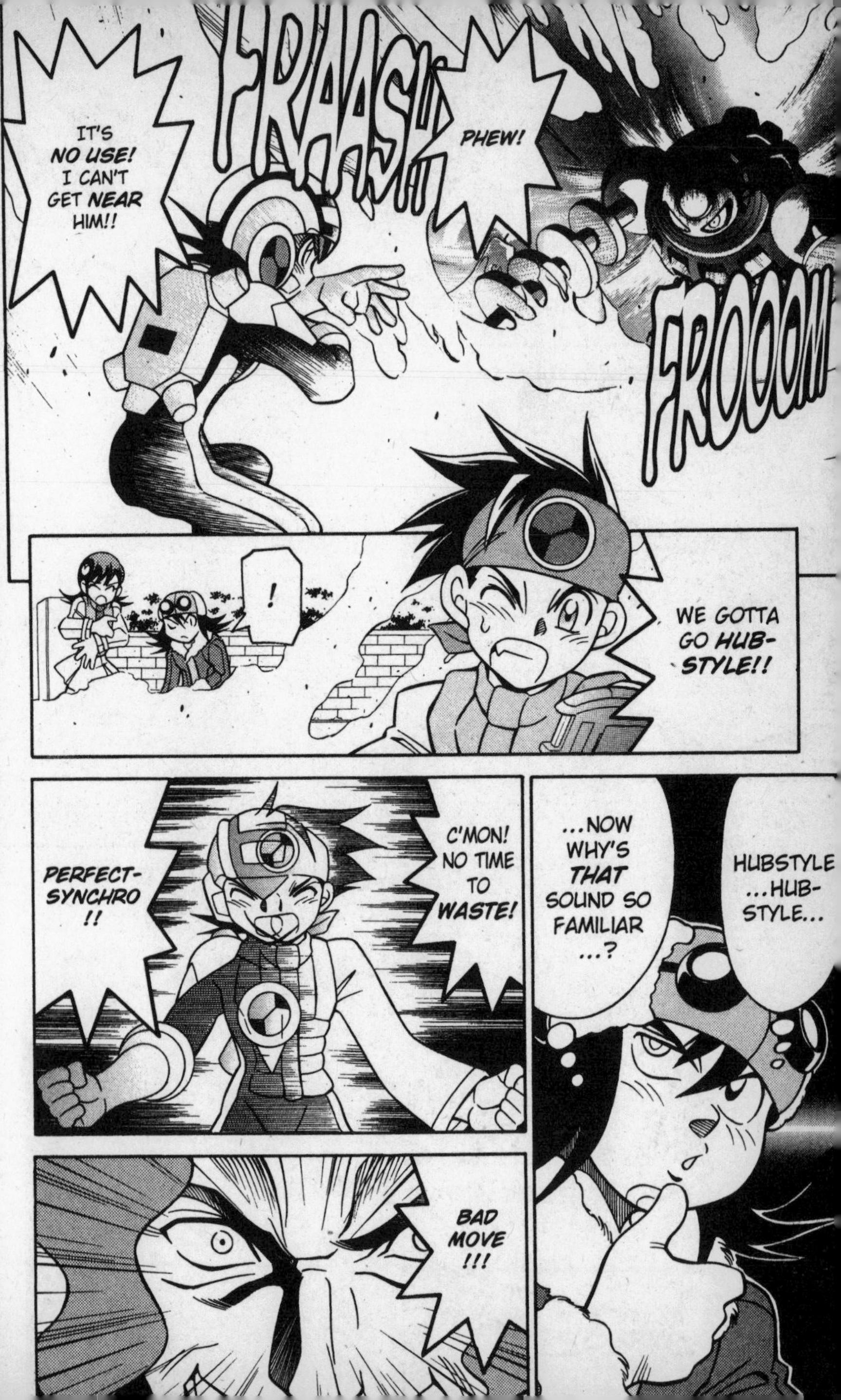
FRAASH
PHEW!
IT'S NO USE! I CAN'T GET NEAR HIM!!
FROOOM
WE GOTTA GO HUB-STYLE!!
!
HUBSTYLE ...HUB-STYLE...
...NOW WHY'S THAT SOUND SO FAMILIAR ...?
C'MON! NO TIME TO WASTE!
PERFECT-SYNCHRO !!
BAD MOVE !!!

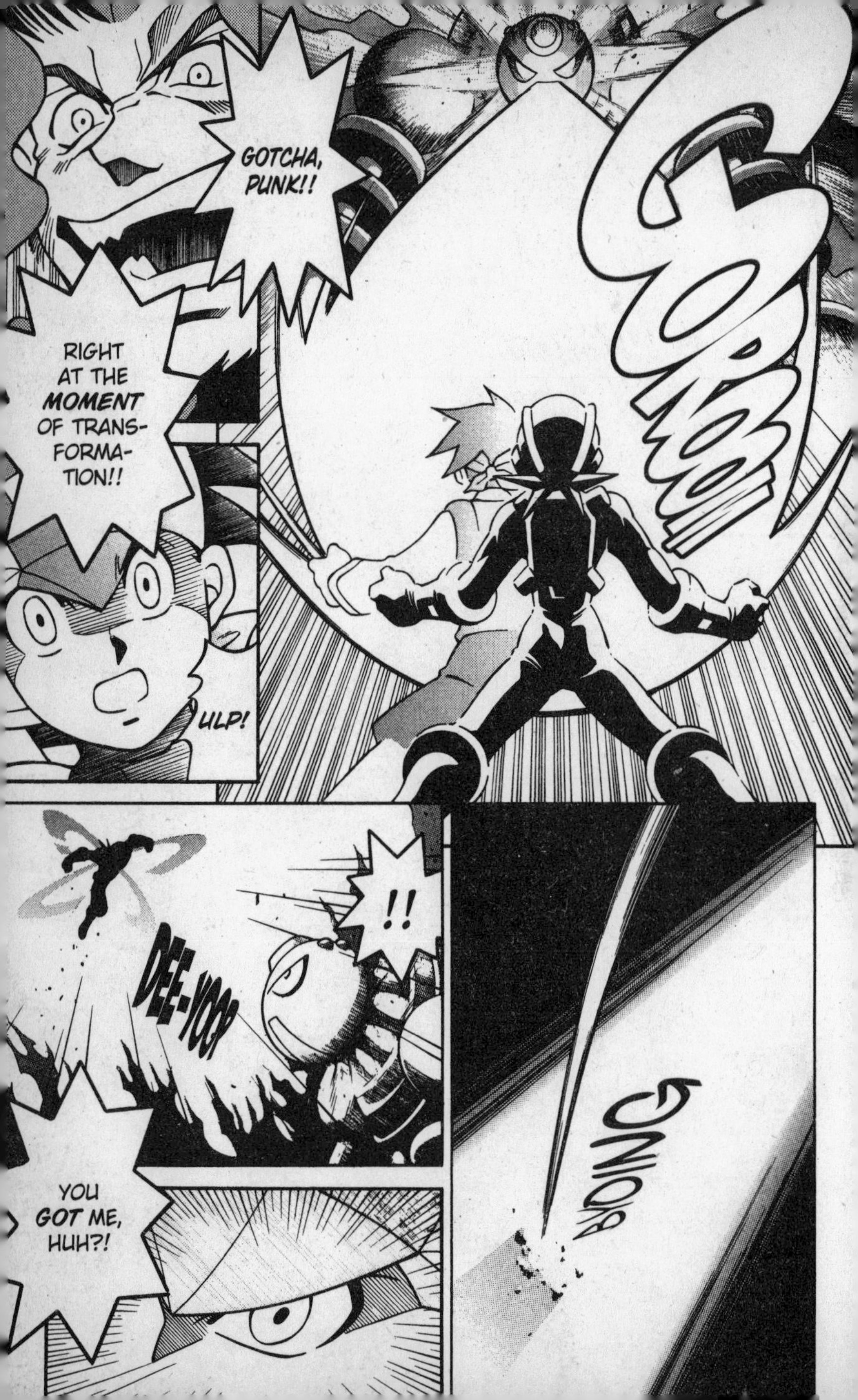
GOTCHA, PUNK!!
RIGHT AT THE MOMENT OF TRANS-FORMATION!!
ULP!
BOING
!!
DEE-YOOP
YOU GOT ME, HUH?!

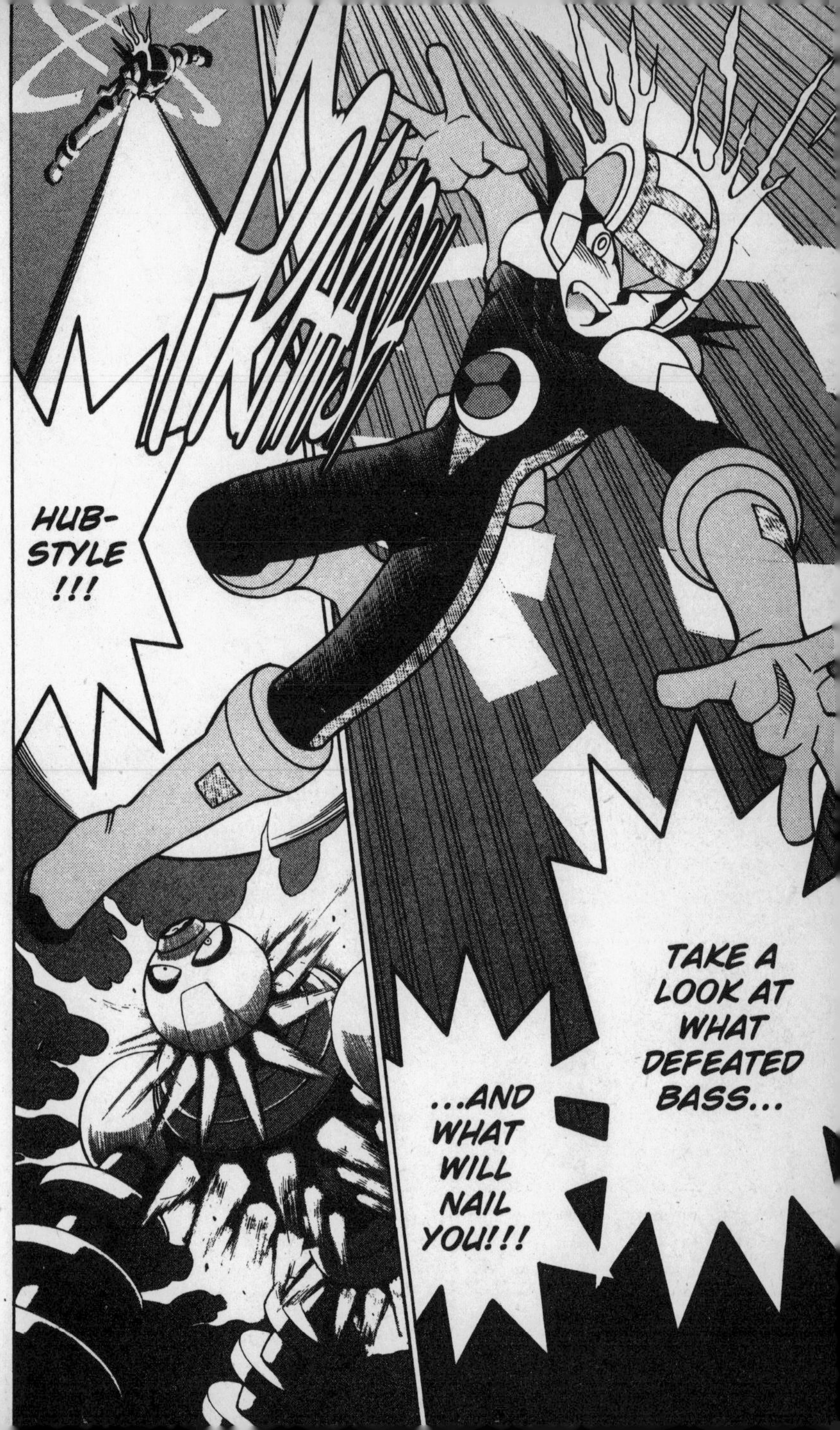
TAKE A LOOK AT WHAT DEFEATED BASS...
...AND WHAT WILL NAIL YOU!!!
HUB-STYLE!!!

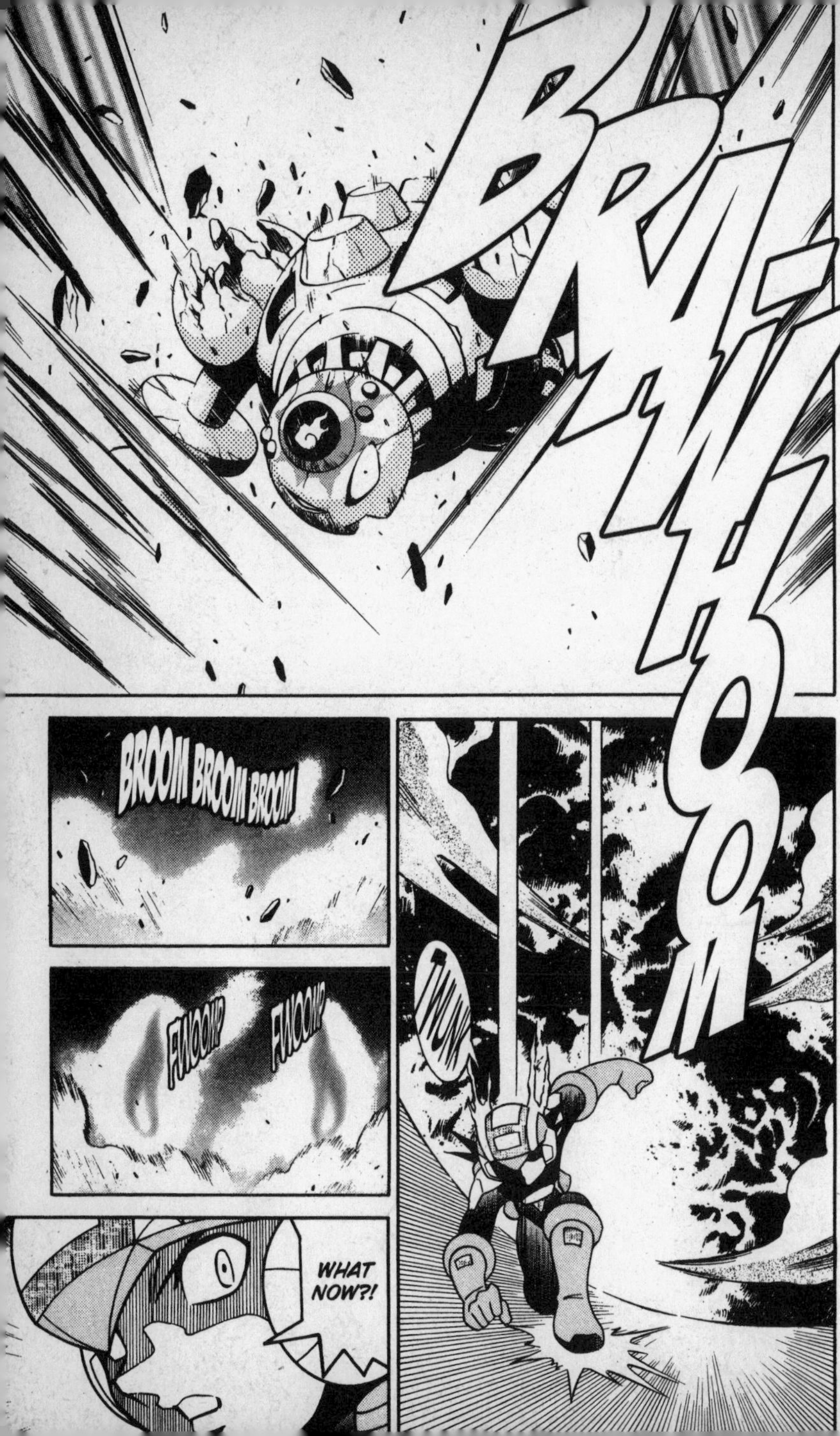
BRA-KA-BOOM
TWUNK
BROOM BROOM BROOM
FWOOMP
FWOOMP
WHAT NOW?!

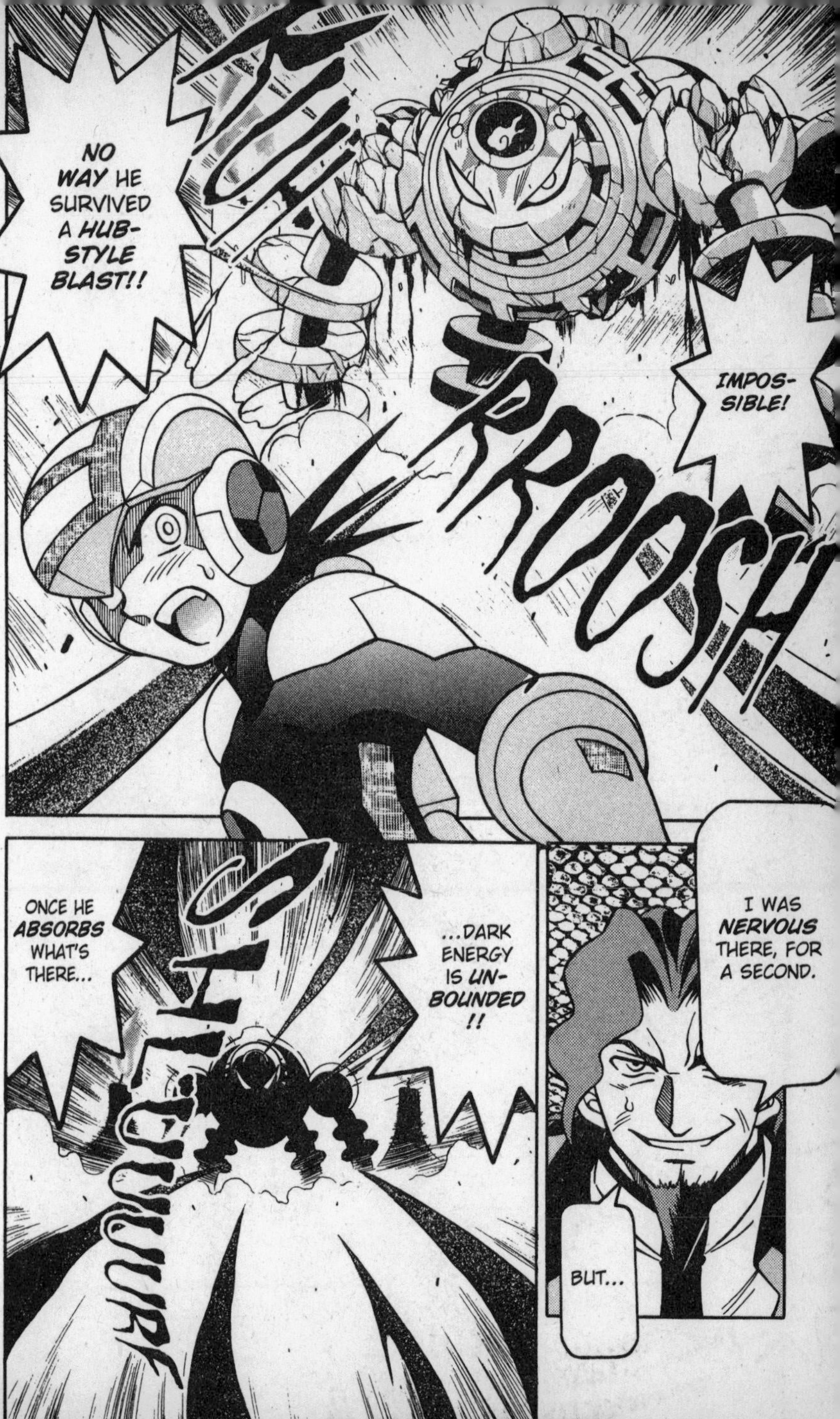
IMPOS-SIBLE!
NO WAY HE SURVIVED A HUB-STYLE BLAST!!
I WAS NERVOUS THERE, FOR A SECOND.
BUT...
ONCE HE ABSORBS WHAT'S THERE...
...DARK ENERGY IS UN-BOUNDED!!

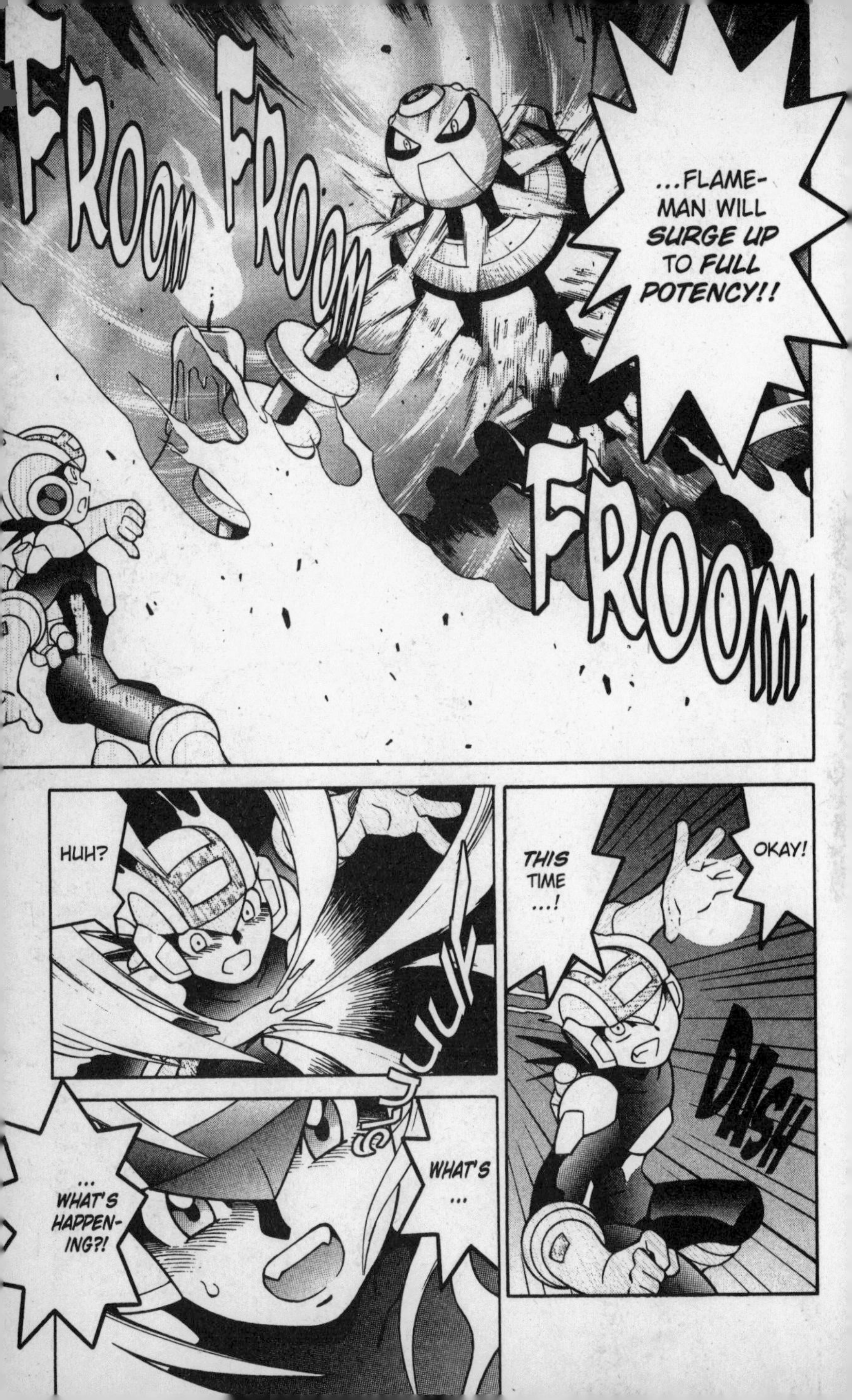
FROOM FROOM
...FLAME-MAN WILL SURGE UP TO FULL POTENCY!!
FROOM
OKAY!
THIS TIME ...!
DASH
HUH?
WHAT'S ...
... WHAT'S HAPPEN-ING?!

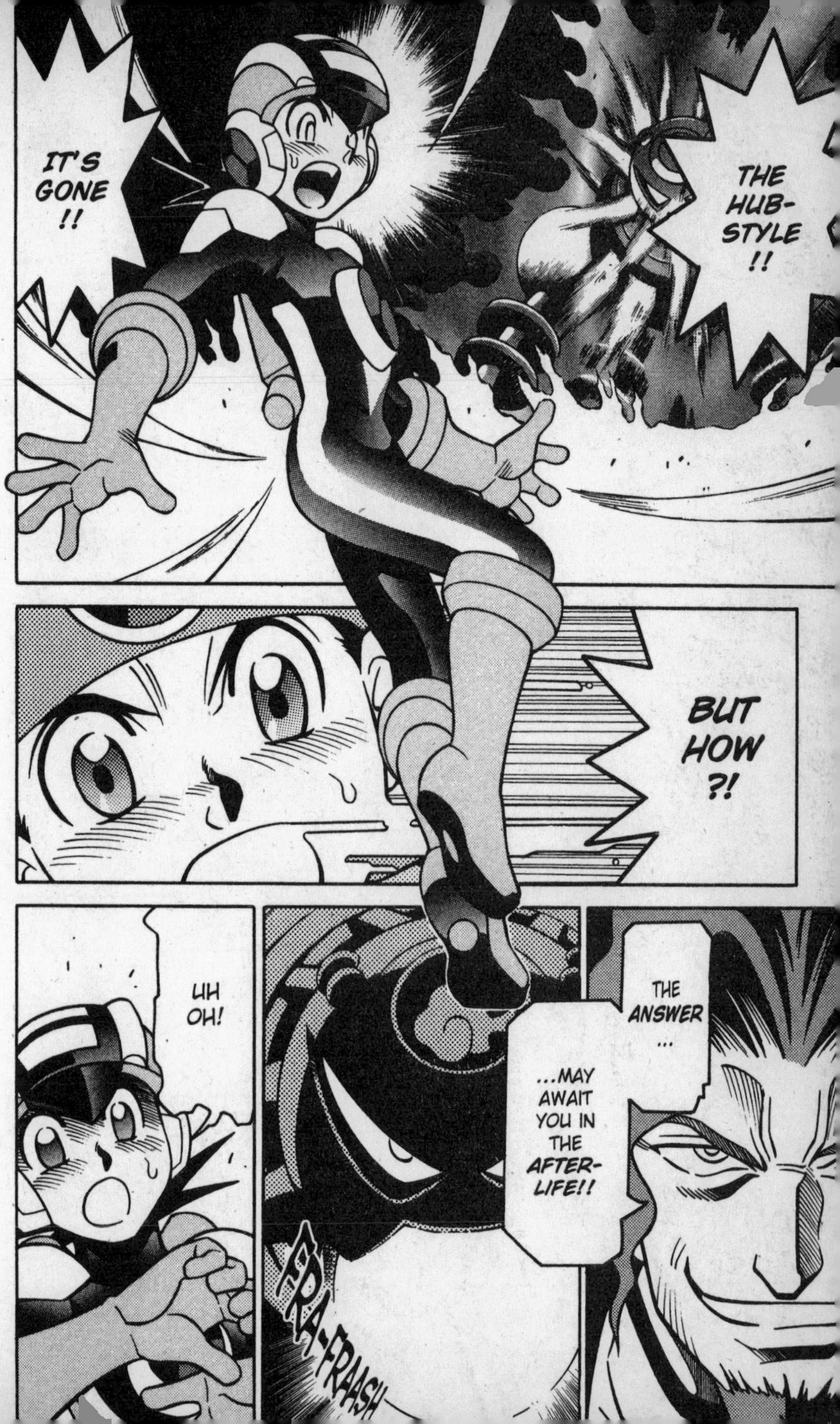
THE HUB-STYLE!!
IT'S GONE!!
BUT HOW?!
THE ANSWER...
...MAY AWAIT YOU IN THE AFTER-LIFE!!
FRA-FRAASH
UH OH!

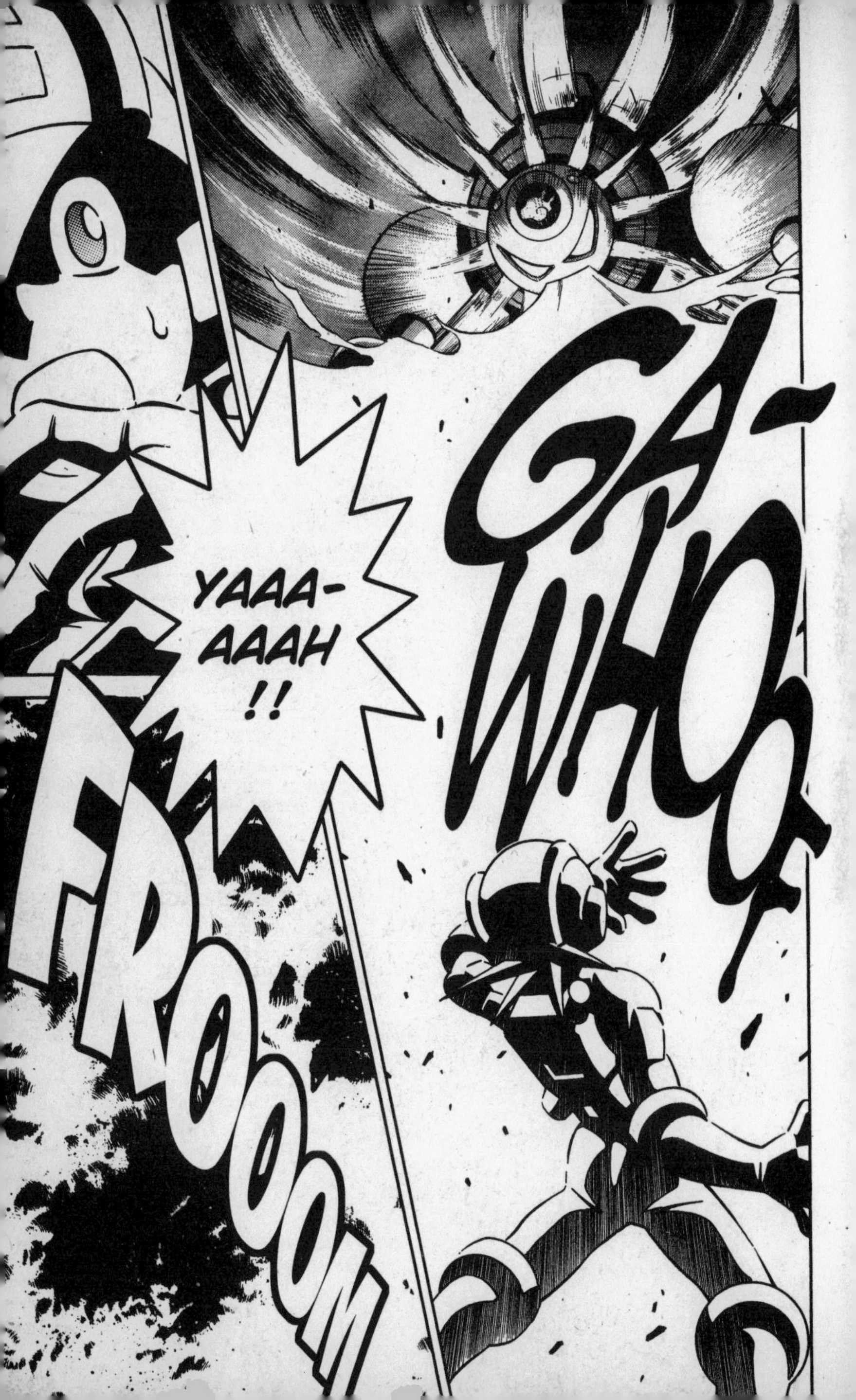
GA-WHOO!
YAAA-AAAH!!
FROOOOOM

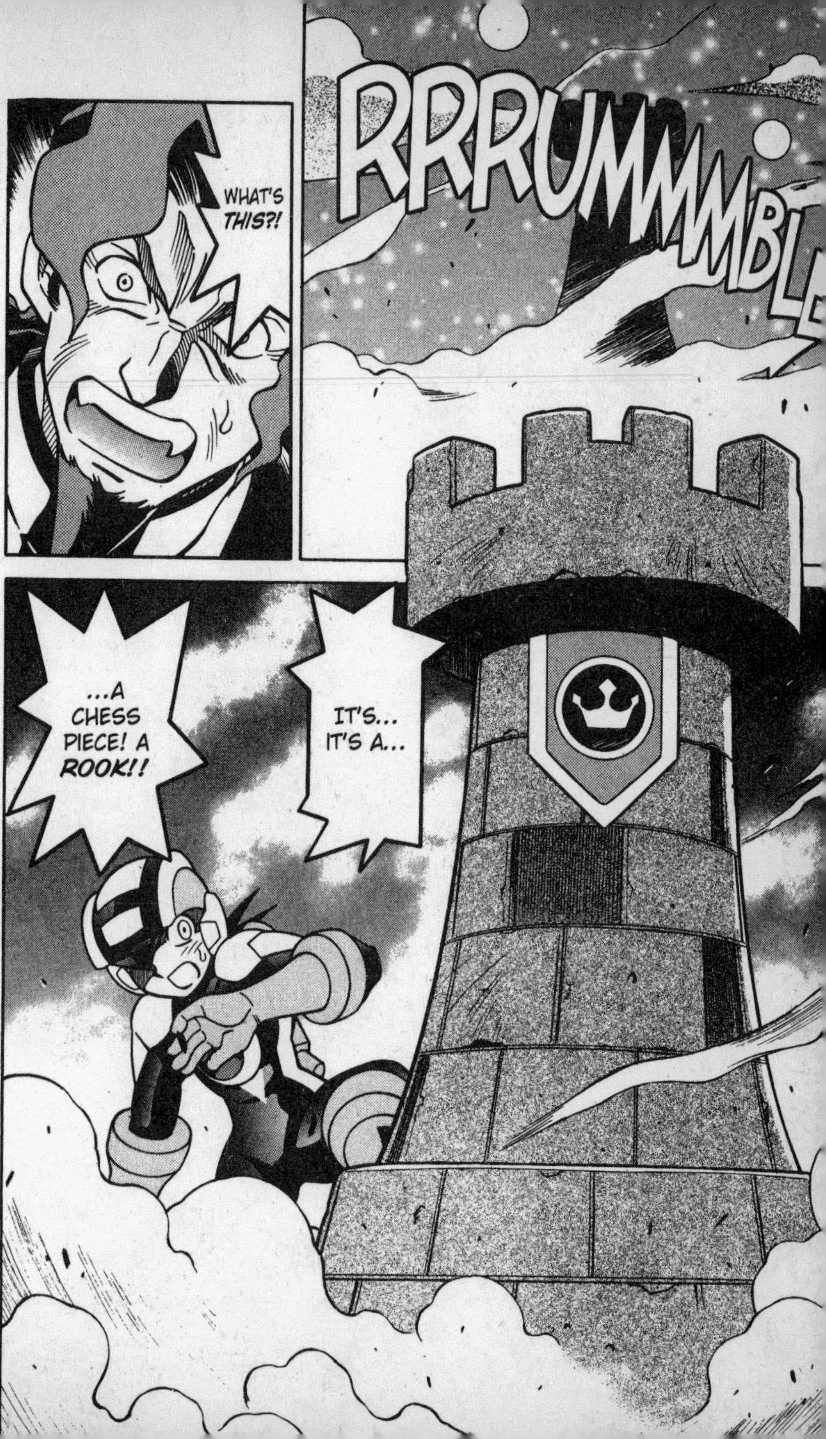
RRRUMMMMBLE
WHAT'S THIS?!
IT'S... IT'S A...
...A CHESS PIECE! A ROOK!!

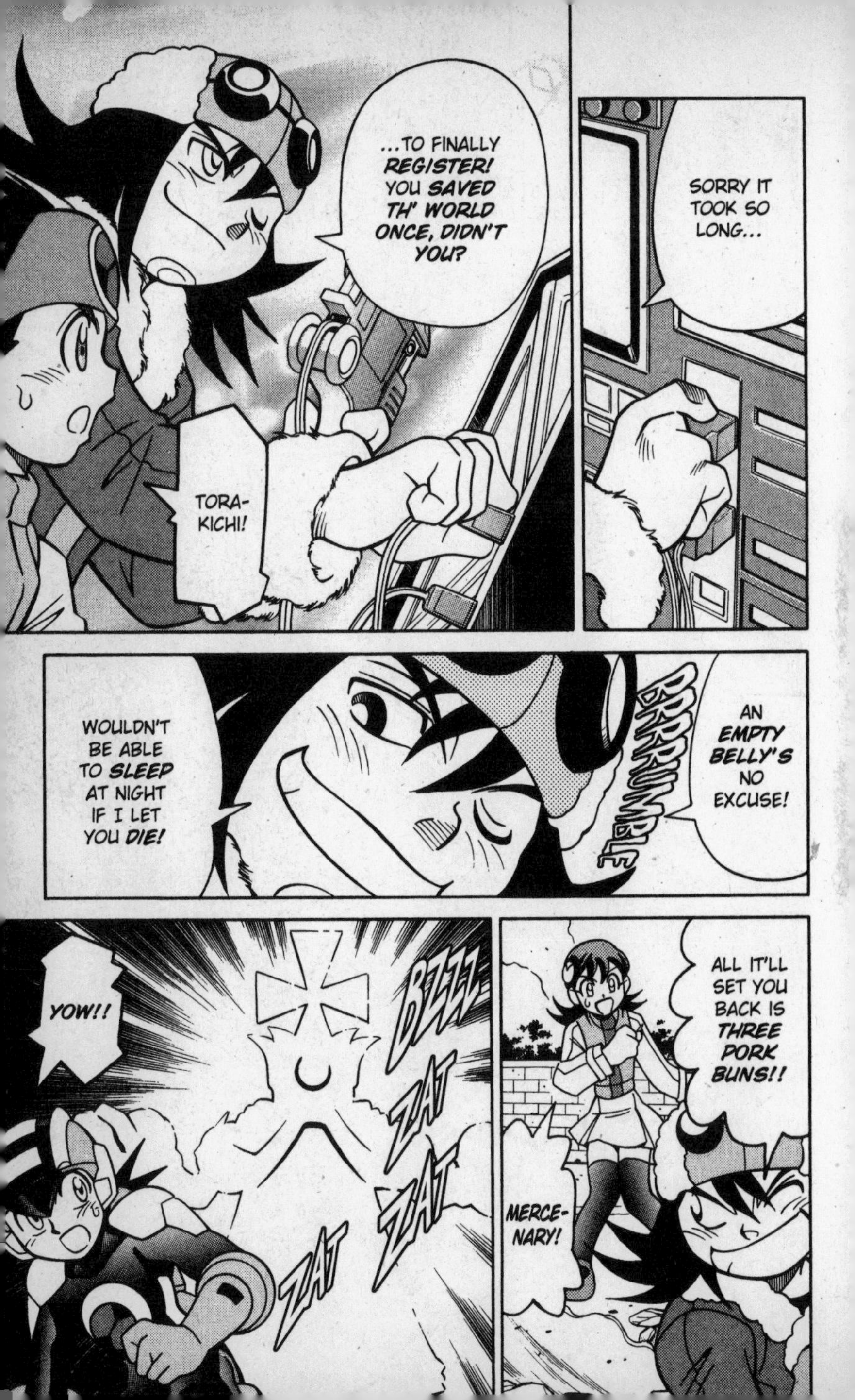
SORRY IT TOOK SO LONG...
...TO FINALLY REGISTER! YOU SAVED TH' WORLD ONCE, DIDN'T YOU?
TORA-KICHI!
AN EMPTY BELLY'S NO EXCUSE!
BRRRUMBLE
WOULDN'T BE ABLE TO SLEEP AT NIGHT IF I LET YOU DIE!
ALL IT'LL SET YOU BACK IS THREE PORK BUNS!!
MERCE-NARY!
BZZZ
ZAT
ZAT
ZAT
YOW!!

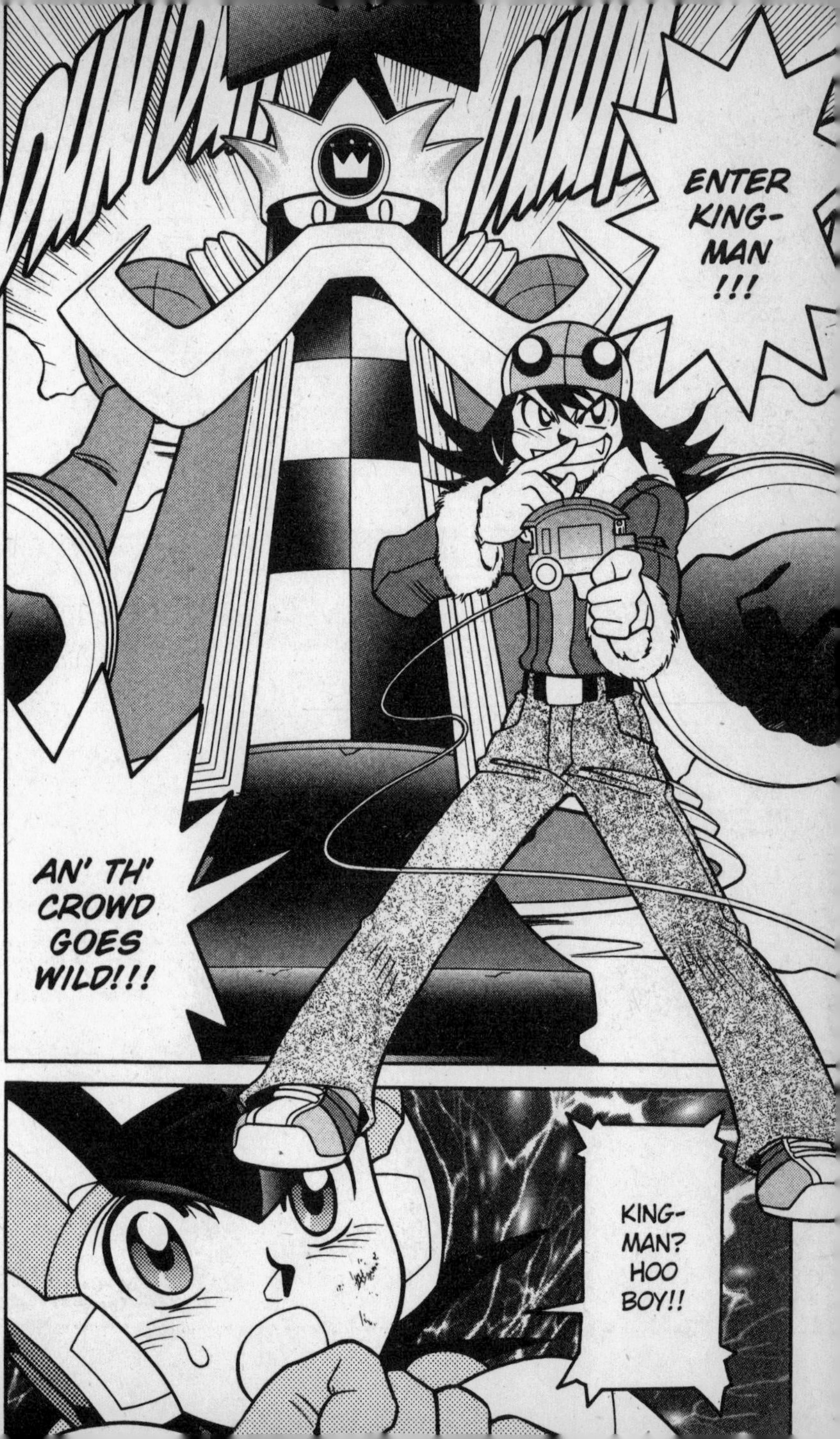
ENTER KING-MAN!!!
AN' TH' CROWD GOES WILD!!!
KING-MAN? HOO BOY!!

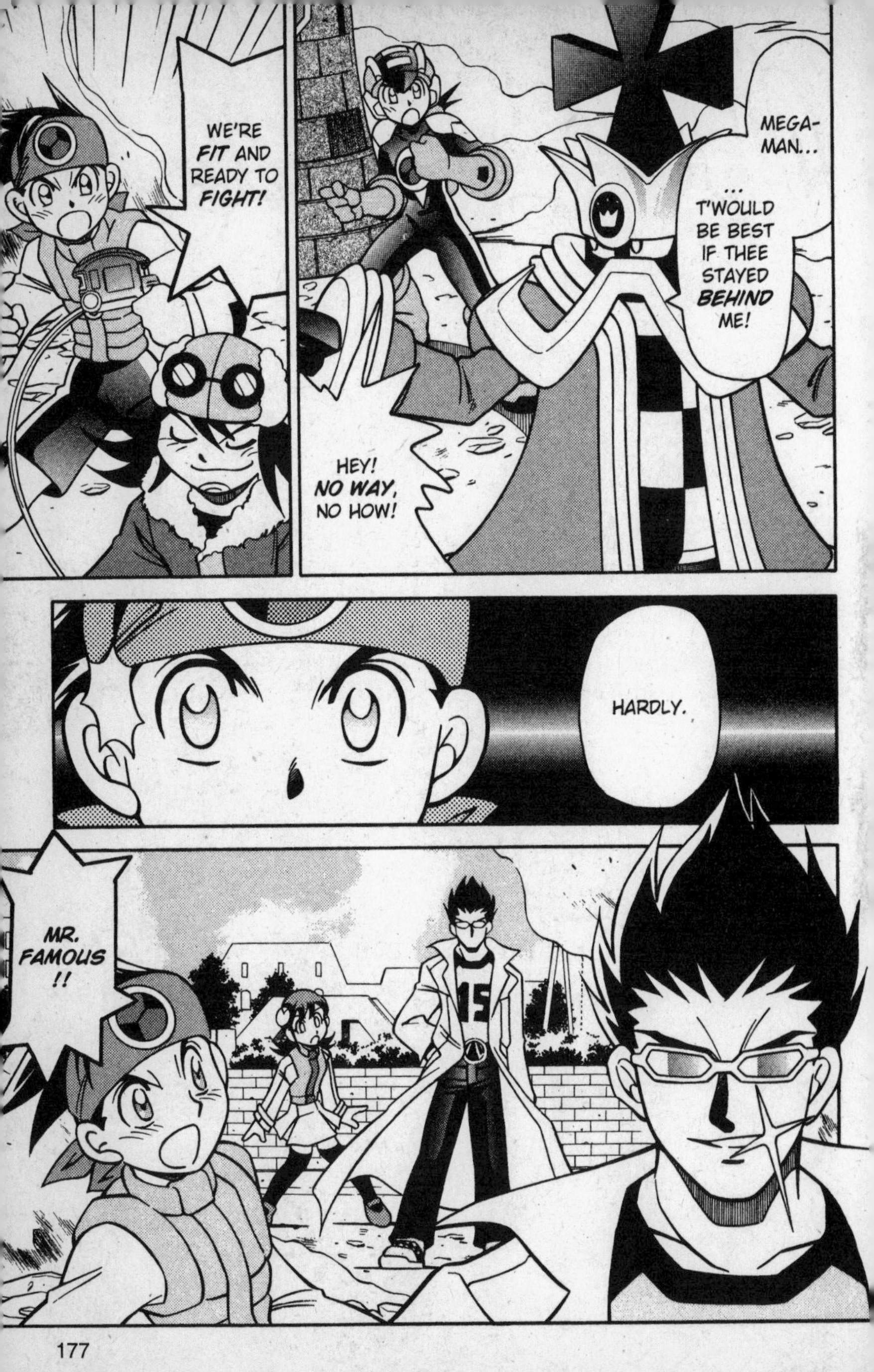
MEGA-MAN...
... T'WOULD BE BEST IF THEE STAYED BEHIND ME!
HEY! NO WAY, NO HOW!
WE'RE FIT AND READY TO FIGHT!
HARDLY.
MR. FAMOUS !!

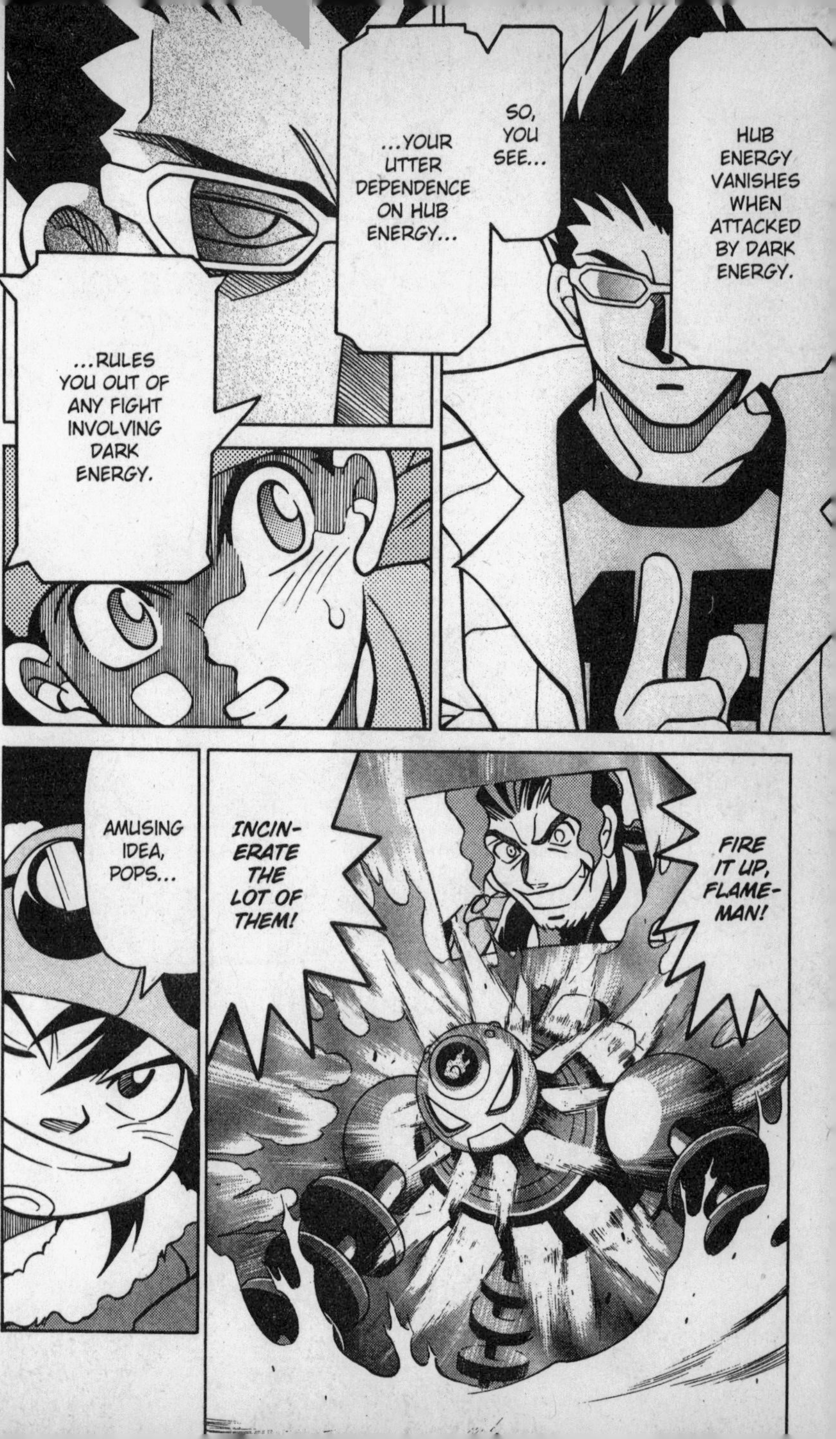
HUB ENERGY VANISHES WHEN ATTACKED BY DARK ENERGY.
SO, YOU SEE...
...YOUR UTTER DEPENDENCE ON HUB ENERGY...
...RULES YOU OUT OF ANY FIGHT INVOLVING DARK ENERGY.
FIRE IT UP, FLAME-MAN!
INCIN-ERATE THE LOT OF THEM!
AMUSING IDEA, POPS...

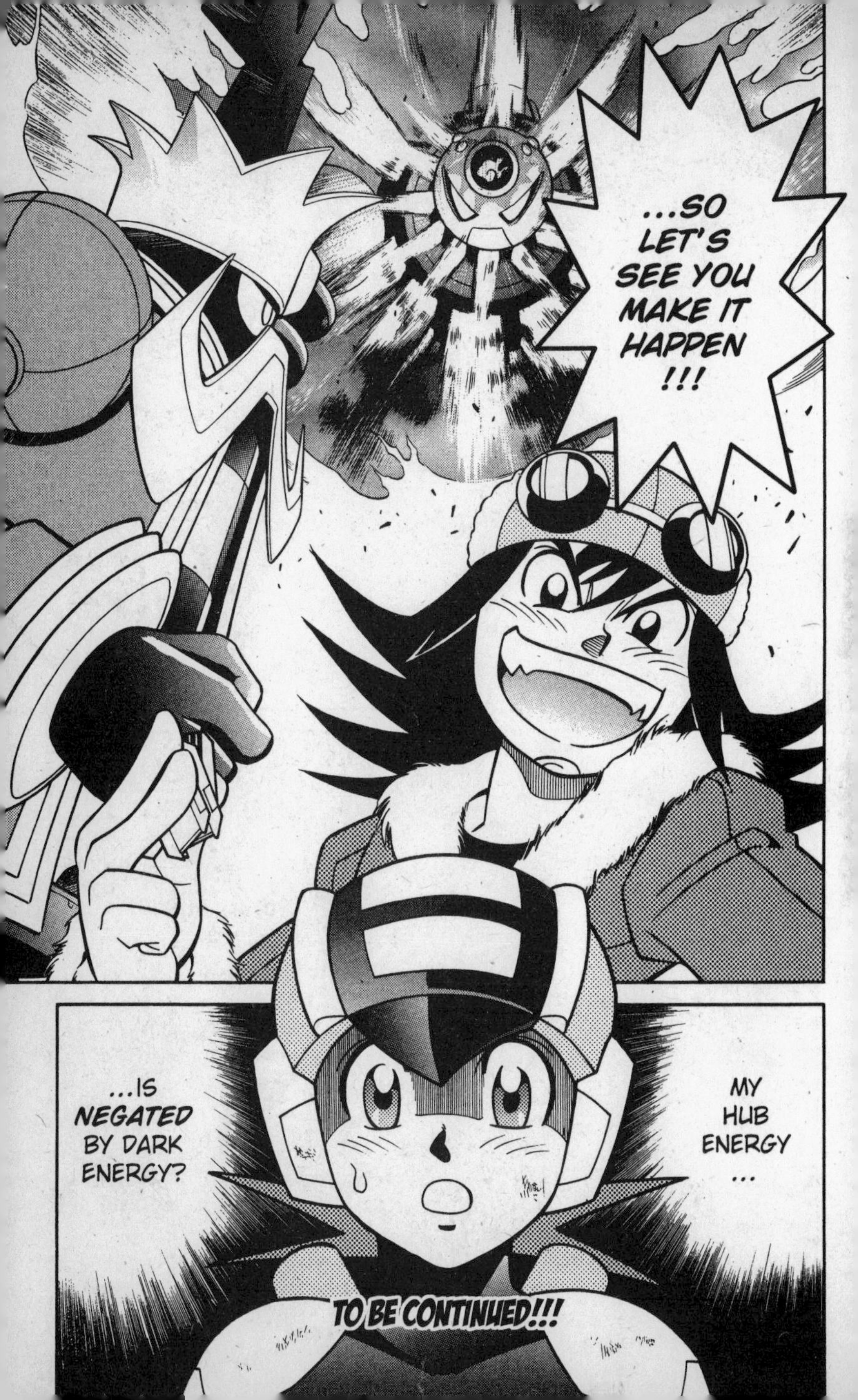
...SO LET'S SEE YOU MAKE IT HAPPEN !!!
MY HUB ENERGY ...
...IS *NEGATED* BY DARK ENERGY?
TO BE CONTINUED!!!

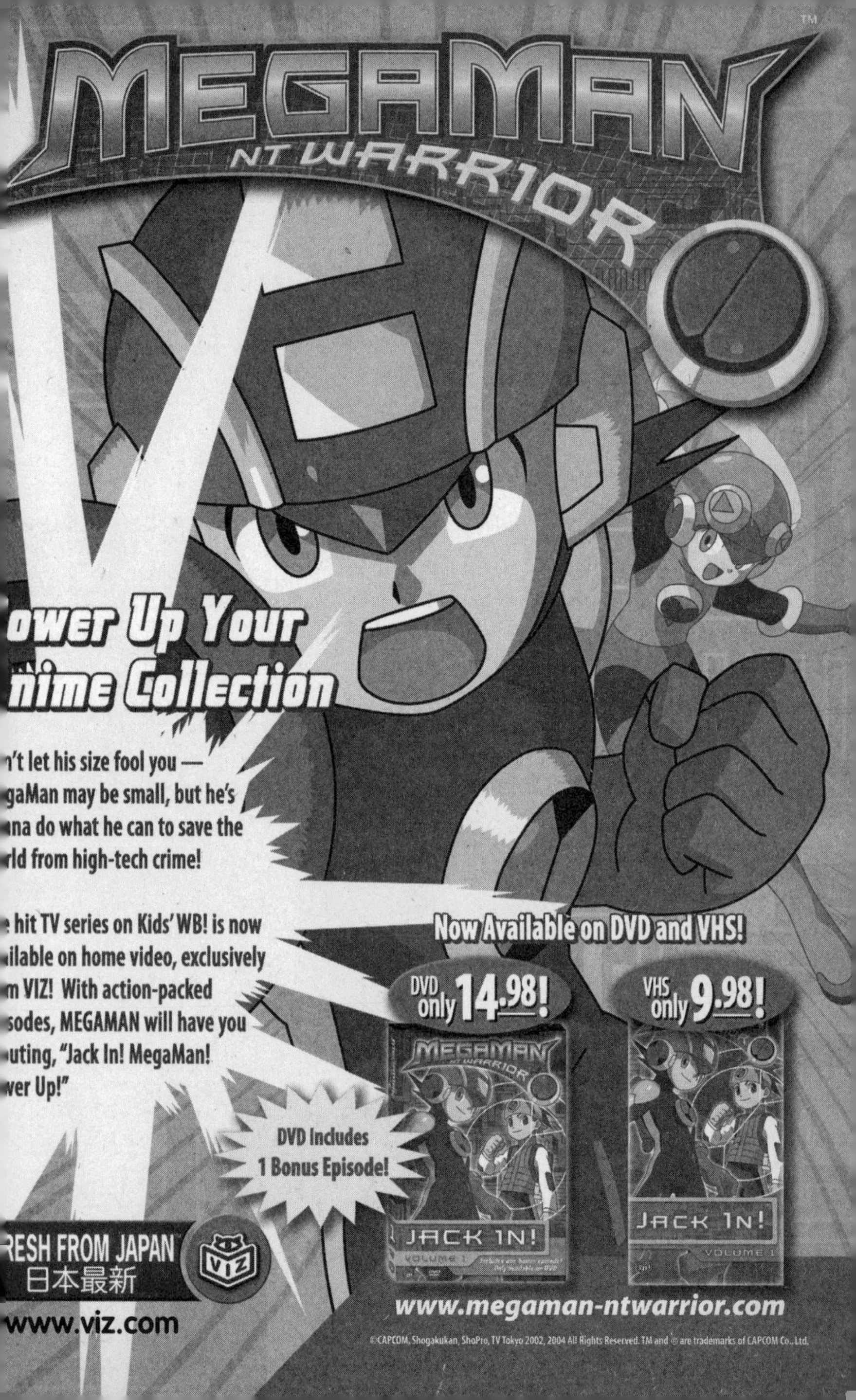
MEGAMAN
NT WARRIOR
ower Up Your
nime Collection
n't let his size fool you —
gaMan may be small, but he's
nna do what he can to save the
rld from high-tech crime!
e hit TV series on Kids' WB! is now
ilable on home video, exclusively
m VIZ! With action-packed
sodes, MEGAMAN will have you
uting, "Jack In! MegaMan!
wer Up!"
Now Available on DVD and VHS!
DVD only 14.98!
VHS only 9.98!
MEGAMAN NT WARRIOR
JACK IN!
VOLUME 1
DVD Includes 1 Bonus Episode!
JACK IN!
VOLUME 1
RESH FROM JAPAN
日本最新
VIZ
www.viz.com
www.megaman-ntwarrior.com
©CAPCOM, Shogakukan, ShoPro, TV Tokyo 2002, 2004 All Rights Reserved. TM and ® are trademarks of CAPCOM Co., Ltd.

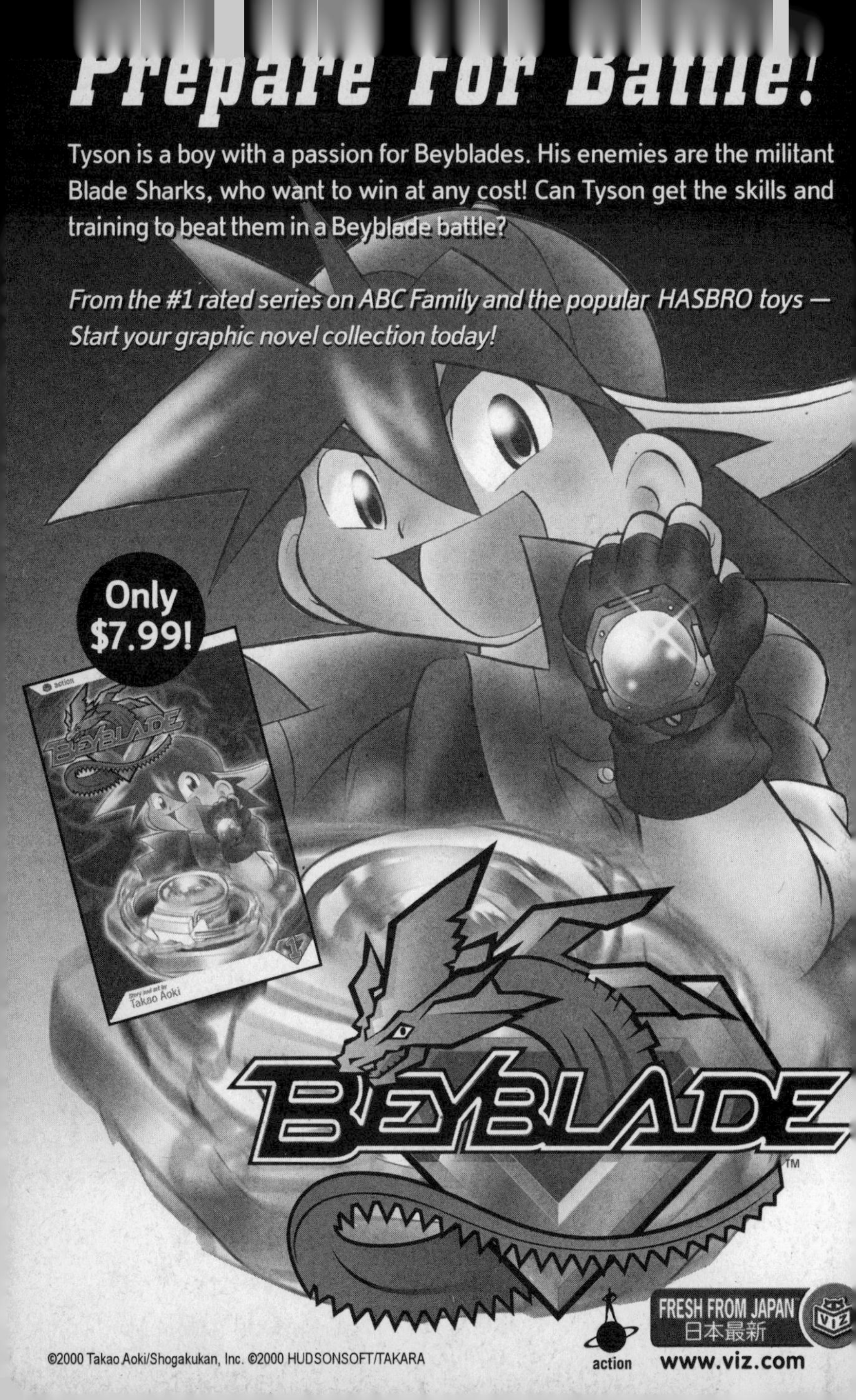
Prepare For Battle!
Tyson is a boy with a passion for Beyblades. His enemies are the militant Blade Sharks, who want to win at any cost! Can Tyson get the skills and training to beat them in a Beyblade battle?
From the #1 rated series on ABC Family and the popular HASBRO toys — Start your graphic novel collection today!
Only $7.99!
action
BEYBLADE
Story and art by Takao Aoki
BEYBLADE™
action
FRESH FROM JAPAN
日本最新
VIZ
www.viz.com
©2000 Takao Aoki/Shogakukan, Inc. ©2000 HUDSONSOFT/TAKARA

# COMPLETE OUR SURVEY AND LET US KNOW WHAT YOU THINK!

☐ Please do NOT send me information about VIZ products, news and events, special offers, or other information.

☐ Please do NOT send me information from VIZ's trusted business partners.

**Name:** _____

**Address:** _____

**City:** _____ **State:** _____ **Zip:** _____

**E-mail:** _____

☐ **Male** ☐ **Female** **Date of Birth** (mm/dd/yyyy): ___ / ___ / _____ ( Under 13? Parental consent required )

## What race/ethnicity do you consider yourself? (please check one)

☐ Asian/Pacific Islander ☐ Black/African American ☐ Hispanic/Latino

☐ Native American/Alaskan Native ☐ White/Caucasian ☐ Other: _____

## What VIZ product did you purchase? (check all that apply and indicate title purchased)

☐ DVD/VHS _____

☐ Graphic Novel _____

☐ Magazines _____

☐ Merchandise _____

## Reason for purchase: (check all that apply)

☐ Special offer ☐ Favorite title ☐ Gift

☐ Recommendation ☐ Other _____

## Where did you make your purchase? (please check one)

☐ Comic store ☐ Bookstore ☐ Mass/Grocery Store

☐ Newsstand ☐ Video/Video Game Store ☐ Other: _____

☐ Online (site: _____ )

## What other VIZ properties have you purchased/own? _____

_____

**ow many anime and/or manga titles have you purchased in the last year? How many were IZ titles?** **(please check one from each column)**

| NIME | MANGA | VIZ |
|---|---|---|
| ☐ None | ☐ None | ☐ None |
| ☐ 1-4 | ☐ 1-4 | ☐ 1-4 |
| ☐ 5-10 | ☐ 5-10 | ☐ 5-10 |
| ☐ 11+ | ☐ 11+ | ☐ 11+ |

**find the pricing of VIZ products to be:** **(please check one)**

☐ Cheap ☐ Reasonable ☐ Expensive

**/hat genre of manga and anime would you like to see from VIZ?** **(please check two)**

☐ Adventure ☐ Comic Strip ☐ Science Fiction ☐ Fighting

☐ Horror ☐ Romance ☐ Fantasy ☐ Sports

**/hat do you think of VIZ's new look?**

☐ Love It ☐ It's OK ☐ Hate It ☐ Didn't Notice ☐ No Opinion

**/hich do you prefer?** **(please check one)**

☐ Reading right-to-left

☐ Reading left-to-right

**/hich do you prefer?** **(please check one)**

☐ Sound effects in English

☐ Sound effects in Japanese with English captions

☐ Sound effects in Japanese only with a glossary at the back

**HANK YOU! Please send the completed form to:**

NJW Research
42 Catharine St.
Poughkeepsie, NY 12601

**ll information provided will be used for internal purposes only. We promise not to sell or otherwise ivulge your information.**